Waiting for the Light to Change

Waiting for the Light to Change

ANNETTE HAWS

CFI
Springville, Utah

The views expressed within this work are the sole responsibility of the author and do not necessarily reflect the position of Cedar Fort, Inc., or any other entity.

This is a work of fiction. The characters, names, incidents, places, and dialogue are products of the author's imagination, and are not to be construed as real.

ISBN 13: 978-1-59955-156-2

Published by CFI, an imprint of Cedar Fort, Inc., 2373 W. 700 S., Springville, UT 84663
Distributed by Cedar Fort, Inc., www.cedarfort.com

LIBRARY OF CONGRESS CATALOGING-IN-PUBLICATION DATA

Haws, Annette.
  Waiting for the light to change / Annette Haws.
    p. cm.
  ISBN 978-1-59955-156-2
  1. Divorced mothers—Fiction. 2. High school teachers—Fiction. 3.
Utah—Fiction. 4. Religious fiction. I. Title.

  PS3608.A897W35 2008
  813'.6—dc22
                              2008009028

Cover design by Nicole Williams
Cover design © 2008 by Lyle Mortimer
Edited and typeset by Lyndsee Simpson Cordes and Melissa J. Caldwell

Printed in the United States of America

10 9 8 7 6 5 4 3 2 1

Printed on acid-free paper

To Allison, my true north, always.

Acknowledgments

I would like to gratefully acknowledge Terrell Dougan, Kate Lahey, and Sallee Robinson, who have critiqued and encouraged and become dear friends. I would like to thank Kim Bouck, who read the manuscript early and often, and my own children—Pete, Andy, Betsy, and Charlotte—who have provided much inspiration and have allowed their traumas to become material. A special thank you to Kathy Merkley for sharing her insights about having a brain-injured daughter and to my parents, Janet and Pete Randall, for a lifetime of boundless optimism. I would particularly like to thank my husband, Charlie, who, in his own bemused fashion, has always encouraged me to follow whatever drummer I happen to be hearing at the moment.

Grateful acknowledgment is also offered to classroom teachers everywhere, who, with little praise or appreciation, educate our children.

first day of school

*S*arah glanced at her watch and inhaled quickly. "Shoe? Einstein?" She held up her right shoe and shook it hard at the golden retriever. "Come on, Einstein. I know you understand. Shoe." But the only words he seemed willing to recognize were *walk* and *cookie*. She pulled up her denim jumper, shoved the Sunday paper out of the way, and knelt down to peer under the faded green couch. Wrinkling her nose at the dust balls and the dog hair, she was delighted when she saw the shoe.

"Slimed but wearable," she announced. She stretched her arm under the couch, reaching for the shoe. The dog stood beside her and woofed, startling her and causing her to scratch her arm on a low-hanging spring.

"No bark, Einstein." She frowned, daubing the bloody scratch with a bit of newsprint. Shaking out her skirt, she shouted down the hall, "Jenny, we've got to go. I can't be late. You've got to get up early enough to be ready." How many times had she had this same conversation? Jenny the Dawdle Queen. Sarah scooped some papers off the kitchen table and stuffed a banana in her purse.

"Mom," Jenny called from her room, "can I ride with Tom?"

Tom, a tall boy with an easy smile and light brown hair, lumbered up the basement stairs taking two at a time. He nodded. "It's okay with me."

"Absolutely not. Someone would have to sit in the back of the truck.

If some dope runs a stop sign, brains could be splattered everywhere. Jenny, grab your bag. We've got to leave."

Jenny raced down the hall, her navy backpack slung over her thin shoulder. Sarah's hand clutched her throat, but she quickly twisted her mouth into a tight smile.

How many wrong turns had brought them to this place? Jenny had picked up a khaki skirt with a smeary catsup stain on the pocket. Her faded plaid shirt was wrinkled. Had she even washed her face? Without looking in the mirror, Jenny stretched the ever-present black elastic off her wrist and pulled her curly hair into a slightly off-center ponytail.

Two weeks ago they had stood in front of Gap, Jenny's brown eyes pleading.

"Sweetheart, I don't have the money for these stores." Sarah gave her standard response: hands raised, elbows bent, head tilted to one side, and a silly grimace on her face. The lousy Charlie Chaplin imper- sonation was the family equivalent of turning her pockets inside out.

Backing away from her mother, Jenny had studied the mannequins in the store window and then sighed heavily as she turned toward the parking terrace.

"Don't you want to look at Discount City?"

"Why?" Jenny grumbled.

Of course, Sarah always managed to scrounge up the necessary funds for every torture device the orthodontist wanted to screw, glue, or clamp into Jenny's mouth. Sarah took tickets at all the high school home games to earn the extra cash because she didn't have a choice. The kid's mouth was a mess.

In the third grade Ryan Schultz, a rotten kid with prominent ears and crooked teeth of his own, had started calling Jenny Dracula. The hated nickname had stuck, permanently attached to Jenny's small frame like a distorted shadow she couldn't shake. The boys in her class didn't get a rise out of Jenny when they called her Dracula. She didn't run, sobbing loudly, to the teacher or chase them, waving her plastic school bag as a weapon; she just faded away next to the school's yellow brick walls or vanished behind the ancient maple tree on the playground.

Now, here they were. Behind yards of wire and multiple elastics, Jenny's teeth were starting to straighten, but everything else—hair, face, clothes—looked rumpled and a bit forlorn. It was the first day of high school. Sarah should have sold the dog. She should have sold a kidney. She should have slapped her silver plastic down on the counter and demanded one of everything in a size four.

"What about a little lip gloss?" Sarah asked.

"Can we just go?"

"A little makeup isn't a moral compromise."

"I don't see you wearing any." Jenny pushed past her and gave the dog a hug.

"Guard the house, Einstein," Sarah ordered. She wanted to sit down on the lumpy couch, cover her face with a pillow, and bawl, but instead she smiled at the big yellow dog thumping the floor with his tail and said, "We'll miss you."

The jarring ring of the telephone halted the rush toward the door.

"Hi, Dad," Jenny answered. Her brown eyes were suddenly animated, and the dour expression on her thin face turned into a grin.

Jenny nodded happily as she listened to the obligatory two-minute phone call, the good-luck-on-your-first-day phone call. *Well*, Sarah thought, *now he can check off the box next to "parenting."*

Bob was probably telling Jenny about his own brilliant high school career. Same old routine. Even when the kids were little, his story was the only story that mattered. Every missed birthday party, Christmas Eve, and little league game was followed by another chapter in the amazing life of Dr. Bob Williams, superhero. Enthralling stories of blood, guts, ambulance rides, perilous emergencies, and fantastic rescues mesmerized Robbie and his three-year-old brother, Tommy. Bob would draw pictures of evil blood clots trying to kill honest farmers, fathers with little children their very own ages. He would tell his children how he pierced the clot with a wire so tiny it was smaller than a single strand of Jenny's baby-fine hair. Eyes wide, Jenny would hold very still as Bob plucked a piece of hair from her tender scalp and held it up for collective scrutiny. He solved every puzzling case. Professors twice his age sought his opinion. Dr. Bob Williams, second year fellow, was single-handedly holding the medical center together with his amazing genius and incredible charisma. Certainly, his hospital whites should be traded for a cape and red tights.

Sarah was amazed only because so many of those modern miracles occurred when her husband didn't answer his pager and obviously was not in the hospital. The only miraculous event—in her opinion—was the superb facility for lying her husband employed to cover the time he had been spending with another woman.

Sarah tapped on her watch. "No time," she demanded. Jenny ignored her, turning to hand the phone to her brother, but Tom refused the phone with an upturned palm and headed out the kitchen door to the carport.

Sarah could hear the motor straining as Tom tried to start his truck. She looked over at the picture on the end table—a handsome young man looking stiff in a starched white shirt and a navy suit; a Bible was opened on his knee and a black and white name-tag hung on his suit pocket.

"I'll dust you when I get home, Rob. I promise," she whispered. "Wish us luck. We're going to need it."

"Mom," Tom bellowed through the kitchen door, "can you and Jenny give me a push?"

"What else?" she grumbled, visualizing a raucous mob of sopho-mores, unsupervised, playing leapfrog over the desks in her classroom. Sarah dropped her bag, papers, and a gray soft-back book, *1994, Healthcare in America*, on the grass near the driveway and waved Jenny over to help. Tom pushed with one hand on the dash and the other on the open driver's door, as Sarah closed her eyes, gritted her teeth, and pushed against the tailgate. Jenny, red-faced, straightened her arms and tried to keep her feet from slipping on the gravel on the street. Slowly, the truck gained momentum; Tom jumped in and popped the clutch. The engine sputtered a couple of times and then engaged.

"Yes!" Tom shouted. "Thanks." He tapped his horn twice and waved. Jenny bent over, panting loudly.

The sun had come up over the rugged eastern mountains, but the morning air was unseasonably cool. Catching her breath, Sarah looked across the valley at the dark clouds piling up against the mountains in the west. Rain in August was an almost unheard of occurrence in Utah. Jenny slammed the passenger door of the old Accord station wagon, and they pulled out over the crumbling concrete driveway into the street.

Two blocks down, at the intersection of Hawthorne and Maple, Jenny slumped down. She held her hand up to hide her face as they drove past a small group of girls waiting for the school bus. *Those little snits*, Sarah thought as she lifted her bangs off her forehead with her free hand. She should have let Jenny ride to school with Tom. Tumbling out of the back of a beat-up truck with a very cool group of junior boys was better than arriving with your mother.

She glanced over at her daughter slouched, with downcast eyes, against the door. Why wasn't Jenny like the thousands of high school girls who had come in and out of her English classes over the years? She winced as the knot in her stomach gave a sharp twist. There were always one or two girls who ended up in the back of the class, girls who didn't fit, didn't have friends. They couldn't look you in the eye. Sarah couldn't remember their names. They never volunteered. They looked unkempt, odd in strange outfits, wrinkled shirts and skirts with catsup stains.

Jenny put her hand up to her mouth and chewed a rough piece of skin on the side of her finger. Sarah bit her tongue to keep from nagging. She had tried everything to break Jenny of the habit. Nothing worked. Oblivious, it was Jenny's automatic response to any kind of anxiety. Her cuticles were chewed and rough, and the tips of her fingers were blunted and misshapen. If Jenny thought anyone might be looking at her hands, she shoved them in her pockets or curled them into fists, but usually they were near her mouth, and it drove Sarah crazy, it broke her heart, and it made her want to scream.

She drove down Fourth North and turned onto East Claremont to avoid the light. She could make it down the hill and across town in ten minutes, but today she only had five. She could see two yellow school buses in her rearview mirror. She accelerated too quickly after each stop sign and nervously raised her foot on and off the gas pedal.

Looking out the window, Jenny wondered out loud if the clouds might mean rain. Speaking in a whisper, she wished she had put on something new and something warmer instead of the faded shirt she'd worn all summer. Sarah looked over quickly. Who would notice the shirt? Probably everyone.

How long would it be until friends on the faculty approached her in the halls with a soft touch on the arm and looks of studied concern: "Jenny's shy, isn't she?" Did they think she hadn't noticed? Like maybe Jenny had left home wearing mismatched socks, and her mother needed a gentle reminder that fourteen-year-old girls still warranted a little attention, because that was always the subtext. Sarah must have done something very wrong to have a daughter whose problems involved much more than mismatched socks. She imagined Mr. Boyston, the pencil-thin, balding biology teacher, approaching her to mention that Jenny had arrived at school missing one of her legs.

"Oh, thank you so much for telling me." Feigning exasperation, she'd slap herself on the forehead. "I just didn't realize—we were in such a hurry this morning, you know." And Mr. Boyston would amble down to the faculty room, a dingy room filled with the odor of stale popcorn, where the regulars, a disjointed jury of men, slouched on worn couches, drank soda, complained about the state legislature, and fished for slippery bits of scandal.

"Does anyone have Jenny Williams in class?" Boyston would ask, and someone would reply, "She's not like her brothers, is she?"

Those men. Worn out. Overweight. Ex-coaches, some of them, in poorly ironed shirts and baggy polyester pants. She knew they gossiped because she'd listened to them when she was new and foolish enough to enter their male domain. Now, she was sure they gossiped about her. She could almost hear the salacious murmurs rustling through the room. "Well, you know Sarah," one would say. "She's pretty high strung and temperamental. Jeff Watts, at the middle school, tried to date her for a while, but she was having none of that. A messy divorce," he'd intimate, wrinkling his nose, implying that divorce had a rancid smell. She could almost see the raised eyebrows and, worse, the lewd winks. Her cheeks burned, and she clutched the steering wheel. A man in her home? How would that help Jenny? But she knew that's what they thought.

Sarah made a left turn into the faculty parking lot. It was full. Only two open spots at the far end. Jenny looked relieved that most of the other teachers' vehicles were as beat up as her mother's. Sarah saw Jenny spot the new cream-colored Camry. She laughed. Holding up two fingers, she said, "Two incomes." They got out of the car and Sarah turned the key in the lock but looked up, hearing pounding music coming from a new bright-blue truck pulling up next to the row of cars by the English wing.

The jarring noise stopped. A long-bodied young man with white-blond hair slid out of the driver's side and, with an easy grace, slung a nearly empty backpack across his broad shoulders. Tyler Colton. Sarah's fingers tightened around her purse strap. Getting out of the passenger side of the truck, his much-shorter friend dropped his breakfast and spewed a creative string of obscenities at the square of potatoes and syrupy pancakes splattered on the pavement.

"Does he think it's going to magically return to the container?" Sarah muttered.

"You're such a loser," the blond said in mock exasperation, and then, looking up at the morning sun, he laughed, pleased to be back at school, pleased to be handsome and young, pleased with the surprise of his own size and masculinity. He looked down the row of cars in the restricted parking lot and saw his teacher. With a quick nod of his head, he acknowledged Sarah, but he didn't smile.

"Who's that?" Jenny whispered.

"Trouble," Sarah replied automatically. "No, not really. His name is Tyler Colton, and Tonto is Braxton Martin."

"Tonto?" Jenny questioned. Sarah reminded herself that her children hadn't grown up watching the same reruns she had.

"You know, politically incorrect, subservient sidekick." Sarah smiled. Then she muttered, more to herself than to Jenny, "I mean, how many students are parking in the teacher's lot on the very first day?"

"Is he your student?"

"Oh, yes. Those two boys are my strongest two-man team, but don't worry about them. They're seniors."

Sarah and Jenny headed into the school. Not stopping to talk to other teachers or students, Sarah nodded and smiled and hurried through the faculty mail room. With an armful of papers and her thick book, she leaned into the vice principal's office. "Tyler Colton's parked in the faculty lot." Terry Schuback, a telephone attached to his ear, rolled his eyes. Sarah strode out of the office and climbed the second set of stairs with Jenny hurrying along in her wake.

The faculty and staff were cheerful. No one was grousing the way they would when the long months of January and February stretched on forever. The floors were polished; the paint was fresh; the school smelled as if cleaning supplies had been liberally applied. The clutter in the halls was organized, no muddy footprints and no fast food garbage strewn across the floor. Garlands of gold and red crepe paper festooned the ceilings, and sponge-painted banners announced *JUNIOR HALL* in large block letters above long banks of lockers. Sarah and Jenny hurried down the main hall in the English wing. She stuck her key in a classroom door with a glass window covered with a laminated poster of a silly-looking princess, holding a long list of demands, with a crown askew on her head. The caption read, *She who must be obeyed.* Jenny smiled at the princess, and Sarah said, "Well, everybody better understand up front that this is not a democracy."

Jenny waited inside Sarah's classroom as the halls filled with students. She fingered the funny-looking stuffed doll with wiggly eyes that sat precariously on the side of Sarah's large metal desk.

"Where did you get this?" Jenny asked. Sarah shoved her purse into a back drawer before pawing through a Teachers-Are-Special mug, looking for a royal-blue marker.

"Oh," Sarah broke away from her mental rehearsal for first hour, "it was a gift at the end-of-year debate banquet. I'm supposed to bash it against the wall when I get angry. You know, smack the doll instead of the students." She laughed at the expression on Jenny's face. "I don't smack anyone. They're bigger than I am. I'd get the worst of it in a shoot-out."

Lockers slammed in the hall; the noise level increased. The classroom door opened and shut, as anxious faces looked in and then retreated to the safety of clumps of friends standing in the hall. Jenny traced her finger around a cheap plastic frame that held a snapshot of her family—Jenny and her brothers and their mother on a beach, sunburned and smiling. Jenny asked an obvious question to fill up the time and avoid leaving. "Is this right before Robbie left? Bear Lake?"

"You've seen that picture before." Sarah glanced down at an outline. "We'll go again when Robbie comes home. Remember, I'll be with Meg in the debate room after school. Don't look for me here." She smiled and gave her daughter a gentle push toward the door, a gentle nudge out of the nest, and immediately thought better of it. She set her outline down and put her arm around Jenny's shoulder and gave her a quick hug. "You'll love high school. This is going to be a wonderful adventure."

The door burst open and five flailing, noisy boys crashed into the room laughing. Jenny chose that moment to flutter quietly away.

"Okay, let's try this one more time," Sarah demanded. With strong-arm motions, she directed the boys with fresh haircuts and new clothes out into the hall and waited with them—a stern expression on her face—as they giggled before composing themselves to enter the room more appropriately. Glancing at the clock, Sarah walked over and flipped on the overhead projector that produced a seating chart on the whiteboard at the front of the room.

"Oh, can't we sit where we want? We won't talk."

Sarah smiled inwardly. *Sure you won't talk . . . or breathe, or burp, or fart.* "You need to sit alphabetically until I can learn your names." She didn't notice that Jenny had left, because suddenly the room was filled with students looking anxiously at the seating chart. Noise, chatter, backpacks being unpacked, frantic calls to friends across the room. The bell rang. The first day of school began.

defection

 C han, a large grin on her face, opened the classroom door and hurried in without knocking. The pretty girl with intense brown eyes and dark, perfectly flipped hair stopped smiling abruptly. "You'll never guess what I just heard at lunch."

Sarah laughed. "You're right. I never will, so you'd better just tell us."

Meg, Sarah's friend and fellow debate coach, tossed a chunk of rosemary bread into Sarah's lap.

"Tyler and Brax," Chan wrinkled up her nose, "are thinking, really seriously, about transferring to Mountain View."

Sarah raised her eyebrows at Meg.

"That's interesting." Meg sat up a little straighter. "Where did you hear that?"

"Well, I was sitting with Rachael, and Tyler and Brax just came over and started to eat her fries and said how really dumb it is that our school district won't let us go to any good tournaments, and all the good tournaments are out of state."

"And," Sarah prodded, "they're going to transfer?"

"Well," Chan started almost every comment with "well," which was a slight improvement over the "hummm" she had used the previous year. "Mountain View lets their kids travel if the parents pay for it. They have a much more student-friendly school board."

Sarah was fairly certain that last sentence was a direct quote, planted by Tyler and Brax, who knew Chan couldn't resist the temptation to report.

"Chan," Meg started, "I wouldn't worry too much about this, and I certainly wouldn't tell a lot of people until the boys make up their minds."

"Well, they're pretty serious."

"You might be right," Meg nodded, "but that's their choice, isn't it? So what event are you going to do this year?"

Not ready to make a firm commitment, Chan turned her head away slightly. "I'm thinking about doing oratory."

"I can see that," Sarah smiled. "Can you give us a few minutes to get a couple of things done before fourth hour comes in?" Sarah walked Chan toward the door. "Don't worry about those boys, kiddo. This is going to be a great year." Patting Chan on the shoulder, Sarah pulled out her keys and locked the door. She made a face at Meg. "What do you think about that?"

"Hello. A power play on the first day of school. Those little twerps think they're so wonderful that we'll prostrate ourselves before the board to keep them. They're in for a surprise." Meg smiled grimly. "Nothing's going to come of this."

"We need those boys. They're obnoxious, but they're our only solid varsity team."

"Would you have transferred to a new school your senior year?" Meg shook her head. "They're not going anywhere. This is the first shot over the bow. Some debate camp advisor has filled their heads with notions of their inherent wonderfulness." Thoughtfully, Meg chewed her last bit of bread. She brushed the crumbs off her long skirt. "We'll be better off without them, if you want to know the truth. I hope they go to Mountain View." Meg dismissed them with a slight wave of her hand. "They were an okay junior varsity team last year, but that was with Sam and Murphy feeding them ideas and briefs."

"They're smart boys."

"They're regurgitate intelligent. They don't have those creative, off-the-wall impulsive brains like Sam and Murphy. Eric is going to be more of an asset. We'll be better off investing time in him. Brax and Tyler are going to be more trouble than they're worth. Didn't some coach blister your ear about them at the summer meeting?"

Sarah nodded, but what seemed obvious to Meg wasn't registering with her. "We have to have strong policy teams. Who's going to help the junior varsity if those boys head south? What about all those tournament points?"

"Well," Meg said, mimicking Chan, "one thing is certain—either they will stay, or they will go." Smiling, she looked at Sarah. "You and I will be just fine either way."

"I don't know." Sarah shook her head.

"Do you remember how hot it was the first day last year?" Meg asked. "We had those big box fans making a racket by the doors." Looking out the small window at the overcast sky, Meg stretched out her legs and pushed one sandal off with her toe. She'd spent much of her time in college wearing a leotard. When Meg hadn't been dancing with the repertory group, she was winning all sorts of academic awards; she was and continued to be wickedly smart. Sarah saw herself as a strange baggage of aspirations, insecurities, and imminent disasters, but working with Meg softened her rough edges.

Whipping her long auburn hair off her neck in one swift twisting motion, Meg stabbed a couple of pencils in to stabilize the knot before she glanced at the clock. Twenty minutes left of lunch. Meg took another bite of her apple.

"Your hair's getting bigger." Meg's palms held an invisible ball that was getting larger by the second.

Sarah laughed. "It's the humidity in the air." She glanced in the mirror on the closet door at the tangled mass of dark curly hair threaded with gray. Her large green eyes set in her oval face looked a little tired and anxious. *Lip gloss*, she thought, gazing at her reflection. *What could it hurt?*

"You run your fingers through your hair when you get nervous," Meg said, smiling. "How are your English classes going to be?"

The first two classes of the day, Sarah taught Sophomore English. Laughing, she likened the experience to pushing a pencil up a steep hill with the tip of her nose.

"Hence, the callus," she said, tapping her nose with her little finger. Keeping students engaged was exhausting, an hour and a half of high-impact mental aerobics. "They're distracted so easily," she complained. "They don't care about sentence structure, or punctuation, or short story arcs. They're thinking about what happened last weekend, what some kid said in the hall, what their friends think of them, what their girlfriends might allow behind the lockers," Sarah raised her eyebrows suggestively, "and what they're going to eat for lunch. Sophomore English is such a losing battle."

The room she shared with Meg was a much better space for Sarah. Large red and gold letters covered the west wall: *North Valley High Debate Team.*

Sarah and Meg were the coaches. This room was home base. The shelves were stacked with an odd assortment of books and news magazines. The mauve carpeting on the back wall had become a catch-all bulletin board covered with photos of students; copies of jokes, articles, and cartoons; and yards and yards of red and gold tinsel stars draped over and around everything else. At the opposite end of the room, bright-blue jagged letters above the whiteboard read, *We have ways to make you talk.* The room was not neat, it was not tidy, and occasionally when the layers of dust made Meg sneeze, she and Sarah would make a short-lived stab at cleaning. Today, stacks of multi-colored handouts lay in piles along the edge of the riser at the front of the room.

Sarah tossed her banana peel into the wastebasket. Better off without a senior policy team? What was Meg thinking? They'd worked so hard. They'd slogged through their first two years with a handful of lackluster students. They thought, more than once, about quitting, but then, in the middle of their third season, a few students had started to place at tournaments. A few trophies had stood, prominently displayed, on the table in front of the classroom. They had been dusted frequently, and the recipients had also been praised and polished.

The last few years had been easier. She and Meg were more competent. They were certainly more confident. And their team started to win, not just individual awards, but large, gaudy, completely beautiful sweepstakes trophies. Almost overnight, Sarah felt like she'd been given a blank check at the Amazing Kids Super Store. The debate team was suddenly a cool place to be, a cool thing to do. That wonderful 20 percent of students who understood that education was the key to their futures wanted debate on their resumes and college applications. Smart, funny kids became news junkies and batted around political issues and personalities like the talking heads on the Sunday morning news shows. It was a heady, happy time. Now instead of getting beaten up at tournaments, every two weeks it was like a noisy birthday party with wonderful surprises all wrapped up for Sarah.

Brief articles, composed by her, appeared in the local newspaper: "North Valley Debate Team Wins State Tourney," "North Valley High Trumps Five A Schools," "North Valley Debaters Take State Again."

At the biannual coaches' meetings, Sarah was no longer an insignificant woman in a green sweater sitting in the back of the room. She had a name and an opinion that mattered. Granted, her pond was very small, but when she wiggled her tail, it caused a splash, and Sarah loved it.

Fourth period started. Papers and schedules were passed out. Information sheets were passed in. Meg was happy to be starting a new year. Sarah was chewing the inside of her cheek. They were riding the crest of two winning seasons, and their enthusiasm should have been infectious, but the afternoon seemed oddly out of kilter. It was always difficult on the first day to look past the acne and the strange hairdos and see the strong competitors some of these students would become, but today especially, Sarah thought they all looked rather flat and dopey. Worries about Jenny, somewhere in the building, pressed at the back of her mind.

Sarah looked at Meg. She could almost see *Building Year* tattooed on her forehead. This was no good. There must be some way to cajole those two boys into staying, but Sarah couldn't get her head around being smarmy to Tyler and Brax. She'd never liked them. It wasn't just that they were obnoxious; obnoxious in a high school was old news. Tyler was condescending with a misogynistic twist that grated on her. Who knew what Brax was like? He just parroted Tyler. She didn't know what to do, but they couldn't take a year's worth of trophies and hand them over to some other coach. She fretted all of fourth period.

By the time fifth period rolled around, Sarah was nervously rearranging the colorful plastic Tyler and Brax tokens on her mental game board, and she almost put them in the small cardboard box inside her head labeled *Arrogant, Self-serving Males Who Are Not to Be Trusted.* They were not the only plastic pieces in that box; actually, there was quite a collection.

The students entering fifth period were primarily juniors and seniors, and unlike freshmen and sophomores, they didn't take their social temperatures every thirty seconds. As mildly excited as many of them were, they made an effort to be nonchalant, to adopt a wait-and-see attitude. Unfortunately, attitude is contagious, and it was immediately apparent to everyone that something was not right.

Meg gave the welcome and the short introductory remarks. Outside, the wind started to gust, and Meg paused as thunder rumbled in the distance. The lights flickered on and off for a second. Always aware of portents, Sarah tried to ignore the weather and choked down a wave of homesickness for last year's seniors.

Meg addressed a form on the overhead projector. "This looks like a calendar, and in fact it is," she said with a short laugh, "but it is going to be used as a contract. After the first two weeks, people will be going seven different directions in this class, so you're going to establish part of your own grading criteria. The whole premise is that by this date—the first tournament—you're prepared to be excellent. We want you to hit the ground running. Every event will have different deadlines, but the objective is the same: excellence. No last-minute preparation."

Before Sarah could make a brisk explanation, Tyler interrupted. "We don't have time for this crap," he said with his lip curled in a surly grimace. "It's just a stupid time suck. We have to file the briefs from camp." The tall blond, who typically used his lieutenants for any risky behavior, threw the gauntlet down on the floor and waited. The blue knit shirt covering his broad chest rose and fell as he breathed rapidly. Heads jerked around to watch him.

Sarah's eyes narrowed. She had a hot, quick temper. In fairness, none of the students in this class had ever witnessed the resulting carnage, but they'd all heard stories. Students who were not examining their hands in their laps were looking back and forth between the teacher and the seventeen-year-old boy. Sarah turned slowly and bent her head slightly toward Tyler, smiling, as if he were a worm she wanted to squish with the toe of her old shoe. Her voice was cold, and she spoke slowly and precisely. "If I am not mistaken, Mrs. Woodruff and I determine curriculum in this class. You are free to spend all of the time you wish filing briefs from camp," she paused, "at home." She paused again. "Because we are going to be researching healthcare in America for the next two weeks here—during class." In a quick turn around, Sarah changed her tone and became artificially pleasant. "You know, I sat in on one of your rounds last year at Region. You didn't understand the issues. You were trotting out tired, old, boring arguments when logic and information would have been more persuasive. Clearly, there's a need for more understanding."

Not one to tolerate criticism, particularly from a forty-ish woman who wore frumpy clothes and scuffed shoes, Tyler stuck out his chin. "We won that round."

"Yes, you did." The *s* rolled out to the tip of her tongue almost like a hiss. "But it wasn't much of a victory. If you'd hit a better team, you would have been throttled. I mean, really, why be mediocre when you can be," she hesitated, "knowledgeable?" She was going to say amazing but settled for knowledgeable, because she suddenly realized Meg was right. This kid was never going to be amazing; he was just going to be a pain—probably all year.

"Let's get into event groups," Meg said. "Your contract forms are up here on the front desk. Draft your deadlines on scratch paper before you write anything in ink."

Suddenly the class of forty students was in motion. The anxiety created by the confrontation heightened the noise level as the students clumped themselves into groups and started looking at the calendar and jotting down tentative lists.

Meg circulated around the class, and Sarah left the room to take the next day's assignments to the copy center. Meg adjusted a few contracts and talked quietly with Amanda Loveless, who just didn't know if she had time for debate in her schedule but wanted to compete. Sarah slipped back into the class, surprised to see only ten minutes left on the clock.

"We need your contracts before you leave today," Meg called out, as Sarah stood by the desk opening mail. She didn't expect anyone to stop after class on the first day, but after watching the other students leave, Brax and Tyler approached Meg, who was stacking disclosure forms.

"We're not going to do any of this," Brax said, waving the empty contract in Meg's face, "because we're not sure that we're even staying at this school." The air suddenly became thick with distrust, and Sarah felt goose bumps on her arms.

Meg said, "Oh?" and waited for the boys to continue. When the boys didn't add to their opening salvo, she finally said, "And?"

"We're seniors—" Tyler began.

She adopted a sincere tone. "Yes, I think I already knew that, but how is that significant?"

"We have our own plans." Brax stuck out his chin. "If we want to go to a big-name university, we have to win at some important tournaments early in the season, and none of them are in this state."

"Okay," Meg said. "What's your plan?"

Tyler edged in front of Brax. "We need to go to at least four out-of-state tournaments before Christmas."

"And you're basing this goal on what information?" Meg asked.

"Bart, our counselor at camp, thinks we have a shot at being a top team, nationally."

Sarah made a small choking noise. "Excuse me," she said, trying to stifle a laugh. "I didn't mean to interrupt. I just caught an absurdity in my throat." But no one heard her.

"Well," Meg said thoughtfully, "I'm surprised to see you here. Those tournaments won't accept independent student registration. You know our district doesn't allow out-of-state travel. The county does. I'm not sure what you want from us. Would you like us to call Mr. Washburn at Mountain View for you?"

Clearly not willing to play, Meg eliminated any leverage the boys had assumed they had. Tyler tried again.

"But you take students to Nationals. That's out of state." Tyler's face reddened right up to his blond roots. He shoved his clenched fist into the pocket of his jeans.

Meg started speaking more slowly. "Our district has chosen—very wisely, I think—not to put itself in a position it can't legally defend. If the county is challenged, they'll be forced to change their policy. Even if your parents are willing to pay for your transportation, our district is still obligated to provide the same opportunity for any student who would like to go. We fund-raise to take any student to Nationals who qualifies. We can't have one team for rich kids and another for kids who aren't." Meg shrugged. "So there you are. Make your own choices."

Sarah tapped her pencil sharply on the edge of the metal desk, but the boys didn't move. They seemed certain that their coaches could remove this barrier if they chose.

Meg sighed heavily. "Thousands of dollars of debate scholarships were awarded to this team last spring. Murphy and Sam have gone to Whitman. It's got a great debate program and a huge endowment. They'll have a free ride through school if they do well."

Brax broke in. "We think we can get into a big name."

Meg extended her palms and tipped her head to one side. "Mrs. Williams and I have some planning we need to finish. I'll be interested to see how you boys solve this. If you choose to stay in our program, you'll need to complete all the assignments Mrs. Williams and I choose to give. Colleges aren't going to be impressed by a failing grade in debate and a poor coach's evaluation."

"Even schools with little names," Sarah whispered. She couldn't help herself, and the wicked smile she couldn't suppress was more of an irritation than either boy could tolerate. Tyler's face became a dangerous shade of magenta, and he clenched his teeth. If he had stepped up and smashed a hole in the dry wall with his fist, Sarah wouldn't have been surprised, but instead the boys bolted out the room, slamming the door as they left. *Three-year-olds in great big bodies*, she thought.

"Sounds like a parent wants to drop the name of an Ivy League school at the country club," Meg said, thoughtfully sliding a pencil in and out of her hair. "Tuition at those top-tier schools is exorbitant."

"You know what the kids call the Colton's new house? Tara West." Sarah wondered if the contractor had built slave quarters out back for domestics and other riff-raff.

"Brax has qualified for free lunch since the second grade," Meg added.

Sarah looked at her over her reading glasses. "How do you know that?"

"I saw his file." Meg winked. "No one was in the counselor's office."

Sarah stretched her arms over her head. "This is going to be one long year," she announced to the empty desks. Relieved to have the day finished, she could smell the rain in the air and wondered if she had closed the windows in her car. Large drops splattered against the window. She turned back to the computer screen and finished entering attendance.

"Little names?" Meg stood over Sarah's shoulder and started to laugh.

Tom rapped loudly on the door at that particular moment and came in, followed closely by Jenny, his small shadow. Sarah smiled at the sight of him. Her middle child was tall and had light-brown hair and inappropriately long eyelashes. He'd been wearing his student body sweater all day, at the behest of the vice principal, to designate himself as a student who could officially shepherd lost freshman and correct small social injustices.

Usually in the middle of a circle of friends, this afternoon he was with only Jenny.

"So how are things? How was the first day?" Tyler and company suddenly seemed unimportant, as Sarah looked hard at Jenny, who was smiling and laughed quietly while Tom told his stories. She stood so close to him that he almost hit her when he gestured. Twenty questions were on the tip of Sarah's tongue, until she noticed the fresh scabs on Jenny's thumb.

"Who do you have for geometry?" Meg asked.

"Mrs. Beales," Jenny replied, uncomfortable as the conversation focused on her.

"Oh, you'll love her." Meg was gushing a little, but it filled up the empty airspace.

Tom nodded. He must have located Jenny right after the last bell. He was probably waiting outside her class. Sarah imagined Tom, wearing his red and gold sweater, coming in the back of the room, making a nonverbal statement to the other students that this was his little sister, then shepherding her through the mob of excited students in the halls. Tom was doing his best to help. *Maybe*, Sarah thought, *this year could be a turning point.*

"Can Jenny stay and help me put up some posters? Everyone else bailed on me."

"Sure. The piano can wait. I'll see you guys at home." Sarah smiled as they walked out the door. Tom hung his arm over Jenny's shoulder, and Sarah knew he would take her down to the office and introduce her to his friends and the vice principal. Jenny would hold the tape and the scissors, and follow Tom patiently around the school, a small grateful slave trying to look inconspicuous, but she would have a smile on her face at dinner.

"So what do you think about Jenny's first day?" Meg asked, raising one eyebrow and listening patiently as Sarah recounted the scene in her kitchen that morning. "You need to hit up that ex-husband for more money."

Sarah sighed. "You know, five years ago, when Robbie was starting high school, I wrote and explained our finances and asked if we could renegotiate our child support. I tried to be nice about it. He was an assistant professor and making a lot more money than when we divorced. Do you know what he said?"

Meg shook her head.

"He said if I wanted to take him to court—with what?—he would ask for increased visitation. He said he'd want the kids for three months in the summer and Christmas every year. He'd talked to his attorney—can you imagine even having one?—and the man told him he was well within his rights. I can't fight him in court." Sarah pushed her forehead with her palm. "He never asked to have more time with the kids until I needed more money. Not once. Robbie had a fit. The boys were both playing baseball then. Do you know what Bob said when I told him that? He wrote to me and said it might be hard to believe, but there were actually baseball teams in Iowa. He's such a jerk."

"The world's cluttered with jerks. I think we've got two in fifth period, but the day's over."

"And we all lived," Sarah said.

Meg gave her a funny look. "Did you think perhaps we wouldn't?"

invisibility

*L*ooking at the crush of students, Jenny groaned softly. She crossed her thin arms over her biology book, lowered her head, and plowed ahead, trying to avoid bumping into other kids. She had a near miss with a large girl with long brown hair and a stricken look on her face who confided loudly to her much shorter friend, "I didn't finish it last night. I thought I would have time this morning, but my stupid mom forgot to wake me up."

The smaller girl had been in Jenny's eighth grade cluster class, but nothing on the girl's face registered recognition as they walked directly toward Jenny. *Do they even see me?* Jenny wondered.

To avoid the collision, Jenny moved behind a flying wedge of freshman boys making their way toward the south bank of lockers. Her left sock was drooping, and she had ink on her fingers, but getting into the girl's lavatory was impossible. Responding to a friend's shout from the stairwell, a tall boy with large ears and a goofy smile turned and noticed Jenny. "Dracula," he sang out above the noise and confusion. Empowered by her red-faced embarrassment, he sang again, "Dracula," and laughed, pleased with himself for being so clever.

Just one friend. That's all she wanted, just one friend. Then she could square her thin shoulders and say, "Randy Larkin, zit city!" Instead, she ducked quickly to the right, her head down, and fell in behind two small blondes in blue and pink hoodies. One was making rapid conversation in a high-pitched voice punctuated with giggles.

"Who do you have for English?" she said, as they moved toward that wing.

"Williams."

"Oh my gosh, I've heard that she's so hard. My sister nearly died in her class."

The friend raised her shoulders and nodded. "It's really bad."

"She assigns books that don't have a video. I mean, you have to like read the whole book. What's that about? Are you going to transfer out? I mean it's not like we don't have anything else to do." The whole time the girl was talking, her eyes were doing a quick scan of the corridor, watching for anyone interesting. A skinny boy with tousled brown hair walked toward them. He moved with a smooth rhythm in time to the imagined music playing in his head.

"Do you know what else I heard about Williams?" The girl's face was suddenly more animated, and she whispered behind her bright-pink fingernails.

Her friend's eyebrows shot straight up. "Oh my gosh. Where did you hear that?"

"It's true. I swear. I've heard it from two totally different people."

Jenny stared at the polished concrete floor, her dark hair falling over her scarlet cheeks. She knew kids thought her mother was hard, and she didn't care, but this was new, some bit of trash floating through the halls about her mom that everyone knew, that everyone was talking about—except her. The math hallway. Thank heaven. She wanted to vanish into a locker and go to Narnia or anywhere that wasn't here. *But,* she thought, *I'm invisible, so what difference does it make?* Dracula could turn into mist and vanish under doors. People looked right through her as though she were a shadowy outline, a placeholder, but what place was she holding? She wanted to escape to the parking lot and hide in the backseat of their car and just sleep until her mother came to drive her home. She slipped into the back of her geometry class. Opening her organized notebook, she pulled out her textbook and turned to the assignment. Then she wrote faintly on a sheet of lined paper, *Isolate = Jenny = invisible.* She rested her forehead on her left hand and traced the word *invisible* repeatedly until she saw Mrs. Beale move to the front of the class.

She heard small snatches of what Mrs. Beale was saying, but her mind wandered to an article she'd found in her mother's cluttered book bag. Looking for a pink marker, Jenny had noticed a couple of under-lined sentences and question marks written in the margins. Jenny was just about to push the mess back into the bag when her eye caught *Jenny* scribbled in pencil, and then a few lines down, her mother had jotted, *solutions?* That would be her mother. There always had to be a plan. Jenny had scanned the text. Her mother had written *learned or genetic?* in the middle of the page. Jenny slumped down on the floor and read the entire article, "Adolescent's Social Network: Friendship Cliques and Social Isolates." There she was, in print, a social isolate perfectly described. No friends, desperate, needy, anxious, prone to depression and drug use. Drug use? Frightened, she had shoved the article back into her mother's bag and run into her bedroom to examine her face in the mirror as though the shape of her nose or the color of her eyes could invalidate the diagnosis. If her mother thought this was genetic, then there was no cure. Was there?

Jenny remembered the story she had heard a million times, about not waving bye-bye when she was a baby. Robbie and Tom had waved until their little arms had about fallen off, but not her. She would just hide her head in her mother's shoulder and refuse to perform. Now she knew why her mother repeated that one dumb thing. She had always been like this, even when she was a baby.

Here she was in high school, her mother's magic solution. Her mother had promised that she would have friends in high school, so where were they? Maybe if she wrapped herself in gauze or doused herself with paint, she would be visible. She rubbed her pencil eraser up and down on the equation until it read *Jenny = visible*, but she didn't believe it and finished erasing the whole thing and brushed the little eraser bits off the desk and put them in her pocket.

At the end of class, Jenny waited for the room to empty before peering out into the hall. Two large seniors boys lounged by a locker, and Jenny allowed the door to close softly. Moving back to her desk, she made a pretense of rearranging the contents of her backpack, assuming that Mrs. Beale wouldn't notice her, but of course, Mrs. Beale did.

Sarah had insisted, during registration, that Jenny have Mrs. Beale for geometry. "She's not just a teacher," Sarah had explained. "She's an experience." And it was true. Reams of multi-colored notifications and schedules that emanated from the office weren't in evidence in Mrs. Beale's room; and yet, students seemed to arrive and depart punctually. There weren't any red and gold pompoms or yellowing school paraphernalia attached to the light fixtures or the walls. In fact, there was really no evidence that this room was used for teaching fourteen-year-olds except for the thirty-five desks arranged precisely in six rows. Candy wrappers, loose papers, forgotten books, and stray writing utensils, typically scattered by departing freshmen, never appeared on her floor. The countertops and cupboards were always dusted and tidy. No one knew if she did the cleaning herself or if dust and grime felt so completely out of place in her presence that they chose to go elsewhere.

As a matter of routine, moments before the bell rang, Mrs. Beale pushed lightly on a sound system, and classical music played while her students changed classes. One well-known Mrs. Beale legend told of the tardy bell ringing just as Puccini started to sing. The expression on Mrs. Beale's face caught the attention of the class until they actually started to listen. When Ralph Murdock and Larry Buchanan made farting noises on their arms to embellish the music, Liz Boxy hissed at them so malevolently they immediately stiffened their hands at their sides and pursed their lips, as thirty-four freshmen students sat enthralled until Mrs. Beale pushed stop. "Beautiful music and mathematics clarify the mind," she said. No one giggled; no one sneezed; no one even breathed loudly. It was just one of several miraculous events that assured Mrs. Beale of canonization in the unlikely event she should ever die.

—◦◦◦—

Mrs. Beale's thick white hair was beautifully styled, and she was wearing a lovely deep shade of eggplant, as she sat down in the adjacent desk and touched Jenny's hand. Her skin was paper thin and cool, and the veins and tendons stood out in bas-relief.

"Jenny," she began, "I invite several students, two from each grade, to participate in a small math competition twice each year. Do you think you might be interested?"

Jenny, immediately suspicious, thought of her mother's penciled handwriting in the margin, *solutions?*, and looked up at Mrs. Beale. "Did my mother ask you?" Then she quickly glanced away.

Chuckling softly, Mrs. Beale patted Jenny's hand. "I really do enjoy your mother, Jenny. I wish I had half of her energy, but no, she doesn't know I'm extending this invitation. Mr. Rose at the middle school called me during the summer. He thinks you're very gifted. From what I've observed this year, I would agree with him. I think you have exceptional clarity of mind."

Jenny smiled and forgot to put her hand up to cover her mouth. "I'd like to be on the math team." She'd be one of Mrs. Beale's math geeks who routinely won large prizes.

"That pleases me." Mrs. Beale smiled. Standing up from the desk, Mrs. Beale's watery blue eyes examined Jenny thoughtfully. "Remember, dear, you must be the protagonist in your own life, the heroine in your own story." She paused for a moment. "And I feel certain that you will be." She touched Jenny lightly on the shoulder, smiled, and walked to her desk as Maria Callas began to sing the aria from *Madame Butterfly.*

Jenny left the room sure that she could slay a few dragons, particularly if they were small and didn't breathe much fire. Her invisibility might be a secret weapon. She made her way to the cafeteria. Pulling her brown sack out of her backpack, she sat down at the long table next to some girls who lived in her neighborhood. She had known most of them since kindergarten and attended church with a few, but no one spoke to her, and shortly after Jenny slipped a straw into her carton of milk, the girls stood up, as though responding to some inaudible signal, a geek alert, and left. Dorothy was the only one who looked at Jenny. With a grim smile on her face, she shrugged as if to say, "Sorry, but there's nothing I can do," and then followed the gaggle of freshman girls out of the lunchroom. Jenny felt as if someone had punched her in the stomach. *They're afraid their popularity will suffer if they're at the same table with such a loser,* Jenny thought. She bit her lip and slipped her sandwich back in the sack and walked out the patio door.

No more cafeteria, Jenny thought the next day as she tucked her legs up Indian style on the grassy bank of the canal and looked into the brown paper sack, as though she hadn't packed it herself. She smiled at her own silliness. No surprises. No short meaningful note telling herself to have a great day. No extra carrots. No fabulous cookie with a half-inch of butter frosting and sprinkles. Just a peanut butter and jelly sandwich, some corn chips, and an apple, but she was happy. The sun warmed her shirt and the back of her neck, as she sat on the canal bank, listening to the water gurgle pleasantly over the rocks. The canal and a copse of wild roses shielded her from the lunchroom windows. Munching slowly on half of her sandwich, she opened *The Two Towers* to the page marked with a lavender strip of paper.

Jenny had just bit down on the second half of her sandwich when she saw a short redheaded boy cutting across the track around the football field, heading for the bridge. She glanced around quickly, realizing she looked like she was hiding, but if she left, she'd have to wander alone through the halls until the bell rang. She set her book on her knees and decided to pretend he couldn't see her.

He was almost to the bridge when he stopped and walked a couple of steps nearer to where she was sitting. His hair was carefully combed, but it didn't help him much. He wasn't very nice looking. Sore purple acne covered his cheeks, and he had a space between his front teeth. Jenny thought for a moment of her constant schedule of appointments to ensure straight teeth and to avoid acne scarring and thought this boy's mother must be one relaxed woman.

"You're Mrs. Williams's daughter?" the boy asked. Jenny put her hand up to shield her eyes from the sun and nodded. She remembered him from the parking lot, but she didn't know his name, and he didn't volunteer it.

"Mrs. Beale said that you're going to be on the math team."

Jenny nodded again.

He continued as though what he was saying would interest her. "We were good last year. We won everything at the last competition. Beale's been doing this for years, so she knows what's up." He paused, waiting for some sort of response.

"She seems very nice," Jenny said.

"She's forgotten more than most teachers know." He dismissed other teachers with a slice of his hand.

Why is he talking to me? Jenny thought. *Doesn't he know I'm invisible?* She chewed the rough edge of her fingernail and then quickly pulled it out of her mouth and squinted up at him. Was he sizing her up? Deciding if she was going to be an asset or not? Warning her that she needed to work hard, not hold everyone back?

He squatted down in the dry grass next to her and picked up her novel, turning it over in his freckled hand several times before setting it back on the grass. "You're probably not worried about colleges and scholarships yet, but this competition is great for applications. I'm applying to some good schools. If the team wins state, I can get a math scholarship and maybe a spot on a college debate team. I might be eligible for grants you don't have to pay back."

If he's on the debate team, Jenny thought, *he must know Mom and Meg.* She started to relax a bit and pulled her hands out from under her thighs. She had heard her mother and Robbie talk scholarships and grants and schools. "It's hard to get a full ride."

"Yeah, but your brother was crazy to stay here. He could have gone to a better school. College is the only ticket most of us get. If you blow it, you're stuck." He reached into his backpack and pulled out a worn novel. "If you like that," he said, gesturing toward the fantasy she had been reading, "you'll really like Robert Jordan." He tossed *The Eye of the World* into her lap as he stretched out his legs and squinted up at the sun. "I'll get it back at our meeting next Thursday. Do you always eat here by yourself?"

"Today's the first."

He sat for a moment as if waiting for her to say something interesting, but she just stared at the apple in her lap. Finally, he stood and brushed the grass off his legs before walking back up to the bridge. "Later." He waved.

Jenny opened the book and glanced down at the name and address printed clearly: Brax Martin. *He lives in a worse neighborhood than I do,* Jenny thought wryly.

"Good luck, Brax Martin," Jenny said softly. "I hope you find your ticket out of here."

back to school night

$t$he confusion of class changes was over in time for Back to School Night, a fall event with shortened class schedules that allowed just enough time for parents to become lost in the labyrinth of stairs, halls, and classrooms created by poorly planned remodeling. By the time the third period had ended, the stream of parents coming in and out of classrooms slowed to a trickle. By the last session, the few parents still in the building were congregated in the foyer eating cookies and drinking watery punch.

Relieved, Sarah untied the paisley scarf around her shoulders; the evening was almost over. She looked up at the clock. "Thank you."

"And why are we thanking the clock?" Meg asked.

"Tyler's parents didn't show, and no mother of Wallace Williams."

———

The previous Thursday, the last day class changes were allowed, Sarah was pounding her head on the desk in front of the computer screen moaning, "Noooo."

Jenny had come in looking for a ride home, and she and Meg glanced at Sarah.

Sarah moaned into the keyboard, "God hates me."

"God doesn't hate you. What did you see?" Meg asked. "A demonic apparition on the screen?"

"Worse. The counselor put my ex-husband's nephew in my second hour."

Bill, the teacher next door, had stopped by to whisper a bit of gossip about a senior football player, but this conversation was more interesting. "Is he a terror?"

"No," Sarah said, "he's a nice kid, but that's a genetic miracle, a strange planetary alignment. His mother is a complete crazy person. She put him in my class on purpose."

"Personally," Bill started, "I don't allow relatives in my classes. They always want to have shared moments, small familial warm fuzzies. It just doesn't work. So, who's the mom?"

"You probably know her. Valerie Williams."

"Oh, Mrs. Beads and Bangles." Bill began shaking his fingers above his head, moving rhythmically in a belly dance, wiggling his skinny hips back and forth, waving invisible veils across his face. He suddenly stopped dancing and sang, missing the high note, "Wearing baubles, bangles, and beads."

"*Kismet*," Meg explained to Jenny, who was laughing hard and in danger of tipping over in the desk.

Suddenly a teacher again in a striped shirt and khaki pants, Bill said, "You, young lady," and he pointed a long finger at Jenny, "have much to learn about the mysteries of the Middle East." He sat down and stretched out his legs. "I had one of her older kids in American history a couple of years ago. I don't remember Mrs. Many Bracelets being an overwhelming nuisance."

Sarah was laughing and pounding her head against the desk at the same time. "She'll come to everything. Back to School Night, parent-teacher conferences, unannounced after school visits, and never mention her son."

"So what's the story?" Meg shrugged.

"It's everything." Sarah laughed again. "All the dirt. She assumes I'm dying to hear it all. We shared an evil mother-in-law in a past life, so she thinks we're linked forever." Sarah shook her head. "Not a friend. Plus, the truth never gets in her way, so you don't know if you're getting the real stuff or a highly colored embellishment. Sometimes she's sent on fact-finding missions." Sarah mimicked students who had a good whine going. "Why won't this all just go away? Wallace Williams in my second hour?"

"Wallace is a nice kid," Jenny volunteered. She pulled at a hangnail on her little finger. "He always says hello to me."

Sarah stopped mid-tirade, realizing Jenny could probably count the kids who spoke to her on one hand.

"So on the familial Richter scale, this woman is an 8.5?" Bill asked Jenny, and Jenny nodded.

"Oh, Bill," Sarah laughed. "I'm so sorry you're married to such a completely wonderful woman."

"Hey, Bonnie puts one toe out of line, and I'll reactivate your application." He gave Sarah a slurpy kiss on the cheek, and as he turned to leave, he caught Jenny's surprised expression. "Your mom's old, kiddo, but she's not dead."

———

Back to School Night was almost over, and Sarah looked around at the empty classroom and said to Meg, "Why do we do this each year? Such a waste of time." The words were barely out of her mouth when a large man stepped hesitantly in the back door. He noticed the two women talking and turned partially, as though trying to decide if he should come in the room or walk back down the hall. All graciousness at these PTA functions, Meg moved quickly to shepherd him into the room.

"Can I help you?" she asked, since he clearly looked lost.

He had broad shoulders, a firm stance, and lightly graying hair. He was a physically imposing person with strong facial features but kind eyes. Wrinkled by too much time in the sun, crow's feet showed even when he wasn't smiling. He was not smiling now, and he looked from Sarah to Meg. "I was trying to find Williams slash Woodruff, and I also need to see just Williams." Then he did smile, very pleasantly. "I understand you two are joined at the hip."

"I don't think so." Sarah looked quickly down at her side. "I don't seem to be attached to anything or anyone in particular. And to whom are you attached?"

He chuckled. "I belong to Jake and Jonathan McLaughlin. I'm Clayton McLaughlin."

Sarah smiled. "I know Jake. He plays ball with Tom. He's in third period."

"I couldn't get here for that class, but I've been trying to visit two sets of teachers. I think you have Jonathan in the morning. He's a sophomore."

Sarah nodded.

"I just wanted to tell you that if either of my boys gives you any trouble, I want you to call me." He paused and took a deep breath. "I'm not looking for any special consideration, just a phone call." He pulled business cards out of his pocket and handed one over to Sarah and another to Meg. He shook hands with each of them and looked surprised when Sarah laughed. She wasn't sure why the simple formality stuck her as funny, but Mr. McLaughlin smiled back.

Looking down at the card, Meg said, "You're the sheriff. I thought I recognized your name."

"Oh," Sarah said, touching her bottom lip with her finger. "How about a trade? We'll tattle on your boys if I can call you for help with our mock trial case in the spring. We always need information about guns, fingerprinting, and stuff like that."

"It's a deal," he nodded, studying Sarah's face for a second.

At that moment the mother of Wallace Williams, wearing a noisy charm bracelet, made her entrance. It was impossible for Valerie Williams to just walk into a room. The woman was all noise and confusion.

"Oh, I'm so glad you're still here," she gushed. "I had to talk to Mrs. Beale. How can anyone that old dream about teaching geometry?"

Valerie's presumption of an intimate relationship irritated Sarah. Valerie thought she held all the cards—plastic—that allowed her intrusive behavior, and she plowed ahead. "Can't they get rid of her? Turn off her pacemaker or something."

The sheriff had moved quietly out the door. Sarah glanced after him for a second before she turned to try and disengage.

"Mrs. Beale?" Sarah countered. "She's a wonderful teacher, a national treasure actually. We're lucky to have her." Sarah pushed a disclosure form toward Valerie. She hoped to sweep her right out of the door like a greasy fast food wrapper and go home. Sarah's legs ached, and a headache, right behind her eyes, throbbed.

She had planned to grab a couple of leftover cookies on her way out of the building to eat instead of dinner, but here she was, shanghaied. The cookies would be cleaned up and inside a professional PTA woman's car before Sarah could get to the lobby. She had taped a note on the refrigerator door for Tom and Jenny: *Graze. I'm at Back to School Night*, so there was nothing waiting for her at home except perhaps a bowl of dry cereal or a peanut butter sandwich. She had her mouth all ready for a pecan bar, or a sugar cookie with pink frosting, or maybe a mint brownie.

"How's Robbie?" Valerie asked, opening the door to a conversation Sarah didn't want to have. Robbie was in Venezuela as a missionary for the Mormon Church. Tom and Jenny missed him, but Sarah ached for him. There was nothing about her son that she was going to share willingly with this jangling woman.

"He's fine." Sarah moved down the row of chairs toward the teacher's desk and her purse, which contained her car keys, an essential item for her getaway.

Meg looked pointedly down at her watch for several seconds. "They'll be locking up the building at nine-thirty." Meg was trying to save her, but Valerie Williams was not to be swayed from her errand.

"Well, his grandparents are upset that he never writes to them."

Sarah just shrugged.

Valerie continued, "We're all so proud of Robbie. No one thought he would choose a mission over basketball, especially after he was all-state. Of course, a mission is just as good as red-shirting for a year." She was clearly repeating a conversation she had heard elsewhere.

Sarah didn't respond. She didn't care. Nothing Valerie said was as important as the vanishing possibility of a mint brownie. Sarah could almost see the plate of cookies levitating down the main walkway toward the parking lot. Eventually Valerie would wind down if she didn't receive the encouragement of a reply, but tonight Sarah didn't feel compelled to wait. She fished in the bottom of her purse for her keys.

"Everyone in the family knows that he doesn't answer his dad's letters," Valerie said. "I don't know why their relationship is so bad."

But Sarah knew, and so did her ex-husband, Bob.

—⁓—

A brisk wind blew the new leaves in the crab apple tree in the front yard. It would be warm and oppressively humid later in the day, but the early summer morning felt cool as Sarah came through the screen door and pulled the worn, gingham robe around her tightly. Picking at a glob of dried pancake batter on the front with an uneven fingernail, she watched her husband glance back at the whole scene: the rusty Toyota Corolla in a carport crowded with kid clutter, a duplex that needed paint, and a small face with tousled blond hair watching him from the living room window. Sarah saw her husband's chest heave, and his heavy sigh was audible.

"You're just going to sneak away? Not say a word to the kids?" she said.

He shook his head slowly. Two days of stubble covered his chin, and dark shadows circled under his eyes. He opened his mouth and then closed it.

"What about us?" Her head gestured toward the house. "How are we supposed to live? I've got three hundred dollars in checking. That's it."

All she could read in his face was exasperation, nothing else. He thought she was being unreasonable. It was June, and she had known he was leaving since February, but she hadn't done a thing. Getting a job, moving, staying, it all seemed like an acknowledgement or a tacit agreement that in some way she was saying, "Okay, leave." But now that he was actually standing on the lawn with a cheap suitcase in his hand, she almost felt relieved. The pleading and crying were over. The questions answered. The excuse was some post-doc fellowship in Switzerland, but actually Bob was leaving her. That he was leaving her for another woman had not penetrated her thick wall of denial until very recently. He was leaving her and the continuous turmoil and inconvenience of two little boys and a baby—for a bleached blonde. How humiliating. She could almost see him tugging at the millstone that weighed around his neck.

"We've talked about this," he said. "You'll have to go back to work for a year or two."

"I'm not certified here. It will take a quarter. I don't have money for tuition, for childcare, food, anything."

"You'll have to get the bishop to give you a hand for a couple of months, and I'll send you what I can."

"Welfare." The word hung in the air between them like an ugly bit of bad weather. With the toe of his shoe, he pushed at a couple of ripe crab apples rotting in the grass.

"Did you ever love me?" she murmured.

"I don't know. I thought I did."

"If you weren't sure, you shouldn't have used up my life." Sarah brushed her hair away from her face. "I know you didn't want Jenny, but you lobbied for Robbie and Tommy. Why did you want to have children with me?"

He wouldn't look at her. He tossed the duffle bag near the curb.

Standing on the front porch, all Sarah wanted was enough energy to twist the knife. Her carefully planned future was walking away from her, and at the very least, she wanted to see him bleed. She pulled her arm across her face, wiping her tears on her sleeve. She looked from him to the unfamiliar car parked by the curb.

"So, is she going with you?"

"I can't afford to take anyone."

Suddenly the weight of her life was unbearable in a standing position, and she slumped onto the concrete front steps. She was so tired. She hadn't been eating. Four long months of not knowing what was so wrong. She grabbed her knees with her thin arms. Her head felt so heavy. Her curly hair covered her face, as she rested her head on her knees.

He turned away from her and opened the trunk of the small red car, and with a nonchalance that belied the expression on his face, he tossed in his duffle bag and the suitcase. As he fumbled in his pocket for the car keys, the screen door banged open. Robbie came running down the sloped yard.

His eyes darted from his mother's face to his father's suitcase. "Don't go."

Kneeling down in the wet grass, Bob said, "I've got to leave, Robbie, but you've got to remember one thing for me. Can you do that?"

Robbie looked into his dad's face.

"I won't be here for the second grade, but I'll be back right after third grade starts. That's a long time, but I'll come back." He hugged the little boy tightly to his chest and kissed the tangle of blond curls. "Will you write me letters?"

Robbie nodded.

Sarah stood up slowly and walked quietly down the grassy slope. "Robbie, I can hear Jenny in her crib. Do you want to go and get her up? I need to tell your dad just a couple of things before he leaves." She kept her voice light and pleasant. Robbie, reassured by the hug, ran toward the house.

As she moved closer to her husband, Sarah's eyes narrowed. "Your children won't remember you," she said, "and they'll grow up hating you. That's a promise."

"Come on, Sarah." His jaw sagged, and he pushed his thick hair back with his hand. "Nobody planned this. It just happened." He leaned against the car. "It's no one's fault."

She was being cast off, thrown away, discarded. Without a second thought, he was turning her life into the stuff of tawdry jokes and knowing half smiles. He stared stupidly at her for a moment before he got in the car and slammed the door.

He gunned the engine, breaking the early morning quiet, and she said softly under her breath, "You selfish, selfish jerk."

She shoved her memories behind her, as Valerie prattled on. Sarah crossed her arms tightly across her chest, and her mouth made a thin red line across her face.

"Dave made such an effort to send Bob all the newspaper clippings Robbie's senior year."

"Hummm." Sarah nodded, but what she wanted to say was, "Who cares? You are not a cookie. You're a pain in the neck. Be gone." She gave Valerie an irritated look.

"Dave felt so sorry for his brother, missing so much."

"Well, right now all that I'm missing is anything remotely resembling dinner. I am just so tired, I could fall in a heap, Valerie, but thank you so much for coming."

Sarah walked over to the door as Meg flipped out the lights. They walked down the hall, but Valerie, oblivious to any slight, tottered right behind them in heels too high and an outfit too sophisticated for a PTA event.

Her streaked blonde hair bounced along as she continued. "It wouldn't hurt Robbie to be polite to his grandparents. They're sitting on a truckload of money."

Sarah stopped at the top of the stairs and slowly turned to make eye contact with Valerie. "Enough," she said quietly. "No one was interested in my children until Robbie started showing up in the newspaper, so let's just not go there, okay?"

Meg's eyes widened. She interrupted Sarah. "You know, we're all tired. This isn't a great time to be having this kind of a conversation." Meg rested a hand gently on Valerie's shoulder. "Why don't you call Sarah on a Saturday afternoon when you have time for a good visit?"

Valerie jabbered for a couple of seconds about making that phone call and fluttered her eyes at Meg as though she was flirting with an old boyfriend. Shifting her leather handbag into her left hand, she marched down the hall.

"What a piece of work," Meg whistled.

"That whole family's sick and twisted. I'm sure Dave loved sending those newspaper clippings to Bob, sticking in the knife. Look at what you're missing, big brother." Sarah sighed, knowing by now all the cookies had vanished into the night.

"Is he the only sibling that lives in town?" Meg asked.

Sarah nodded. "You know, my reaction to Bob or any of his family is the emotional equivalent of headache, nausea, and diarrhea."

"Oh dear." Meg felt Sarah's forehead. "Well, just because you're paranoid—" and she handed an imaginary microphone to Sarah.

"—doesn't mean they're not out to get you." Sarah laughed, pushing the handle on the exterior door. The night was cool and the stars were clear. Most cars had left the parking lot.

"I don't blame them for wanting to be a part of Rob's basketball career. His senior year was amazing," Meg said, as they walked toward the parking lot. "Doesn't Rob ever write to his dad?" she asked.

"Why would he?"

They walked across the grass as the janitor shut off the lights and slipped the chains through the handles on the front doors.

needs not met

*L*ow profile was the mental picture Sarah had of herself at church. Unfailingly pleasant to everyone, she kept her opinions to herself and sat reverently on the back row. It came as something of a surprise when the telephone rang late Thursday afternoon, nearly dinner time, and the bishop asked her if she had time that evening for a visit.

She knew being a Mormon bishop wasn't an easy job. An ecclesiastical responsibility for four or five hundred people was nothing to sneeze at. Two nights a week, the bishop scheduled ten or twelve appointments to counsel members of his congregation or to ask people to accept assignments. He visited members in the hospital and checked on elderly people. He was busy all day on Sunday. He scurried around doing all this in addition to his day job and raising his own family.

Of course, the bishop didn't make appointments to chat. Something was up. She had assured him that she could be available and at the chapel at seven-thirty. Now she quickly tried to put the puzzle pieces together as she sautéed onions and green pepper in a shallow pan for a tuna casserole. Sarah inhaled the smell of onions and frowned as she thought about the possibility of one more added responsibility.

She had been teaching the thirteen-year-olds in Sunday School for the past five years, a harrowing job that no one in his right mind wanted, but Sarah and the budding adolescents had reached an uneasy truce, because they might encounter her as a teacher at the high school next year. Now, as she tossed the macaroni into a colander and rinsed it in warm water, she wondered why he had called.

———

Sitting at the kitchen table, Jenny separated the bits of green pepper into a small heap on the side of her plate, and Sarah decided not to mention it as she swallowed her last green bean and pushed back her chair.

"Would you tell Tom his dinner's in the fridge?" she asked needlessly. Tom's first instinct when he came home was to open the refrigerator door and stare at the interior as if some fabulous dessert with chocolate sauce and whipped cream would suddenly appear on the middle rack next to the cottage cheese and yogurt.

"Where are you going?" Jenny looked up from her plate.

"The bishop wants to see me."

"What for?" Jenny's immediate accusatory tone surprised Sarah. *Does she think I have some large sin lurking around that needs confessing?* But Sarah didn't say, "I haven't done anything." She just shrugged and reached into the closet for her jacket.

"Don't say anything, Mom." *Please* was in Jenny's voice and she had that beaten-up look on her face that was becoming more habitual as the school year went on.

"What do you mean?" But Sarah knew exactly what Jenny meant. On the rare occasions when Sarah opened her mouth at church, strange quotable things leapt off the tip of her tongue and took on a life of their own.

"You know." Exasperated, Jenny spoke in a voice that was almost a whisper, "Like don't say that men standing around in the foyer on Sunday morning look like a penguin convention."

"What's wrong with a little color?"

"Mom, no one is bugged by all the white shirts except you."

Sarah breathed in through her nose and closed her mouth. One little slip and her kids remembered it forever. How many times had she been embarrassed when Jenny did her turtle routine when people tried to talk to her? But that would be keeping score, so she just grumbled, "Okay, okay. I won't say anything."

Setting her plate next to the kitchen sink full of dirty dishes, Jenny shuddered slightly before she picked up her book and headed down the hall without glancing back.

—⁓—

Pleased that there weren't other congregators stacked up in the foyer when she arrived, Sarah sat down and dropped her purse by her side. Resting her arm against the back of the nubby brown couch, her fingers touched the pebbly texture of painted brick. All the interior walls were painted brick. Industrial-strength construction. She could be sitting in any one of a thousand foyers in a thousand buildings. They were all exactly the same. Economy of scale. The same colors, the same carpets, the same furniture, the same absence of any pictures, stained glass, ancient paneled wood, or potted plants. A culture of sameness. The warm blanket of that familiarity, that sameness, had been so comforting when she first moved home. It had been a known quantity, a safe haven for her children, a place to heal. Now something had changed; she didn't know what. She felt smothered.

Sarah looked down the hall as the door of the bishop's office opened, and he emerged with a short seventy-five-year-old woman balancing herself precariously with two canes.

"I feel very optimistic about your situation, Helen." The bishop comforted her with a carefully placed pat on her back as he walked her down the short hallway. The woman leaned against the wall, adjusting her canes, before she pushed her arm into the sleeve of her lilac-colored sweater and gave Sarah the suggestion of a smile, and then she was gone, out the door.

"Well, Sarah, I'm so glad that you could come on such short notice."

"I try and keep Thursday open for misplaced appointments," Sarah said as she looked over her shoulder at the woman making her way carefully down the dark sidewalk

It really wasn't his fault that he wasn't his predecessor, Bishop Rudman, a kindly older man with a shock of white curly hair, who had been a big favorite with Sarah and her children. On Sunday mornings when Jenny was barely more than a toddler, she would escape from her mother and find the bishop. Standing patiently, she would tug softly on his pant leg until he looked down. Scooping her up in his arms, he would continue whatever conversation he happened to be having. Unfortunately, that wonderful man had moved to a retirement community shortly after being replaced by this more recent edition.

Sarah tried to smile at Bishop Richards, a short balding man, and walked into the office ahead of him. Hearing the click of the door closing, Sarah had an ominous feeling in the pit of her stomach. She felt cornered.

"So how are things at school this year?" he asked, looking at her intently.

Sarah wondered how many minutes were going to be devoted to pleasantries before he got down to business. She wondered how he would respond if she asked him to cut to the chase, but she didn't. Sarah knew the drill.

"You know, the best thing about being a teacher is that every year is a clean slate. A whole new set of kids. Nothing ever stays the same. It's great."

"How many years have you been at the high school?"

"Too many to count."

"Are you still enjoying the students?" His look was so piercing that Sarah felt for a moment as though she were being questioned by burly police detectives in a drab green room with a naked light bulb dangling from the ceiling.

"Yes, usually. There are moments, you know." Sarah forced a smile, but her teeth felt dry and her lips didn't slide together easily.

The chitchat continued for a few minutes, and her mind wandered off to a bathtub that needed scrubbing and a set of sophomore essays that needed correcting before first period in the morning. He pulled her back into the present with a question that startled her.

"Do you ever date, Sarah?"

"Do you have someone in mind?" she retorted. Then she added without thinking, "Hopefully with piles of money."

His startled look softened quickly, and he laughed. She couldn't help smiling back, and then she noticed the sheen of moisture on his high forehead. He ran a finger around one side of his collar and grimaced as though his red and blue stripped tie were too tight. Why was he so nervous? Was she making him uncomfortable?

"No, running a dating service isn't a part of my stewardship. But it really isn't good for a woman your age to be alone." He drummed his fingers on the armrests of his chair and chuckled artificially before giving her an embarrassed smile.

Sarah looked at him blankly and started to blush. "Excuse me?"

"Your children are going to leave home before you know it. You'll be all alone. They'll have lives of their own that won't include you. Which is, of course, what we as parents hope for. It would be nice to have a companion your own age." He stopped speaking and looked at her as he moved his bifocals up and down on the bridge of his thick nose.

"Is this why you wanted to see me tonight?"

"No," he continued, "we're thinking about making some changes in the Sunday School." He paused to allow Sarah time to speak, but she didn't say anything. She was biting her tongue, thinking about Jenny's disconsolate face at the kitchen table as she slowly moved bits of green pepper around the rim of her plate.

He went on, "We think that someone else should have the opportunity to teach the thirteen-year-olds."

The momentary relief she felt at being freed from an unpleasant responsibility every single Sunday morning was in immediate conflict with her dismay at being dismissed.

"Have you had complaints?" Sarah responded, straightening her back, and she wondered how long her replacement would last.

"No, no. You're a wonderful teacher, but I've worried about making a person who teaches all week teach on Sunday too." But when he spoke, his eyes flickered away from her toward the gallery of old black-and-white bishops staring down from the wall.

Something else was bothering him; something he couldn't mention. "Are we through?" she asked, reaching down to pick up her purse.

"Not yet. Would you consider being on the activities committee?" he asked quickly.

"The activities committee?"

"You'd help plan and execute three large ward parties each year. Brother Oglethorpe could really use your excellent organizational skills. He asked for you specifically."

Sure he did. Brother Oglethorpe, the terror of the over-forty singles crowd. His mother let go of the leash and died two years ago, and he had been searching for a replacement ever since. He wasn't a bad-looking guy, and his feet flying across the organ pedals did bring Fred Astaire to mind. Sarah didn't know whose type he was, but he certainly wasn't hers.

Sarah scrutinized the bishop's face and didn't speak for a minute. "No problem," she said standing up and moving toward the door. "I'll be happy to help plan parties." She left the office and shut the door firmly behind her.

Tom had her car, and Sarah refused to drive the truck, so she was on foot. She set off walking the three blocks toward home. Walking alone in the dark probably wasn't the smartest thing that she had ever done, but tonight a lurking stranger with evil intentions didn't seem as dangerous as the people who populated her life. There was some logical thread here—single mother, Oglethorpe, Sunday School—but she couldn't figure it out. She suspected a conspiracy.

It had been clear today at lunch that Meg had an agenda too. After tossing her apple core into the metal wastebasket, Sarah had found, with some effort, a relatively clean spot of carpet by the back wall. She was so tired. She just wanted to lie down for ten minutes, and she stretched out on the floor with a couple *Time* magazines propped under her head and closed her eyes. She was experiencing that lovely drowsy moment just before sleep, when Meg batted at her with a rhetorical question.

"Why don't you invite Clayton McLaughlin to go to the movies? He seemed like a nice guy."

"Not the issue. I'm sure he's a nice guy. His kids are nice," Sarah said, wishing Meg hadn't chosen this particular moment to do a character analysis of the sheriff. The sun was coming in the window, heating the small section of mauve carpet where Sarah was lying.

"I think he's interested in you."

"Meg, I don't know him at all," Sarah said, mildly irritated at the loss of her nap.

"But he thinks he knows you. Both of his sons have you. You're probably discussed every night at dinner. I sensed a connection at Back to School Night. You were this close to flirting with him." Meg held up her finger and thumb a fourth of an inch apart.

Sarah sat up and leaned her elbows on her knees. "Back to School Night? I didn't even know he was a widow-were-er," Sarah tripped over her tongue, "at Back to School Night. Give me a break. This place is so charged with sexual energy the building almost pulses. It's warped your brain." Sarah continued her lighthearted grumble. "I mean how can anybody learn anything with half the student body on testosterone overdrive? We should be teaching in a nursing home. We'd be more productive." She gave up on the nap and shook out her skirt as she stood up.

"Well, assuming that you were flirting with the sheriff, it would be okay. You need a life of your own," Meg said.

"I have a life."

"No, actually, you have your children's lives, and I think it could get a bit crowded. You need a life of your very own." Meg was in her lecture mode. "A divorce that happened twelve years ago shouldn't be a life sentence."

"Wait a minute. You're assuming that because I'm single, I don't have a life. Being single isn't a punishment. Do you know that single women are the happiest demographic in our society?"

"Where did you get that?" Meg sounded like a rebuttal speaker.

"*Parade* magazine."

"That's not much of a source."

"It makes sense to me. You've never been single. How would you know?" Sarah scored her point and started to summarize. "You and I have such different world views. You had a mother who served up religious platitudes your whole life. 'Jesus loves you.' 'If you have enough faith, all things are possible.' 'If you get married in the temple, you will live happily ever after.' I grew up on a solid diet of imminent disasters. Did your mother ever tell you not to run with scissors?"

"Of course."

"Well," Sarah continued, "I got the don't run part, but I also got the story of my mother's nameless cousin who left partially opened scissors on the couch. They slipped down between the cushions. The unsuspecting father was impaled. He had to be rushed to the hospital, but only after he lost quarts of blood. The cushions were ruined forever, and I can't look at a pair of scissors without feeling a sharp pain in my bottom that's totally unrelated to Tyler Colton."

"Ouch." Meg put a hand down over her denim skirt to protect her own backside.

"And that's nothing compared to how I feel about escalators. A picture of a little child's mangled hand was near the bottom of the escalator in the library. We couldn't just pass it by. We always had to stop and look at it. Then my mother would tell me about another child who wasn't paying attention on an escalator and got her ponytail caught in the teeth. She was scalped and had to wear a wig for the rest of her life. I've just given you the short story. My mother's version included blood and screaming and the key no one could find to turn off the machine. Gruesome. The inside of my mother's brain was a dark and scary place."

"And this was the person who took care of Jenny?" The moment the words came out of Meg's mouth, Sarah could see she wanted to suck them back in.

"I was doing the best I could," Sarah said defensively. Sadly, she envisioned a miniature version of Jenny standing at the front window in her grandmother's home watching the other little preschoolers fly through the neighborhood with bath towels pinned around their necks. Jenny never felt the wind lift her sweaty curls as she raced through backyards evading pirates or Indians or space aliens. She never stuck out her little chin trading threats in a neighborhood war, and her big wheel stayed safely parked by the back porch. She watched at the window because her grandmother's arthritic knees didn't allow the old woman to chase a four-year-old.

"I'm sorry," Meg said.

"Oh, it's okay. I just don't need any more complications in my life. You see a couple of dates with a nice man as being harmless, but I see myself opening a door to layers and layers of complications and trouble."

"You might be turning your back on something good."

"I've heard that before. When I was first divorced, people used to line me up. A million Joe Shmoes and each one had a sad story. One night I was sitting in a dumpy restaurant listening to some guy, and I thought, *I could be at home reading Treasure Island to my kids. Now that's an exciting story.*"

"Haven't you ever been attracted to anyone?"

"Well, yes. A student's father. He was drop-dead gorgeous."

"And?" Meg leaned forward.

"His wife had some terrible neurological disorder and was sentenced to a wheelchair for life. He loved his wife, but he thought we might be able to have a mutually satisfying relationship."

"Oooo." Meg frowned. "Where? At the gym?"

"We didn't get to the logistics. I just told him there was a word for that kind of relationship."

"Personal trainer?"

"No, adultery." Sarah smiled grimly. "He was very offended."

"The sheriff might be different."

"It's not worth the risk." She walked over and unlocked the class-room door.

———∿∿———

Now, walking home along neighborhood streets, she frowned as she rewound both conversations in her head. Was she so obviously in need of fixing? Walking past the streetlight, she stood in the dark, looked up at the sky, and called out, "You're kidding about Brother Oglethorpe, aren't you?" She knew God had a sense of humor because, after all, He had created skunks. Sarah stood silently for a couple of minutes, enveloped by the softness of the night. She looked up again. "Could You please move your finger just a little to the left of the Smite Sarah Button?" and then, remembering to whom she was speaking, she added a "please." She stood for a moment staring up at the stars and felt a little less important, a little less imposed upon. Looking back down at the sidewalk to avoid tripping over any serious cracks, she pushed the strap of her purse further up on her shoulder and hurried along in the dark.

lost in the mail
utah, 1981

*O*pening the screen door, Mrs. Ritzman craned her neck, look-ing up the street for the postman, and then looked down the street at Sarah and her little children. She puffed a quick breath. She had such a difficult time getting Sarah out of the house before the mail arrived. Plowing through old cardboard boxes in the basement, Tommy had set up a howl when he couldn't find her husband's old canteen, and as she kissed away the tears on his small cheeks, her daughter's new grief brought back the old. Her grandchildren needed the quiet kindly man her husband had been, but she couldn't bring him back any more than she could magically alter their father.

Mrs. Ritzman, Sarah's mother, was a short, stout woman with unnaturally dark brown hair shaped like a football. Her thick glasses magnified her pale watery eyes and gave her the appearance of an elderly beetle. She was a timid soul. Her world was small, composed of a few friends, the ward, and her family. Frequently, the postman was the only person she chatted with all day—that is, until Sarah had moved home in August with her two little boys and a toddler.

Mrs. Ritzman felt nothing but love and compassion as her tired eyes watched her daughter and the three little children pull the rusty red wagon loaded with a thermos and a brown paper grocery sack filled with tuna fish sandwiches and graham cracker cookies. Another block down Oak Forest Drive was Adam's Park, the destination for the small troop anxious to play in the leaves on that October afternoon. Jenny's short plump legs dawdled along, and Sarah swept her up and settled the baby on her hip as the little boys maneuvered the old wagon Mrs. Ritzman's own little children had used. She waved as Sarah looked back toward the house.

Weekdays were easy. Until the superintendent found her a permanent assignment, Sarah was substituting at whatever school called, but Saturdays were a bit of a problem. Mrs. Ritzman had to change her long-standing hair appointment.

The old woman knew it was her religious duty to forgive, but her bitterness was occasionally so intense she wanted to spit bile. Her little Sarah coming home, a failure. Mrs. Ritzman shook her head and stuck her hand inside her shirt to feel for heart palpitations. Just on Thursday, she had been to see her old friend, Mrs. Furhiman, drooling and vacant, at the care center. She'd had a terrible stroke a few days after Easter. High blood pressure was a silent killer. Every time Mrs. Ritzman woke during the night, listening to Sarah's muffled sobs, she hated her son-in-law more and felt her blood pressure rising. How could she forgive him? Honestly, how could anyone forgive him? Sarah needed to find another husband, a better husband. She pursed her lips together tightly. Mrs. Dutson, her oldest friend, had a son, an unmarried man, who, if a bit fastidious, at least held a steady job.

She should have seen this coming. All winter Sarah had been dropping hints that something was not right. "Don't keep looking for houses. We might not be moving home after Bob finishes his training," Sarah had suggested. "He's thinking about staying in academics." Sarah was trying to let her down gently. "He might do some additional training at another program, maybe somewhere in Europe," Sarah had intimated a few weeks later. Then the earthquake hit with multiple aftershocks: Sarah's marriage was over. Carter, Sarah's brother, headed east on a Greyhound bus to collect Sarah and her little children.

This was not the way this story was supposed to end. Mrs. Ritzman felt cheated and humiliated. For years she had trumped her friends because her daughter was married to a doctor. When he graduated from medical school, lengthy discussions had been held about what dress she should wear to commencement. The round of telephone consultations had gone on for weeks. When her son-in-law chose a sub-specialty, all her friends had offered advice. Surely, her palpitations had influenced his decision to become a cardiologist. For the last couple of years, Mrs. Ritzman's opinion on medical matters was given a great deal of consideration by her friends. After all, her son-in-law was a doctor. Now what was there to say? Some days she didn't answer the phone.

She'd held on so tightly to the pretty picture of what Sarah's life would be. Dreams of Sarah's eventual home had sustained her and made her own quiet poverty less grinding. Now this. Shame. Embarrassment. He had abandoned her for another woman, a younger woman. Just like a character in the soap operas she watched every afternoon. Sarah was humiliated. Mrs. Ritzman was humiliated. She hated him. She leaned against the railing on the front porch and waited for the postman.

"Good afternoon, Mrs. Ritzman. Looks like you have another letter from Switzerland." Nodding, he handed her a catalogue, two bills, and the letter with foreign stamps. She grasped the letter and rushed into the house, as quickly as arthritic knees would allow. Setting the rest of the mail on the kitchen table, Mrs. Ritzman slit open the envelope. A letter and a check for two hundred dollars fell on to the counter. After glancing at the amount, she tucked the check carefully into her apron pocket. She reached for matches next to a wooden chicken on the small decorative shelf. Lighting a single match, she brought the flame to the edge of the two-page letter. She held it carefully over the disposal but read the first sentences until the flame burned the tips of her fingers, and she dropped the match. It hissed in the bottom of the sink. *I miss the kids so much. Another associate has a little two-year-old girl with brown hair. They have been very kind to me and invite me over frequently, but it about kills me to think of Jenny and how much she will change before I get home. I miss the boys too. I didn't have any idea how difficult this would be.*

She read the strong masculine hand that described his research opportunity, asked questions about his children, and, at the end of the second page, wondered about the possibility of marriage counseling when he returned. The letter was an overture, a suggestion that reconciliation might be possible. Mrs. Ritzman snorted loudly. He missed his children, but how long would that last? Until the next willing skirt sashayed past. Sarah was well rid of him. The fifth letter he had written, without receiving any response, burned briskly over the sink. Sarah pushed her little children on the swings at the park, as her mother turned on the disposal, and the last hopes for Sarah's marriage flushed through the pipes and made their way to the sewage treatment plant.

Convinced that a clean break was the least painful solution for her daughter and her little grandchildren, the older woman patted the pocket that contained the check. She would endorse it with Sarah's name and spend every penny on Sarah and the children.

Then tucking her pocketbook under her arm, she strolled down the street to LaPreal's Beauty Salon, a one-chair operation in LaPreal's basement, to have her hair done. If she wound her hair in a net and slept on a silky pillow, the hairdo would last until the following Saturday.

"How's poor Sarah?" LaPreal asked sympathetically as Mrs. Ritzman relaxed her head back into the sink.

"The man has no honor, and in the long run she will be better off without him. She's young and pretty. She can do better." The shampoo smelled like rosemary as it lathered under LaPreal's practiced fingers.

"Who was the other woman?" Like everyone else, LaPreal assumed that a man doesn't leave home unless he's going to another woman.

"A stupid nobody. He'll regret this. Sooner than he knows. He'll want Sarah back, but it will be too late. He isn't even going to be a real doctor. He's going to be a doctor to rats or dogs from the shelter," she scoffed dismissively.

LaPreal adjusted the water temperature and rinsed the suds down the drain. "After Sarah put him through all those years of medical school, he doesn't want to be a real doctor?"

"His mother should be ashamed," Mrs. Ritzman said, resolving to talk to Mrs. Dutson the very next day at church.

tomatoes, zucchini, and bullies

*S*arah stood behind Meg's shoulder and stretched her arms above her head as Meg scrolled down a document they were both reading. Lockers slammed in the hallway as students left the building.

"This is really good. She needs to tighten up that first story, but this one's going to fly. Good for her." Sarah felt like cheering.

"Chan's paid attention to what's winning. She's a smart kid."

"Go back up to those numbers." Sarah moved her finger along the screen as the door opened and Bill's head popped in.

"Good afternoon, ladies."

He was almost on his way back down the hall, when Sarah, pointing at a large bulging sack, said, "Do you want any tomatoes or zucchinis?"

He came back in, glanced into the sack, and said, "Sure, we'd love some tomatoes, but no to the zucchinis." He dropped his voice down a register. "We don't do zucchinis at our house." He ticked the items off on his fingers. "No zucchini bread, no zucchini casseroles, and no zucchini a la mode." He looked around the room. "Where's Jenny?"

"She took the much-hated bus to her piano lesson."

"You know you can buy this stuff at a fruit stand," Bill informed Meg's and Sarah's backs.

They both looked up from the screen as Sarah said, "Have you ever been flat-out broke? Have you ever been on church welfare or skipped town without paying your bills?"

Bill shook his head solemnly as though he were a small child being scolded.

"Well, that's why I have a beautiful garden and half a dozen fruit trees, and about a bazillion mason jars that I'll be filling every Saturday morning until Halloween. It's all about having a wolf at the door."

"You throw these tomatoes at wolves?" Bill questioned Sarah seriously. "I think a zucchini would be a better grenade."

Sarah tipped her chin down and started to giggle.

"My goodness, Sarah," he said pulling a large, perfect tomato out of the sack, "you grow these yourself?"

"You sound just like my neighbor. Every year he asks me," and Sarah feigned a dark husky accent, " 'How do you coax such luscious tomatoes out of the earth? So ripe and firm.' But he's not looking at the garden when he says that. He's looking at me, dirty face, scraggly hair, and *all*." Sarah lurched a few steps as though staggering under the weight of gigantic tomatoes.

Meg clicked off the computer. "Maybe cherry tomatoes." She ducked as a paper snowball shot past her ear. "Okay, okay, hang on to your illusions."

Kathy Murdock, the world history teacher, walked in the door to investigate all the laughter. "What's going on?"

"Sarah's neighbor is into her tomatoes," Bill said raising his eyebrows up and down as though he were Groucho Marx.

"He's so creepy," Sarah said. "He has all these motorized gardening weapons. He trims his vinca with a chain saw. His plants all cringe when they see him coming. We call him the serial gardener."

"What does he call you?" Kathy asked.

Bill butted in with his arms outstretched, "The cute little divorcee with the giant tomatoes!"

"You can say what you want," Sarah felt mischievous, "but I love my garden, and I would never brutalize my vinca."

In fact, Sarah had been thinking that if she could get home before four o'clock, she would have time to pick a last batch of beans before they got fat and waxy. She might be able to get them blanched and in the freezer before dinner. She was already feeling the late afternoon sun on her shoulders, and she smiled to herself. She did love her garden, particularly in the fall.

If everything fell into place, after dinner she could reward herself with a couple of hours with a new novel. Sarah smiled and waved a hand at Kathy and Bill as they departed, and she then leafed through the last dozen sophomore essays sitting on the desk. At that moment, Kristen, a senior, stuck her head in the classroom door. Her broad smile was noticeably absent.

"Hey," said Sarah, wondering if Kristen had been waiting outside for Kathy and Bill to leave.

"I have bad news," Kristen said uneasily, as she dropped her bag and sat down where Meg and Sarah were working.

"Hit me," Sarah said, curious about this out-of-the-ordinary visit on a Tuesday afternoon.

"Someone let all the air out of your tires."

"You're kidding."

Kristen grimaced. "They did a few other cars, but your car is the only one with all four."

Sarah clenched her jaw and squeezed her eyes shut before she spoke. "Now what?"

"Call the tire store," Meg said. "See what they can do."

Sarah grumbled into the receiver for several minutes. When she turned back around, angry lines creased her forehead.

"They're swamped. They have a portable air compressor they can bring over, but they can't get here until maybe five-thirty. They're going to charge me fifty bucks. I'd like to strangle the jerks who did this."

Meg looked out the window before she spoke carefully, "Whoever did this thinks they're just being extremely clever. No serious harm done."

Sarah huffed, "My house was egged last weekend. Einstein gobbled up the mess and got sick before I could clean it up. I had to take him to the vet. Not so funny."

Meg looked hard at Kristen. "What do you think's going on?"

"I think Tyler Colton is really angry."

The side of Sarah's mouth curled up in a grimace. "You think he's behind this?" Wasn't it enough that he disrupted her class every day with sneering asides and infected the younger students with his abysmal attitude? "Are Mrs. Woodruff's tires flat?" she asked.

Kristen held up a single finger. "You're the one who calls him on it whenever he's out of line." Kristen shook her head. "I'm not criticizing. He deserves it."

But they all remembered the previous day when Tyler had called

Mike a disgusting name, and Sarah swooped down on him like a small avenging angel waving her finger in his face for the entire room to see. "You can't contaminate an enclosed classroom any more than you can smoke in a restaurant, because we are all forced to consume your ugliness. Clean up your act."

Red faced, Tyler had tried to frame his complaint more appropriately, but Sarah had cut him off with a wave of her hand. "Forget it. There's no justification for that kind of language." Today, retaliation.

Meg gestured for Kristen to continue.

"Tyler thinks, because he's a senior, he should get to run the show this year. Things should go his way," Kristen explained.

"I don't understand why he should think that. Sam and Murphy didn't run the show last year." Meg was adamant.

Kristen laughed. "They thought they did. We all thought they did." And Sarah and Meg smiled at the memory of the two boys who had been in and out of trouble the four years they were in high school but had also managed to win the first place trophy at Governor's Cup and the State Championship Title. They smoked cigarettes in the parking lot, wrote research papers for hire, and published an underground newspaper. Everyone on the debate team loved them.

"Tyler and Brax are just not a Sam and Murphy." Sarah spoke of the recent graduates collectively, as everyone did.

"No, they're very different," Kristen agreed, "but Tyler and Brax still think they should be able to do what they want, and they think you're stopping them."

"What do you think?" Meg prodded her.

Kristen went off on a lengthy tangent that initially didn't seem pertinent to Sarah, who was pushing her fingers against her temples, thinking of her flat tires.

"When I was in eighth grade," Kristen started, "there was a new girl in our math class; actually she was in several of the upper-track classes. She was really tall and had a funny sense of humor and was always laughing, in spite of being new, which is really awful, particularly in middle school. Maybe she was laughing because she was nervous; I don't know."

Kristen had been tracing the scribbling on the desk top with her fingertip, but now she looked up. "I don't know what caught Tyler's attention. He was in those classes too. She was great at math. Maybe it bugged him that she was smarter than he was. Maybe it bugged him that she was tall. Who knows?" She shrugged. "Whatever it was, Tyler started to make her life miserable. He called her a lerp."

"What's a lerp?" Sarah asked.

"It sort of implied that she was a tall geek. You know, that she would fall over her own feet, but she wasn't like that at all. Really, she was sort of graceful, and she played club soccer and all that. There wasn't any rational basis for what Tyler did. I think he did it because he could."

"So what did he actually do?" Sarah asked.

"Well, he started out calling her a lerp," Kristen repeated. "He asked other kids on her soccer team why they were hanging out with such a loser. He'd say those things right in front of her. He'd shove her when she'd walk by. He'd knock her books out of her hands. If she'd say anything back, he'd get nasty."

"It sounds like he was already nasty," Meg said.

"No, it was much worse than that. Gross stuff." Kristen grimaced and stuck out her tongue. Meg raised her eyebrows. "Things finally came to a head one day during an assembly. Tyler and two of his friends sat right behind her on purpose, and Tyler started to complain that he couldn't see over her head. He told her that she should take her ugly head off so he could see the assembly. She finally had enough and turned around to tell him to knock it off, and he hit her right in the face with a dirty gym sock stuffed with grungy underwear. He hit her hard. A bunch of us saw the whole thing. She started to cry, of course, and then those boys laughed like it was the funniest thing they had ever seen."

Meg sighed heavily. "Middle school is a horrible place."

"Her mom and dad were in the principal's office about two seconds after the last bell. Tyler was in a lot of trouble. His parents always get him out of everything, but they couldn't get him out of that. Her parents said they were going to press criminal charges against Tyler, and they were going to sue the school."

Meg held up two fingers. "Assault and a violation of the Utah Safe Schools Act."

Kristen continued, "So the principal transferred Tyler out of all the classes he had with her. They were all the higher track classes, and Tyler was so angry. He thought they should move her. She was the one who was new. He had to have his locker by the office. He was one furious kid."

"Did that end it?" Sarah asked, still fuming about her tires.

"Are you kidding? It just got worse. Tyler didn't do any of the stuff himself, but he organized it. He had his minions keep it up. I mean, and she was new. She didn't know who to avoid. She didn't know who the friendlies were. I saw those jerks trip her and shove her down the main stairway by the front door. If she hadn't caught the handrail with her foot, she could really have gotten hurt, and they just thought they were so funny. By Thanksgiving she had quit laughing, and by Christmas she transferred."

"That's an awful story," Meg said quietly. "What finally happened to her?"

"I don't know. She's probably still in therapy somewhere, or in a group home for people permanently scarred by middle school. But the worst part is Tyler acted like he had pulled off some big coup. He was like this big hero. They laughed and joked about it for months."

"Why didn't anyone help her?" Sarah asked.

"It's middle school. Helping her would have made you a target too. No one would take that kind of risk. Actually, I've felt guilty about her for years. I was in a lot of her classes, and I liked her. I promised myself that I wouldn't stand by and watch something like that happen again. The thing that's really unfair is that nothing happened to Tyler."

"No consequences," Sarah said.

"Except that people don't like him," Meg added.

"And he can never get a date," Kristen finished.

Sarah raised her eyebrows. "So this is the guy who thinks he should call the shots in our program this year?"

"Tyler's mean. You really need to watch your back." Kristen looked directly at Sarah.

Meg quickly covered Kristen's hand with her own. "You don't need to worry about us. We're big girls, and we can take care of ourselves."

Kristen collected her bag and stood up, but when she reached the door, she stopped and said seriously, "No kidding, watch your back."

Sarah felt a sliver of fear prick her neck and ripple down her spine. After the door closed, Sarah turned to Meg. "Are you worried?"

Meg shook her head very slightly. "I don't know."

Sarah glanced up at the clock; it was four fifteen. She'd be snapping beans at ten o'clock.

stolen keys

Sarah pushed her way through a clump of sophomores to unlock her door. It was hard to be on time Monday morning. She dropped her purse on her desk and took a swig of water from a plastic bottle. The room smelled stuffy from being shut up all weekend. She looked longingly out the window at the clear blue sky and autumn leaves turning a dusty shade of red. A perfect morning for a tromp with the dog. What a waste. The second bell rang. She grabbed her folder and the seating chart.

Sitting on top of an empty desk, Sarah placed the stapled papers on her knees and flipped over to the page marked with a paper clip.

"Okay, our story is going to turn right here. Did LaVon threaten Carpenter?" Half of the bleary faces looked like they might have a faint memory of the story from the previous Friday, but unsure of the facts, no one volunteered. Looking at the blank, sleepy students, Sarah wondered if someone put tranquilizers in the water on Monday mornings and why first hour had to start at seven thirty. These kids wouldn't wake up until nine o'clock.

She repeated the question. "Did LaVon threaten him? Does that give us a clue as to what might happen in the rest of the story? These boys have to be really angry. Their fathers have been arrested. What do you think, Tim?"

Blushing, Tim raised his shoulders up around his ears and turned for just a second to look at his friend before he answered, "He grabbed his hands."

"Very good, Tim." He grinned, and she continued, "Does everyone remember LaVon grabbing Carpenter's hands?"

Without the consideration of a knock, the door opened, and Melissa, a pretty blonde, tiptoed into the room. "Oh, Mrs. Williams, I am so sorry. I need the keys to the prep room." She smiled, showing all of her perfect teeth, and apologized. "Mrs. Woodruff was into it with one of her AP Government kids, and I hated to go in."

"Sorry, Melissa. You'll have to wait until third hour. Why aren't you in class?"

"Well, of course, that's where I should be, but I left my English essay in there last Friday, and Mrs. Ward will skin me if I don't have it for peer review next hour. I am so sorry."

Reduced in size by several remodeling projects, the prep room, adjacent to the debate classroom, could only be used for storage. Gradually, debate students appropriated the space. The previous year it had become something of a clubhouse, an invitation-only inner sanctum for policy debaters, Murphy and Sam's headquarters. Meg insisted the room remain locked to prevent students from moving in permanently and setting up housekeeping.

Sarah fished in the pocket of her khaki pants and pulled out an overburdened key ring. Tossing the keys to Melissa, she said, "I want those back in five minutes."

"Absolutely. You're saving my life." Melissa jangled the keys at Sarah and smiled, displaying the beautiful orthodontic work again.

Sarah thought she saw a boy in the hall as Melissa closed the door. She tried to find her place on the page, but her thoughts were jumbled. A pimply boy on the second row suddenly tugged on the necklace of a girl sitting in front of him, which caused considerable shrieking, and Sarah worked to regain control of the class.

The rest of the day was surprisingly uneventful. In fifth period Rachael Beck was explaining her newest legislative bill. An entertaining girl with a large irregular nose and curly brown hair, she was not one to let the truth get in the way of a good story. The previous year she had gained a fair degree of notoriety. Walking into the congress round at St. Mary's High, she discovered, to her total dismay, that she was stuck in the last row. No trophies were going to be found there.

Rachael immediately told the adult in charge that she was blind in her right eye. Could she please be seated closer to the front? In the midst of spinning this magnificent whopper, she managed to contort her face just enough to make the lie plausible. She made the swap, received much sympathy, and delivered several excellent speeches, including one on handicapped access. By the end of the day she had accumulated enough points to win a second-place award and an appreciative audience on the bus ride home.

A different audience was enjoying her presentation this afternoon, as she explained the absolute need to balance the minimum wage for workers at the bottom of the food chain with a maximum wage for greedy CEOs of large American corporations who were gobbling up an undue share of the corporate profits. She had a stiff way of cocking her head and waving her finger in the air to punctuate her most important points, which made the students egg her on. Meg, involved in writing suggestions on a yellow note pad and laughing at Rachael, didn't see Tyler make subtle thumbs up gesture to Brax, and Brax give a slight nod in response. But Sarah did, and she felt uneasy.

The next week started out badly and went downhill fast. Sarah, and every other teacher in the school, knew that the unfinished summer remodeling project would cause endless confusion and tardies, but no one anticipated a fire.

On Tuesday, the state fire marshal threatened to close school if the contractor didn't reconnect the alarms immediately. On Wednesday, as if on cue, a fire started in the front courtyard in a pile of dead grass near a handrail a metal worker was welding. The thick black smoke panicked the lunch secretary, who grabbed the phone to announce a school-wide fire alarm over the PA system. Knowing the marshals were threatening to close the school, Sarah didn't have to be persuaded that this was the real thing. A note of urgency was in her voice as she told her students to leave the building at once.

"Oh, let me see, where is our collection point?" she wondered. The halls were packed with students and teachers who were unsure of evacuation patterns because that particular memo had not yet been circulated. Grabbing for their possessions and knocking each other around with their large cumbersome bags, students tried to exit the building. It was mayhem and an unexpected holiday from schoolwork.

On Wednesday, Sarah and Meg were climbing up the stairs after a brief excursion to the faculty ladies' washroom when Bill Cottle stopped them.

"I am not sure what I really saw, but I think when my class was heading out during the fire alarm yesterday, I saw a couple of your junior debaters sneak into that textbook storage room." He put his nose down and gave them a knowing look over the top of his half glasses. "Do you think that's possible?"

"I don't see how," Meg answered. "I can't think of any of our students who would have a compulsive need to save math texts in a fire." She laughed, Bill laughed, and Sarah didn't laugh. A small anxious feeling rapped inside her head.

On Thursday, as the third-hour novice debate class was in the midst of a productive discussion about rehabilitation vs. punishment in the American penal system, the door swung open, and the red-faced ex-basketball coach, who also happened to teach calculus, stalked into the room huffing. His collar was wet with sweat. Meg looked immediately at Sarah, pointed her finger at her chest, and mouthed, "Heart attack."

"Both of you," he bellowed. "Both of you come right now. I want you to see this." There was no reason his command had to be instantly obeyed, but Sarah and Meg violated their contractual agreements with the North Valley School District and left a classroom of students unsupervised to follow this man into the storage room.

A large bomb of adolescent angst had exploded. Coke cans had been thrown at open closets stacked high with used math texts. Spilled drinks had dried on the carpeting. Meaningless obscenities were scratched into a portable whiteboard. Paper and fast food wrappers were strewn over the floor, and the wastebasket smelled like urine. However, one corner of the room was tidy. Briefs were carefully arranged in orderly stacks. File folders were neatly labeled, and several large Rubbermaid containers were partially filled.

After fifteen years of teaching in public schools, Sarah wasn't surprised by much, but this mess did surprise her and didn't make the large callused finger waving in her face any easier to bear. Mr. Neilson's ranting became progressively louder, but Sarah wasn't hearing him. Partially concealed by the door and Mr. Nielson's broad back was a list of ugly obscenities—about her. Sarah glanced from the whiteboard to

Meg, who was resolutely squaring her shoulders.

"Who's going to clean up this mess and pay for the damages?" Mr. Nielson was not going to be appeased easily, or perhaps, Sarah thought, he was enjoying his indignation too much to let it go.

Please, Sarah sent up a silent prayer, *don't let him turn around.*

"We'll have students in here to clean this up, and parents called this afternoon," Meg said, pursing her lips.

"I can't believe you let students in here unsupervised." Almost shouting, he pulled a spoiled text out of the closet. "Someone's going to pay for this." And he slammed the book on a table.

"We've never had this problem before. A little clutter maybe, but nothing like this. We're as upset as you are." Meg spoke with a mature calmness that belied the slight tremor in her hands and the red splotches on her neck.

"Well, see that's it's cleaned up today."

"That's our plan." Meg included Sarah in her response, although Sarah hadn't spoken a word.

He marched his large storm cloud down the hall and back to his calculus class.

"Maybe I'm missing the obvious, but why do we get to be responsible for this? These kids have four other teachers during the day. Why isn't this their fault? Someone let them out of class. This mess took some time."

Meg sighed. "The only thing that worries me more is what a great story this will make in the faculty lounge."

"Well, the story could have been worse."

"How?" Meg questioned.

Sarah closed the door, exposing the whiteboard. The color drained from Meg's face as she silently read the list. Meg picked up a blue rag and started to erase the board.

"Divorce makes me so vulnerable." Sarah was feeling a little shocky. "What if my kids had seen this?"

"Hey, half the people on the faculty are divorced, but I wouldn't want your kids to see this either. It's so disgustingly crude." Meg's voice was soft. Both women had forgotten that a classroom of thirty-five sophomores had been left to their own devices.

Meg erased the board quickly and turned when Sarah started to speak. "What on earth are we going to do about this? I mean, what recourse do we have? You've heard about Tyler's parents. They'd excuse their kids' behavior with their dying breaths." Sarah paused. "I want those two brats out of our program."

Meg responded slowly, "Of course you do. So do I, but I'm not sure what to do. You know, they're just three-year-olds in great big bodies. This is just big talk. They're just announcing that they're sexually knowledgeable, but it is ugly," she conceded. "Let's think about it."

Meg looked up. Someone tested the doorknob and, finding it unlocked, pushed the door open. Tyler leaned his broad shoulder against the doorjamb and observed the situation without speaking. Sarah was sure the remarks written on the whiteboard had been a hilarious diversion the previous day. After his clique had a good laugh at her expense, he was sneaking in to erase the evidence before he got caught. He looked at the blue rag in Meg's hand and saw the expression on her face. He drew in a quick breath and looked, for a second, like he was going to head back out the door.

Meg pulled herself up into Sarah's favorite authoritarian pose and demanded in a don't-mess-with-me tone, "This disaster gets cleaned up right now, or you will never be allowed the use of this room again."

Tyler opened his mouth to argue.

"No conversation. Just do it right now."

Tyler took a quick glance toward the whiteboard. "We just came over to grab a couple of files. I told Mr. Gobbel that we'd be right back." He stuck out his chin, challenging Meg, his hubris reasserting itself. It was all Sarah could do not to reach up and slap his face. She wanted to grab him and throw him down into a chair and beat him with the lid of one of the Rubbermaid boxes. He outweighed her by fifty pounds, but anger made her thin arms and legs feel like unregistered lethal weapons. She wanted to rip that smirk right off his face and throw it over in the pile of fast food garbage.

"No problem," Meg said. "That is, of course, your choice. My choice is to go and get the principal and show her how you value the use of this additional space. I think I can guarantee you that if this is not perfectly clean, including the dumped drinks, you'll never see the inside of this room again." Meg bit off each word.

"You'll have to write an excuse for Gobbel."

Sarah sneered, "We'll be more than happy to explain the nature of your problem to Mr. Gobbel and all of your other teachers." She had listened to Tyler about as long as she could. "While you're at it," she added, "make sure these boards are clean, and," Sarah paused for effect, "I don't ever want to see this kind of filth written on these boards again—about anyone."

Crude language and adolescent male braggadocio were standard fare in a high school. Teachers walking down the hall at lunch could have their hair curled for free by listening to student conversations, but this was different. This was insulting language used about her by a student in Sarah's own program. Tyler didn't seem to realize a line had been crossed. Sarah plucked at her skirt, trying to think of some way she could retaliate that didn't involve jail time or unemployment compensation.

"What's the big deal?" Brax materialized from some unknown location and pushed his way into the room.

"Look, I'm your debate coach, not your mother. Thank heaven." Sarah's eyes narrowed. "Why don't you go home and ask your parents why writing filth for other people to look at isn't okay?" She intentionally changed her tone and her facial expression to one of innocent query. "Of course, I'm assuming they'll know."

"Do you want to give the novice class their assignment, or would you like me to?" Meg said, giving Sarah an out, which Sarah took and stomped down the hall. The expression on her face subdued all conversations in the classroom. The assignment was passed out and explained briefly. Her clipped "any questions" sounded more like she was asking for blade testers for a guillotine, and no one raised a hand.

Meg walked quietly in the back door of the classroom. She motioned to Sarah. Sarah moved down the aisle between desks toward the back of the room, making sure that the students were starting to work and not just stuffing the assignment into backpacks to conveniently forget that evening.

Sarah and Meg looked at each other. Meg broke the silence. "They're cleaning it up. You know, what they wrote isn't really about you. You're an attractive woman. No one can believe you're unattached."

"Not the issue."

"They're not targeting you because you're divorced."

"Please," Sarah said, her lips in a tight line, "I wasn't fishing. I was horrified." She was so angry her hands were shaking.

The next day, Friday afternoon, Sarah was struck by the absence of noise. She looked around the classroom fifth hour and decided half the kids had started the weekend early. Word had gotten around that there was more trouble between the teachers and Tyler. An oppressive layer of bad feeling hung over the class like an inversion holding in a dirty layer of smog. Brax was absent, and Tyler worked quietly on a brief at his desk. Rachael Beck started to tell a joke near the end of class but stopped mid-sentence for no apparent reason.

The disastrous week enhanced the thank-heaven-it's-Friday relief Sarah felt when the final bell rang. Usually, they didn't lock the door or hurry to leave the building. Today was an exception. Sarah followed the last student over to the door and managed to snag her soft gray knit dress as she pulled her keys out of her pocket. "Oh great," she murmured inspecting the damage to one of her few good dresses. The key ring was bent slightly, and she ran her fingertip over the rough edge.

"What a really bad week." She locked the door and turned to show Meg the pulled thread across her skirt. "Just when you think things can't get any worse."

Meg didn't respond. She was pulling a last piece of a gingerbread cookie out of a sack and offering half of it to Sarah. "I think we've got a problem," Meg said thoughtfully.

"I think we've got more than one. I think we have a spoiled brat destroying the varsity squad, and I don't know how we're going to get rid of him before he ruins our program." Sarah started to launch into a litany of grievances about Tyler, when Meg interrupted her.

"I think we have a more immediate problem. I think several kids have keys. That's the only way they could have gotten into the storage room. A week ago, it was relatively clean. That mess didn't get made in one day. All those fast food wrappers and junk? Those kids have been hanging out in there, probably after school." She flipped her shoe off and on. A key that opened the storage room would also open all the classrooms in the social sciences wing. Student access to the entire wing? The other teachers would kill them.

Sarah sighed. "They'll never admit it, and I don't think we can catch them without a surveillance camera, which we don't have."

"If we do catch them, they'll just say we gave them the key. Did we give them the key?" Meg looked at Sarah with an odd smile.

"I don't think so," Sarah said, feeling uneasy but trying to remember. "You know, I've always given kids my keys to open that prep room when I'm in the middle of class." She paused, but she was so tired it was hard to think. "Last week Melissa came over first hour right in the middle of class and said she left an English paper in there that she needed right that minute. She said she didn't want to bother you."

"When did you get your keys back?"

"She didn't bring them right back. She gave me some song and dance about forgetting when she returned them third hour. Could she have had them copied that fast? That doesn't seem like something Melissa would do."

Meg raised one eyebrow. "Who does it sound like?"

"Tyler and Brax," Sarah admitted. "You think Melissa was duped into going along."

"Sure. 'Hey, Melissa, will you get Williams's key to the prep room? She hates me.' Melissa wouldn't blink twice."

"They'll lie if we confront them."

"Yes, but we're in the clear if an entire class of sophomores heard her get your keys under false pretenses. I guess we're covered, but how will we get the keys back?"

"I'm too tired to think about this now. I've got to be back down here in three hours to take tickets at the football game."

Meg studied her friend thoughtfully. Sarah felt like she was being assessed for damage control.

"Let's go. Where did you park?"

"I'm over by the English building," Sarah said. They walked down halls that were now devoid of students. The last bell on Friday was like a starting pistol being fired at a foot race.

"Is there faculty meeting?" Sarah asked. "I didn't check my messages before I left."

"A short one. Monday morning. Seven o'clock."

north valley 14, sarah 0

*t*he stadium lights came on half an hour before game time. Sarah and Jenny cut across from the teacher's parking lot down the grassy hill to the bridge. Jenny stopped abruptly.

"Come on," Sarah said. "You can do this."

Jenny breathed in and out several times as though she were preparing to swim across the English Channel, underwater.

"Sit with one person who looks a little lonely. Think about making her feel happy. You'll be surprised. Everyone needs friends." Sarah gently shoved Jenny toward the stairs below the bridge. She closed her eyes so she wouldn't see Jenny tentatively making her way toward the bleachers. *All this hand wringing just makes it worse*, Sarah thought. She watched the cheerleaders call to each other as they passed string and scissors back and forth, tying balloons to the top railing on the bleachers.

People were arriving wearing parkas and heavy sweatshirts and carrying stadium blankets; the evening's brisk chill belied the seventy-degree temperature of the earlier September afternoon. Students were arriving excited about the game, excited about the dance after the game, excited by the lights, the pep band, the hotdogs being sold, and the mix of friends outside the normal routine of the classroom and homework. The pep band, playing the school's fight song, couldn't completely fill the night air, and conversations and laughter mingled with the notes of music.

Warming up, the North Valley players bent, stretched, and ran in place on the grass under the lights, in uniforms not yet grass stained or splattered with mud. The boys exaggerated their efforts, playing to the crowd, as people started to fill the bleachers. A shrill whistle blew, and the team ran back to the locker room for one final pep talk.

The old canal cut through the rear of the campus and separated the buildings from the playing fields. Wind moved through the branches of the tall poplar trees, planted years ago, that lined each bank. From her vantage point on the bridge, Sarah could look down toward the football field and see Tom in his red and gold student body sweater hammering rebar into the edge of the grass, as his friend attached yellow plastic rope to keep the students off the field if the game took an exciting turn. Sarah had a wry smile on her face as she watched her son. The previous spring Tom thought he was winning a popularity contest, but actually he was winning a job. He and the other student body officers had assignments at every game and every event. They hosted class reunions. They cleaned up after activities. They were cheap labor, which was how she regarded herself. It was only the second home game of the season, and she stuck out her tongue at the sturdy metal money box placed on a student desk. She wondered how many million tickets she had sold over the years.

Sarah sold a ticket and stamped a woman's hand with a very small bear's head in red florescent ink. As the woman moved on, Sarah stopped for a moment during a lapse in the line to breathe in the fall smells. She nodded at the biology teacher who stood across from her checking student ID cards and flicked a large kernel of popcorn off her chest with her finger. *North Valley Faculty* was embroidered on the front of her red fleece jacket. When she glanced up, she recognized the county sheriff, Clayton McLaughlin. He was talking to Ron Brown, the assistant basketball coach. Ron was gesturing with his hands in a wide arc. He punctuated the air with his index finger. She couldn't hear what they were saying and felt as if she were watching the television with the audio on mute.

The sheriff looked over at her and smiled. He excused himself from the conversation and got in the line to purchase a ticket. After several parents chatted, bought tickets, and moved on, he leaned down and spoke to her, "It's your turn to take tickets?"

"Yes, and I get all the turns. I'm a professional. Don't try to do this at home." She remembered her conversations with Meg and the bishop and wiggled uncomfortably inside her jacket. Was she being too flippant? He wasn't saying anything. Sarah continued, "Are you here in your official capacity? If you're going to break up any fights, I don't have to charge you for a ticket."

The home team raced onto the field, crashing through a bear's head painted on butcher paper. The fans roared. The burst of noise drowned out Clayton's reply, and Sarah stood to watch the next few moments on the field. The pep band played loudly, and Bill Cottle started his sardonic commentary from the small press box perched on top of the bleachers. Both teams positioned themselves in carefully practiced formations, and the whistle blew. Sarah laughed at all the commotion. Ron Brown moved over to her side of the bridge to get a better view. Bruce Crapo, a biology teacher, left his position and came over too. Suddenly feeling outnumbered by males, Sarah stepped back to her small desk and sold tickets to several latecomers.

"Are your debaters going to have another winning year?" A short plump woman smiled as her hand was being stamped.

"It's so hard to say this early in the year. We lost strong seniors last spring. It's always something of a surprise." Sarah smiled. She couldn't remember the woman's name but knew she was either the mother of a student, the mother of a former student, a former classmate, a distant relative, or a complete stranger who read the local newspaper.

"Small towns," she laughed to Bruce when the woman moved on. "I think that I know everybody, and usually I do, or at least I'm two degrees away."

"What's a degree?" The sheriff was back.

"Oh, if you don't know someone firsthand, you probably know someone that knows them. Or you know someone who knows someone who knows them. That would be two degrees. It's just silly."

"So, if you're my son's teacher, then we're in a two-degree relationship?" He looked at her seriously. "If I buy you a bag of popcorn, does that make our relationship a single degree?"

He's kidding me, Sarah thought, *but not flirting*. Whatever Meg said, Sarah detested flirting. It was demeaning and led to unpleasant gossip, and today she felt raw and vulnerable as though her skin had been stripped away with a dull vegetable peeler. She held up a greasy brown sack and said, "I don't usually eat popcorn. I have a tendency to dump it in my lap. But thanks anyway." She locked the little box and slipped the key on a blue ribbon into the back pocket of her jeans. Pushing the desk out of the way, she stumbled over a small crack in the concrete. Clayton grabbed her arm to steady her, but he let go quickly when he saw her grimace.

"I'm fine," she said, raising her palm, and leaned against the railing to watch the game. She counted to twenty and looked over her shoulder, but he was gone, walking over the bridge toward a group of men standing near the field.

She scanned the crowd, trying to spot her kids. Tom was a stand-out in his school sweater. He was supposed to be keeping the students on the track and off the field, but he was working the crowd like a seasoned politician. Smiling, laughing, punching someone on the shoulder, he moved up and down the rope barrier. If there were a sudden touchdown, all attempts at crowd control would be lost. Sarah smiled simply at the thought of him and looked anxiously for Jenny.

Jenny was sitting at the edge of a group of freshman girls. None of the girls leaned over to laugh or whisper to Jenny. A smile was frozen on her young face, but she was sitting there with a small red and gold pompom she had pilfered from Robbie's room, shaking it like a trooper. *That's okay*, Sarah thought. *It's all just fine. She just needs time.* The sick, anxious feeling in the pit of her stomach eased, and for just a few seconds, she let go and loved the fall evening and was actually glad that she was firmly fixed in this particular moment in time.

The light in the lamppost flickered. A cold wind moved in the trees. Where was the vice principal? Two minutes on the clock until the half. He needed to collect the money box. She was stuck here alone, exposed to the wind until he did. She wished she were cocooned in a crowd of warm bodies in the bleachers, sitting next to Jenny. Sarah looked back toward the building. The light went out and the shadows lengthened. She wrapped her thin arms around her middle and wished for a heavier coat.

"Hey, Mrs. W.," said a familiar voice.

She turned quickly. "Jason!" She smiled, pleased at the sight of a former student. He stood close to her and bent over slightly so she could hear him over the noise and the wind.

"How's Robbie?" Jason asked. His cheeks were red, and he rubbed the tip of his nose.

"He's great. He writes interesting letters. I think he's happy. I mean the food is awful, but the people are very kind." She looked at him apprehensively. "How are you?"

He nodded and smiled.

She paused carefully and then said, "I thought you'd be going."

"So did I," he answered, "but I'd have trouble with a few of the questions in the bishop's interview." He raised his eyebrows significantly.

Sarah couldn't match his frank stare and turned her eyes away.

"I'm going to Scotland on a semester abroad. I might stay a whole year if I like it."

"Where in Scotland?"

"St. Andrew's," Jason replied.

"That is so wonderful. What a great school." She felt a moment's pang that her own children would never do a semester abroad, but she shook it off. "That's kind of like a mission. You'll make interesting new friends, see new places."

"That's what my mother keeps saying. She's compensating." Jason grinned. "It wouldn't surprise me if she tells people that I'm on a mission. But I'll have to figure out some place else to go for the second year." He laughed.

"You'll come back with a brogue." Sarah smiled and dipped her head slightly, looking down at her hands. "I think there's a castle right there—with a ghost and everything. It sticks right out over the North Sea."

He laughed at her. "You've been reading travel brochures."

"No, gothic romances." She gave him a furtive look. "Don't tell anyone."

He laughed again and punched her shoulder gently. "I wanted to check in with you before I left."

"You've changed. You've filled out." She put her hands on each of his shoulders and made him stand up straight. "You're not the skinny kid who brought home our first trophy."

"Skinny, but great potential, right?"

"Amazing potential." She grinned at him.

A wind gust lifted Sarah's hair off her neck and bounced the red balloons still tied to the bleachers. Suddenly the crowd roared. Joe Anderson had broken away and was racing toward the North Valley

goal. Students were on their feet, screaming. A boy from the opposing school was racing across the field, attempting to cut him off. Joe
tucked the ball firmly next to his chest, not daring to look back. The
students stood in the stands, the pep band director lowered his baton,
and everyone was caught up in the footrace. The halfback was running,
stretching out his hand. The tips of his fingers were barely touching the
back of Joe's jersey as Joe crossed the line. Popcorn flew into the air,
and students on the bottom third of the bleachers surged onto the track
and the edge of the field. Tom had his back to the crowd, watching the
action on the field, cheering and waving his arms. Players clumped
around Joe, jumping up and down. The music started up. The cheerleaders tried to get into a formation to start their routine, but the crush
of students made any coordinated movement impossible.

"Students need to vacate the track," came Bill's voice over the
microphone, "or run the risk of being kicked in the teeth by the cheerleaders. Students need to return to the bleachers."

Sarah rolled her eyes. "Whatever," she said to Jason. "How do you
herd cats?"

Everyone was watching the action on the field as the teams formed
for the kickoff. Tom wasn't watching Tyler, Brax, and a couple of other
senior boys, but Sarah was. They were attempting to cross the rope barrier and stand near the players' bench.

She stood on her toes to get a better view. Shoved hard by Tyler,
Brax bumped into Tom's shoulder, causing Tom to lose his footing,
stumble, and fall. Surrounded by his group of friends, Brax had a nasty
smirk on his face. Tom jumped up quickly and motioned for the boys
to move behind the rope. Sarah saw Brax's lips move and saw the smile
leave Tom's face. Then Tom smiled broadly, put his left arm tightly
around Brax's shoulder, and leaned over to say something only Brax
could hear, but the other boys saw the fist Tom made with his right
hand. *He's going to punch him*, she thought. Tom outweighed Brax by
twenty pounds. Quickly, Tyler and another tall surly boy grabbed
Tom's arms.

Sarah inhaled quickly and started for the stairs, but Sheriff
McLaughlin, walking along the rope line, firmly motioned for the boys
to move behind the yellow rope. Reluctantly, the boys released Tom.
McLaughlin folded his arms across his broad chest and then smiled at
Tom. Ignoring the boys who had been absorbed back into the crowd,

Tom smiled at something McLaughlin said.

Sarah relaxed her shoulders and quit holding her breath. Crisis averted—for the moment. She should trust Tom; he had good people instincts, but he was no match for Tyler and Brax's ugly behavior. She pulled her jacket around her tightly, feeling rattled as she remembered the comments on the whiteboard and wondered what Brax had said to Tom.

"Are you okay?" Jason leaned into her as he watched Sarah watch Tom.

"Oh, I'm fine. We've got a couple of real jerks this year, and that's hard, but what else is new. It's always something." Sarah's smile had left her face. "They'll be gone in May."

"If you live." Jason was quoting Sarah, and she laughed.

"Oh, I'll live. I always manage to survive, don't I? A woman resigned to her fate."

"I've got to leave. I'm meeting some friends at the student union." He raised his eyebrows at her questioningly, held out his arms for a hug, and enveloped Sarah before she could step back. Her nose squashed against the front of his leather jacket.

"You'll be missed," Sarah whispered into his chest, but Jason heard her and gave her an additional quick squeeze.

"You'll answer a letter?" he called out as he walked back across the bridge.

"Sure." She waved and watched him as he ran up the stairs and across the lawn. She lost sight of him as he turned around the corner of the building. Sarah sat down on the desk and looked toward the game. She wanted to leave, but she'd promised Jenny they'd get a hot chocolate on the way home. Of course, Sarah would freeze to death by then. She wished for the tenth time that she had brought a heavier coat or a blanket.

She watched the crowd of students on the track milling around the Snack Shack. Jenny was still perched carefully on the bleachers, but Tom was climbing toward her with a couple of his friends, shoving each other and laughing. Tom made his way over to Jenny. One of Tom's friends grabbed her pompom and threw it at a girl sitting three benches below. The girl jumped up and turned around with a fierce look, ready to do battle. Jenny started to laugh and automatically put her hand up to cover her teeth. The girl reluctantly tossed the pompom back. Tom reached out to catch it as it sailed back over the heads of fans who had the good sense to duck. A rowdy group of senior girls started a chant on the front row.

"Kill, Kill, blood makes the grass grow.

"Kill, Kill, blood makes the grass grow."

Sarah laughed. The girls were singing the words over and over in direct competition with the cheerleaders, who were trying unsuccessfully to get the crowd to spell G-R-I-Z-Z-L-Y. Tom scooted Jenny over to make room, and the girl next to Jenny smiled broadly at the inconvenience.

The referee blew the whistle, and the teams moved toward the locker rooms beneath the gym. Sarah didn't notice the man walking up the steps until he was standing at her side.

"Seven-zero; that's not bad for the first half. I'm surprised Mountain View didn't score on that fumble," Clayton confided, assuming she was a fan and not just a ticket taker.

"Yeah," Sarah responded. She turned up the collar of her jacket to keep the wind off her neck. The ugly list on the whiteboard kept appearing, uninvited, in her head. The sheriff seemed uncertain but not inclined to move away. She ought to thank him for backing up Tom earlier in the game.

He tried again. "Tom doesn't play football? He's a big kid."

"No, too many demolished knees. Tom sticks to basketball and soccer." She looked up at him. "I mean that's bad enough. There are plenty of injuries in soccer." The conversation ended again. If he wanted to talk about health care in America, or funding for extracurricular activities, or the slimy debate coach at City High, she would be happy to engage, but she had never figured out football.

Clayton paused a moment and plunged in again with the same go-nowhere topic. "Do you think we can hold on to the lead in the second half?"

Sarah had no idea. Before he had intruded on her thoughts, she had been watching her children and walking along cobblestone streets in a village in Scotland. She was worried about Jenny. She was worried about that group of boys giving Tom a hard time. And she was worried about turning into a frozen replica of a teacher, but she wasn't concerned about holding onto the lead. Not tonight.

"Who knows? Maybe just the great football god who lives in the end zone. Honestly," and Sarah laughed, "I just don't get this game. Everyone lines up and then, *crash*, everyone falls down."

He stood silently at her side for another five minutes until she started to pull on a loose curl and rock up and down on her toes. When he looked down at the top of her curly hair and spoke, he had obviously been rehearsing a short invitation. "Ron Brown and his wife would like to go out for a pizza after the game. Would you like to come? I mean, with me and them?" He tripped over the words, and Sarah could see that he was embarrassed.

She started to say, "I'm sorry, but I just don't date," but she stopped herself, realizing that response would sound like he had invited her for something besides a pizza. She stopped after the, "I'm sorry, but . . ."

He looked almost through her.

She started again. "It's not you. I know you're a very nice person. I just make it a policy not to date." Now it was her turn to be embarrassed, because he hadn't really asked her out on a date. Stopping on the way home for a pizza with friends was not a date. She lowered her head and shook it quickly as if to erase the mess she was making.

"I mean," she said, "I told Jenny we would stop for a treat on the way home."

Clayton shoved his hands deeper into the pockets of his jacket. Sarah thought he would move away, but he just stood there. She was so bad in silly social situations.

"Really," she said, "another time a pizza would be nice."

"But you don't date," he said quietly.

"No, but I have been known to eat, you know, with friends." She was glad that it was dark on that bridge and hoped that he couldn't see the deep blush working its way up her neck. She sighed heavily and looked up at him. "You know, I went through a really ugly divorce," she said, as though that explained her disjointed responses.

He came back quietly, "But wasn't that a long time ago?"

"Yes, but it left me with brain injuries and a really bad limp." She wrinkled her nose and crossed her eyes, and he started to laugh.

"So, you don't ever want a crutch or a little physical therapy?"

"No thanks, it seems to work better if I just stumble along by myself." He was still laughing, and she was still blushing, and she didn't really like the twist he had given her metaphor. He continued to stand next to her, not speaking, as the teams raced back onto the field.

"Any money?" Terry Schuback, the vice principal, was finally coming up the sidewalk toward the bridge.

"Yes, yes," she said a little too eagerly. She turned to give the vice principal the money box and caught the sheriff watching her as she pulled the small key out of the back pocket of her jeans. It was his turn to blush.

a man, a puppy, and a mother-in-law
utah, 1981

*b*ob parked the little red convertible around the corner from his mother-in-law's house. Uncomfortable driving Claire's car, he drummed his fingers against the steering wheel. He didn't want any cracks about Claire or her car. He just wanted to see his kids.

He had called twice from JFK International Airport, and Sarah had hung up on him both times. He couldn't believe her. She hadn't sent him a snapshot or a word about the kids since he'd left, but she'd managed to cash his checks. And she'd left, left Iowa. She'd taken his kids and gone home to her mother. He'd racked his brain trying to think of a way this could work. How do you get little kids back and forth? He only had three weeks of vacation a year. How can you have a relationship with little kids three weeks a year? One thing was certain, when Sarah had a good burn going, she could be brutal. She wasn't going to make any of this easy.

He took three deep breaths. Letting his mind play, he imagined his children. He had thought hard about the first few minutes of this visit. It had been over a year, and the kids were so little. Robbie would be thrilled to see him, but Jenny and Tommy might be shy. Once Robbie recognized him, Tommy and Jenny would be comfortable too, but still, he worried.

He lifted the large shopping bag, filled with toys and clothes, over the seat. He had shopped by himself, taking hours to finger soft fabrics in little garments and choose toys Swiss children loved. He'd found a children's book, one of Robbie's favorites when he was little, written in German. He imagined reading it with Robbie and talking about the words and how similar the two languages could be. He had wrapped the packages carefully in bright colors, and he was pleased with the effect as he set the bag on the curb.

The gray crate was more difficult to manage. He lifted it out of the backseat and took a moment to open the wire gate and remove the fluffy chocolate lab puppy, holding it close to his chest and petting it softly. It was plenty old enough to leave its mother, but a ride in the backseat of a convertible was pretty traumatic. He sat down on the cement curb and cuddled the puppy, or maybe the dog was cuddling him. He needed it. He was rattled. If he hadn't written twice to tell Sarah and the kids exactly when he was coming, he would have been tempted to turn tail and go back to his mother's. He was excited, but guilt churned away in the pit of his stomach. The minute he made that last turn out of the canyon and saw the granite Mormon temple sitting on the bluff in the distance, a wave of remorse hit him like a dam breaking. Driving down into the valley, he wondered what he would say if he ran into his old bishop. "Yeah, I'm in an adulterous relationship with a wonderful woman, and my wife has moved my children two thousand miles away from me, probably out of spite." Where would he go from there? Why hadn't there been any Sunday School lessons about what to do when you fall out of love with your wife? When he was a kid, a temple marriage was the finish line, a guarantee for living happily ever after. *It shouldn't be a life sentence*, he told himself.

Now, sitting on the curb, his feet felt like lead. He hoped Sarah's mother was long gone wherever creepy old ladies go, but seeing her wouldn't be nearly as bad as seeing the look in Sarah's eyes. Maybe he could just take the kids and the dog and go to the park down the street. The weather was perfect. It wasn't cold, no wind. They could play with the dog and the playground toys. He envisioned Jenny, two and a half, playing with the puppy, tumbling and laughing. *That would be the best*, he thought, *get hamburgers at McDonald's and go to the park. Get out from under the looks.* He stroked the little dog. How could you not love a puppy and the guy who brought it?

He took several deep breaths, in and out. He could do this. He tucked the little dog under one arm, held the bag in his other hand, and walked around the corner up to the screen door.

There she was, Mrs. Ritzman, waiting for him, sitting on an old brown chair by the front door just like a large purple spider. The tips of her polished orthopedic shoes were showing under the cuff of her polyester pants. He'd always hated those shoes. Her legs were pressed tightly together, her hands were folded in her lap, and her thin lips were moving slightly. *She's rehearsing*, he thought, and steeled himself for the drama.

She looked up and saw him. The puppy yipped, and he shifted the presents into his other hand, trying to juggle the dog and the gifts. She just stared at him, saying nothing.

"Can I come in?" he finally asked.

She nodded and held the screen door open. He looked around the empty front room and then at her.

"They're not here," she said resolutely.

"Where are they?"

"Gone."

"Okay, I'll play." He'd never liked this old woman. He had married Sarah with the firm conviction that she would never be like her mother. "Where are they, and when will they be back?" He faked a pleasant tone.

"It is none of your business where they are, and you'll be gone before they return."

"Look, I just want to see my kids. I have the right to see my kids."

"Your kids? You have no children."

He panicked for a moment, thinking something had happened, and then it occurred to him that this dumpy old woman was having her big moment. *Okay*, he thought, *I'll wait through this and then she'll tell me where they are.*

She continued, "Last Father's Day I picked Jenny up from the nursery at church. You remember church?"

"Yeah, I remember church." *Play along*, he told himself. *Don't make her any crazier than she already is.*

"All the fathers came to the nursery for a song and a treat. When I picked up Jenny, she put her hands on my cheeks and asked me, 'Where's a daddy for little Jenny?' Do you know what I had to tell her?"

"No, but I bet you're going to tell me." The puppy was starting to squirm. Since no one had asked him to sit down, he set the bag on the floor and started to stroke the puppy, holding it tightly against his chest.

"I told Jenny that she had no father, but I told her about all the people who love her: Grandma, Robbie, Tommy, and her mommy."

"But Jenny does have a father, and I'm here, right now, ready to do all the daddy stuff. If you'll just tell me where they are, I'll take this little dog, before she piddles down my shirt, and go see them. How's that?" He'd had enough of this old woman.

"You think you can walk in here and spend an afternoon and then just leave again. You are so selfish. You want to break all their hearts again? If you have any love left for any of them, leave them alone."

"Look, I promised Robbie I would come back. Here I am. I'm not leaving until I see my kids."

"They're where you'll never find them," she huffed. "Robbie never mentions your name."

He rolled his eyes. He couldn't believe any of this was happening. His mother-in-law was like a character in a B-grade horror movie. Was Sarah nuts too? Where was she? He'd written twice saying he would be here Friday at eleven o'clock.

"Hey," he said, "did Sarah even know that I was coming today?"

Mrs. Ritzman looked down at her hands, and she didn't speak again for a long minute. "You think that you're bringing presents, but all you bring is new hurt. I understand that woman you're living with is pregnant. Did you come to tell your children and wife that?"

His hands started to tremble. He wanted to smack her. He'd forgotten the efficiency of a small-town grapevine. His face flushed a deep red. "I just want to see my kids."

"Well, you can't have everything you want. You made your choices. Now you have to live with them."

His heart was pounding. He was so angry he had a hard time speaking. The little dog gave a tiny bark. "Can I leave the presents and the puppy? You don't need to tell the kids they're from Satan. She's a nice little dog."

"Three minutes after you leave, those presents will be in the garbage, and I'll be on the way to the pound with that dog."

His free hand clenched into a fist. "You tell Sarah that she'll be hearing from my attorney. You can't keep me from seeing my kids."

He stormed out the front door and across the lawn. Tossing the bag of gifts into the car, he set the puppy on the grass and then pounded the ground repeatedly with his fist. He wanted to scream and throw a brick through that horrible woman's front window. He leaned his head back and bellowed for all he was worth, but it didn't do any good. His three little kids didn't jump out from behind the bushes. The street remained quiet. The puppy batted a moth with her paw. He held the dog up to his face. "We tried, little girl, didn't we?" After gently putting the puppy into the crate, he walked around to the driver's side and got into the car.

He bit down hard on his bottom lip. He had to leave early Tuesday morning. Iowa City was a two-day drive. He had to find an apartment, buy some furniture, and get Claire settled before he started his first stint in the cardiology clinic. He had a week off at Christmas, but Claire was due the first week in December. He couldn't come back then. He had counted on the next three days with his kids. Now he'd have to spend the weekend listening to his mother run through her litany: why he should never have married Sarah, blah, blah, blah. He ran his fingers through his hair, pulling it back from his forehead. He'd call Jack Perry, but what could an attorney do on a Friday afternoon? Even an old friend? Magic legalese? Mrs. Ritzman would stonewall, he was sure of it. Crazy old broad. He shoved the gear shift into first and pulled away from the curb.

——⁓——

Thirty seconds after Mrs. Ritzman heard him drive down the street, she picked up the phone and called the house in Island Park.

Sarah answered. "Hey, Mom, what's up?"

"Are you having a good time?"

"Oh, we're having a great time. I love being with Bethany again. It's been so long. Our kids act like long-lost relations, which I guess they are." Sarah laughed at her own small joke. "We've seen lots of deer and one large moose—from a distance. Tomorrow we're going to try and drive partway through Yellowstone. Maybe have a picnic at Old Faithful."

"Hold on to those little children around the hot pots and geysers."

"Oh, for sure. I'll be really careful." Sarah paused a second before she said, "I'm so glad you pushed me to come. This has been so great for the kids."

"Well, I didn't think you needed one more teacher convention. You needed a vacation."

"You're right, and we're having a great time. Jenny keeps asking why Grandma didn't come to the vacation house. We all miss you, Mom."

"I miss you too, sweetheart." Mrs. Ritzman hung up the receiver and sat down on the couch. Breathing heavily, she rested her hand against her chest and felt her heart flutter, but it was all right. Her daughter was safe.

glitter and disaster

Sunday afternoon was Sarah's favorite slice of time. Perusing the Sunday paper, she jotted down the last question for the current events quiz Monday morning. Einstein rolled over on the rug and nosed into the side of his yellow fur, making disgusting noises.

"Einstein, gross," Jenny said, turning up her nose. She was sitting on the floor beside the dog, painting her toenails a soft shade of lavender. Coiled toilet paper between each of her toes kept them from rubbing together and smudging her polish. Sarah thought it was such an odd incongruity that a girl who had such disregard for her hands could make such efforts with her feet.

The big dog stopped his own grooming rituals and thumped his tail on the rug, nearly disrupting Jenny's gentle painting motions. Einstein lumbered over to the cardboard box in the closet, shoved his toys around with his nose, and came back with a grin on his face and his leash in his mouth. He stood in front of Sarah and whined.

"Come with me to walk the dog?" Sarah suggested. "It would help your toenails dry."

"Shoes?" Jenny responded.

"Sandals?" Sarah mimicked her tone exactly. "It is a completely beautiful afternoon."

"Nah, I don't think so. Dorothy might call."

"Didn't you talk to her this morning at church? What earth shattering events could have happened in the last three hours? Why don't you call her when we get home?"

"You don't get it, Mom. She's having some kids over to her house tonight. Maybe she'll call me."

Sarah did get it. She had been an amused observer of the high school social hierarchy for years. Dorothy was small and blonde, and because she had an older sister, she was socially savvy. Plus, she had a nice home, cute clothes, a sophomore boyfriend, and two parents. Jenny was standing in line for the crumbs from Dorothy's plate, and Sarah wasn't amused, not one bit.

"I'll be back in a little while," Sarah said. "Walk!" One of two words that Einstein clearly understood. He barked excitedly and hurried to the door. Clicking the leash on his collar, Sarah and the big dog jumped down the two concrete steps and started down the street.

The day was warm, but not hot like August afternoons. Leaves were starting to change color, and some had dropped to the sidewalks and lawns. Einstein had to stop, sniff, and investigate each leaf that had any resemblance to a fast food wrapper. It made for a slow walk, but Sarah was in no hurry.

She didn't get it. The girls in the neighborhood were clearly third string, and Jenny still wasn't a player. Even at church they barely acknowledged her. Sarah shook her head, pushing away the anxious thoughts and angry memories of the previous week, and looked up at the blue sky through the leaves. She exhaled. *It's all going to be okay.* Robbie had a difficult time his freshman year, and then he managed to grow four inches in a single year and become a local basketball legend. Jenny had nice features, and she was smart. *She'll find herself,* Sarah thought and turned the corner. Before she died, her mother's home had been just a couple of blocks down Acorn. Clearly, Jenny had inherited her grandmother's dark curly hair. She hoped Jenny hadn't inherited anything else.

"Enough, enough!" Sarah said out loud as she shook her head hard to toss out the old ghosts and worries.

She turned on to a side street when Einstein pulled on the leash, indicating that he needed a dog moment. Sarah looked over her shoulder discreetly and feigned searching in her pocket for a plastic bag. In spite of the new city ordinance and in spite of the fact that Sarah really was a law-abiding citizen, she couldn't bring herself to pick up a half pound of steaming dog poop and carry it home. Einstein finished as Sarah sneaked a quick glance over her shoulder to see if there was anything that could identify the excrement as coming from her dog, specifically glitter.

Two days ago Einstein had filched a tube of glitter from Jenny's scrapbooking supplies. She kept the glitter, card stock, and tape in a cardboard box that, in all fairness, did resemble Einstein's box of toys. The theft wasn't discovered until Jenny found the plastic stopper, and of course, the tail-tale evidence on a corner of the front lawn.

Sarah had been sitting on the couch with the side window open when she heard a small group of young soccer players stop in front of her house. They couldn't imagine why dog poop would glitter, and they speculated that perhaps this was the dog's way of decorating his yard for some unannounced fall holiday. A little boy with sandy-red hair, looking at the mess, said, "Party poop." Another boy sat down on his haunches in that peculiar way children have that would permanently cripple an adult, picked up a small stick, and started to poke the fresh pile, looking, Sarah supposed, for a prize inside. Then the children sauntered slowly on down the street, looking for the next small miracle.

Satisfying herself that there were no figurative fingerprints in the pile, Sarah tugged on the leash and said, "Come on." They had walked an additional half of a block when a clean white SUV pulled up next to her. A nice-looking young man rolled down the window and pulled a shiny gold badge out of his pocket. Sarah puckered her mouth over to one side. Her fist clenched on the leash. "Busted," she muttered under her breath but decided not to confess.

"Do you live around here?" he asked pleasantly.

She nodded, determined not to make any voluntary incriminating statements.

"Do you walk around here often?"

Great, Sarah thought. *Now I'm going to catch it for all the unidentified poop from who knows how many dogs in the neighborhood.* She decided to change her tactic from stonewalling to charm, and she smiled at the officer. "I do walk around here frequently, but I live about three blocks west of the park."

He leaned out the window and said, "Could you do me a favor?"

Right, she thought, *forty hours of community service with a shovel and fluorescent-orange garbage sacks.*

He laughed at her quizzical look and started to explain. "I'm a narcotics officer. There's a drug house about three blocks down this street. They have surveillance cameras, and if they see my vehicle driving past more than once, they'll get suspicious. If you don't mind, maybe I could walk past the house with you. You and your dog could be my cover."

Sarah paused for a minute. "Well, I'll need to see more ID. I wouldn't want to be an unfortunate item in the newspaper. You know, local woman bludgeoned to death while walking large dog." The officer laughed, and Sarah continued, "Clearly, I should turn off CNN once in a while."

He flipped open his wallet, as he punched several numbers into a cell phone and handed it to Sarah. "Dispatch," he mouthed. All this was happening as the officer got out of his SUV, locked the car, and tucked his badge inside his shirt.

"Yes," Sarah stammered, "I just wanted to know if David Bradshaw is a narcotics officer?" After listening for a moment, she handed back the phone.

"So how about letting me hold the leash?" he asked, but Einstein was having none of it. The dog sat down next to Sarah, straightened his front legs, and refused to move. Several sharp tugs only increased his resolve. Sarah finally had to stoop down beside him, scratch behind his ears, and tell him that it was his civic duty to let this man hold his leash. *This dog understands every word*, she thought as she nodded at the officer, and Einstein took off at a fast trot with the officer holding the handle of the retractable leash.

"So how do you know this house is a drug house?" Sarah whispered.

"Irritated neighbors. Strange cars coming and going after midnight. Plus, we get tips from other sources."

Sarah's heart pounded a little faster. She wasn't sure she wanted a new career in law enforcement.

The house resembled other houses in the neighborhood, but the yard hadn't been watered or cared for. No bright red geraniums in terra-cotta pots sat on the front stoop. Someone had been doing some bodywork on a Camaro and left greasy tools and the car parked on the dead lawn. Curtains were drawn, but they sagged and drooped sadly. A red flag wasn't flying above the roof, but it might as well have been. *I wouldn't want this house next to mine*, she thought. Two additional cars were parked in the driveway, and a blue truck was out in front.

The screen door opened, and she gawked at the two young men coming out. One had a tight dark knitted hat pulled down over his hair. The other kid was shorter and stockier and wore a North Valley sweatshirt with the hood pulled up.

Startled, she started walking again, quickly, and didn't look as the boys climbed into the truck and drove away in the opposite direction. But she experienced the same antipathy she felt when they walked into class every afternoon.

"You know those kids?" the officer asked her immediately.

"Yes," Sarah said hesitantly. "I teach at the high school. I never thought of those boys as drug users." Then she shook her head dismissively. "Of course, smoking a joint is like having a beer now."

He gave her an odd look. "You teach at the high school?" he said incredulously. "Kids get pot from other kids. Dealers set up surveillance at a house like this because they know if they get caught, they're going away for a long time."

"Those boys weren't buying pot?"

"No."

"Then I have a serious problem on my team." She spoke as much to herself as she spoke to him. She closed her eyes and wondered what else she didn't know. She hated policing her team. She thought of herself as a mentor, not teacher-slash-cop.

"What are their names?" he asked.

"How will this involve me?"

The officer looked at her directly. "I don't have to involve you at all."

"What will you do?" Sarah asked.

"Well, I can't compel them to talk to me. I can't take them in. I can invite them to talk. Then it's their call. I'll call the principal and have a periodic locker check done, but again, we don't have much probable cause. The principal can look in the locker for anything immediately observable, but he can't check inside a backpack or anything like that."

Sarah's mind tumbled ahead. She imagined the vice principal opening the locker and discovering an incriminating collection of colorful drug paraphernalia, maybe a bright blue bong or a beaded pipe on the top shelf next to a trig text and a Joseph Conrad novel. Were the boys too smart for that? They were so arrogant, but would they be careless?

She looked up at the officer. "You'll tell the boys that you got their names from the license plate number? Do you think they saw us?"

"I don't think they noticed us."

"They were Braxton Martin and Tyler Colton. Tyler's family is very affluent."

He shrugged. "Then he's probably buying for his friend."

Sarah groaned.

They made another right turn and were back on the street just a couple of blocks away from the officer's parked car.

"Hey, thanks for coming," he said.

Sarah nodded grimly, but her shoulders sank under the load. *One more problem*, she thought. The tally in her head was going into the red. Drugs on the team. Not enough probable cause. Those boys were too clever to implicate themselves.

She abandoned the rest of her walk and hurried home to call Meg with this newest revelation. If the boys were kicked off the team, it would have to come from the vice principal. That's why he got paid the big bucks. She and Meg would have to be neutral, aggrieved bystanders bemoaning the destructive influence of drugs. She could play that part.

Sarah opened the door and tossed Einstein's leash back into the battered box before she realized that all the lovely Sunday afternoon relaxation had been sucked right out of the room. She had been worrying about how to share the adventures of Einstein, Wonder Dog, and Sarah, Crime Solving Mom, minus the specifics, but something was very wrong besides drugs on her team. Tom was sitting on the couch, but he wasn't lounging in the cushions with his feet up, perusing the sports section. He was sitting up straight, tensely studying his cuticles. Jenny was pulling the wound-up toilet paper out from between her toes, not looking at her mother.

"What's up?" she asked.

Tom bounced his fist against his mouth before he spoke. "Dad called."

"And?" Other considerations vanished. "What's he up to now?" *I have enough trouble*, she thought. *Why can't he leave us alone?*

"He's thinking of moving back here."

"What?" She collapsed on the straight-backed kitchen chair, as though all the air had been let out of her lungs. She started to inhale quickly, sucking air, as though she had just run a marathon. The joints in her knees liquefied. She stared at her children and, after a few seconds, realized that she was panting. She worried about the big earthquake hitting the Wasatch Fault. She worried about Robbie vanishing in Venezuela. She worried about an oil embargo and melting polar icecaps, but she never worried about this. He hated Utah. He was a big-deal academic doctor. He did research, and he published papers, and he never made enough money to up his child support. He'd lived in Iowa for fifteen years. No, make that almost seventeen years. She couldn't stretch her head around this terrible piece of news.

"What did he say, exactly?" Her tone was offensive.

"Don't interrogate me," Tom bristled. "I didn't do anything. I just answered the phone."

"What did he, in fact, say?" she persisted. She rubbed her sweaty palms on her thighs.

"The hospital is looking for another cardiologist. They called him to see if he was interested."

"Phooey. He had to make the initial contact."

"Do you want to tell me what he said, or do you want me to tell you?"

"Sorry, keep going."

"He hasn't made a decision yet. They're just thinking about it. If they did come, it probably wouldn't be until next summer, maybe the first of the year. He wanted to know how Jenny liked high school. He wanted to know if I'm going to play basketball this year." This last bit of information irritated Tom, and Sarah was pleased.

"Play basketball?" she snorted. "You're the best they've got."

"He's trolling. I think he wanted to know if Jenny and I want him to come." Tom, the most sensitive of her children, probably wasn't off the mark now.

"He's got some nerve to think he can walk into our lives, without so much as a by-your-leave."

Jenny cut her off. "You're always so hard on him. Maybe he just wants to live here. It might be cool to have a father who's a doctor."

"He's always been a doctor. That's one of his big problems. He's always been a doctor who incidentally is a father with three kids out there in the stratosphere somewhere—"

Jenny cut her off again. "You know what I mean, a doctor," she said, "right here in town."

Sarah knew what Jenny was thinking, and the thought came at her like a well-placed wrecking ball. A doctor, with status, and money, and a big house, and nice clothes, and a highly polished, very blonde second wife. Suddenly, through the eyes of her daughter, she saw her shabby efforts to make a home. She couldn't compete, and until this moment, she had never felt like she had to. This would never be okay. She slowly lifted herself up off the chair as though she were at least a million years old. "Where did you leave it?"

"I don't know what he'll do." Tom's voice was resigned. "He's in negotiations with the hospital, but they're pretty desperate to have him come."

Sarah leaned over to unbuckle her sandals and tossed them in the corner. Of course, that was how Bob would see it. Everyone was always desperate for Bob; everyone always wanted a piece of his limitless wonderfulness. She couldn't look at her children. She walked down the hall and flopped on her bed to think this one through.

For the first time in a long time, she had no control over her life. She was a punching bag for egotistical males. She needed to circle the wagons, to push back at all these multiple layers of trouble, but she wasn't sure how.

She hadn't closed her door and she heard Tom whisper to Jenny.

"You don't need to rub her nose in it. What's the matter with you? Don't you know how hard it will be for her to have Dad live here?"

Jenny mumbled for a moment, "I just meant—"

"You're such a . . ." But Tom didn't finish his sentence and left all the possibilities of what Jenny was and wasn't hanging in the air for her to consider. He stomped down to the basement to finish homework while Jenny waited another hour for a call from Dorothy that never came. Sarah read the same two pages in a novel until ten o'clock, when she gave up and slipped under the covers.

She should call Meg to tell her what she had seen at the drug house, but every time she reached for the phone, she stopped. She wasn't ready to explain this latest personal disaster. Squeezing her eyes closed did no good. The crowd in Sarah's brain kept milling around, punctuating the air with loud outbursts like angry parents at a PTA meeting. How long had it been, she wondered, punching her pillow with her fist, since she had been alone in her head?

Jenny, Jenny. What to do about Jenny? She saw the ugliness from the prep room, the hooded boys leaving the drug house, and Tyler's sullen face. Arguments with her ex-husband went round and round in her mind without resolution, occasionally interrupted by a tall sheriff analyzing her soberly from a distance. Tucked into the back of her head were her own desperate wishes to run away, maybe to Scotland, and never come back.

Finally around three o'clock, when it was much too late to take a sleeping pill and still function at 6:30 AM, she got up and paced in the living room. She sat on the couch and flipped through the pages of a book. Abruptly, she pitched the paperback across the room. It slammed against the kitchen wall. Einstein barked and scrambled down the hall, looking for an intruder.

"Hush, Einstein," she whispered crossly, as though he had started the ruckus. Desperate for sleep and angry at her impossible circumstances, she shook her fist in the darkness. Finally, for a few hours, as the outside sky turned a pale gray, exhaustion won, and Sarah fell asleep on the couch.

honey

*h*e was not the first student to fail a current events quiz, and so he looked up Monday morning, surprised to hear himself being addressed.

"Mr. Newton," Sarah demanded, "are you aware that in three years the fate of our nation will be in your hands? It might be expedient for you to have some understanding of the problems facing our nation. In fifty years all the coral reefs will be gone. The ice caps are melting. Eight hundred million people suffer from chronic hunger. And asteroids are coming perilously close to the earth." Sarah held up her thumb and finger a fourth of an inch apart and shook them at Mr. Newton. "How are you going to solve any of these problems if you spend all your time playing Grand Theft Auto?" Sarah's voice got progressively louder as she waved his test paper like a red flag.

Mr. Newton, who usually went by the name of Jack, shielded himself from her wrath by putting a hand in front of his forehead, but the look on his face said, "Hey, who changed the rules? I thought you liked me," and he reverted to basic teenage strategy: I'm not the only one, and this isn't fair. He pointed his finger across the aisle at his friend Mike. "He was playing too."

"Well, both of you need to get your heads out of video games, or wherever else you keep them, and pay a little attention to what's going on in the world. I just hope when the asteroid hits, it takes out all the people who spend their lives in front of a screen!"

Students were sitting a little straighter, and their furtive glances ricocheted around the room as if silently asking each other, "Is she for real?"

Mike looked up with a loopy smile on his face. "Mrs. Williams, if the asteroid hits, no more world hunger."

"No, Mike. It would bring universal hunger, and we would be reduced to eating each other," she retorted, thinking Mike should be the first one in the pot.

Changing directions abruptly, she gave the class instructions for a group activity and then stepped briskly from group to group, pouncing on any student who wasn't anxiously engaged.

After third hour, Meg grabbed her arm as the last skittish student escaped. "What's the matter? I thought you were going to skewer that Newton kid and have him for lunch." Meg examined Sarah's face more closely. "You look terrible. Why are you so angry?"

"In a nutshell?"

Meg glanced at her watch. "That's all the time I've got. I've got to skip lunch and go trade cars with Gary."

"Well, I spent a half an hour with a narcotics officer yesterday afternoon. Plus, my ex-husband is moving back to town." Sarah took a step closer to Meg until she was inches away from Meg's nose. "So what do you think about that?"

For the first time in a long time, Meg had absolutely nothing to say. She stared at Sarah. Finally, pulling keys out of her pocket, she said, "I've got to go," but she didn't move. "Who's using?" she asked.

"Our two favorites. Maybe more."

Meg raised her outstretched hands up to her shoulders. "And this is bad?"

"Not enough probable cause to arrest them or even question them. I feel like I was handed a broom to whisk them right out of the room, and it vanished in my hands." Sarah looked down at her palms as if something had just gone *poof!* She glanced furtively around the room, looking for a hapless victim to strangle.

"I've got to go," Meg said. "Gary's meeting me in the parking lot in five minutes. I'll be back as soon as I can." Clutching her keys, she hurried out of the room.

—⁓—

Sarah felt bone-weary tiredness that afternoon as the varsity class came in. Her anger had burned itself out. She had left home too early. She thought she could do some catching up before faculty meeting, but the pile on her desk just seemed to grow. The news about her ex-husband felt like a canker sore on the inside of her lip, and her mind wouldn't leave it alone. She shuffled student essays around on the desk at lunch, but she couldn't focus. Finally, she closed her eyes and just let her mind spin.

Meg came back thirty seconds before the second bell rang. Sarah passed her the current events quiz, as Meg, making her way to the front, good-naturedly stepped over backpacks and long legs extending into the aisle.

"We're two weeks away from the end of the trimester. If you have any late work, it's got to be in one week from today. That's our cut-off." Meg set the class in motion.

"Can we apply tournament credit to this trimester's grades?" Rachael asked.

"Sorry." Meg smiled knowingly. "That would be like charging a grade. You can charge shoes, but you can't charge grades. You kids set up your own contracts. You can't expect to change the rules of the game the last week."

Tyler rolled his eyes at Brax.

Responding on cue, Brax challenged, "You can if they're bogus rules."

Meg's smile vanished, and Sarah stood up from the desk and walked toward the back of the class. Meg held up her right hand and continued, "Sorry, but this is the hand that keys in the grades, and I'm not changing the policy regardless of what Brax thinks."

Sarah added, "Or what Tyler tells Brax to think."

The class laughed, and Brax scowled. Tyler smiled and nodded his head up and down, miming a belly laugh.

Meg cut off the disruption. "Okay, let's get this quiz out of the way. Number one to five. The secretary of the treasury made a comment last week about the condition of the economy. I don't need an exact quotation, but paraphrase what he said."

She continued at a calm, steady pace, repeating each question. Sarah stood at the back of the room, ostensibly fixing a loose piece of red edging on the bulletin board. Meg told the class to exchange quizzes and started discussing the answers. Sarah saw Tyler moving a book to cover his quiz. He was filling in the answers on his own paper.

The little cheat, Sarah thought, and she interrupted Meg. "We don't have much time. Why don't I finish correcting these after school?" She walked over and pulled Tyler's blank quiz off his desk. She didn't say anything. She just smiled. He flushed a dark pink and looked away.

Meg pulled the class's attention away from the small drama occurring on the third row. "If you go to the library or the prep room, sign out on the whiteboard. Say where you'll be and be where you say." It was a familiar drill, and students were up and moving before she finished her sentence. Policy debaters started to move toward the prep room. Sarah hurried past them.

"Let me get the door unlocked. No one's been in here today." Returning to the room, keys still in her hand, she spoke pleasantly to another clutch of students. "I want everyone to draw topics and speak the last half hour of class." She picked up a handful of questions written on slips of paper and walked toward students, standing beside a couple of metal boxes containing news magazines.

"Who wants to choose first?" Her stomach clutched. *I sound like Mr. Rogers*, she thought, *too cheerful*.

Meg glanced up from the student she was helping and looked at Sarah anxiously. She walked over and whispered, "What's up with the quiz?"

"Tyler and a couple of other kids were cheating. They made of show of trading papers and kept their own. They were filling in the answers. They've been doing it the last two weeks."

"Did you see them?"

"No, Rachael told me. Someone always tells."

The back door slammed open, and four students burst into the room. Not waiting for Brax to be his mouthpiece, Tyler shoved his large storage box in front of him. Panting and furious, he said, "Some creep poured honey into our files. Everything's trashed."

Using a voice that would calm wild beasts, Meg said, "I can't believe anyone would do that." She moved toward exhibit A and knelt by the box containing hundreds and hundreds of evidence briefs. She lifted a manila file out of the middle of the container and opened it. At least she tried to open it. The paper inside stuck to the folder. "Are they all this bad?" If they were, hundreds of hours of work would have to be repeated, if duplicates could be even be made. The students in the back of the room grew silent.

"I don't know. I haven't had time to look at every single file." He was so angry and red-faced the smattering of acne on his cheeks disappeared.

"Okay, pull everyone in." Meg continued to speak slowly and deliberately. She motioned for Sarah to sit by her on the riser. All the students moved back into the class. Some sitting in desks, some standing.

"All right," Meg said. "Let's think this through. Who would do this, and who had access?"

"Well," Sarah started, breathing rapidly, "we locked up Friday night before we left. No one else has unlocked those rooms before I did, unless a janitor was in there. The building is unlocked on Saturday for Adult Ed, but these rooms aren't used."

"You didn't unlock the room," Meg said to Sarah, "and I know that I didn't." She turned her gaze toward the rest of the class. "Does anyone have any ideas?"

"Well, are there any other keys?" Kristen spoke, enunciating each word. Tyler turned a menacing look on her that would have wilted a weaker student, but Kristen said, "Don't give me your scary face, Tyler. I was there in the second grade when you threw up during the Pledge of Allegiance."

Meg looked at her closely. "What exactly do you mean, other keys?"

Kristen looked around the room at the other students, and then she pushed up the sleeves of her pink angora sweater as if preparing for hand-to-hand combat. "We all know there are duplicate keys. I think whoever did this deed is a person who has one of the duplicate keys or a person who was passed a key. I mean, how many of these keys are there? Ten? Twenty?"

"Ugly wench," curled out of Brax's mouth softly.

"There won't be any of that kind of talk," Sarah said. "Particularly as Kristen seems to be telling the truth. That's the only logical explanation. Mr. Cottle saw several of you going into the prep room, which was locked, the day of the fire drill. It will take about two seconds to have him in here to ID the kids he saw."

"Let's have those keys now." Meg slapped her hand out. Several junior varsity students tossed quick, guilty looks at each other. Melissa, whose mother taught keyboarding at the junior high, started to squirm.

"I want those keys right now," Meg insisted, "or I'm going to start calling parents." But no one made a move to surrender his key and run the risk of retaliation.

"Go ask Bill to step in for a minute," Meg said quietly to Sarah.

"It's not that big of a deal," Melissa drawled. "I have a key, but I didn't mess with Tyler's files." She made a show of reaching into the bottom of her large bag, lifting out several books, and pulling out a key tied on a bit of red yarn. She put the key in Meg's outstretched hand. "Come on, you guys. Busted. Party's over." She tried to sound like it was no big deal, but she failed.

Several other students scrambled through their belongings. More keys surfaced.

"So, Harry," Meg said as he handed over his key, "where did you get this?"

He shrugged.

"Are you getting their names?" Meg glanced at Sarah, who was scribbling on a legal pad. Surprised, students looked over at Sarah. A list was being kept?

Sarah nodded. "Every single one, but I didn't hear Harry's answer. Where did you get that key?"

"Same place everyone else got theirs."

"That's pretty much a non-answer to a very simple question."

"This is so lame." Kristen jumped into the fray. "We all know that Tyler had ten keys cut. He's been bragging about it for days. I mean, haven't we all heard him rant about how stupid Mrs. W. was for giving Melissa her keys?"

Sarah watched Kristen carefully. Risky behavior. Students never ratted out other students, but Kristen didn't seem to care. She paused and looked at the teachers to see the impact of her remark. "The stupid one is the person who handed over a key to a friend," her tongue slid all over the word, "who was happy to dump honey into his files. Now that's really dumb."

Meg stopped the argument. "Okay, I have four keys. I want six more. No one is leaving this room until I have them all. That's it."

"I have a job," Brax said. "I have to be there at three-thirty. I'm not hanging around here."

"No problem. You can give me your key on your way out the door. After the bell rings, of course." Meg smiled grimly.

Brax gave Tyler a quick look. Tyler responded with a subtle nod. The metallic blue key ring jangled as Brax pulled off the duplicate and tossed it into Meg's outstretched hand. That was the signal. The rest of the keys were turned in quickly and without much bravado. The tension eased, but Tyler was embarrassed, his stature was diminished, and he had a look of grim resolve.

"So what about my files? Are we all going to stay until someone admits to trashing my files?" He looked slowly around the room.

In all her years of teaching, Sarah had only really disliked two or three kids, but this kid, this arrogant, rude, clever kid, was at the top of her list.

"So nothing's going to be done about my files? How bogus is that?"

"I guess we could dust for fingerprints, but I don't think anyone in here has a criminal record yet. There is nothing, on file, to match." Sarah started to smile at the pun, and several other students giggled nervously. Flashing an angry look around the room, Tyler was quiet. Everyone knew Tyler would get even. The question was, with whom?

Relieved when the final bell rang, students left quickly. On a typical weekday, students stayed after class to ask a question or chat, but not today.

Meg shook her head quickly and looked down at the ten keys in her cupped palm. "Those boys and a handful of their followers are ruining this experience for everyone. We're going to see kids transfer out at the quarter. Plus, if rumors start going around about drugs, it will really hurt us. This is so bad. We really should talk to Terry about this. Give him a heads up, because I'm sure he's going to get parent calls."

"Isn't there any way we can get rid of those boys?" Sarah asked in a tired voice. Then she laughed. " 'Will no one rid me of this tiresome priest?' " Meg smiled, and Sarah continued, "If we can't get rid of them, they're going to be trouble all year."

"Hello, when did teachers ever have rights, but there has to be a punishment for copying those keys and passing them out, even if we can't get them for drugs. I wish we had photographed that whiteboard on Friday," Meg said almost to herself. "What do you think?"

"I think every kid with a key should have to miss at least the next tournament." Sarah stopped and thought. "And I think that Tyler and Brax and Melissa should have to miss the next two."

"That's Gov's Cup."

"That's right."

"That will be trouble."

"They've been asking for trouble all year. Making those keys was over the line. We can't keep looking the other way hoping that things will improve. They won't. If there isn't a serious consequence, they'll poison next year's team too."

"Well," Meg said as she walked back to their large metal desk. She sat down hard on the chair and rummaged into the back of the drawer behind Sarah's purse. Pulling out a shopping bag, she dumped two empty plastic honey bears onto the desk and looked up at her partner. "We need to talk about this."

hamburgers and confessions

*g*ently pushing Jenny ahead of her, Sarah walked in the kitchen door. Meg stood at the sink.

"Hey. We're almost ready." Meg talked over her shoulder. "Jenny, do you want to carry these hamburgers out to Gary?" She gestured at the plate of beef patties with her vegetable peeler.

Wearing Robbie's old T-shirt, Sarah sat cross-legged by the large round table in the kitchen of Meg's old two-story home. It was a wonderful room, very welcoming, not too tidy or clean. Unopened mail was stacked randomly on the edge of the counter. Scattered magazines, books, and unfinished homework shared the tabletop set with paper plates and napkins. Meg had invited Sarah and Jenny for hamburgers and a picnic on the back lawn. Meg's little boys thought Tom was a human jungle gym, so he begged off, claiming an English paper as an excuse.

Sarah, afraid she was in for a "do better" talk, wrinkled her nose as she watched Meg peeling carrots with a vengeance.

"What did that carrot ever do to you?"

Meg turned, her carrot pointing directly at Sarah, and opened her mouth to speak but snapped it closed.

"So," Sarah asked, "are you going to drive that carrot through my heart?"

Meg shook the carrot at her. "There were a hundred ways to finesse those keys without trashing their files. The moral high ground is gone. *Whish!*" and Meg passed her free hand quickly over her head.

"I thought it would feel great." Sarah rested her hands on her legs. "You know, to get even, but it didn't. I was a wreck by fifth period."

"I can't believe you did this." Meg glared at her. "What are we going to do now? I've never seen you so wired. Tyler's not the worst kid we've dealt with. You usually manipulate kids that arrogant like a lump of Play-doh. I mean, honestly, he's smart, spoiled, and vain. We can outflank this kid, no problem, but not if you're a walking emotional land mine."

"You're wrong about Tyler," Sarah replied. "He's mean. He's using drugs. Do you remember when that task force talked to the faculty about gangs? If they could just pluck out the leader, the problem would go away. I think Tyler's functioning like that on the debate team. He's always got his little retinue with him. He sends out his minions to do his dirty work. The kid's scary."

Meg used the carrot like a pointer. "He's not more than we can handle. If anyone had found those bears, that class would have exploded. How on earth would we have explained that?"

"Denial."

"Oh, Sarah, nailing that kid isn't worth the risks you're taking. Don't trash our program over one bratty kid."

Sarah's fingers raked through her hair nervously. "Things are spinning out of control. Tyler is evil. Bob moving back into my world makes me nuts." Sarah twisted a lock of hair into a little knot around her finger. "I know the Romans aren't coming to burn the Christians. The Nazis aren't invading. I don't have to arm the kids with AK-47s and send them to become partisans in the mountains behind the golf course, but there's a piece of this that feels like that. It really does." Her tone had a tinge of desperation. "I don't want Bob here."

"You're the one spinning out of control." Meg chomped down on the carrot.

———

"So, why now?" asked Meg's husband, Gary, as he set a tray loaded with dirty dishes next to the sink. "Why after all these years does the prodigal father return?" He pressed his thick gray mustache down with his index finger and his thumb, his habit when pondering a difficult question.

"Well, it's not local boy done good," Sarah responded with a toss of her head. "He's way past that. He assumes everyone knows that local boy has done fabulously well."

"Fabulously?" Gary rolled his eyes and chuckled. He couldn't stay serious for long, and the altered inflection of a word or a funny gesture turned almost anything into a joke. "Give us an unbiased thumbnail of this guy, Meg." He shifted, unintentionally, into the mode he used to question his graduate-level classes.

"Tall, good looking, a high school hero, smart, confident, but he was several years older than I was."

"You're forgetting arrogant, self-absorbed, and cheap," Sarah added.

"Hmm, what does Sarah think?" Meg said, and Gary laughed.

Sarah scowled. "I forgot one: narcissistic."

"Again, why now? What's changed in his life?" Gary repeated.

Sarah glanced into her hands as if some answer were written on her fingertips. "He's never been interested in seeing the kids much, and that's suited me just fine." She pondered Gary's question with a frown. "I don't know. Maybe he wants to get his foot in the door while Robbie's gone?"

"Well, he's interested now. He's moving next door," Gary said.

"I just want him gone. Dead, buried, detassled in the middle of some Iowa cornfield." She sighed and ran her finger around the edge of a paper plate.

"Detassled?" Meg and Gary exchanged a quick smile before Gary said, "That might really cobble a guy."

Sarah giggled in spite of herself. "No *corny* puns. Not this late at night."

Laughing, Gary pounded his forehead with the palm of his hand.

"What do the kids think of Dr. Iowa?" Meg prodded gently.

"Robbie hates him. Bob offered to pay for his mission, but Robbie said that if his dad's money were the only way he could go, he'd stay home, thank you very much. He wouldn't even let Bob come to his farewell. He said if Bob walked in the front door, he'd go out the back. The end." She felt nasty but somehow validated by repeating Robbie's refusal.

Gary leaned back. "Ouch. That's a lot of extra luggage for a boy to haul around on a mission."

"Come on, you guys. Robbie hasn't done anything wrong." Sarah stuck her chin out. "Robbie was crushed when his dad left. If Robbie doesn't love his father, it's Bob's fault."

"Blame aside," Gary continued, "it's pretty hard to find a positive spiritual feeling when you're carrying all that excess baggage inside your head."

This wasn't exactly new turf, but they were notions Sarah pushed away. Her relationship with Bob was black and white. He was a person to guard against, to exclude, and to stomp on if she had the chance.

She shook her head. "These kids are my life. I've raised them by myself. Who does he think he is to waltz in here now and have a piece of their lives?"

"He's the only dad they'll ever have," Gary said.

"They're better off without him. When a guy leaves like that, it's not going to be business as usual."

"What does Tom think?" Meg asked.

"Tom, Tom." Sarah stirred a carrot stick in a small puddle of ranch dressing. "He doesn't remember his dad living with us. He was too little. I think he sometimes senses a void, but he's moved on. He's a pretty busy kid. To tell you the truth, I think Tom's more worried about me."

"Jenny?"

"I don't know about Jenny. She's sick and tired of being broke, but she's not old enough to make her own money. She sees the doctors' kids that live on the hill and thinks that looks just right."

"Surely they see him occasionally," Gary said. "Doesn't he come to visit his folks?"

"He was here last summer for a few days. He took Jenny out to dinner and a movie. Movies are great; you don't have to actually talk. Tom was at basketball camp. Bob was irritated that Tom wasn't available, but he never checks the kids' schedules before he makes his plans. He wanted Tom to leave for an evening, but that's not fair."

"Tom wouldn't go?" Gary clarified.

"I didn't ask Tom. I just told Bob that Tom couldn't leave camp. Bob's so self-centered."

Sarah looked out the window at Jenny and Liz, Meg's oldest daughter, sitting on the lawn pulling up blades of grass and biting off the white ends while they chatted. Jenny looked completely at ease with the younger girl. She was laughing and gesturing with her hands. The little boys were playing on a large rope swing that hung out over a gentle slope. The old tree bent slightly and swayed as the boys ran and grabbed the rope to dangle for just a second and then roll down the hill. Laughing, they would run up to punish their small bodies one more time. It was all so peaceful. How could Sarah explain all the unfinished business with her ex-husband in a home like this?

"Have they ever been back to Iowa?" Meg asked. "It's so beautiful."

"Kids don't care about rolling corn fields and Grant Wood. They went a few times, but it didn't ever go well, and the last time there was a huge blow-up."

Gary raised an eyebrow, and Meg leaned forward a bit, so Sarah continued. "They were there for two weeks, and Bob didn't take the time off. They were stuck with Claire."

"That's a long time if you're not used to kids," Gary said.

"It's also a long time for kids not to be with their friends," Meg said. "When was this?"

"The summer before Robbie's junior year," Sarah remembered. "The boys played a lot of basketball, but it's too hot and humid to be outside during the day. I'm sure Jenny just prowled around trying to be inconspicuous. Right before they came home, Claire threw away Jenny's retainer. The woman is so dumb. Of course, the boys know how much money we've spent on Jenny's mouth. She sucked her fingers like a crazy person until she was five."

Rosie, a little girl with long curly red hair, had been sitting on her father's foot. She stood up, surveyed the adults, stuck her thumb in her mouth proudly, and then popped it out.

"Yes, Rosie, we know you're a big girl, and you don't suck your thumb anymore." Gary patted her on the head.

Sarah ignored the interruption. "There was an ugly scene about the retainer. When the kids came home, Bob called several times. Actually, every day for almost a week, but Robbie wouldn't talk to him. Some details leaked out, but they never talk much about the time they spend with their dad and Claire."

She rolled her eyes and smiled wickedly. "They do make fun of Claire. If someone is oblivious or makes a really stupid remark, the boys will say she's pulling a Claire." She shrugged. "I never really knew what happened. Jenny never said a word. But the next summer,

Robbie refused to go. It wasn't fair to make the other kids go without him."

"So now he's going to come back," Gary finished. "Instead of giving him 10 percent of the kids and keeping 90 percent for yourself, you're going to have him in your life, big time. Ouch." Gary scooped up Rosie. She had been listening to grown-up talk long enough, so she bit her dad right above his left kneecap to get his full attention. He draped her across his wide shoulders and started to turn slowly in circles, laughing at her screams.

Meg smiled. "Don't get her wound up this late. We'll never get her to bed."

"Bath time." He hauled her, giggling, up the stairs, and the two women sat listening to laughter and the sound of water filling the tub.

"Do the kids ever see Bob's parents?" Meg asked. "Don't they live somewhere around here?"

"They used to. They live over the mountain now." Sarah gestured with her hand as though "over the mountain" was near the end of the world. "It's a gated community, very posh. They moved after he retired, to live near their daughters," Sarah said. "They made a couple of overtures when the kids and I first moved back, but it was so awkward. They've never liked me, and finally I had to tell them they didn't have visitation rights and please not to bother us anymore."

"How could they not like you?" Meg said, surprised.

"Oh, I think they always thought Bob found me in a bargain basement. You've got to remember, I'm a Ritzman. My mother was a widow living on social security and a very small pension."

"But you were a star in college."

"Well, I certainly thought I was," and Sarah patted herself on her chest, "but the wedding was a nightmare."

"All weddings are nightmares."

"Yes, but . . ." Sarah looked down her nose to indicate that as awful as some weddings were, her wedding won the prize. "I didn't wander around with a picture in my head like a lot of girls did. You know, colors, receptions, dresses." Meg nodded, so Sarah went on talking. "But my mother had a clear picture in her head. She nearly killed herself. She made the wedding dress and the bridesmaids' dresses. She and her friends decorated the cultural hall at the church with these large roses—they made out of tissue paper and sprayed with lacquer, so they were sort of translucent. They stuck them on a trellis Brother Mortensen made." Sarah grimaced.

"How did they look?"

"Well, if you stood across the room and squinted with only one eye, if was sort of okay."

"That bad?"

"Oh no," Sarah replied. "It gets worse. They set up a trousseau table with a place setting of my dishes, and a couple of quilts, and thousands—I'm not kidding—of dish towels that my mother had been embroidering my entire life. The same ladies who made the tissue roses made a very marginal dessert buffet. Bob's parents walked in and were absolutely horrified. My mother kept fawning over both of them, and they treated her like she had leprosy. It wasn't just sort of awful. It was completely awful." She started to laugh. "I mean, what can I say? We were doomed. Bob was humiliated, and from that moment on, he was doing me a large favor. He was rescuing me from the dishtowels."

"I'm so sorry." Meg frowned sympathetically, but her eyes were laughing. "Did the dish towels say Sunday, Monday, Tuesday, Wednesday?"

"Oh, yes."

"My aunt did a set of those for me. Small bears holding teacups."

"Plus, you know, I don't have a single pioneer ancestor. There aren't any prominent polygamists hiding behind my family tree."

Meg extended her hands, like, "So what?"

"Oh, come on," Sarah answered. "If you can't stand up on the Twenty-fourth of July and tell a story about your very own relative, near death, pulling a handcart in a snow storm, you're right next to nothin'. And that's what Bob's family thought of me."

Meg sighed and changed the subject. "Your kids aren't in any danger from this man. They're too old. He might spoil them with some stuff you can't afford, but who cares? He can't really throw them off course. To tell you the truth, the boys won't really have much time for him. I don't know what the story is with Jenny. She's not like her broth-ers, but if she needs masculine attention, wouldn't it be better to get it from her long-lost father than from a scholarly sixteen-year-old with more than math on his mind?" Meg turned her face to the side, as if to say, "You know what I mean?"

Sarah nodded slightly. She knew, and both alternatives worried her.

Meg plowed ahead. "Sarah, the problem is you. You're tied to this man. You've got to cut loose."

"Easy to say. Difficult to do. I get furious if he even calls the house. I want to yank the phone out of their hands and beat the kids over their heads with it. I'm angry if the word *dad* comes out of their mouths."

"He's the only dad that they'll ever have. You haven't been too eager to produce a stepfather."

"That would just make things worse." Sarah shrugged. "We've had this conversation before."

"Well, what are you going to do? What about seeing a counselor?"

Sarah rubbed the ball of her thumb against the tips of her fingers. "Money."

"So how about going to the temple once a week? It's quiet and peaceful. Maybe you could work things out there. Mediate a little. Make some good choices."

Sarah rolled her eyes. "I tried that once after we moved back. I hit a logjam with the fidelity part. I kept remembering the day we got married. Was I the only one that promised to be faithful?"

"So I take it you haven't been back much." Meg smiled wistfully.

"What's the point if those promises are broken so easily?"

"It's not about him." Meg was emphatic. "It's about you. You have got to let go. Your issues, that's what you've got to resolve. Like it or not, he's coming back to live right under your nose, and you have to figure out a way to deal with it, or you won't survive emotionally, and that's what could hurt your kids, not Romans with torches."

"I know, I know." But Sarah couldn't step out of the small black box she had constructed. She started to ease herself out of the chair and set her wadded napkin on the paper plate. "You've been great to listen. I'll think hard about what you've said." She was starting to feel pressured and tired. It had been a long day. "I need to collect Jenny and head out, so you can get your kids to bed."

Meg wasn't ready to let her leave. "So what's up for tomorrow?"

"Well." Sarah pursed her lips as she made a mental list. "We need to see Terry after school and make sure he's on board with whatever we decide to do about the keys. Wednesday we need to keep the culprits after school and tell them what the consequences will be."

"And then we leave the country."

"Right. You're thinking Nova Scotia." Sarah laughed and leaned into Meg's outstretched arms for a quick hug.

"Tomorrow will be better. We'll take control." Meg was reassuring, but Sarah wasn't buying any of it.

chicken salad and rhodes scholars
summer in iowa, 1990

a dribble of perspiration rolled down the side of his cheek. Only a stalk of corn could thrive in this kind of heat and humidity. Bob's sweat glued his pants to the car seat, and he lifted his left leg, hoping the air conditioning would dry him out. He had tried to leave work early, hoping he could take Claire and his kids to the pool at City Park. He couldn't sit through another movie or another night of board games with Robbie making thinly veiled remarks about how much he didn't want to be there. *The boys tolerate me, but just barely*, he thought. The heat shimmered off the asphalt on Arbor Circle. He turned his car slowly into the driveway. No signs of life, but it was too hot to be outside.

He opened the garage door and tried to walk into the kitchen. Mayonnaise-coated pieces of chicken and fruit were all over the floor, stuck to the linoleum. Broken bits of a blue ceramic bowl were scattered amid the chicken carnage. He had come upon a large domestic explosion. He peered around the doorway to the living room. No bodies, bleeding or dismembered, on the carpet. He felt like he needed to tiptoe.

"What's going on?"

No one responded.

This was not like Claire. She was immaculate. If it weren't for the current risk of salmonella, he could grab a napkin, a fork, and a glass of ice water and have dinner right off the floor. Not like living with Sarah.

Thank heaven. How many times during his residency had he plowed through piles of laundry on the couch, looking for a pair of clean socks? He shook his head to dislodge the memory, particularly as Sarah's children were here and participants in the mystery of the exploding chicken salad. He walked carefully down the hall. He glanced into the guest bedrooms full of his children's suitcases and clutter, but no children.

Hearing soft gulps of crying, he opened his bedroom door. Claire, her eyes swollen and her face blotchy, was curled in the fetal position on their bed. Her short blonde hair stuck up on one side of her head. He looked at her affectionately. A complete meltdown. When she saw the concern on his face and heard his voice, "Oh, honey," the serious crying started up again, and it all came out in heaving sobs. His vicious ex-wife had put these horrible children up to "all this." They had been horrible all week. A nasty little piece of plastic covered with chewed bits of breakfast cereal had been churned up in the disposal. It made a racket, but how could she have known it was Jenny's retainer that cost fifty dollars to replace? Robbie was a vile child. Tom was not much better. Jenny was a tattle. Robbie had called Claire a Rhodes Scholar, and those children had all laughed. The teary deluge continued for ten minutes. The conclusion was inevitable. The monsters had to leave, and yesterday wouldn't be soon enough. This wasn't too tough to figure out. Outflanked and outgunned, Claire had lost her temper and done to the chicken salad what she couldn't to do his children.

Torturing stepmothers wasn't new in the history of blended families, he told himself. The kids had been set up to dislike Claire. He knew Sarah well enough to know that. His racquetball partner had told him to take the two weeks off. Great advice, but all the new residents and interns started this month, and he had to be there. Last month would have been a better, but that time slot conflicted with Tom's baseball schedule, and Sarah wouldn't budge. But torturing Claire—that was like kicking a puppy. He ran his fingers through her blonde hair and kissed the top of her forehead as he pulled her into his arms and held her. She cried harder.

"You've done enough this visit. I shouldn't have left them with you all this time," he whispered into her hair.

"I'll go and clean up the floor," she sobbed into the soggy mess she had made of his shirt and tie.

"Stay put. I'll clean it up and order a pizza." He was curious to see how his children would respond. But where did he go from here? Clearly, Robbie was the ringleader. He had watched his children carefully the last week, and Robbie called all the shots. So what if Bob didn't have much parenting experience? He would be professional, he thought, straightforward, treat Robbie like an adult, like the hundreds of interns and residents he had guided over the years. Mulling this over, he poured a half-cup of strong-smelling ammonia into a bucket and cleaned up the remnants of the domestic outburst.

Bob wasn't angry when he called Robbie and his siblings to come upstairs and eat. He wasn't sure what to expect, but Robbie's studied nonchalance didn't surprise him. It was a pose he would have assumed at the same age. Foolishly, in the back of his mind was the hope that this eruption might be an opening to clear the air, man to man. It was only after two large pizzas, a couple of liters of soda, and an order of breadsticks had been consumed that he held the screen door open and nodded to Robbie, indicating that they were headed to the screened porch for a conversation out of earshot.

"So, what's this all about?" He opened carefully, looking directly at his son.

Robbie shrugged.

Bob tried again. "Claire's pretty upset."

Robbie looked at his father squarely and said, "That's your problem, not mine. In three days I'm outta here."

"You know, Robbie, she's not a bad person. She's tried hard to make your visit pleasant."

"You know, Dad," Robbie mimicked, "the woman's a moron. This vacation," and he stressed the word *vacation*, "hasn't been easy for us either. You haven't bothered to spend any time with us. Why did you have us come? We don't want to bond with Claire. That would be like trying to have a relationship with a . . ." He looked around to find an object to complete his metaphor. "A chair, a plant."

Bob sat quietly, waiting for Robbie to continue, unwind, spew all this anger. He put his hands together and set them deliberately in his lap. He'd never been on the other side of an angry adolescent male. He didn't understand. Robbie was waiting for his provocation to hit its mark, and when it didn't, he upped the ante.

"Do you know what she does all day? She cleans. That's it. She cleans. How can you stand living with her? What do you talk about?

The latest trends in vacuuming?" Rob paused. He looked at his dad, waiting.

Bob didn't know where to go from here. Was he supposed to defend Claire? But he wasn't worried about Claire. She was pretty resilient. Should he yell at this kid? He didn't feel like yelling. He slapped nervously at a mosquito buzzing by his ear.

Robbie sat still for a moment and then said quietly, "You should see my mom in front of a class. My friends can't believe how smart she is." Rob looked at his dad. "How could you throw away my mom to marry a bimbo like Claire?"

"That's enough. I'll have a conversation with you, but I'm not going to sit here and listen to you call Claire names." Finally, Bob was rising to the bait. He breathed rapidly through his nose with his jaw clenched.

"Do you honestly think you can take the moral high ground with me?" Robbie's anger was way ahead of his father's. Bob slowly realized that his son had been honing his arguments for years, rehearsing what he would say if he ever had an opening. The kid was smart. Bob was starting to feel sick.

"You abandoned us." Robbie snickered with contempt. "You left us with no money and went on some tour of Europe with her."

"No, that's not true. It was a fellowship. You don't understand. You don't know how difficult your mother could be," Bob stammered, caught off guard by his son's candor. "There was always an agenda with your mom, always some plan, always a list. I couldn't live someone else's list. I had to live my own life, my own way. Your mother had this set picture of what our life was going to be, and she couldn't look right or left. We wanted totally different things." Floundering, he relied on the old, worn-out standby. "You're too young to understand. You don't know Claire. She has a lot of wonderful qualities. She's patient and kind. She's quick to smile." He tried smiling to reinforce his point.

"Oh, okay. So tell me, Dad." Robbie spoke sarcastically as if using the word *dad* to describe Bob was the world's greatest travesty. "If Mom got just what she deserved, what did Tom and I do? What great sin did Jenny commit? She was only one when you left. Tom's the nicest kid in the world. Why did he get hung out to dry? What did we do to mess up your grand plans for your life? What about the lies you told me? 'I'll be back when you're in the second grade, and everything will be just great.' Yeah, right. The only person you've ever cared about is yourself.

You sit here with all this money," Robbie gestured with his hands as though his father lived at the Ritz, "and just take care of yourself. Do you know that I was the only kid on the basketball team who didn't have the money to go to camp? The only one."

That final insulting denial was the punctuation that ended whatever relationship they had. Robbie stood up. Bob pushed himself up out of his chair. They were almost the same height, but Robbie was slender, wiry, and quick. More of his mother's genes blended into this boy. His facial features resembled his father's, but Robbie lacked Bob's easy arrogance, his smug confidence. Robbie's raw hurt stood out plainly on his sleeve.

"You think I'm too young to understand?" Robbie said. "I understand you perfectly. You threw us over for a hot babe with big . . ."

Bob slapped Robbie hard across his face. Robbie staggered back against a wicker chair, tripped, and fell down, narrowly missing a large terra-cotta pot of bright-pink geraniums. Bob's whole body was shaking. Robbie looked up at his father, and with a complete loss of control and dignity, he started to cry. The angry adolescent was suddenly a small seven-year-old boy, standing on the grass begging his dad not to leave.

Bob's anger vanished. He wanted to hold on to his son and cry with him. Cry for all the lost years, and misunderstandings, and basketball camps, and whatever else was so desperately wrong, but as he moved toward his boy, Robbie backed up, almost fearfully. Then he turned and ran off the screened porch into the twilight. The screen door banged in his wake.

"Robbie, come back!" Bob shouted. His call went unanswered over the noise of the bugs and crickets and the thick humidity of the Iowa night.

He pressed his hands against his head to squeeze out his stupidity. He beat himself up for the next couple of hours, pausing occasionally to look up and down the street, hoping to see Robbie walking back in the light of the street lamps. He didn't notice or hear the door open slowly, or see Tom sit carefully on a small stool.

"Dad," Tom said quietly, "where's Robbie?"

"Gone." Bob looked up. "I didn't know about basketball camp."

"Yeah, that was pretty bad."

"I send your mom money," he said, trying to make the lame excuse sound plausible.

"It was just a bad month. Money's always pretty tight at our house. Camp is before summer quarter starts. It's before Robbie makes much money doing lawns. The washer died, and the car needed a new fan belt. Camp had to go. Robbie understood."

"You were all in on the financial stuff about Robbie going to camp?" Bob tried to get his head around these family dynamics. "So, Robbie wrote to me?"

"And you turned him down."

"I didn't understand. I didn't know that everyone was going. He didn't explain." The nausea came back in waves. He had really screwed up. He rubbed his hand over his forehead and avoided looking Tom in the eye.

"Well, Mom said it was a long shot." Tom shrugged. He was so matter-of-fact, almost fatalistic. "I think it just made things worse to see how you and Claire live. You've got stuff we'd never dream of having." Tom expected this visit to be uproar. Bob finally understood. Tom knew his brother was ready to explode.

So many surprises. How could he have missed so many signals? When had Robbie gotten so old and bitter? *How long has he hated me?* Bob wondered. He and Claire didn't have an affluent lifestyle. He wasn't even a full professor. He and Claire didn't drive expensive cars or travel much, but then he realized he had never been inside the shabby little rambler where his children lived. When he picked them up, they were ready and came out the door before he could step out of his car. He never saw Sarah, and that was fine with him. Claire bitterly resented any money they sent to his kids. She thought child support was payment for polite behavior, cheerful letters, and lots of thank-you notes. If the kids were rude, cut off the money. He felt like the rope in a continual tug-of-war.

"You probably ought to head to bed." The moment the words came out of his mouth, he knew he had made another mistake. He was dismissing this son who was ready to talk, treating him like a little kid.

"No problem." Tom slid off the stool and closed the door quietly, as Bob stared out into the darkness.

It was nearly midnight when the telephone rang. Bob heard Claire's sleepy voice. "Just a minute. I'll get him." He walked into the kitchen and lifted the handset sitting on the counter.

"Doctor Williams." Habit overrode concern, and he assumed this was a call from the hospital. He still expected Robbie to come home chagrined and humiliated but in one piece.

"You probably don't remember me," the voice began. "I was in the elder's quorum when you first moved into the ward. I'm the bishop now. Bri Miller."

"I'm sorry. You've caught me at a bad time." Bob, forgetting the lateness of the hour, started to go into his standard refusal about anything relating to his lapsed membership in the Mormon Church, but the bishop interrupted him.

"Yes, I know. Your son's here at my house."

"What's your address? I'll be right over."

"Hey," the bishop's voice was soft, "if you do that, I'm afraid he'll bolt. Why don't you let me keep him here tonight where he's safe, and we'll work things out tomorrow? I have to go to work in the morning, but I could come by on my way home. I work in the dental clinic. I could swing by the hospital if that's easier for you."

"No, I took the next two days off to have some time with the kids before they go back." Too little, too late. Bob's head pounded. "What time?"

"I'll be there about five-thirty."

"Thanks," Bob muttered, wondering if Robbie had called his mother.

"Sure," the bishop said. "I've got kids too. This sort of stuff happens all the time. Don't worry."

It should have occurred to him. You get in trouble away from home, find the bishop. It's what he would have done when he was sixteen. Bri Miller—it wasn't a name he remembered, but he sounded okay. Bob turned off the lights and walked slowly down the hall to bed.

———

The bishop was late, not much, maybe fifteen minutes. It was another scorching afternoon, and he left his sport coat on his front seat. He hurried up the sidewalk under the canopy of tall maple trees but didn't reach the door because Bob, who had been waiting, came down the steps to meet him. Bob didn't want Claire or Jenny or Tom to hear this stranger. He didn't want them to hear about Robbie's anger, enough anger to force a boy out into the night.

The man, stopping on the sidewalk, had kind eyes and dark hair that waved down nearly to the top of his prominent glasses. The bishop extended his hand. Tall and slender with the gauntness of a distance runner, he smiled as they shook hands. Bob remembered him vaguely.

The bishop started, "My wife remembers your kids. She was pleased to see them Sunday. They've really grown." Bob stared at him. Pleased to see the kids? An angry mess had landed at his house uninvited late at night. Bob mentally filled in all the gaps. Seeing his children, everyone in the ward would remember Sarah, the pretty young mother with the "difficult circumstances." He was the question mark. The blank face. The inactive name on all the rolls. The bad guy.

"I'm Bri Miller," the bishop continued, but Bob couldn't do the polite exchange. He felt exposed and raw, certain his son had ranted at length about his failures.

"How did Robbie get to you?"

"He called Cindy from the 7-Eleven, and she went and picked him up." The bishop's face was empathic. "I'm so sorry you're having a difficult time, but understand that there isn't a father alive that hasn't gone through this. Boys this age can't become adults until they defeat the older generation, or at least leave us limping."

Suddenly Sarah materialized out of the humidity and made a crack about Henry II and his sons who were constantly trying to topple him off his throne. She'd been here the whole week. Her funny phrases coming out his children's mouths, her politics in their heads, her venom poisoning them. She'd orchestrated this entire disaster. Now she was in his head too. He saw Sarah wrapped in her ratty, old housecoat standing on the grass, her cheeks wet with tears. "Your children will hate you," she had promised. And Robbie and Tom did, but Jenny? Jenny had slipped her mother's grasp.

The bishop's voice was kind, and he smiled, waiting for Bob to respond. When Bob didn't, he continued. "Give him a little time, and your son will forgive you. I'm guessing you've already forgiven him."

Galled to be the recipient of so much sympathy, Bob imagined what Robbie had told this stranger. Regardless of what he said, this man's sons had never run away from home, run away from a father this gentle. This guy had stuck it out, and his kids probably loved him.

"So, is Robbie coming home?" Bob asked. The moment the words were spoken, he realized Robbie didn't think of his house as home, and he wasn't coming back.

"He's pretty upset. Let him stay with us for a couple of days. My wife will take him to the airport. He doesn't remember me, but he remembers Cindy and our boy who's a year younger than he is."

Cindy. Cindy Miller. Of course. She had been Sarah's friend. Bob wondered if she'd already called Sarah.

The bishop laughed at Bob's look. "We're locals. We've lived here forever. You're kind of unusual. Medical residents come and go, but you stayed." The air felt thick and humid, and his white shirt had dark circles under his arms. He stepped closer to Bob to be in the shade.

"How about if I just come over and straighten this out with Robbie?"

The bishop had been analyzing a weed growing in a crack in the sidewalk. He looked up. The half smile left his face. "I think that would be a mistake. I don't think he would respond well. Remember he's just a kid. Give him some time. He'll work through this. He's a wonderful boy. You'll both get over this bad patch."

"Well, it looks like I don't have many options."

"This is a good choice. Give him a couple of weeks, and then call and tell him how sorry you are, when he's ready to listen. He won't hear anything you say now."

This guy clearly didn't get it. Sarah would pounce on this and drive the wedge in more deeply than ever. One more layer of separation. How could he have been so stupid about basketball camp? He hadn't thought it through. He hadn't remembered. He lived to play basketball when he was Robbie's age. His shoulders sagged, and he turned slowly to walk back into the house, but the bishop stopped him with a hand on his shoulder.

"I'm so sorry. Cindy and I were thinking that the next time the kids come, maybe your family could come over to our house for dinner, hamburgers or something. We could meet your wife—"

"Claire," Bob interrupted.

"Claire," the bishop repeated. "Our kids could make friends. I think it would make a difference if they knew some kids their own ages."

Bob couldn't respond. He brushed the perspiration off his forehead with the back of his hand. "Well, I guess we'll see somebody at the airport? You or your wife?"

"We'll have him there on time." The bishop retraced his steps slowly back down the sidewalk.

Bob watched him, shielding his eyes from the glare with his hand.

Jenny waited, tucked in behind the drapes. Bob looked down at her. She held a Scrabble box in her hand, a small inadequate offering, but he tried to smile as he sat, exhausted, on the couch and patted the cushion next to him.

"Well, cupcake, I guess I owe you a new retainer."

"It's not really a retainer. It's more like a space holder."

"So tell me about your mouth," he said, engaging his child he knew the least.

"I sucked my fingers way too long," Jenny confessed, "and the roof of my mouth got too pointy. So the dentist put a thing in that Mom had to screw one notch every two days. Now I have a spacer to keep it wide until my mouth's old enough to start braces." Her teeth were too large for her thin face, and her incisors pushed out against her top lip.

"Well, the good news is that teeth can be fixed. When you're sixteen, you'll be beautiful. Will you have anything to do with me when you're sixteen?" He reached over and pulled Jenny against his shoulder. He put his face into her hair and smelled the scent of shampoo, soap, and summer, and felt overwhelmed with love for this little shadow of a girl.

He held her until she said in a quiet voice, "It'll be okay, Dad."

He wondered again at the relationship between Robbie and his brother and sister. Robbie was more than an older brother. He wasn't a father, but he was clearly the leader of this small tribe. Would there ever be a place for their father, and what would that place be? He wanted to be more than the Great Evil One, a role he was sure Sarah had assigned. Maybe they would never let him be a dad. Maybe that was all lost.

Jenny wiggled a bit, and he released her.

"Should we help Claire with dinner?" he asked. "Can you pull an old man off the couch?"

Jenny jumped up and stood on his toes. She grabbed his hands and pulled with all her weight until her bottom was almost touching the carpet. She laughed as Bob feigned losing his balance and landed them both on the floor. Bob smiled and rumpled her curly hair. Jenny had her mother's hair, but the brown eyes in that little face were his.

meetings and phone calls

*d*uplicating keys? Absolutely, there has to be an immediate consequence." Terry spoke without much conviction. He sat back in his desk
chair and sighed before he looked over the notes he'd jotted down on a
yellow pad. His office was a clutter of high school paraphernalia: pictures of former student body officers, a couple of large bears dressed in
school colors, and a bookcase holding faded yearbooks from the beginning of time.

He flipped through both student files, then with his thumb and
forefinger pushed his gold-rimmed spectacles back up his broad nose.
"Well, I can guarantee you this," he said, looking at Sarah and Meg as
he tapped his fingers on the paper, "if the Colton kid is as smart and
spoiled as you say, this will translate into at least two meetings and a
dozen phone calls." He glanced out the window. "None of the admin-
istrative classes prepare you for the bulk of this job: pain-in-the-neck
phone calls." He raised his eyebrows as if asking Meg and Sarah if they
really wanted to travel this road.

He turned a couple of pages over with the eraser on his pencil. "You
might be wrong about Brax. He's qualified for free lunch since first
grade. Single mom. No address for a father." He scanned the information sheet. "He was a National Merit Scholar finalist." Terry whistled
softly through his teeth. "Pretty unusual from that part of town. You
might want to cut him some slack."

Sarah didn't dislike Terry, but she'd dealt with the vice principal before. She knew what he was thinking. Hadn't she been around here for ten years? Didn't she know that she wasn't going to straighten out anything? Nothing ever got straightened out. Things just got pushed aside for the next crisis.

"These boys have been a problem from the get-go. If we don't stop this right now, the year will go downhill fast. Plus," Sarah added emphatically, "they're using drugs." She described her involvement with the officer Sunday afternoon, but Terry shrugged it off. No proof. He glanced at his notes.

"Of course, the problem is that you gave them the keys." Terry was mildly accusatory. "It's too bad you can't use the drug issue, but I can't do anything because you saw two boys walking out of a dumpy house."

Meg intervened. "I've been handing my keys to kids to unlock that prep room for years. We've never had a problem before—"

"That you know about," Terry interrupted.

"I think we'd have found out, even the next year. Things like that always surface."

"Well, I hope you're right." He rubbed his knuckle with his left hand. "So what are you going to do tomorrow?"

"We'll keep the ten offending students after school. The kids that received the keys will miss one tournament. The boys and the girl that took the key and made duplicates will miss the next two," Meg said.

"Well, that's what would happen to an athlete for a rules infraction. So, I guess that's fair." Terry pushed his chair back, signaling the meeting was over.

Sarah and Meg walked over to the mailroom.

"Boy, he's got that down to a science," Sarah remarked, pulling several large envelopes out of her box. "X problem equals this many inconvenient phone calls."

"Yes, and if it happens in our room, it's our fault," Meg added. "But, you know, I don't like conflicts with angry parents."

"Nobody with half a brain does, but that's Terry's job. He's supposed to run interference." Sarah tossed some junk mail into the wastebasket.

"But will he?" Meg glanced over her shoulder at vice principal's closed office door.

The hands on the clock above the door moved so slowly that Sarah thought the clock was broken or on strike. *Maybe just a work slowdown,* she told herself as the morning crept along. Ostensibly, meeting the offending students after school was a good idea. The rest of the team would be protected from unpleasant bouts of temper. The culprits would have all evening to grouse over the phone or complain in the hall, and then it was a done deal. She looked out their narrow window anxiously at the darkening sky. The temperature had dropped. She shivered and rubbed the goose bumps on her arms. She hated trouble hanging over her head, dragging on her mind all day. She was sure she'd been alone, but what if Tyler hauled a chagrined Mr. Orton, the janitor, into the room to claim that he had seen Sarah with honey on her hands? How could she have been so dumb? Meg kept giving her cautious looks as though she expected Sarah to start speaking gibberish or strangle a student with her stocking.

The bell rang. Coming in with a false cheerfulness, most of the varsity class went to work quickly and a little too loudly. Kristen kept passing out her winning smiles. Tyler and Brax strolled into class ten minutes late. After Meg announced the meeting after school, the instigators spent the rest of the hour in slow motion. Tyler made a show of throwing sticky file folders into the large trash can he pulled in from the hall. Brax scowled at anyone who spoke to him. Melissa peeled the red polish off her fingernails.

Finally, the last bell rang and the room emptied slowly. Sarah stood to her right as Meg tersely announced the consequences for duplicating keys. After consultation with the school administration, and Meg made it sound like an audience with the Pope, missing a tournament was the appropriate response, and missing two was the consequence for the people who intentionally took the key—with malice and forethought, she implied—and made the copies. It was clear-cut with no room for argument, but these were students who lived to argue, and they regarded Meg's remarks as merely the opening speech.

"Why does it have to be the next two tournaments? Can't we choose any two tournaments during the season?"

"Scholarships hang on Gov's Cup. Can't Gov's Cup be an exception?"

Arguments ricocheted around the room. Students interrupted

Sarah and Meg and each other. Fifteen minutes grew into an excruciating forty-five.

Finally, Sarah extended her arms and flipped her fingers up like a conductor concluding a symphony. "Okay, let's get one thing straight here. Mrs. Woodruff and I didn't create this problem to ruin your lives. You created this problem." She pointed at the students. "You own this. We don't."

Meg added, "Gov's Cup and The Weber Classic are the first two policy tournaments. The end. I'm sorry you made the wrong choices, but you have no one to blame but yourselves." After a few seconds, Meg signaled Sarah with her eye, and they both walked, with firm resolve, to the back of room, collected their things, and stood by the door. Tyler shoved past two girls who were waiting for Harry, and one girl tripped against Sarah.

"Sorry," she drawled, realizing she had stepped hard on Sarah's toe.

It's a good thing I'm impervious to pain and rudeness, Sarah thought as she suppressed a sharp cry.

—*᠕᠕*—

Glowering, Sarah slammed the car door. Dry leaves piled against the adjacent chain-link fence. Dark-gray clouds amassed above the western mountains, and Sarah heard a rumble and saw a flash of lightening. "I give up," she whispered and wished she could hit a button by her left ear and stop the instant replay in her head. She ran her fingers through the tangle of curls made worse by the humidity.

She turned left on Main Street. Such a funny old town. Bright, well-lit stores on the street level denied the dingy second stories with dim windows and a name or a date embossed in brick that had lost any meaning decades ago, as though each store wore a dark shabby hat leftover from the Depression.

Two chairs were empty at the Clip and Curl. Walk-ins welcome. A quick stop? *I'm worth $11.50.* She thought briefly about gray hairs so numerous that plucking was no longer an option, but she didn't have enough energy left to chat with a stylist. Maybe on Saturday. Waiting at the light on Fourth North, she drummed on the steering wheel and planned the rest of the afternoon. Jenny was at her piano lesson, and Tom was playing basketball, so Sarah had a good hour and a half before she had to fix dinner.

Shaking free the memory of the surly faces that had glared at her after school, she turned into the driveway and ran into the house as the first drops of rain hit the English essays she hugged against her chest.

"Hurry, Einstein." She held the door open as the dog skidded across the kitchen floor and ran over to the patch of dead grass, his designated spot. "Oh, good boy." She fished in the box for a doggie cookie and held it up to encourage him to hurry and not go sniffing around. He gave several large woofs in the direction of the paperboy and trotted back into the kitchen.

Einstein loped over to the couch, where Sarah flopped with her feet up, to have his ears scratched.

"Those kids are jerks, Einstein. I don't think they've ever heard no in their lives. Complete brats." He nudged her hand with his large nose for more ear scratching, but Sarah's arm hung limply over the edge of the couch. "Bad meeting, Einstein. Not a good day," Sarah complained, and Einstein wagged his tail.

Hearing the rain hit the windows, Sarah pulled back the curtain. She loved changes in the seasons, and she would have been content to listen to the rain drum softly against the window all afternoon. She was so tired. The phone started to ring. Sarah ignored it. Instead she fell back onto the couch and held a soft pillow over her stomach. It was quiet in the house for five minutes until the phone rang again. Sarah put the pillow over her face and pulled the edges over her ears. The big dog stood by the couch until she reappeared. She stretched out her arms and gave some serious thought to making macaroni and cheese for dinner, not the stuff out of a box, but real macaroni and cheese with a couple of hot dogs chopped up between the noodles. It was a nice sort of casserole for a cold afternoon. The phone rang a third time more insistently, as though the caller had an urgent need that wouldn't be ignored. Thinking of Jenny walking home alone, Sarah got up off the couch.

"Hello." She answered slowly.

"Is this Mrs. Williams?" the voice demanded. Sarah opened her mouth to say, "That depends on who wants to know," in her best John Wayne imitation, but she couldn't be John Wayne without a quick draw and a sidearm. How unfortunate. She held the phone away from her ear and frowned. "Yes, this is Mrs. Williams."

"Well, this is Mrs. Colton, and I want you to know that there is no way that we are going to allow . . ." *I know where this is going,* Sarah thought. *I've met you a thousand times before.* This conversation would ruin a perfect rainy afternoon.

Using her most officious voice, she interrupted, "Mrs. Colton, hmm, I have a hundred and forty students. Several students with that last name, so you'll have to be more specific."

"My son is Tyler, and he came home this afternoon—" Sarah cut her off.

"Let's see, Mrs. Colton, I don't think that I've ever had the pleasure of meeting you at any of our parent meetings. Is that correct?" Sarah had learned long ago that interruption was key in establishing dominance in unfriendly conversations. Sarah was determined to be the dominant female in this one.

"I am not calling about parent meetings."

"Yes, but, Mrs. Colton, if you had made the effort to attend, you'd know that we have strict policies about students cheating on tests. Actually, I'm very pleased that you called this afternoon. I was going to call you in the morning about Tyler's quiz."

"I'm calling about the keys and the tournaments." Mrs. Colton's voice raised a decibel or two, but she couldn't lose her temper because it was already lost.

"Oh, Tyler didn't come home and tell you that he was caught, red handed, cheating on a test?" Mrs. Colton sputtered, but Sarah pressed her advantage. "Is this a recurrent pattern? Are you aware that Tyler cheats? What do you and your husband intend to do to help him?" Sarah knew that Mrs. Colton knew she was being jerked around, but a small piece of Sarah just didn't care.

"I don't know what you think you're talking about. I am calling about the Gov's Cup tournament, and I just want you to know that we paid a lot of money to send Tyler to debate camp, and he is going to be at that tournament. I don't know who you think you are making a decision like that without talking to parents, but you don't have the right to make those kinds of decisions." The woman's voice felt like a pinched nerve, and Sarah held the phone out from her ear and let the woman rant for a full minute and a half, before she broke in.

"Mrs. Colton, I am so sorry. I can't talk to you right now. I have to take my daughter," she lied, "to the orthodontist this very moment.

Why don't we meet with Mr. Schuback Friday after school? If that isn't convenient with Mrs. Woodruff or Mr. Schuback, I'll call you in the morning." And she hung up the phone, right in the middle of Mrs. Colton's tirade. It was not a wise thing to do, but she just didn't have the energy for that woman tonight. Tyler and his family had consumed more of her time in one day than they deserved. She pulled her arms across her chest and dropped back onto the couch.

―*⁓*―

"I understand you hung up on Mrs. Colton last night," Terry responded when Sarah called to set up the meeting.

"Terry, she was on a total rant, and I had to leave for an appointment." Sarah continued, "The woman was out of control."

"That's not her story. She says you were rude and condescending. When I refused to fire you on the spot, she called every member of the school board. I know, because three of them called me." He paused. "It was a long night."

"Sorry."

"She said that you accused her son of cheating without any proof. She said that you wouldn't address her concerns. She went on for quite a while."

"Terry, she was over-the-top rude." Sarah's tone was matter of fact. "Plus, the kid does cheat."

"Well, it's a good thing for you that you had a winning season last year. It also helps that Mrs. Colton seems to be something of a regular." He paused and then spoke more patiently. "If you just let parents like that go on until they wind down, you can inject some sort of reason. Try that next time."

"Okay, I hear you. I just don't like home calls."

"Well, you live in a one-zip-code town. You're not going to get away from that." Sarah could hear someone enter Terry's office, as he ended the call. "We're on for two-thirty. Bring Meg and don't be late."

Sarah put the phone down and looked at Meg, who had been standing by Sarah's shoulder listening to the handset. Sarah pushed a lock of hair behind her ear. "Now what?"

"Well, that certainly explains Tyler, doesn't it?" Meg observed. "My son, right or wrong. No, it's worse than that. My son is never wrong, because if he were ever wrong that would mean that I have not been the perfect parent, which clearly I am. So, there you have it. Plus, if this woman is a screamer, Tyler's learned that if he waits out the yelling, nothing else happens."

"Tyler's a complete mess. He's never learned right from wrong. Or . . . if he has," Sarah raised one finger, "it makes no difference to him. A sociopath."

"I don't know if I would take that line at the meeting Friday." Meg smiled. "I mean it would be interesting. You could say, 'Your son's a sociopath, and you're a screamer.' But where do you envision the conversation going from there?"

"Well, the kid has issues with female authority figures."

"I don't know if I'd bring that up either." Meg pursed her lips before she laughed. "What are we going to say? Let's think this through." They sat down with a legal pad in front of them and chewed through the problem as they shared whatever they had grabbed that morning for lunch.

At twelve fifteen a knock was followed by the entry of Bill and Kathy. "I understand you have a meeting," Kathy began.

"That is really fast," Sarah said, "amazingly fast."

"Gracie knows all. Tells all that she knows." Bill loved to make fun of Gracie, the shrewd school secretary who didn't produce any discernible work but had her thumb on the pulse of the entire school.

"Well, it gets better," Kathy continued, ignoring Bill's interruptions. "Evidently, the Colton family has recently moved to a lovely estate in the south end of the valley. Country living, you know," she said, giving her nose a snobbish tilt. "The youngest Mr. Colton, a charming lad by all accounts and a carbon copy of his older brother, now has to take the bus to school. You know what those buses are like. The buses are too big, the rides are too long, and there are too many kids. So, this boy has been alleviating his boredom by throwing things out the windows at passing motorists and whomping other kids on the head with his books." She looked at her audience over the top of her green half glasses. "Of course, the precious little man lost his bus privileges."

"Not an unreasonable response on the part of the much-maligned bus driver." Bill nodded.

Kathy continued without missing a beat. "Unfortunately, the very exclusive carpool for one spoiled child conflicted with Mrs. Colton's schedule with her personal trainer, and so the parents talked to the middle school principal in a flurry of righteous indignation."

"A real toot. I just wish I had been there." Bill loved high drama, as long as it wasn't in his classroom.

"This is what really had people going in the faculty room at lunch." Kathy simulated a drum roll on the desktop with two pencils. "The parents didn't think that their son had behaved badly. Oh no, the problem is inadequate adult supervision. They suggested teachers ride the buses each morning and afternoon with the little darlings. And then he said if the district would just pay them ten bucks a ride, there would be a line a mile long of teachers begging for the opportunity."

"We were afraid several people were going to go right into orbit," Bill said.

Meg rolled her eyes, ripped the top sheet off the legal pad, tore it into several pieces, and then tossed them high into the air just like confetti.

"A blamer and a screamer," Sarah said. "A nasty combination."

"Well, now you know what you're dealing with," Kathy said, wagging her finger in their direction.

"Forewarned is forearmed," Bill said, and nodded as he and Kathy edged out the door.

Kathy turned at the last moment before the door closed. "Don't take any you-know-what from those people." And she was gone.

blanche dubois violated again

*M*eg tugged the classroom door handle to be sure it was locked, dropped her keys into her purse, and folded her jacket over her arm.

"You and I will be fine. Just remember, we only want what is best for Tyler," Meg said. "Tyler is our friend." She glanced at Sarah and stopped mid-step. "What's going on in your head?"

"I was just thinking that I'm going to behave perfectly at this meeting." Sarah smiled wickedly. She looked over her shoulder at Meg and turned down the main hallway, the heels of her best navy shoes clicking on the linoleum.

Taking a quick step to catch up, Meg tugged on Sarah's sleeve. "What do you mean by perfectly?"

"I was just thinking that Elizabeth Bennett might enjoy coming to this meeting."

"Oh no, you don't. I remember when Blanche DuBois came to parent-teacher conferences."

"But I didn't have her down. I know Elizabeth. She's always so lively in difficult situations." Sarah tipped her head toward Meg.

"No, we're not going in character today. Just remember," and Meg repeated in a sing-song voice, "we only want what's best for Tyler." And they hurried down the hallway past the few students still collecting their belongings and slamming locker doors.

Chairs were arranged carefully in Terry's office. He had pushed his large metal desk back by the window and cleaned off his stacks of unfinished business. His office faced the north entrance to the school, and large windows looked down on students covering their heads with backpacks, sprinting toward the parking lots through the rain. Terry cracked the window open just an inch to let in a little cool air. He pulled out his chair, returning to his position in the circle with the Coltons, as Meg and Sarah walked in. Terry stood for a moment, but Mr. Colton did not.

Money, Sarah thought, *these people are all about money*, as she decided where to sit. In addition to an angry expression, Mrs. Colton wore a black gabardine blazer and enough gold jewelry hung around her neck to make drowning a distinct possibility if the rain continued and her car happened to stall near a ditch. Her long peach-colored nails clicked on the side of her metal folding chair. She stopped clicking to scowl at Sarah and Meg.

A paunchy man in a light-blue sweater huffed through his nose impatiently. *Dear, dear*, Sarah thought. *Mr. Colton wants everyone to know that his time is valuable, and no money is being made while he's forced to sit in this room with three silly women and one incompetent administrator. How wonderful to go through life as a successful purveyor of carpet cleaning supplies.* Sarah wondered if he knew about his wife's innumerable calls to the school board. Sarah shook her head and whispered "tut tut" to no one in particular.

Meg quickly introduced Sarah and herself. She thanked Terry for being a mediator and taking time away from his many responsibilities to help them resolve this problem. She complimented the Coltons on their active interest in their son's welfare.

Meg's preamble was too long, and Sarah felt awkward standing in the middle of the circle like a little kid playing "I have a little doggie, and he won't bite you, and he won't bite you, but he will bite you!" She thought Mr. Colton wouldn't hesitate to take a bite out of her leg or grab the scruff of her neck with his teeth and give her a good shake. She was imagining him pulling his lips back and exposing sharp fangs when Meg nudged her into the chair next to Terry.

Meg extended her hand and gushed, "You must be Mrs. Colton. It's very nice to meet you. We've enjoyed having Tyler as a student." When Meg released Mrs. Colton's hand, Sarah looked for puncture wounds from those peach-colored nails.

Sarah slipped her arm around Meg's shoulders and whispered in her ear, "I think Elizabeth's here."

Meg gave her a quizzical look.

"You."

The left side of Meg's mouth twitched slightly before she assumed a serious expression. "I'm very sorry that we're forced into such an unpleasant situation this afternoon." Meg had positioned Sarah between herself and Terry, but unfortunately, Sarah was sitting directly across from Mr. Colton, and the two made eye contact immediately.

Sarah smiled sweetly. "May I offer you something? A drink? A candy bar? I think there are Twinkies in one of the vending machines. I'm always so hungry after school."

"No," he said gruffly, "thank you."

Sarah crossed her feet neatly at the ankles.

Terry opened his mouth to take charge when Mr. Colton said, "All right. Let's talk about this tournament. Tyler and his partner are going, so how can we satisfy any other problems that you two have?"

His condescension caught everyone off guard. Meg recovered first.

"Mr. Colton. We don't have a problem. Tyler created a problem for himself—knowingly." Meg rolled into her what-is-best-for-Tyler strategy. "I'm sure you don't want Tyler to receive the impression that such inappropriate behavior is to be winked—"

"Let's see. Who was hurt by Tyler's behavior? Tyler," Mr. Colton declared. "He's the one whose files were vandalized. He's been punished sufficiently." Mr. Colton stopped and glared at Sarah. "I can't believe the stupidity of giving students keys to the building. You were asking for a problem. I also want to know what you've done to discover and punish the person who poured honey into those files. They destroyed hundreds of hours of work."

Sarah flushed and Meg jumped in. "We teach a full schedule. For the last seven years, we've allowed students to unlock the prep-room door when we're with a class. The room is locked specifically to protect student belongings and math texts. Tyler and Brax, to be honest, have abused the extra space, not just by copying the keys, but also by writing abusive, obscene things on the boards and filling the room with their garbage. That behavior is inappropriate, and we'd be remiss if we ignored it."

Revelations of drug abuse were poised on the tip of Sarah's tongue. She was dying to detonate that small bombshell, to trump this conversation, but she wasn't supposed to know. She had to be patient.

Looking over at Sarah, Mrs. Colton started in a haughty voice. "That's what *she* did when I called her. She brings in all these other things to make Tyler look bad." Her voice rose, and the pitch was grating. "She's not willing to talk about the tournament." She sat up straighter in her chair and started clicking her fingernails until silenced by a fierce look from her husband.

"These behavior issues are much more important than attending any tournament," Sarah said, breathing in and out slowly. She needed to stay calm. "I know you think this is a side issue, but Tyler cheated on a quiz." She pulled a folded paper out of her skirt pocket. It was wrinkled a bit, and she wished she had taken a moment to flatten it in a book. She started to explain. "I'm sure you can see this is Tyler's writing. He kept his paper and was filling in the answers as we corrected the—"

Mrs. Colton interrupted, "Well, Mrs. Williams, he said that he didn't do it." The mother tossed her glossy red hair and crossed her hands over her knee.

"We both saw him filling in the answers," Sarah said. Meg, who hadn't seen anything, didn't contradict her.

"So don't give him credit for the quiz." Mr. Colton dismissed the cheating and Sarah with the same breath. "The issue is the tournament. I'm suggesting that the boys miss another tournament during the year, or that they do some sort of community service," he added magnanimously, "of your choice."

"Mr. Colton, it's our job to police our own program," Sarah insisted. "We travel with thirty-five adolescents almost every weekend during our season. If we can't trust a student, he can't travel with us. It's that simple. If he can't keep our rules, he needs to find another extracurricular activity or debate at another school." She flipped her thumb toward the door, upping the ante. Terry loosened his tie nervously and stretched his neck. Mr. Colton glared at her and tapped the crystal on his Rolex.

He tried another tactic. "These two boys are probably one of the best policy teams in this state, if not in the nation. They want to buy what you're selling. You teach debate. They want to debate." He scrutinized Sarah, who had her eyebrows raised. "You're not thinking clearly.

This tournament is the most competitive of the year. You should want your best team to compete." Mr. Colton almost growled at Sarah, as he pointed his finger at her menacingly. "What kind of coaches are you?"

"Winning coaches, and you can take your finger out of my face."

"We sat down with Mr. Schuback," Meg gestured gracefully at the vice principal, "when this happened, and together determined what would be consistent with school policy. If a student athlete has a disciplinary problem, which clearly this is, his coach can suspend him for the next game or two. It doesn't matter if the next game is the region playoff or the state tournament. That approach seems to be effective, and of course, we all want to send Tyler the message that there will be consequences for inappropriate behavior."

"That's been the traditional approach, but I don't think its carved in stone," Terry offered. Meg and Sarah both stared at him. "I don't think I understood the importance of the tournament the boys would be missing when I suggested that response. I don't think some type of really rigorous community service would be out of line."

Sarah started, "Perhaps, if you had suggested this before, Terry, but we've already announced to the students what the consequence will—"

"You shouldn't have acted unilaterally," Mr. Colton snapped, sitting on the edge of his chair. His wagging finger was out again. "This decision should have involved the parents. We should have had this meeting before you told anyone anything. We, at the very least, should have had a phone call."

"Terry," Meg interjected, "do you typically call parents when there is such a flagrant violation of school policy?"

"Show me." Mr. Colton turned around in his chair so he faced Meg. "Show me, in any policy statement, where consequences are delineated for duplicating keys. The problem here is a lack of discipline in your program." The finger—still out of its holster—pointed first at Meg and then at Sarah. This guy was used to having things his way. Sarah was sure his conversations were typically with employees whose livelihood hinged upon flattering this man. Keep the boss happy. His wife used the telephone like an Uzi. They were a dangerous combination, Sarah thought, and they had no regard for anyone foolish enough to be involved in public education.

Sarah had only seen Meg lose her temper two or three times, but now Meg was livid.

"Mr. Colton," Meg said, "we have a hundred students in our program. We have one of the most winning programs in the state. The football team has eight coaches for eighty participants. There are just two of us. However, if you're not pleased with how we run our program, please feel free to have your son participate in another program. Actually, at the beginning of the year, Tyler suggested that he might like to go to a program that allowed interstate travel."

"It's not fair to ask Tyler to move during his senior year," Mrs. Colton said.

"No one is moving anywhere," Mr. Colton snapped at his wife, who was working a large diamond ring around and around her finger. "Do you know who I am?" he said turning to Terry in an exasperated manner. "I can't waste any more time here. I have another appointment. Let's be straight," he said, excluding the three women, "if you can't come up with a solution that allows my son to complete at the Governor's Cup tournament," and he glanced at his Rolex watch, "by four o'clock, you'll have a telephone call from my attorney."

"Well, I think community service is a compromise we can all agree on." Terry smiled as though he had just negotiated an amicable settlement. "The press box at the football field needs painting. Let's have those two boys down here at eight o'clock on Saturday morning." He slapped the desk with his palm as though he was personally leading the charge. "I'm assuming that one of you ladies will be available to supervise that project?"

"No, Terry." Meg gathered her books and purse. "Neither of us will be available." She motioned to Sarah, and they both stalked out. Sarah started to hyperventilate when she reached the hall. Meg grabbed her roughly by the elbow and pushed her toward the outer door and the set of concrete stairs that led to the lawn. Neither spoke until they reached the grass.

"I can't believe this." Sarah's cheeks were burning.

"Not here." Meg was resolute. "Let's get away from the building."

They hurried through the wet leaves, as Meg almost shoved Sarah toward the parking lot. They hadn't spoken to each other for the past few minutes, but when they saw the large silver Mercedes parked next to a curb, clearly painted red, Sarah hissed at the license plates: Clean-1.

"Tell me why I'm not valuable, and why everyone kowtows to that carpet cleaning jerk?" Sarah bristled.

"American education. That's why Johnny can't read." Meg shook her head. "What a cretin. He ought to pull his head out of . . . the sand," even in a rage, Meg chose not to be vulgar, "and clean up his mess of a son." Then Meg walked over and kicked the Mercedes's right front tire. She gave a small yelp of pain and pulled off her shoe in the wet parking lot to massage her toes.

Sarah started to laugh, and as she laughed, Meg started to laugh. Soon they were hanging on to each other, howling with laughter, as Sarah walked and Meg limped to the old Accord. Tears ran down their faces, as they laughed harder with each remembered remark.

Sarah turned the key in the lock and opened the door. They flopped down sideways, Meg in the backseat, one foot on the pavement, her damaged foot across her lap. Sarah wiped the tears off her face with the hem of her skirt.

"What was that about 'we've enjoyed having Tyler as a student'?" Sarah scoffed. "I could practically see your nose growing."

Meg stuck out her tongue.

They didn't see the Coltons approaching the Mercedes, until Sarah glanced up as Mrs. Colton stepped gingerly over a large puddle. Mr. Colton pointed his keypad at the car door, but he was staring at Sarah and Meg, who were laughing in Sarah's beat-up old station wagon.

"He looks like he wants to come right over here and throttle us, doesn't he?" Meg smiled and waved. Mr. Colton gunned the car out of the parking lot.

Sarah mused. "Tyler knew this would happen, didn't he? He aimed his parents at us just like a shotgun."

Meg shook her head. "You almost have to feel sorry for him. The only life lesson that kid's learned at home is manipulation, or worse."

"What do you mean?"

"What they're really communicating with all this intervention is that Tyler's incompetent. He can't be trusted to solve his own problems."

"That's interesting," Sarah said, watching the Mercedes drive away. "You know, things could be worse. We could be married to that guy."

"Do you think," Meg wondered, "she ever damages the inside of her nostril with those fingernails? She could deviate her own septum."

Sarah started to laugh again. Trust Meg to have the correct anatomical terms.

surprises and basketball

She bent her head down as she hurried over to the JV's first pre-season game. Most of the leaves had fallen and been collected in large plastic bags, but a few wet leaves and residual candy wrappers from the Halloween dance were whipped about by a sharp wind. The wind was bringing in a storm, and Sarah squinted through the bits of snow pelting her face and settling on her maroon sweater. She trotted the distance between the administration building and the old gym. The cold air stung her exposed skin, and she had already missed the first half. Her cheeks were red, and the knot of hair on the top of her head was coming loose. She felt rather disheveled and damp curls stuck to her neck and the side of her face.

She had driven Jenny to her cousin's house after school, and now she was late.

———※———

"No way," Jenny had said adamantly the previous night, swiping the air with her hand, glaring at her mother. "No way am I going to stand around while you take tickets. I don't have anyone to sit with, and I'm not going to hang out with my mother. You want me to advertise to the whole school that I'm a social zero." Jenny had found an adult voice, and Sarah didn't know what to make of it.

"Are you premenstrual?" she questioned, and Jenny made a guttural noise like an internalized scream and clenched her fists, before her anger spewed out in torrents.

"You told me high school would be different. You told me I would have friends. You said it would be fun, an adventure." Jenny looked like she had something nasty sitting on her tongue as she hissed, "It was all lies, lies. The only thing different about high school is there are just more ways to be left out. I hate high school."

Jenny started to turn away, but then she stopped. She glared at Sarah. "People whisper about you. All the time. I hear whispering about you in the halls. No one ever says anything about Mrs. Woodruff, just you. You make me sick."

Open-mouthed, Sarah had stared at Jenny, until Jenny ran down the hall and into her bedroom, slamming the door. Planted to the ground, Sarah wondered what on earth Robbie was doing in Venezuela. She needed him here.

She sat down on the faded couch in the living room and analyzed a grape jelly stain on the cushion as though the stain might provide a clue, some missing bit of pertinent information. Who was this unknown person inhabiting Jenny's body? Where was this wild-eyed paranoia coming from? Whispering? Good grief. Half an hour later she called her sister-in-law, Nan, and pleaded in a cheery voice for a sleepover. "Jenny seems to have maxed out on basketball," Sarah had explained. "Who could blame her?" Sarah had laughed.

But today Sarah blamed her. The boys never screamed at her. What about loyalty? Didn't Jenny owe Tom some support at his first game? They hadn't spoken in the car until, arriving at Nan's home, Sarah said, "See you tomorrow." Jenny had grabbed her bag and slammed the car door.

———

Checking her watch, Sarah left the wind and the chilly air outside, as the heavy oak doors to the gym closed behind her. The smell of ancient sweat from subterranean locker rooms assaulted her nose. Twenty worn concrete steps separated the doors from the basketball floor. Grime-covered windows blocked out the incoming storm.

This Friday afternoon only a handful of students and parents filled the lower half of the bleachers. Sarah strode around the edge of the floor during a time-out and settled onto a bench by some other mothers.

The janitor who cleaned this building was almost as old as the building itself, and the gym was smelly, dirty, and filled with the noise of basketball shoes squeaking and pounding down and up the old wooden floor. Ten minutes left in the game. From the half, the score had been tied: one shot up, the ball turned over, one shot up. No foul shots. It was too close. No mistakes. Jake threw the ball in to Tom. Tom turned, sweat shining his red face and wetting his hair. As the boys worked the ball up the floor, the coach sprang off the bench.

"Run the play!" he yelled. The forward passed back to Tom. No one was open. Tom squared up to make a shot. A Highland player stepped to Tom's side and pawed the ball, knocking it out of Tom's hands. A shrill whistle blew. The opposing coach was off the bench and onto the floor.

"That's no foul!"

"Sit down!" The referee shouted and signaled to the scoring table that Tom had two shots. The noise lessened. If Tom scored, they would be up two. Jake walked over and slapped Tom lightly on the backside. Tom took a couple of deep breaths as he bounced the ball several times. Sarah held her breath and crossed her fingers. Tom pulled up and released the ball in a perfect arc off the tips of his fingers like Robbie had shown him a million times on the driveway at home. The ball was airborne for a half an hour before it hit the rim and circled slowly.

"Drop," Sarah whispered, placing a maternal charm on the ball. The ball wobbled dangerously and finally tipped through the net. A woman, known only as Ryan's Mom, smiled at her as the opposing coach signaled for a time-out. Hustling over to the bench, Tom found his mother's face and nodded at her thumbs up. Sarah relaxed for the first time since she had left her classroom after fifth period.

"Do you think he'll start to sub in?"

Sarah shrugged. She looked down by the doors to see how much time was left on the clock. Clayton McLaughlin had just come in. He caught her eye and smiled. She acknowledged his smile with a quick nod and a pleased smile of her own. Starting to turn back toward the bench and the boys, her eyes were pulled toward Clayton and the tall man standing beside him.

She knew him. She knew everything about him. She couldn't see his face, and his light brown hair had a smattering of gray, but the cast of the broad shoulders and the trim figure were too familiar. His expensive leather jacket was tossed over his shoulder, and his khaki pants were perfectly pressed. He and Clayton both turned toward the game as the whistle blew, and she saw the clean profile if not the sprinkle of freckles she knew covered his face. She ate every detail. Pulling a curl from the side of her face and pushing it behind her ear repeatedly, she stared at him until the slice of pizza and pint of milk she had eaten for lunch started to churn in the pit of her stomach. Her heart pumped frantically, and she felt an overwhelming desire to be anywhere but here.

"You okay, hon?" Ryan's mother gave her a concerned once over. "You're as white as a sheet."

"I think I'm going to be sick." In imminent danger of hurling her lunch over the bleachers, she stumbled over four or five parents and scrambled up the old wooden benches, heading for the clearly marked exit, as her stomach heaved. She slipped and cracked her shin on a metal stair. The noise reverberated through the gym. She turned back quickly. Clayton and her ex-husband both noticed her rapid departure, and Tom, watching his mother with concern, didn't see the Highland player at his left elbow. She stumbled up the remaining stairs, holding the corner of her sweater over her tightly closed mouth, as she heard the coach yell, "Get in there for Williams." The burly coach grabbed another player off the bench by his jersey. Tom had lost the ball. Red faced, the coach started to berate Tom. "What's the matter with you!" He shoved Tom toward the bench, but Sarah couldn't wait to see what happened next because her mouth was full of vomit, and it was all she could do to keep her lips pressed closed.

Grateful, as she pushed the bar on the exit door, that the alarm system didn't screech, Sarah felt the cold wind and snow hit her face. She almost jumped down the five concrete stairs to the battered garbage can. She spit out the contents of her mouth just as another wave of partially digested lunch came up. Holding on to the rusty, grimy can, she threw up over and over again, her eyes squeezed closed. Finally, her stomach was empty, but her body continued to heave. The wind picked up again and bit under the edge of her sweater. Snow melted and ran down her neck. She started to shake violently, afraid if she let go of the garbage can, she would fall.

At that moment she felt a rough, warm hand touch her forehead. Another hand circled her thin waist and almost carried her the short distance to the bottom of the concrete steps. Behind her closed eyes, she had a fleeting memory of her other life when a concerned young husband helped her through the waves of nausea that accompanied each new pregnancy, but the tips of the shoes she saw were worn, and the lining of the jacket being tucked gently around her was a faded flannel.

"I'll be okay in a minute," she said in a constricted voice. She was embarrassed by that fleeting second of false hope. "I'll never eat pizza again in my life."

"I'm going to take you home," Clayton McLaughlin said.

"I'm all right. I have to take tickets at the varsity game. I have a car here."

He didn't seem to hear her. She thought for a moment that perhaps she wasn't making sense. He put his hand under her chin and lifted up her face. "I'm taking you home. You're a mess."

She nodded, looking at the splatter of vomit on the bottom of her pants.

"The game's almost over," he said. "People will be coming out this door."

She covered her face with her hands, but they smelled disgusting, and she pulled them away. Groaning, she shook her head.

He didn't smile. He walked her quickly to his patrol car and opened the door. He pulled into the street past a small, white BMW she had never seen in this parking lot before.

The ride home was short. Sarah didn't make any self-deprecating jokes. Any comment would open the door to advice she didn't want to hear. She didn't apologize when he stepped into the house and saw the boxes of dry cereal from breakfast and the dishes from last night's dinner on the kitchen counter. The fluffy piles of dog hair in the corners were such a fixture it didn't occur to her to be embarrassed. Exhausted, she flopped down on the couch as Einstein loped up the stairs to greet her. "Thanks for helping me, but Einstein will take care of me now."

"I'll tell Tom to bring the car home?"

She nodded and handed him her keys. Clayton started to leave, but he paused at the door and spoke softly, "We're not all like Bob."

She looked up at him. "Bob wasn't even like Bob. Who's to know?"

He left without saying anything else. He was putting his car into gear and driving away when she put her head into her palms and shook with sobs as the golden retriever pushed at her hands with his nose.

———ww———

It was late and the room was dark when Tom came in from the carport, shaking the snow out of his hair. Sarah was asleep on the couch under an old green flannel quilt. Awakening with a start, she realized how strange it must seem to have her lying on the couch alone in the dark.

"How was the game? I can't believe I missed one. How could anyone play if I wasn't there taking tickets? I'm such a fixture." The light banter wasn't fooling him, and she stopped talking and pulled the quilt up around her shoulders. Her tall, handsome son studied her face—her eyes must be swollen—dropped his red gym bag heavily on the floor, and sat on the faded overstuffed chair. He examined his hands and didn't speak for a while.

She wanted to be strong, unflinching in this latest disaster. She didn't want him to see her being such a wimp. She was their security, but this afternoon he had watched her fall apart.

She tried to fill the empty space. "Did you get any playing time in the varsity game?"

Ignoring her question, he said, "Mom, I just don't hate him like Robbie does. I don't even have any memories of him when I was little. The only thing I remember about Iowa is seeing Uncle Carter drive up in that U-Haul."

"Lucky you."

"Yeah, I guess I am lucky. I don't have this stored-up reservoir of bad feeling. I mean, I don't really feel anything about him. He's been a sort of non-person in my life. I saw him once when I was in the first grade, and I think, twice when I was in the second. Hit and miss since then. Robbie always seemed like the one he wanted to connect with, not me." He paused and looked at her sitting under the blanket.

"So what's your point, kiddo?"

"This is my point: if it's going to make you physically sick to have him at my games, I'll tell him not to come. It's just that easy, Mom. He's not coming for me."

"What do you mean, he's not coming for you?"

"I don't know. Somehow he's making up for Robbie. Some sort of weird penance."

"Did you talk to him?"

"Sure, he came up to me after the game, before we went over to the big gym to warm up the varsity."

"What did he say?"

"Not much. They're here looking for a house. The hospital wants him to start in January." He scrutinized her face. "Mom, you knew they were thinking about moving here. Sooner or later they were going to start showing up at stuff. That's a big part of why they're coming. You can't be surprised."

His momentum petered out. Her shoulders drooped under the blanket. She knew he was waiting for her to come up with some plan. That was her MO. She would say, "Okay, how are we going to deal with this?" And then a plan would come out of her mouth as though she had a whiteboard behind her and was sending her little army into battle, but nothing happened, not tonight. No plan. No strategy. She was defeated and exhausted before a single skirmish had been fought. Tom looked over at the missionary portrait of his brother sitting on the small chest by the front door.

"I miss Robbie so much. I want him at my games. I even miss him telling me everything I did wrong."

Sarah could hear tears in his voice. Robbie's absence left such a jagged void in their family. Robbie had been Sarah's first lieutenant, the surrogate father for the other kids. She loved both of her sons, but she leaned on Robbie. Tom was trying to tell her that she could lean on him too, and that he understood this was a big deal. She wiped her nose on the quilt.

"I just feel so invaded," Sarah said, sniffing. "We've made a life for ourselves. It's not perfect, but it's ours, and I think we've been pretty happy . . ." She knew she was fishing, and she didn't care.

"Are you kidding? We're happier than families with twenty dads."

"I just don't know how he'll fit in. What will we do with Claire? What will happen when Robbie comes home? This complicates everything. Why didn't they stay in Iowa?"

"I think the thing with Robbie's farewell really hurt his feelings."

"Did he say that to you?"

Tom shook his head. "Not in so many words."

"Why did Robbie have to take such a hard line? Bob could have come, slapped everyone on the back, slithered back to Iowa, and left us alone." She tried not to sound desperate.

"Robbie hates him, Mom, but I don't think Jenny does."

"No, you're right there. Jenny doesn't hate him."

"What are we going to do, Mom?"

"I don't know." She closed her eyes. "I just don't have a clue."

tyler tossed

*t*he Mondays after a tournament were a lost cause in varsity debate. No one was interested in doing serious work. Everyone wanted to tell stories. As the students shared, the real challenge was in getting them not to all speak at once.

"I couldn't believe it," Melanie continued, talking emphatically with her hands. "She had this great beginning. She used some really obscure Aesop's fable as an intro. She had the hand gestures and facial expressions down cold. I mean it was perfect. The rest of us were going to be toast, and then she just stopped. Halfway through, she just stopped. She didn't fake it. She didn't try to keep going. She just stopped."

"Did she stop right in the middle?" kidded Harry, who was sitting on the front row.

"Yes, she did. And so I got the trophy." Her tone was so chipper that the class laughed. She placed her trophy on the riser next to four other new additions and took a deep bow as the class applauded. Sarah winked at Melanie. Standing at the back of the room, she was smiling for the first time in three days. The vise-like tension that had gripped the back of her neck relaxed. *This is why I'm here*, she told herself. *This is the payoff.*

"That won't happen to her twice," Meg interjected. She'd seen that girl compete before. "She'll be ready next time. Don't count her out."

The stories continued, a random, spontaneous sharing. The late fall sun shone in through the small, square window in the back of the room. Sarah turned in the spot of warmth until the sun hit her shoulders. She put her hand on the back of Eric's chair. He was a tall boy, a National Merit scholar who maintained a studied reserve and dressed elegantly to emphasize his differences from the rest of the students. He had a delicious sense of humor he rarely shared, and he could be ruthless if angered. A year ago on the bus, he had turned swiftly on Tyler, who had whispered "faggot" as Eric passed him in the aisle. Without pausing, Eric had sliced back. "Oh, the predator." The words rolled off his tongue like honey. "But your prey keeps eluding you, surely a sign of taste in the female species." Tyler had given him a wide berth since then, at least to his face.

Eric leaned back and whispered, "Mrs. Williams, I think Lakeview's coach is writing their cases for them."

"Really? That will come back and hurt them."

"It already did. That tall Asian kid didn't know where he was going in the rebuttals."

The students talked about what they had learned about the competition. Some would make subtle changes based on what they had observed and win another day. Less motivated students wouldn't, and their names would be absent from the trophy shelf.

Near the end of class, Meg snapped her fingers quickly and interrupted the stories to discuss the schedule for the rest of the week.

"Well, things are in full swing. Parent-teacher conferences are Thursday evening. We'll be on shortened schedule Wednesday and Thursday. Use that extra time at home to prepare. We go the next three weekends. If you signed up for Gov's Cup this weekend, we need your motel money by Wednesday. Everyone is guaranteed five competitive rounds. That means two rounds Saturday morning before eliminations start. Remember, no pay-per-view movies. We don't want any tired kids who thought it was funny to stay up half the night. The bus leaves Friday at one-thirty. Any questions?"

Rachael Beck, curls bouncing, waved her hand before starting to speak. "Who's going with us to Gov's Cup?"

"Mrs. Williams is going this weekend," Meg answered.

Leaning back in his seat, Tyler covered his mouth with his hand and whispered loudly, "Lock your doors, boys."

Sarah snatched her hand away from the back of Eric's desk as though her fingers had been singed.

Eric crossed his arms tightly across his chest. "Hate language," he whispered. "It's the only way he knows how to talk."

Several students twittered and glanced back at Sarah. Kristen and Rachael looked uncomfortable. Chan rolled her eyes.

"Get out," Meg said, a deep flush on her face. The laughter stopped.

Tyler didn't move. His blue eyes widened in surprise. He opened his mouth and then closed it.

"I'm not kidding. Get out. Right now."

He hauled his long body up in his desk and brought both hands to his chest. He feigned a wide-eyed innocent look, as he turned toward the class, palms up, and said, "What did I do?" He shook his head slightly. " I think we all need to chill," he said loudly. A few of Tyler's cronies laughed grudgingly.

Meg didn't blink. She pointed her finger toward the door. Tyler moved slowly, taunting her, a panther stretching his muscles in the sunshine. He was enjoying himself immensely. He slid his pencil into a small pocket in his backpack. He stacked his quote cards carefully into a neat pile and slowly pushed one arm into his jacket.

Sarah had opened her mouth to lash at him, when Meg said, "In five seconds, I'll call for the vice principal. If that happens, you'll be suspended, and that means no tournament this weekend. That's in the policy handbook." She held up her right hand shoulder level and ticked off each finger, counting silently. When the fourth finger went up, Tyler was out the door, but he waited in the hall, waited for his companions to congratulate him on "scoring one" on the coaches, waited to laugh at Sarah's discomfiture. She could see him. She could see the raw smirk on his mouth.

Twenty minutes left in the class, but the good feeling vanished. Meg passed back the tournament ballots. Always eager to see the what the judges had written, the students read scores and comments, and the room was quiet. The bell was a huge relief. Meg followed Chan down the aisle between the desks to where Sarah was sitting.

"Don't pay any attention to him," Chan said, her books pressed tightly against her chest. "It's such a tired old joke. I don't know why anyone would even bother laughing." The word *old* stuck in Sarah's frontal lobe. *Old* joke? Chan kept going. "He's so mean and crude that no one will go out with him." She nodded knowingly but paused, noticing Sarah's facial expression. "He's such a jerk. Most of us think you're wonderful. You're the best." She gave Sarah and Meg a forced smile and then walked away to complain to her friends about Tyler and his small gang of debate geeks.

Sarah turned her back on the handful of students who were still examining ballots and whispered to Meg, "Did I hear him correctly? 'Lock your rooms, boys'? "

Meg pursed her lips and nodded toward the few remaining students. She pulled out the pencil stabilizing the knot of her hair and whipped it up again more tightly, jabbing the pencil back in. Furious, Meg was still flushed, and she fanned her face with her hands. "Did you see him stalling?"

Sarah closed her eyes tightly and sat without moving until the students left, and the door closed with a click.

Sarah said, "When did I become an *old* joke? Do they think I'm some sort of deviant preying on adolescent males? Do they think I have an acne fetish?" She pinched her earlobe tightly with her thumb and finger.

"This is news to me." Meg stopped and thought for a moment. "I wish I had grabbed a camera and kept a record of that garbage those boys wrote in the prep room. I just wanted to get it off the wall as soon as possible. Ha. How stupid am I? It would have been enough to get them booted. Plus, it's libel. They're intentionally damaging your professional reputation. This is nasty, nasty stuff."

"Why? What did I do to them?"

"You can't stand either of those boys. It's all over your face every time you interact with them. But, hey, I don't like them either."

"They certainly aren't Sam and Murphy," Sarah said ruefully.

"That might be part of the problem. Everyone loved Sam and Murphy. No one likes these guys." Meg flipped a pen slowly in her hand. "Plus, I think Chan is right on the money, amazingly enough. I mean, Brax is a troll. Tyler's dangerous. So they do a lot of crude talk to compensate."

Sarah shook her head. She hated this, feeling victimized and powerless. "You know, Jenny's been hearing this stuff."

"You're kidding. Anything specific?"

"I don't know. She told me Friday that people 'whisper' about me. That was right after she told me that I make her sick."

Meg rubbed her forehead with her palm. "Oh, I'm so sorry. That's the last thing Jenny needs. We've got to do something."

"When did this come?" Sarah showed Meg a note from the office, a request from the principal for a brief meeting with Sarah Tuesday afternoon.

"A kid brought it in this morning. What's that about?"

Sarah shrugged. "Who knows? Probably something to do with the battle in sophomore English. No one can agree on curriculum. Boyce and Milligan teach in their own little boxes and think what they do is no one's business but their own. You know, same old, same old." Sarah tossed the note in the trash and started tapping her pencil on the desk.

Meg looked at her closely. "You've been quiet all day. What else is going on? How was the game Friday? I was surprised you didn't call to hear about the tournament."

"I was at the JV game just long enough to humiliate myself and my son." Sarah tried to laugh, but nothing came out.

"What happened?"

Sarah looked at the clock. In fifteen minutes she had to take Jenny to her dermatologist appointment. "In a nutshell?" she asked.

Meg nodded.

"Bob came to Tom's game. I got violently ill and threw up my socks in that garbage can by the outside stairs. The good Sheriff McLaughlin found me, picked me up in all my disgusting vomit, and drove me home. Not charming."

"Did you talk to Bob?"

"Nope, seeing him was enough."

"How long has it been?" Meg asked.

Sarah wiggled all ten fingers and then said, "Actually, twelve years." She looked at her hands as if she had momentarily misplaced a couple of fingers. "I've made a point of avoiding him."

"That's not going to be possible now."

"You're right," Sarah replied, wondering how many donuts she could stuff in her mouth at one time and live. "He and the lovely Mrs. Doctor Williams are moving here in January."

"Nova Scotia," Meg said.

"Yes, it's the only answer. I'll move to Nova Scotia. I should have gone yesterday." Sarah collected her bag and took her coat out of the closet. As she walked out the door, she turned, "I'll be back tomorrow."

"Yes, I know you will. I'll be here too." Meg gave her a wry smile.

Sarah didn't have time to waste. She hurried down the stairs and then paused on the last step. They always had to wait at least half an hour at the dermatologist's office. She bit her bottom lip and walked into the school's front office. It was empty, which was unusual. *Gracie must be out on a fact-finding mission*, Sarah thought. Taking the High School Association booklet from the hook on the wall, Sarah traced down the listings with her finger. St. Mary's. Sitting on the edge of Gracie's immaculate desk, she punched in the long-distance number. When a student voice answered, Sarah identified herself. "This is North Valley High. Can you take a message? I need to call in a drop for the tournament on Friday. We won't be bringing a Senior Varsity policy team. You can leave that slot blank. Thanks very much."

She hung up the phone and continued to walk out the door. The sun was shining. The sidewalk was wet from the melted ice and snow. Her shoes crunched the salt sprinkled on the pavement that morning.

libel and denials

*A*fter the last bell rang Tuesday afternoon, Sarah walked down to the office. She closed the door quietly and faced Mrs. Merrill, the principal, sitting behind the large oak desk.

"Please sit down, Sarah." The principal smiled pleasantly and tapped the mouse by her terminal several times with her long finger. Then she folded her hands graciously on the desk. Her note didn't mention any specific reason for meeting, but Sarah had imagined several scenarios: the principal needed support corralling all the sophomore English teachers into teaching the same curriculum, or Sarah and Meg had scheduled more tournaments than their budget allowed, or the worst case, there was a new complaint from the Coltons; and initially, the Coltons were what Mrs. Merrill addressed.

"So have things calmed down upstairs?"

"Define calm. We've had four days without any major blow-ups. That's a good sign. I don't want to criticize Terry behind his back, but his reversal really caused some problems for us."

"I think the most important thing now is to move forward. More than a few of the faculty have let Terry know that he botched it. I don't think he'll make the same mistake again any time soon." Mrs. Merrill raised her eyebrows slightly and waited a few moments before she spoke. "I understand Meg asked a student to leave your class yesterday."

"Yes," Sarah spoke hesitantly. She had hoped that particular disruption would slide under the rug unnoticed. How did Mrs. Merrill know? Had she heard what Tyler said? "Meg was totally justified."

"His mother called me," Mrs. Merrill explained. "She feels he's being singled out for punishment. Evidently, he wasn't the only student who was being inappropriate. Is that correct?"

"No. It was just Tyler." Sarah wanted to complain. She wanted to demand that Tyler be removed from her team, from her life, from the planet. She pursed her lips and waited.

"I'm sure the situation was difficult, but there's a liability issue. If a student is in the building, he needs to be in a supervised situation. Another time, if you need to remove a student, please call Terry or Mrs. Ruskin to come and assist you."

"That would chew up half a class period and give the kid a huge amount of negative attention," Sarah protested.

"Well, fortunately, it's not a situation that happens frequently. That's the first time either of you has asked a student to leave, isn't it?"

"Yes, but if I had a larger leg, I would have drop-kicked him out the door."

Mrs. Merrill chuckled quietly, and Sarah started to forgive her for being officious.

"That isn't why you wanted to talk to me, is it?" Sarah asked. "Your note came yesterday before fifth period."

Mrs. Merrill paused and stacked a couple of papers neatly. "You're right. Tyler Colton isn't the reason I wanted to talk to you. Sarah, I want you to know that I pay little attention to gossip. But I need to warn you that there's an ugly rumor circulating, and it's widespread enough that I've been receiving phone calls for the last two months. I don't believe the rumor, but the superintendent called yesterday morning and wanted me to discuss this with you."

The steel coil cinched around Sarah's stomach since the first day of school tightened. She was being cut in half. The smile left her face, and she didn't respond. She became aware of soft music playing and noticed the interesting glass jar filled with tootsie rolls that looked almost like a piece of art deco sitting on the credenza. *What else?* she thought. For a moment she saw an ethereal finger poised next to the Smite Sarah Button. She looked up at Mrs. Merrill and steeled herself.

"It's being suggested that you've engaged in a sexual relationship with a student, actually a former student." Mrs. Merrill's voice was kind. She reached over and covered Sarah's hand with her cool palm. "Sarah, can I get you something to drink? You've lost all your color."

"It's not true," Sarah whispered.

"I believe you. It would be inconsistent with anything I know about you. This kind of innuendo is an ugly tool someone's using to discredit you. I don't know how it got started or why. If we make assumptions, they'll probably be incorrect."

"And the lucky victim is?"

"A couple of names have surfaced, but Jason Wolcott is the one most frequently mentioned. Several anonymous people supposedly saw you with him in the canyon this summer." The words came out of her mouth reluctantly.

"Jason?" Sarah bit her bottom lip. "He was one of our best kids. He's Robbie's friend. He's my friend. He's one of those kids that stays connected." Clearly the wrong thing to say, but Mrs. Merrill nodded.

"I'm so sorry, dear. There's nothing to be done but hold your head up high and move ahead. It's impossible to pin down a rumor. That would be like trying to nail Jell-O to the wall. It just doesn't work."

Mrs. Merrill was working hard at being kind, but this was only the second item on her list of unpleasant things to do on Tuesday afternoon.

Holding up her head was the easy part; shoving past all the trash on the interior would be difficult. She thought of Jason in Scotland safe from this mess. She wondered what whispers her children overheard in the halls. She remembered the interview with the bishop, and a hot surge flooded her cheeks. He had heard this ugliness. That's why he had called her in. The walls, closing in for the past months, were crushing her like the interior of a trash compactor, and she was being squashed between empty cans of tuna fish and rotten vegetables. She couldn't get enough air. She opened her mouth, but nothing coherent came out.

"This has been the worst year. I must have done something really horrible in a past life to deserve all this. I must have been Genghis Kahn's first lieutenant and slaughtered masses of innocent people. Really, the year I got divorced was terrible, but this year is a close second." She rattled on completely out of kilter.

"Sarah, I've already said I don't believe this rumor, but I must caution you. If a student were to actually come forward with an accusation, I'd have to suspend you, with pay, of course, until an inquiry could be held. It's a liability issue. My hands are tied. I would have to act."

"And even if I were totally innocent, my reputation would be shot. Discipline would be impossible. I'd have to leave. And who would hire me?"

"You'd leave with glowing references from me. You might not be able to live in a desirable area, but I think you could find employment."

"Blanding, Scipio, outer darkness."

"I don't think it will come to that. I just want to caution you. Be circumspect in all your dealings with your students." Her expression was grave, and Sarah needed a smile in the worst way.

Mrs. Merrill pulled her mauve sweater around her shoulders and came around her desk. She patted Sarah lightly on the shoulder. "Hopefully, you've hit the bottom and your year will start to improve. Be very careful. Keep some distance from your students." She smiled again and held the door open for Sarah.

Avoiding people by heading to the third floor, Sarah crept nervously along next to the lockers. She wanted to hide. Why was all this happening? Was there some large cosmic lesson she hadn't absorbed? Was she getting proud? Did she need this fall? This humiliation? Did her children deserve this? She was panting and trying to hurry, but her feet, encased in blocks of concrete, wouldn't move. She couldn't run. Finally, she reached the classroom door. She hoped Meg had already left, but she heard voices inside.

"Remember, keep your hands inside a box the size of a television." A girl laughed, and Sarah heard Meg speak again. "Move, but not that much. You want your audience to be comfortable. If you're all over the room, you make people nervous."

Rachael Beck, in a rush to meet her ride, pushed the door open and ran down the hall, waving at Sarah. Sarah stood outside the open door, her hands clenched at her sides. Startled, Meg looked up and moved toward the door.

"Chan, why don't you look over the third and fourth paragraph on the second page? I need to talk to Mrs. Williams for a minute." Meg moved to the door where Sarah stood. "What on earth did she want?"

Meg asked quietly. Before Sarah could answer, Meg said, "You're hyperventilating. Look at your hands."

Sarah's hands were in some sort of weird spasm. Her chalky white fingers were contorted and pulled in tightly toward her palms.

"Chan's here. I can't put a paper sack over your head. Breathe slowly." And Meg started to take deep, slow breaths as though she were leading Sarah in a Lamaze exercise. After a moment, Sarah's hands started to tingle, and Meg asked again, "What happened?"

There wasn't much to tell. Sarah repeated the accusations. Meg stood still and stared at her for a couple of minutes after Sarah stopped talking.

"You need to take a couple of days of sick leave."

"People will think I'm staying home because I can't face this."

"No. No, they won't. This is old news to everyone else. No one will think that."

"But was this old news to you?" She couldn't believe Meg didn't know, didn't know about Jason, and didn't know about Sarah being an old joke. Everyone knew. Everyone was whispering.

Meg's eyes shifted quickly toward the door. "No, of course not." Meg stuffed her hands in her pockets. "Let me think for a minute." Then she put her arm around Sarah's waist and pulled her into the classroom, and in a voice a little too loud, she said, "I can't believe any of this. It is so absurd!"

Chan looked up from her printout and tilted her head toward Meg, who started to laugh.

"Honestly, Chan, just when you think you've heard everything." Meg laughed again. "Have you heard this? That Mrs. Williams is having a fling with an old student?"

Chan rolled her eyes. "It's so lame."

Meg kept it up. "Where does this craziness come from?" She smiled at Chan, waiting.

"I don't know, but I could guess," Chan offered with a grimace.

"These kinds of lies are just so vicious. A teacher at Sky Crest High was hounded out of his job over this kind of nasty rumor. It turned into an absolute witch hunt. He has seven little children. He had to put two in foster care because he couldn't support them. I mean, it's just terrible, and he's a wonderful teacher."

Sarah tried to follow Meg's lead, but she couldn't laugh, so she said,

"Do people think I'm a crazed predator?" She tried to smile, sitting down hard on a desk and said, "What next?" Because she really did wonder what other canons were aimed at her. She changed the subject. "How's the oration?"

"She's going to win with this one," Meg said. "It's thoughtful, well written, and interesting." She turned to Chan. "You've done a wonderful job. You should be very proud of yourself. I think we can take a break now, but we'll see you tomorrow."

Pleased with the praise, Chan didn't look at Sarah. Smiling broadly, she packed up her books and left. When the door was closed, Meg waited a few minutes before she spoke. "Well, a solid refusal just went out on the wires. You need to stay home for a few days."

"It's those boys, those horrible boys. They've done this." Sarah shook her fingers until the tingling quit. "I can't stay home. Tomorrow's parent-teacher conferences."

"You look awful—guilty as sin actually." Meg was trying to make her laugh. "Stay home. Sleep. Read a book. Clean out a couple of closets." Meg put her arm around Sarah's shoulders and gave her a hug. "I'm sure they need it."

"I can't. I can't miss parent-teacher conferences. That would be like putting an admission on the front page of the *City Times*. You know, I'm sure I heard Jenny and Tom talking about this the other night, but I didn't put it together. I wasn't paying attention."

"Give it up. You can't monitor every conversation in your house." Meg stopped. "Why don't you just talk to them? Preempt the gossip."

"Let's see. How would I start that conversation? 'Okay, kids, I'm not having a wild affair with Robbie's old friend.'" Sarah shook her head. "I don't think so."

Meg touched her lip with her finger. "At least let's call the sub-line for your English classes in the morning." She moved toward the phone, made the call, and then turned toward Sarah. "You know what would kill these rumors faster than anything else?"

Sarah shook her head.

Meg continued. "A small diversionary romance. Why don't you go to the movies with the sheriff for a couple of Friday nights?"

"Oh, Meg." Sarah put her head down on her hands. "I just don't have the energy for all of this. I'm not going to use him to dig myself out of this mess. I don't need any more complications."

"Well, it's not like you'd be breaking his leg." Meg walked out the door with Sarah, who still looked pasty and sick, and they headed down the hall toward the parking lot.

"Who was the teacher from Sky Crest?" Sarah asked as she dug into the bottom of her bag for keys.

"Oh, no one. I just made him up. I just wanted to give Chan a little emotional leverage."

"No starving children?"

Meg gave her a wink and a sad smile. "Good luck with the flu. I'll see you tomorrow afternoon."

parent conference and chinese conspiracies

Sarah's nose kept dripping, and she had a tissue balled up in her fist. She had caught a cold, and she kept touching her forehead, sure she had a fever. Not many parents had come to her table, and she was glad. All she wanted to do was go home and drink a quart of TheraFlu. The sheriff had been meandering around the gym talking to other teachers and parents, patting acquaintances on the back, and he wasn't even up for reelection, but Sarah avoided catching his eye, although several times she was aware he was looking at her. She couldn't face him, not after the Big Barf episode. He must have figured that out, because he never showed up in her line. She wondered if he had heard the rumors, and she wondered what he thought. She wondered what everyone thought who looked her way. She turned slightly in her chair and blew her nose.

Sarah and Meg sat at adjacent tables. Williams, Woodruff, and Wuthrich (the music teacher) were seated in a row. The gym was cold. It was drafty and voices echoed. Sarah had her coat tucked over her legs, but her feet were freezing. Bleachers had been pushed back, and tables from the lunchroom had been placed around the edges of the wooden floor. Chairs were positioned in the center of the room where parents could wait until the teacher they wanted to meet was free.

Mrs. Badger sat down at Sarah's table and smiled tentatively. Sarah sniffed, nodded, and pulled Kurt Badger's grade printout from the stack of papers. Pushing the sheet toward Mrs. Badger, she pointed to the percentage score with her pen.

"As of today, Kurt's getting a C. Barely."

"Ohhhh," Kurt's mother said, clearly disappointed. "He told me he did well on the vocabulary test last week."

"He did," and Sarah pointed to the test score, "but look at all these little zeros." She circled them in green ink. She didn't use a red pen. She thought red ink made papers look bloody. "He's not doing his homework."

Mrs. Badger carefully wrote "not doing homework" on the bottom of the page as though she were recording a secret formula or a concept so difficult and complicated that it would defy memory. This was the sixth time in the last hour that Sarah had repeated this exact conversation. The face was different, but the message was the same: no homework. This mother, however, made a serious mistake. She asked Sarah if she had any suggestions.

"Suggestions? Are you serious?" Sarah asked.

The mother was underlining "not doing homework" for the second time to demonstrate how serious she really was.

"You should throw his Playstation or Xbox out your second-story window and cancel your cable TV."

Surprised, Mrs. Badger pulled back from the table. "Maybe we could use time playing video games as a reward for finishing his homework?" she said hopefully, trying to avoid the more radical cure.

"Oh, I'm sure that will work for about two days. This kid's going to fail my class if he doesn't hand in his assignments." Sarah was too feverish to bother with diplomacy. "Get rid of the video games. All of them. The handheld stuff too."

"He'll just go over to the Moffats to play."

"Tell Mrs. Moffat to toss hers. Start a mothers' revolution in your neighborhood. You know, when the Pied Piper stole everyone's children, the town had a fit. These games are stealing our kids' brains and turning them into mush, and no one gives a hoot." Sarah coughed roughly and swiped at her nose.

Mrs. Badger hummed for a moment and started to say, "Well, I just don't know—"

Sarah cut her off. "You are incredibly powerful, Mrs. Badger. You are the food source," Sarah said as though it were a designation assigned by the United Nations. "Without you, Kurt would be starving and homeless, and worse, he wouldn't have a ride to the mall. He'd have to walk. Put your foot down. You can do this." She pushed the printout closer to Mrs. Badger and nodded at her encouragingly.

Mrs. Badger collected her purse and coat. "Well, thank you."

"No problem." Sarah checked out her pocket, looking for a fresh Kleenex as the next unsuspecting mother sat down. A large smile spread across this mother's face like a smear of strawberry jam, and she nodded her head up and down when Sarah glanced up.

Sarah looked at her closely. "Kandi Stevens, right? Second hour?" The mother kept smiling and bobbing, and Sarah thought the entire family needed to tighten up a few loose screws as she pulled out the grade sheet. "I think I had your older daughter a few years ago." The bob became a nod, although it was difficult for Sarah to distinguish between the two.

"How's Kandi doing?" the mother finally asked. "She needs a solid B in your class if she's going to have the grade point to try out for cheerleader." She pulled up her shoulders and smiled at Sarah as if they both should be rooting for Kandi.

"Well, I can't pass out grades like cookies, and right now, Kandi is getting a solid C."

The mother's smile turned into a pout.

"You know," Sarah said, "there is life after high school. Kandi needs to get better grades, so she can get a good *job*." But Sarah wasn't getting through. This mother couldn't conceive of anything more important that having her daughter be a cheerleader, so Sarah tried another tactic. "Have you heard about the Chinese conspiracy?"

The mother's eyes widened.

"You should watch CNN." Sarah lowered her voice. "The Chinese are plotting to take all of our good jobs, so we'll only be able to shop at Bert's Big Box Stores. We'll become a nation of low-end shoppers. Notice the next time you're in Bert's. Everything's been made in China. They're using video games to stupefy our kids, so we can't compete with them. Go home and get rid of your video games. It's your patriotic duty."

"But Kandi doesn't play video games much."

"Then take away her phone. She'll earn better grades. I guarantee it." Sarah dabbed at her nose and thought for a moment of rolling up two little wads of Kleenex and plugging each nostril to stop the dripping. That would be a great look. It wouldn't do anything to stop the Chinese, but it should end any gossip about her as a sexual marauder.

She watched Kandi's mother hurry over to a group of women waiting in line for the adult roles teacher. *There*, Sarah thought, *now I've given them something new to talk about.* She raised her hand to her forehead. She felt chilled. What was this? If you faked the flu, were you automatically doomed to have a nasty cold? Some sort of fatalistic retribution?

She couldn't see outside, but a light smattering of snow had been coming down when she walked over from the main building two hours earlier. She imagined large fat flakes making the roads impassible by now and was relieved that parent-teacher conferences were never rescheduled. The erratic fall weather had turned cold. Another heavy snow would overload the branches and cause all sorts of havoc and downed power lines, but she didn't care. Her trees could spare a few branches. Thinking how lovely it would be to have the power go out right that minute, Sarah closed her eyes.

She didn't see trouble coming. Valerie Williams thought it was very funny that Sarah was "asleep at the switch." Valerie sat down as Sarah shook her head. Too much makeup covered Valerie's face. She had several novelty rings on her fingers that coordinated with a gaudy pin on the collar of her embroidered vest. A furry cuff edged the boots that she was wearing, and Sarah noticed snow melting in the fur. *Not enough snow*, she thought, *to keep Valerie away, but enough to keep me from getting up the hill on bald tires.* The moment's reprieve was shattered. She could see Valerie's mouth moving at breakneck speed, but she hadn't decided to listen to her yet. She got the high points: snow, ice, cruise. The woman just kept motoring along.

Sarah flipped through the piles of grade printouts and found the *W*'s. There it was: Williams, Wallace Williams. She had started calling him Wally, and he had been persuaded to quit calling her Aunt Sarah. She had made the point by telling him one morning that divorce severed any familial connection, and she had emphasized the notion by slicing her hand across her throat in a quick gesture. Wally got the message.

Sarah slid the printout toward Valerie and interrupted her pointedly by saying, "Do you want to talk about Wally's grade?" Sarah spoke slowly and emphatically as though Valerie was hearing impaired. The woman didn't blink. She didn't pause. She didn't even make much sense.

"Do you want to talk about Wally?" Sarah tried again. "Your son." She rested her cheek on her hand and braced herself for the continuing onslaught. Looking past Valerie to see if other parents were waiting, Sarah glowered, for the first time that night, at the empty chairs. She sneezed loudly and pulled a dry Kleenex out of her pocket.

After about five minutes, Sara's mind was brought back from her feverish reverie by the words *Bob* and *the old Widsoe home*.

"What about the Widsoe home?" Sarah asked.

"They've made an offer on it."

"I didn't know it was for sale," Sarah said wistfully. It was a beautiful old home, built in the late twenties with dormer windows, a slate walkway, and more charm that any house should be allowed to have. It was in an older section of town. The willow trees were tall and graceful, and the yards were much larger than the postage stamp lawns in the newer subdivisions on the hill. It was so lovely that it was almost a landmark. Sarah's mouth felt dry, but her eyes were watering. She wished she had some juice, and she was aware that Meg didn't have a parent and was watching her. Meg broke into Valerie's barrage with the question Sarah couldn't ask.

"Why did Bob decide to move back to North Valley now? I thought he had made Iowa his home?" Meg slid her chair a little closer to Sarah.

"Well, I think you can put it into two words: *money* and *kids*. The hospital made him an offer he couldn't refuse. After all these years in academics, genteel poverty has lost its appeal. I mean there are big bucks to be made, right?"

Meg questioned her again. "What about the kids?"

"Well, they're growing up without him, aren't they? And she can't have any, can she?"

If Valerie answered her own questions quickly enough, there was no chance of anyone else getting a word in, but as she took a breath, Sarah broke in. "Claire can't have children?" She was caught. The hook was firmly embedded in her bottom lip. She sneezed again. Her joints ached. She had always assumed that it was a choice, a conscious choice not to have children because Bob already had three, and children were, after all, extremely inconvenient.

"Didn't you know?" Valerie tugged on the line. "I bet she's had at least five miscarriages. I'm surprised your kids didn't tell you. She had a hysterectomy last spring." Valerie drilled it in. "I think Bob always thought there would be time, time to have more kids, and time to get to know your kids, and then suddenly time ran out on old Bob." Sarah pulled back from the table.

"Know his own kids?" Meg questioned.

"That mess with the farewell was really a wake-up call. He knew he had to make things up. He didn't realize how old they were getting until Robbie was going on a mission. He saw them so rarely. So he started looking for something closer." Valerie paused, noticing the line accumulating behind her, people waiting to hear about the Chinese conspiracy.

Valerie prattled on. "He's afraid of children and grandchildren who won't know him, to say nothing of wanting to spend time with him. I mean, what a mess!"

Sarah stared at her. Then she wrinkled her nose and poked a Kleenex at her watery right eye. Valerie had braved the snow to deliver this message, and now she should leave. Sarah opened her mouth to speak, but nothing came out except a short, dry hacking cough.

"Everyone in the family knows there's no love lost between the two of you. So how hard are you going to make it for him?"

Sarah dipped her chin slightly and looked at Valerie out of the corner of her eye.

Meg broke the impasse. "My goodness, families are endlessly interesting, aren't they?"

"She hasn't answered my question," Valerie insisted.

"Perhaps there aren't any answers. Maybe there are just feelings," Meg spoke gently to Valerie, who was making a production out of gathering her purse, coat, and Wally's grade printout. Valerie tapped on the top of the table with a long artificial red fingernail.

"Oh, and by the way, stop telling people to throw their video games out the window," she said, pointedly looking at Sarah's runny nose. "You're making yourself ridiculous."

Sarah's patience was at an end and a small thread of saliva was working it's way down the corner of her mouth as she threw caution to the wind and sneezed without covering her mouth. "Well, you're certainly the reigning authority on that, aren't you? No one knows more about being ridiculous than you do."

Valerie's mouth dropped open and her eyes narrowed.

"Oh dear, look at all the parents waiting for Sarah," Meg said, stifling a laugh. "Sarah, you have at least six people who want to see you, and it's almost quarter to nine." Meg turned toward Valerie. "Thanks for coming by. I can't tell you how many times Sarah has told me how much she enjoys having Wally in her class and what a good student he is."

Sarah looked over the top of her glasses at Meg. Meg couldn't tell her because Sarah had never said either of those things, but the remark stopped Valerie from launching a counter attack.

"Well, good-bye, Sarah," she huffed before jingling away. Sarah could only nod and stare after her.

"Sarah, you're sick. You've got to leave," Meg whispered.

"Yes," Sarah replied. She blew her nose and turned to infect the next parent.

escalation

*t*he large yellow North Valley school bus pulled up to the curb as a light flutter of snow was starting to fall. The brakes lurched and the door mechanism gave a hiss and opened to disgorge excited students who were busy collecting belongings and stuffing papers into backpacks.

Sarah coughed roughly into her hand and then picked up the microphone at the front of the bus. "Okay." Her raspy voice caught the students' attention. "I'll get our packet and meet you on the north side of the main staircase."

She pulled up her sleeve and glanced at her watch. "We only have fifteen minutes, so help each other get those policy boxes out of the back of the bus. One more thing. Behave! If you do something stupid, no one will ever remember your name, but everyone will remember that you came from North Valley High. Oh," she looked over the students beginning to stand, "no hats leave this bus." Tyler, Brax, and two junior varsity members happy to assist the older boys in asserting their masculinity, were wearing baseball caps. "If I don't see the hats on your seats when you leave the bus, I won't give you your numbers. I mean, good grief, who needs this today?" She shook her head and stepped back to let the students pass as she made good on her threat to check for hats.

Mike, a junior, came right up and stuck out his chest as he argued about his innate right to wear clothing on his head, but she cut him off.

"I'm not having this conversation again. I'm not changing my mind. If you're so attached to your hat, stay on the bus and wear it all afternoon. I'm sure Ray," indicating the bus driver, "would love the company." Ray smiled and nodded his assent. Mike blustered, until Sarah smiled and said, "Be gone, fussy child. Save your arguments for the tournament." Against all his macho inclinations, Mike grinned and passed her quickly to retrieve his two large Rubbermaid boxes from the luggage compartment under the bus.

St. Mary's had been hosting Gov's Cup for at least a million years, and Sarah loved coming. It was a wonderful old parochial school that had, amazingly, escaped the gruesome effects of remodeling and retained some of its architectural charm. Newer buildings, hidden by trees and small grass-covered hills, were tucked behind the original structure. Student parking lots were an inconvenient block away. As a student teacher here twenty years ago, Sarah would have taken a job at this school in a heartbeat, but English positions were rare. She thought fondly of Mrs. Bowman, her cooperating teacher, who had refused to leave until she was led doddering out the side door, mumbling incoherently about adjective clauses and gerund phrases.

Sarah hurried down the bus steps and wrinkled her nose at the diesel fumes coming from the exhaust pipes. She glanced up at the sky before she ran into the main building, head down. Her camel blazer was small relief against the cold.

Her mop of hair was pulled back behind her ears with a couple of clips, exposing petite gold earrings she seldom wore. She felt very dressed up but was sure that her sore red nose was more noticeable than her outfit. She was sick of the stigma of being a divorced, single parent. Being a professional woman was more of a badge. She needed to be more assertive, less paranoid. She had decided that morning, as she was getting dressed, that her private life was no one's business. "Make the jump," she had told the woman in the mirror. As she headed into the foyer, she whispered to herself, "Margaret Thatcher, Madeline Albright, Martha Stewart." A new mantra—strong women who could be ruthless when crossed. She felt the outside of her jacket pocket, checking for a couple of packages of tissues.

The gray marble foyer was a mass of students milling around, their plastic boxes loaded with debate briefs, plus dollies and a couple of red wagons to transport the boxes. Sarah made her way up the stairs past clusters of students talking and joking with each other, belying their anxiety. She got in line to register behind two other coaches.

A heavy-set woman with a long brown ponytail greeted Sarah, "North Valley High, how are you?"

"We got here in one piece and all the hats are on the bus, so I guess that's a good start." She liked this teacher from the southern part of the state. She felt a bit overdressed next to the woman's faded sweat suit. Red Canyon High was a five-hour bus ride, and this woman had opted for comfort.

"You're the team to beat. How are you going to do today?" the woman asked.

"I think one of our novice teams might have potential, but we've got some real attitudes in our varsity class, and you know how that poisons the well." Sarah rolled her eyes.

"I've had a few seasons like that. It takes a whole year to come back from a bad bunch. Drugs?"

"It wouldn't surprise me. Nothing would surprise me." Sarah made a stab at fairness. "I haven't seen anything, and no one has come to me—yet." She fished in her purse for her registration check.

"Is it that tall, good-looking blond kid?"

Sarah, surprised, looked up at her quickly.

Cotton Country continued, "I watched him at State last year. I was short a judge and had to pick up a ballot. The kid's arrogant. He's his own worst enemy."

"Oh yes, that would be Tyler. I'll try and get around to watch him today," Sarah answered uneasily. Cotton Country was suddenly occupied with her registration materials. Three teachers were busy working the table, and Sarah moved over to a redheaded woman on the right.

"North Valley High?" The teacher looked up at her and smiled. "You won this last year." Smiling, Sarah passed over the school check to cover her fees, picked up her manila folder, and looked inside for the school code and student numbers. She ran down the stairs, her heels clicking on the marble stairs. Excited students were starting to crowd around the bulletin board where the first rounds were being posted. A clutch of her students watched for her. They made Sarah think of ponies, energized, prancing in the starting gate, waiting for the starter's pistol.

She pulled her school's slate out of her folder. The first position on the top of the list was for the senior varsity policy team. She skipped it. She read out the other names and numbers quickly, and just as quickly, the students jotted the numbers on their hands, grabbed their stuff with a wave and a smile, and headed over to the postings. St. Mary's student body officers were circulating with maps of the old school and giving directions to students impatient to get to their first rounds on time. Tyler and Brax were standing several feet away, waiting. Tyler's arms were crossed tightly across his chest, his hands tucked in his armpits. Brax nervously fingered a pimple on the back of his neck. She felt flushed and hoped her face wouldn't betray her. When the last student scurried away, she turned to face them.

"You're not on the list," she said, extending their school's slate to the boys.

"You've got to be kidding," Brax exploded, but Tyler was busy examining the paper, looking for an easy solution or an obvious mistake, anxious to join the other kids, anxious to be on his way. Finally, he looked down at Sarah.

"What's going on? Can you fix it?" Tyler scrutinized her warily.

He knows, she thought, *or if he doesn't know, he suspects.* She spoke slowly. "Well, it's a mistake. Unfortunately, at a tournament this large," she raised her hands in a shrug, "it happens all the time. Usually, there'll be a couple of teams that drop out at the last minute. I'll go see if you can pick up one of their numbers." She looked around, pretending to be unsure of her surroundings. "They're tabulating in the library. Don't go anywhere. I'll be back."

She glanced over her shoulder at the two frustrated boys talking with their hands, sitting on their boxes, watching the other students leave. *Margaret Thatcher*, she thought, *Martha Stewart, Madeline Albright.* She smiled grimly as she trudged up the stairs.

The library was a musty two-story room. Dark wood paneled the walls and tall freestanding bookcases stood in rows. A large section of windows looked east at the mountains, and the library tables that filled the center of the room were covered with white cards and pencils. Small groups of teachers were gossiping quietly, and other teachers had found the large overstuffed couches and were reading the newspapers, a quiet reprieve before the onslaught of the first-round ballots. Sarah drifted cautiously over to the table that held the cards for the senior varsity policy teams. She glanced at it for a moment, unsteady in her resolve. She could add those boys right now. She could run downstairs with a number. She could erase what she had done, but the words *old joke* were still lodged in her head, like a pebble caught in the tread of her shoe, and every time she remembered, she felt a fresh scratch of humiliation. She turned away from the table, straightened the paisley scarf around her neck, and taking her time, ambled back to the lobby twenty minutes into the first round.

"There weren't any drops," she lied, "but I think I can get you in this round. It will be a last minute thing, so don't wander off."

Her decongestant was working. Her nose had quit dripping, but her head felt stuffed with cotton, and she was sleepy. These boys were so dumb. Didn't they realize she was their only advocate at a tournament? She visualized the principal's face saying, "There's an ugly rumor circulating about you, Sarah." What was the advantage in insulting her? She remembered Tyler's remark in class. "Lock your doors, boys." Her face burned.

Tyler watched her, and Sarah looked toward the postings. "This stuff happens all the time. Don't take it personally. I'll come and find you after they post for the second round." She turned her back on them, not willing to commiserate and express sympathy she didn't feel, and walked to the library. She found a chair in the corner by a large window and watched the snowflakes drift down through the late afternoon light before she took a Patricia Cornwell paperback mystery out of her purse. Tucking her legs up under her, she opened the book to page thirty-six and ran away.

She was pulled back from a gristly murder scene as college students, hired to judge, started bringing in ballots. Sarah crossed over behind the bookcases, assiduously avoiding the dark, oily haired man who was working the senior varsity policy table. She always avoided Edmund Kensington. He gave her the creeps. His dark hair was combed straight back from his forehead, gelled into compliance. Whenever he talked to her, he put his hands on her arm and pushed his face inches from hers. Winning ballots had a way of vanishing when his team was behind. Today in particular, she didn't want to talk to him. He'd ask about her missing policy team. She moved over by Red Canyon, who was working at the Lincoln-Douglas table nearer the doors. Sarah read the ballots out loud, while the older woman recorded the results. Thumbing through the stack, she looked for Eric's name. Sometimes she thought his research bordered on overkill, but he had started winning last year. She crossed her fingers behind her back. Eleven ballots later, Sarah noticed Harry jumping up and down outside the door, waving his arms to get her attention. Students weren't allowed where ballots were being tabulated. She walked over to see what he wanted.

"Tyler and Brax want to know if they have a ballot for the second round."

"Are their legs painted on? When did you become an errand boy?" She dismissed his question. "So, how was your first round? How did you do?"

Harry looked around her at the coaches busily handling hundreds of ballots. "You tell me, Mrs. Williams."

"Oh, Harry, you wouldn't want me to be unethical, would you?" Sarah punched him lightly on the shoulder. "You've got enough on your own plate without being a gofer for Tyler and Brax. I told them before. I'll be down after the postings go out for the second round."

She walked back to the table where she was working.

"Any problems?"

"Oh, nothing really. Nothing I can't handle."

—◆—

A coach took the new postings down to the bulletin board in the main hall. Sarah waited until the crowd had dissipated and walked slowly downstairs. Tyler and Brax were standing by the bulletin board, anger and frustration hardening their faces. They looked ready to do battle with someone, anyone.

She preempted their strike. "You're B11. You're affirmative. You're going to be debating R9. The only catch is this: they have to use an annex." She coughed into her Kleenex. Tyler quickly wrote the number on his hand in ink.

"You're in room two. South of the this building." She checked her watch. "The second round started ten minutes ago. Be quick. Get your stuff." She made a pushing motion with her hands to hurry them on their way and bit the side of her lip as she watched them move down the hall. *How can you hurry pushing four large boxes on two dollies?* Her stomach tightened. Ten years ago, St. Mary's had chosen not to raze the old school. Instead, they had used an old playing field as a site for four new buildings joined with walkways. The boys would be lost looking for a nonexistent location.

She stationed herself by the entrance to the library in anticipation of the trouble she had set in motion. She pulled her mystery out of her purse, but splattered blood and hair matted on an axe handle couldn't hold her attention. She read the same page over and over, her eyes wandering down the hall. She walked over to the dismal buffet, but the dried cheese and coagulated vegetable dip looked so unappetizing she wasn't tempted. She picked up a carrot stick and gnawed halfheartedly before tossing it in a garbage can.

Twenty minutes before the second round ended, Tyler and Brax appeared at the door. Out of breath and flushed, they waved to her. Sarah feigned a look of horror. "What on earth are you doing here? Why aren't you in your round?"

Tyler panted breathlessly. "We looked everywhere. There are four buildings out there. They all had a room two. Only one was open, but they all connect. We looked everywhere."

"You should have stayed until you found your round. This is so bad. What can I do to fix this?" She shook her head seriously. They followed her, as she slowly made her way down the hall out of earshot of the coaches in the library.

Tyler spoke first. "It's not our fault."

"Is anything ever your fault?" Sarah raised her eyebrows. "Sure, they should have given more explicit instructions, but you know how nuts tournaments are. People always assume what's simple and familiar to them will be simple and clear to everyone, and it's not." She shook her head and kept walking.

"Can't you do something?" Tyler's tone was so conciliatory that Sarah stared wide-eyed. Was this the boy she sparred with every day in class?

"I don't know," she said. "You've missed the first two rounds. It would be grossly unfair for you to waltz into the third round with two wins never having opened your mouths. People will just scream." Sarah pursed her lips as though deep in thought. Brax kicked a locker, and the noise echoed down the hall.

"Oh, please," Sarah barked. She looked at the dent in the locker and hoped he'd broken a toe. "Being melodramatic doesn't serve any useful purpose." She adopted a conspiratorial tone and patted the air with her palm. "Go back downstairs. Don't talk to anyone, even kids on our own team. I don't want anyone complaining that you've had an unfair advantage. Pretend that you've been debating all day. Whatever you do, just don't let on. I'll pull in all my favors and see what I can do." She was matter-of-fact, but her tone suggested that chances weren't good. "I'll be down and find you after they post for the third round."

Sarah spent the next forty-five minutes avoiding everyone. She loitered in the faculty women's restroom, messing with her hair. She mimicked Mr. Colton's assertive bluster to the mirror: "Tyler and Brax are going to Gov's Cup or you'll hear from my attorney." She grimaced at her reflection. *Well, they're here. The spoiled brats.* She pinched a little color back into her cheeks and applied lip gloss to her mouth before she walked back into the library.

She hadn't helped tabulate the second round, and Red Canyon looked at her carefully. Sarah returned her look, smiling faintly.

"I'm sorry I wasn't more help. I'll be back in a minute and count on me for the third-round ballots." Again, following the coach with the listings, she hesitated several moments until students had jotted down their destinations and were leaving, before she looked around the foyer for Tyler and Brax. She found them sitting on the marble steps. Tyler had his chin cupped in his hand. Their boxes, filled with hundreds of carefully prepared briefs, sat on the steps below them.

She didn't wait for the boys to speak. "What's your take on the conversation you had with the South High coach last year?"

Tyler frowned. "Brax talked trash to one of the girls on his team."

Brax blushed, shaking his head.

"Did you really suggest that she'd had relations with half of the football team? That little girl was a lily-white bishop's daughter, and she went home and cried for three days. Then she quit debate." Sarah looked Brax right in the eye. "When her coach confronted you, you didn't apologize, did you?"

Neither boy spoke.

"Well, he was happy to tell everyone about it who would listen. That little incident has just come back to bite you." Her palms started to sweat. The South High coach had scorched her ears for a solid half hour at a summer meeting, but he hadn't said anything today.

"Come on, Mrs. Williams." Brax elbowed her side awkwardly. "We were just heckling her a little. You know, to throw her off her game. To give us the mental edge. Nobody takes any of that stuff seriously."

"She did," Sarah replied. "Her parents did. Her coach did. Do you think that you can say crude things like that about real people with impunity?"

"Everyone does," Brax said. "You should hear what the football players say to each other."

"Sorry," she responded. "Different venue. You know," she whispered and both boys leaned toward her, "we were the team to beat today. This little problem takes our team right out of the running, and opens the way for City High or Claremont to win, and City High's coach, Edmund Kensington, is running the varsity policy table." Sarah's script didn't include the large sneeze she barely had time to cover with her hand. She pulled a tissue out of her pocket and covered her nose.

"Isn't there anything we can do? Can't we complain to someone?" Tyler persisted.

"Like who? The governor?" Sarah rolled her eyes. "I don't have his number." She wiped gently at her sore nose. "Stuff like this always just comes down to he said, she said. There's no way to prove that another school sabotaged us." She included herself as a member of the injured party. "It's a done deal. I don't know what you want to do now. Staying around here for two days is going to be pretty boring. I don't have the authority to release the bus to take you home, but maybe one of your parents could come down to get you? I don't know."

Two totally dejected boys looked at her. They couldn't even verbalize a response. The train had left the station, and they weren't on it. For about two seconds she felt a flush of pity.

"Oh, one more thing," she added. "I can only release you to a parent, not a sibling, certainly not a friend. If I don't see the parent who comes to get you, you won't be able to travel to any more tournaments this year. That school policy's carved in stone. Do you understand?" Both boys nodded their heads. She touched her nose gingerly. *I need a little lotion*, she thought.

That evening a light snow dusted the pavement in front of the motel foyer as Sarah, from the windows in the mezzanine, watched Mr. Colton help Tyler load the large boxes into the trunk of his Mercedes. Brax glanced over his shoulder toward the motel where the rest of the team was having a noisy, happy dinner in the coffee shop. Mr. Colton brushed the snow off the windshield and stared hard at Sarah, standing in the window. She managed a sullen smile and waved.

"Have a nice drive home," she mouthed, "in the blizzard."

He cupped his hand by his ear, indicating that he couldn't hear her. Sarah waved again.

revenge and resistance

*J*ust before the bell rang for fifth hour, Mike and Harry sauntered into the classroom, carrying a large two-foot trophy with a gold statuette on the top and at least four small wreaths on the sides. First Place Junior Varsity Policy was prominently written on a brass plaque. Smiling but silent, Mike nudged his partner, Harry, who was laughing and pointing at the trophy to students who had not attended the weekend tournament. Harry turned down his volume but continued to stick out his chest and shove his thumbs under imaginary suspenders.

Meg quizzed Sarah with her eyes.

Sarah chuckled, "Oh, they're trying hard to feel guilty about winning when the great ones didn't get to open their mouths, but Harry can't do the sad routine when he's so pleased with himself."

"I thought you'd call me yesterday. What happened at the tournament?"

"I'll tell you later." Sarah avoided Meg's eyes and headed up to the front of the class.

Eric, sweeping his dark auburn hair out of his eyes, walked into the room with another large trophy under his arm. Sarah, still laughing, stepped up on the riser to call the class to order. Only this additional height allowed her to be at eye level with Eric, who was enjoying the praise of his teammates, as he handed his trophy to Sarah, and she pretended to stagger under the weight.

"Eric, this is wonderful. First place Lincoln-Douglas debate, senior division. No one deserves this more than you do." Class members started to clap. Sarah grinned at the class. "I was so proud of all of you. Several judges stopped me on Saturday to tell me how impressed they were with your performance. Mrs. Woodruff and I couldn't be more pleased. City High took the sweepstakes trophy, but that doesn't take anything away from your successes. Mike and Harry, take a bow too." Harry jumped to his feet quickly, flashed his warm smile again, and bowed deeply. Mike cuffed him lightly on the shoulder and laughed.

Ten minutes into the class, the door opened. Tyler and Brax swaggered into the back of the room, carrying the remnants of their lunch.

"You need to leave that food at the door." Meg stood. Without a word of apology or an explanation for being this tardy, Tyler shot her an insolent look and didn't move. Mike, who was telling the story of championship round late Saturday night, saw Tyler scowling at the back of the room.

"They dropped two of their arguments, and we won," he said abruptly and sat down.

"Gentlemen, how nice of you to join us. Come and take a seat." Sarah gestured to their empty desks, determined not to have the moment spoiled. Tyler crumpled his fast food garbage into a tight ball and tossed it in a long arc across the room into the wastebasket.

"Three points," Mike offered.

Tyler kept his drink in his hand and meandered down the aisle to his seat. Brax slid into a desk in the back of the room and stuck a handful of French fries in his mouth.

Sarah deflected attention from Tyler and back to the students who were trying to continue the positive feeling from the beginning of class. "Rachael has an idea for a interesting bill for legislative forum. Tell us your premise, Rachael."

Rachael, the funny brunette, who always enjoyed attention, stood up quickly. "I'm going to write a bill to limit the compensation for CEOs."

Tyler guffawed from the side of the room. "Let's add that to the list of the ten really stupid ideas of Rachael Beck. Good luck getting that passed."

Her mouth open, Rachael turned toward Sarah.

Sarah smiled. "Actually, getting the bill passed isn't really the name of the game. What we want is something that will stimulate a lot of argument."

Eric raised a hand carefully. "I'd have to raise the question of constitutionality."

"That's interesting." Sarah coughed and sipped juice from a bottle. "What do you think about that? Is there any other legislation in place?"

It was quiet for a moment, and then Chan spoke as an idea popped into her head. "Minimum wage!"

"Excellent, Chan. If it is constitutional to establish a wage at the bottom of the pay scale, shouldn't it be constitutional to establish a cap for the top?" Thinking, Sarah paused for a second. "Are there any models where this has been tried successfully?" Students were starting to shake their heads. "I think that perhaps Japan has a similar sort of law. Rachael, your premise will take a little research, but the idea's a good one."

Tyler, too cross to be ignored, stuck his figurative foot out to trip up the forward motion of the class. "My dad has his own company. It's privately held, and if he runs a tight ship, it's no one's business how much money he makes."

"Okay," Sarah responded. "Let's say Tyler's father employs a design engineer who comes up, during working hours, with an idea for the perfect widget. This is such a great widget that every household in America will want to own at least one. Everyone in this company works very hard, and millions and millions of dollars in profits are made. Is Tyler's father the only one who should benefit from this success?" Sarah glanced around the class.

Tyler half-stood up out of his desk. "They're lucky to have jobs."

Sarah nodded. "There are a lot of interesting directions this could take. Is it moral, ethical, or practical for the CEO of a large corporation, public or private, to make millions and millions of dollars a year, while the lowest paid employee only makes minimum wage? Should it be more proportional?" Sarah stopped and looked at the class. "Let's pursue this. Eric, would you look up the compensation packages for the CEOs of some large American corporations. I think that I read somewhere that in some cases it's over four hundred times the lowest paid employee. I think the shock effect of those numbers in a proponent speech would be great. Does anyone have a parent who belongs to a union?"

Harry raised his hand reluctantly. Trade unions weren't popular in Utah, and she hated putting him on the spot.

"Run this past your parent tonight and see what they have to say, would you?" Sarah smiled at Harry. "Rachael, see if you can find out how CEOs' salaries have risen in the last twenty years. I think we can have some fun with this. Great idea, Rachael."

Rachael made a few quick notes in her folder and beamed artificially at Tyler's scowl.

Meg walked to the front of the room with the current events quiz in her hand, and Sarah stepped back to the desk and sat down, groaning softly. She had gotten home late Saturday night, church was early Sunday morning, and she was starting to droop. Meg directed the class activities until the last bell rang. Talking and joking, students filed out, leaving the two trophies standing proudly on the riser.

Meg walked slowly back to the desk, slipped out of her shoes, and reached into the drawer for a couple of chocolate chip cookies left over from lunch. She offered one to Sarah and put her feet up on a chair. She sighed deeply. "How do you feel about being unemployed?"

"What do you mean?" Sarah regarded Meg out of the corner of her eye.

"Why didn't you work Tyler and Brax into the second round on Friday? It would have been easy."

"I didn't want to. Those boys shouldn't have been allowed to debate at Gov's Cup, and they didn't."

"Good grief, Sarah, you threw a tournament on purpose?"

"Don't you remember how horrible that nasty Mr. Colton was at that meeting? Call it poetic justice, divine retribution."

"I call it revenge."

"And revenge is best served cold." Sarah's lips made a thin line across her face. She slapped a pencil down on the desk.

"But no one knows that you've scored," Meg said.

"That's not important to me."

"You're acting like a terrorist."

"What do you think creates terrorists? They're people who have no power or resources to protect themselves or make any reasonable changes in their lives. We tried to deal with those boys in an up-front, direct way, and we were plowed." Sarah paused. "But I'm not a terrorist."

"You're not?"

"No. I'm more of a saboteur. If I were a terrorist, I'd call the radio station or send a note to the Coltons claiming victory." Sarah sneezed loudly and rubbed the tip of her nose.

Meg laughed sarcastically. "You won't need to call the Coltons. They called the principal Saturday morning, complaining vigorously that you didn't make the tournament director fix the error. They smell a rat, Sarah. Do you think you can avoid being discovered?"

"Of course." Sarah pretended to be scared by glancing over her shoulder at the door and shuddering. "Think of me as a member of the French Resistance in World War II. They weren't terrorists. They were heroes."

"Now you're a hero?"

"Absolutely," Sarah said with confidence she didn't feel.

"Did you call in the drop?"

Sarah thought a minute about lying, but decided against it, and nodded.

"You planned the whole thing?"

"Yes, I did, and I'm not sorry. I am so sick and tired of being a victim. Those people, that creep and his jerk of a son can behave any way they want to me, and I have absolutely no recourse, because I'm just a teacher. Tyler can say any horrible, disgusting things about me and trash my reputation, but I have no rights, because I'm just a teacher. If I complain, it's just going to be the sad look and 'it goes with the job, honey,' or 'they're just kids.' "

"But, Sarah, they are just kids. Just dopey kids."

"I guess you weren't at that meeting with the parents. I guess you didn't see the really awful stuff those boys wrote about me on the whiteboard. Who do you think started the rumors about Jason? Just kids? I don't think so."

"Those rumors are their idea of an off-color joke. They don't have a clue that they've damaged you professionally."

Sarah turned her head slowly away from Meg. "Would you be defending those boys if they had said those things about you? How would you feel if your children were hearing that you're a completely wanton forty-three-year-old?"

"I'm not saying it's okay, but you keep upping the ante. You want to get even, and that's a dead end. Sarah, these people are their own worst enemies. The parents are obnoxious and the kids are a mess.

You've dealt with this stuff before, and it's never tipped you over. I know Tyler's horrible, absolutely horrible, but he's not worth your job." Exasperated, Meg threw her hands up in the air and looked around the room. "I can't do this anymore. Mrs. Merrill asked me this morning what I thought had happened at the tournament, and I had to tell her that tournaments are crazy and mistakes happen. I lied to cover for you." She shook her head. "Honey in the boxes, and now you've thrown a tournament. This is going to blow up, and I don't want to be one of the casualties. I can't keep you from doing this stuff, but if you're going to do it, you're going to do it without me."

Sarah glared at her. "So that's it?"

"Look, we've had a great run, but I don't know where this is going to end. Robbie's gone, and Bob's moving here. Maybe you can't deal with debate on top of all that."

Sarah grabbed the side of the desk. "I walked into church yesterday, and people can't look me in the eye. People that I've known for years. Jenny drags herself in. She's humiliated to be seen with me. Tom tries to compensate by being everyone's best friend, even the little old ladies. That's all new. Courtesy of Tyler and Brax. We get home, sit down to lunch, and the phone rings. Dr. Iowa has called to say they've bought the Widsoe house. Jenny's euphoric. She can't wait to have a non-sleazy parent in town. I am now the sleazy parent. How crazy is that?" She looked hard at Meg. "And now you're going to dump me for giving those boys a taste of their own medicine."

Meg's shoulders sank. "Dirty tricks don't make anything better."

"Maybe it will slow them down," Sarah said. "It feels like they're in cahoots with Bob. Like I'm being set up." Sarah rubbed her nose with the back of her hand. "I'm sick of being a victim, a doormat! I've been that jerk's victim since I was eighteen. I'm sick of it." Sarah's eyes narrowed. "That man turned down his invitation to this little party twelve years ago. Now he comes barging in, turning my life upside down, stealing my children right out from under my nose. And there's not one thing I can do about it. Nothing. Victim again, particularly if I'm a social pariah," Sarah sputtered. "But I don't have to let the Coltons occupy Paris without doing anything."

"Misplaced aggression." Meg scrutinized Sarah. "Don't you see that you're the one with all the advantages?"

Sarah rolled her eyes.

"You've had those kids for twelve years to raise without any interference, and they're good kids. All the money in the world won't make Tyler Colton a person like Tom. How many kids would vote for Tyler if he ran for anything?" Meg made her thumb and index finger into a zero. "He's nasty. When Tyler says his filthy little things about you, no one who knows you believes him. He thinks he's talking about you, but he's really saying volumes about himself, his lack of character, his trashy mouth, and his parents." Meg shook her head. "Your kids love you. The kids at school love you. You don't see the looks that flash around the room when Tyler acts up. He's got his little handful of gangsters, but the rest of the kids don't like him."

Meg pushed the pencil more tightly into her twist of hair. "Jenny and Tom can love Bob a little and not love you any less."

Sarah listened. Fragments of truth banged around in the back of her head. She propped her chin on her hand and looked past the geraniums out the window at the gray sky.

"Look," Meg said, "I'm going to the next two tournaments. You're staying home." Sarah started to protest, but Meg stopped her. "Three years ago when Rosie had pneumonia, you took over everything for three weeks. This is worse. You're staying away from Tyler Colton. Stay home, get ready for the holidays, and spend some time with Jenny."

Sarah didn't answer. She looked at Meg for a minute and then she squashed her cheeks together until she looked like a guppy. All thoughts of her noble resistance fled. She wasn't Madeline Albright. She was just a mess. *I'm alone*, she thought, *all alone*. Her eyes watered, and her whole body seemed to sag heavily against the chair. She stood to put on her coat and reached into the drawer for her battered purse.

Meg sighed audibly. "I'm sorry. I won't quit, but you've got to promise me, no more sabotage. This is my team too."

"Okay."

"And promise me you'll at least think about calling the sheriff to go to the movies. You've got to give people something else to talk about."

Sarah shook her head and walked out the door.

christmas break or christmas broken

*t*he actual number of days left until Christmas didn't matter. The day before the break was complete mayhem. It was a day of slacking off and general goodwill toward men, students, and teachers. Students were singing "Jingle Bells" in the hallway. Treats appeared magically on desks. Piles of wrapping paper and ribbon materialized in the corners of rooms. A movie, *The Princess Bride*, was playing in the front of the room.

"Any big plans?" Meg asked. She moved several papers around the desk, looking for a pen.

"No. I'm not painting anything, sewing anything, or cleaning anything. I have two great books I've been saving."

For three weeks they had only exchanged little superficial pleasantries. An uneasy truce. Sarah wasn't sure exactly how Meg engineered it, but she seemed to have taken over the varsity class, and Sarah spent more and more time with the novices. Meg was separating Sarah and Tyler Colton, as though she were sitting between two misbehaving children in church.

"When does Robbie get to call?" Missionaries were allowed one phone call to their families at Christmas.

"Christmas Eve."

"What did you send him?" Meg asked casually. The burdens seemed lifted. They were happy to have a two-week break from the debate season, lesson plans, students, and each other.

"Lots of silly stuff. I put in a couple of new ties and some socks. Tom and Jenny got him a few things. His companion's mother sent him a breadmaker last year."

"You're kidding?"

"No, I'm not. Isn't that nuts?" Sarah raised her shoulders and laughed. "I guess it nearly drove the kid crazy packing that thing around."

Sarah had on a green and red plaid dress, a bit faded but still festive. She laughed at Billy Crystal's character in the movie. Meg tossed a popcorn ball at her, and Sarah caught it with the tips of her fingers.

The back door opened, and Jenny and Tom came in with Estee, Tom's new girlfriend, in tow.

"Mom, will you excuse us for the rest of the day?" Tom was a bit breathless, and Sarah guessed they had run up the stairs.

"What's up?" Sarah asked.

"Well, Dad called last night," Tom said. "They could use some help moving in. If it's okay with you."

"Their movers are there today," Jenny explained.

"You're going to leave all this hilarity to go and work?" Meg asked.

Sarah's face suddenly felt like an ironing board. He was coming. Sarah knew it, but she had pushed him out of her head. Now he was here. She'd be tripping over him.

Tom watched his mother. "We're not doing anything in any of my other classes."

"It's a nice thing to do," Jenny chimed in, quoting Sarah when she wanted the kids to help neighbors or relatives.

"What about the Christmas dance?" Sarah nodded at the cute girl at Tom's elbow.

"Oh," Estee replied, "we'll have plenty of time to get ready. I mean, that's not a problem for me." Estee's hands were outstretched as though she were saying, "I'm Switzerland." *But she's not neutral*, Sarah thought. *She's curious.*

"I'll call down to attendance for you," Sarah said.

"Mom, you're the best." Tom leaned over to give her a quick hug but glanced back at Estee and punched Sarah's shoulder lightly instead. Sarah looked at Meg out of the corner of her eye and bit her tongue.

"Jenny, will you check in with me by five-thirty, please?" Sarah asked as the three scooted out the door.

Jenny nodded. "Thanks, Mom."

"That is so cool to have a mom right here," Estee said in a husky voice.

Meg nodded at the closing door. "How long have they been an item?"

"A couple of weeks."

"How did we miss having her in debate?" Meg asked as the three vanished down the hall. "I'd kill for that voice."

"That's just the half of it. She's smart too." Sarah shrugged. "She has sort of a math family. Her dad taught engineering at the university." But she wasn't thinking about Tom's new girlfriend. Sarah was standing on the curb outside the beautiful old home on the Boulevard, next to a large moving van, watching her children drive up in Tom's rusted out Toyota truck.

"He doesn't teach there anymore?"

"Oh no," Sarah said absentmindedly. "He died when Estee was little."

"How?"

"Cancer. I guess he died by inches." Sarah sighed. "Tom thinks that's their common bond. Neither of them has a father. Of course, until today. Return of the phantom father with a big house and money to spend."

"Why did you marry such a jerk in the first place?"

More of Meg's moral superiority, she thought, twisting a red and white candy wrapper between her fingers. "Packaging," she said thoughtfully. She put the bit of toffee in her mouth and sucked on it for a minute. "He was just so completely adorable. Handsome and athletic. You have no idea. But not safe, not safe at all."

"Well, this is new."

"You know, I was engaged to someone else." Sarah tried to smile at the surprised look on Meg's face. *See*, she thought, *I'm not a romantic disaster after all*. The noise of *The Princess Bride*, the snatches of Christmas carols in the hall, and the chatter of kids laughing almost drowned out Sarah's voice.

Meg pulled her chair closer. "Anyone I know?"

"Steve Watkins. A very solid citizen. He was a bishop a few

years ago. I think he might be a stake president now. He lives over in Atherton. Lots of money."

Meg nodded, waiting.

"He was crazy about me." Sarah batted her eyes and laughed. "I didn't have a ring, but we were going to get married after he graduated in the spring and ride off into the sunset in a U-Haul."

"Were you going to drive forever, or did you have a destination?"

"He was going to dental school in Nebraska. Now he has a beautiful home, a nice wife, and I think, five kids." Sarah opened her mouth in mock horror. "Five!"

"But you didn't go?"

"Nope."

It was a warm summer morning, and the front door was open, letting in a soft breeze. Mrs. Ritzman was in her gardening clothes ready to go out and weed her tomato plants. The doorbell rang and a masculine voice asked for Sarah.

"She's busy." Sarah's mother flipped the lock on the screen door.

Sarah pounded up the stairs and gestured her mother back to the kitchen. "Mom, don't run interference for me. Who's here?"

"Bob." Mrs. Ritzman raised her voice. "Steve called."

Bob. Horrified, Sarah pinched her cheeks and ran her fingers through her wet hair. Her cutoff jeans were too short, and the old white T-shirt she was wearing had a tear in the back. "Oh great," she said to herself, walking to the door.

"Hey, stranger." Faking nonchalance, she stood behind the screen door, waiting.

He had filled out. His jaw was stronger, and his eyes were a deeper shade of brown. He was carrying a large paper sack in his hand.

"Sarah, I have the perfect picnic." Wearing an old hat with a floppy brim and a faded high school T-shirt, he smiled and gestured toward his mother's car. He opened the top of the sack, tantalizingly. "Barbecued chicken, Fritos, peas in the pod, and two gingersnaps."

Sarah stepped out on the stoop, sat down on the warm concrete, and patted the step beside her. She sighed heavily as she looked over at him and hoped he didn't notice her drooling. "I'm not going on a picnic with you. I mean, it's great to see you and all, but I'm dating someone else. I'm getting married next spring."

"You're kidding?"

"No, hang around and I'll send you an invitation."

He watched her with anticipation and smiled as if she had just told him a joke and left out the punch line. "Well, then going on a picnic with me is a completely safe proposition. We'll eat chicken, talk about old times, and you can tell me about whoever this guy is."

Oh, that smile. He smelled the same: his mother's laundry soap, his shampoo, and some musky male something. She wanted to rub her nose against his shoulder. The proximity of his body and the way his eyes played on her face melted her stony resolve.

He already knows about Steve. She smiled to herself, but she said his name anyway. "The guy is Steve Watkins, and I can be gone for two hours. That's it. I have a ton of work."

"I didn't know you had a job."

He has been asking around about me. He's been gone for two years, and now he's trying to round up his old possessions. Sarah looked up at him. "I get tuition and a stipend for being a student body officer, and they get a pound of my flesh," she said, pinching the skin under her arm, "but I could use a break." She stood up and headed toward his car. Bob was right behind her, jostling his sack.

"I'll be back in a little bit," she called over her shoulder. Mrs. Ritzman clutched the screen door.

—⁓—

The afternoon was warm and lazy. A couple of men were fishing off the bridge. Bob drove across, heading to the Bird Hollow picnic area up in the mountains. They splashed across a small noisy stream and spread an old plaid blanket on a worn patch of grass. Pine trees and a few bushes separated them from the Saddleback Trail.

Bob devoured most of the chicken, pelting the bones at a persistent squirrel. Sarah tossed raw peas into her mouth. She flipped the ones at him that fell on the blanket. Half a package of Fritos later, Sarah squinted up at the sun through her fingers.

"So what happened to Elder Goobler from LaVerkin after he went home? Who did he kiss first, his girl or his horse?"

"We were all afraid to ask." Bob chuckled. He slid next to her and followed her gaze up through the trees. "Is there a message in those clouds?"

"Just the time. This has been fun, but I've got to go home." They'd talked about old friends and old times, but they hadn't talked about Steve. She felt unsettled, almost guilty. She tried to think about Steve's warm smile and the secure feeling of his arm around her shoulder. She brushed some dirt and grass off her legs.

"Come here," Bob said. She ignored him. Stuffing some pea pods and the little white bag back into his sack, she turned her back on him. He pushed himself over behind her and slowly squeezed her shoulders.

She jerked away.

"Come on, Sarah, you're as nervous as a cat. Relax a minute, and then we'll leave." His hands were strong and warm. He pressed his thumbs down each side of her spine and kneaded her shoulder muscles. She had forgotten about his hands. She relaxed and leaned back toward him. He rubbed the back of her neck. Then he lifted her hair and brushed her skin with his lips.

She turned toward him. "Whoa, we're not doing this." But he kissed her and held her so close she could feel his heart beating. "I'm not doing this," she said, but she put her arms around his neck. Her knees felt like jelly, and his fingers were flirting with the edge of her T-shirt. Her heart was going a mile a minute. She couldn't breathe.

A red light flashed in the back of her brain. *Steve. What am I doing?* She pushed hard against Bob's chest with both hands, but he wouldn't release her. She turned her face away from him, panting. She caught her breath. "Why did you quit writing to me?"

His mouth tickled her ear. "I wrote the last letter."

"Yes, but you were waiting weeks to answer. You changed. You didn't come to see me when you got home. Now this?"

"It doesn't matter, Sarah. I'm here now."

"You bet it matters. I need to understand."

He shrugged. "I don't know if you can understand. After you live someplace for a year, it starts to feel real and home doesn't. I felt like I was going to be there forever." He lowered her in his arms and kissed her again. She felt limp and closed her eyes.

She kissed him back, but when his arms tightened around her, she opened her eyes and sat up straight. "I can't do this to Steve."

"You already have."

She shook her head. "I don't get it. I don't know why we're here. I want to go home."

Bob held her head in both of his hands, forcing her to look into his eyes. "I realized I'd made a terrible mistake. You're the person I'm supposed to be with."

"You're some kind of an arrogant jerk. You waltz back into my life and turn everything upside down?" Her chin started to quiver. "You broke my heart. I cried and cried for weeks. I thought my life was over."

He pressed his ear against her chest. "It doesn't sound broken to me. It sounds like it's firmly in my camp." He grabbed her head again with both hands. He kissed the tip of her nose. He kissed her cheeks and each eyelid. "I think the only thing that needs convincing is right in here," and he kissed her forehead softly. "Sarah, your body is madly in love with me."

She tried to slug him. He grabbed both of her arms and laughed.

"But he's such a nice guy," she whispered into his neck.

"So am I."

"No, you're not." But Bob started to tickle her and pretended he hadn't heard what she said.

Sarah felt Meg's eyes drilling into her head, so she shielded her face with an empty Christmas plate. "So that's it. That's the story. He was going to love me forever, and then when I wasn't looking, he and that dumb blonde stole my life. Now, they're back for my children."

Meg grabbed Sarah's hands. "Oh, Sarah, I'm so sorry." She whispered, "You're still in love with this guy."

Sarah rolled her eyes. This was all so ridiculous, so stupid. She had learned to push him out of her head and only rarely felt some residual phantom limb pain, but now he was right here. She could keep her life intensely busy, but she would still see his car, hear his name, and see him.

"Sarah." Meg tugged gently on Sarah's hands. "Sarah, look at me. You've got to do something," Meg insisted. "You've got to see someone, get on a medication, or something."

"An anti-love potion? I don't think they sell those over the counter. I think you need a prescription."

"Maybe you could be hypnotized." Meg continued to talk, almost to herself. "I didn't understand. You never talked about him before. You've been repressing this for years. I'm surprised you haven't exploded before now."

"So, now I'm exploding?"

"Exploding isn't the right word, but Sarah, it's all coming out. You've got to let go." Meg looked her in the eye. "If you don't, you'll alienate your children. You really will."

Sarah gritted her teeth. "Stop lecturing me. I'm not going to explode or implode. I just feel a little left out and used up, but I'm sure I'll survive. I always do." She tossed a piece of fudge into her mouth.

christmas day disrupted

Sarah grumbled to herself and anyone else in ear shot almost constantly. The laid-back routine over the two-week Christmas break was disrupted by the sudden invasion of another parent with an agenda and invitations. Sleigh rides, movies, restaurant reservations. Was he trying to make up for twelve years in five days? For years she had been able to dismiss Bob at Christmas and the inappropriate, expensive gifts he sent with a lift of her eyebrows. "Maybe we can exchange it for something that you can actually use."

But now she had to make plans. The relaxed, quiet Christmas day with a fifteen-pound turkey cooking slowly in the oven had to be arranged around the kid's three-hour afternoon visit to Bob's house. She glowered at the front window as Tom and Jenny backed out in Tom's old truck. She didn't wave. She waited until they turned the corner, and then she flopped down on the couch. The best-seller Meg had given her didn't hold her attention. She read the same page over and over as she absentmindedly scratched Einstein behind his ears. "This is so unfair," she complained bitterly to no one. She popped *Holiday Inn*, her favorite Christmas movie, into the VCR and watched for an hour until Fred Astaire tried to set himself on fire with firecrackers during a tap dance. *One more egotistical male display*, she thought and hit the stop button.

The phone rang twice. She didn't answer it. She'd talked to Robbie the night before. She wished she could talk to him now. She'd really unload if the other kids weren't around. The Christmas Eve phone call was just too positive, too uplifting, and too spiritual. She could tell Robbie wanted to talk about this unsettling turn of events, this affluent pink elephant that had invaded their family. Instead, they talked about Robbie's life as a missionary. They talked about the constant diet of rice and beans and the impoverished conditions of the people in the small town where he was serving. He talked to Tom about the basketball team, Tom's performance at the last game, the assistant coach and his opinions, and defensive maneuvers. The amount of time those two boys could talk about basketball amazed Sarah, but she didn't interrupt.

After her turn, Jenny had handed the telephone back to Sarah so she could tell Robbie good-bye. She wouldn't talk to him again until his next official call on Mother's Day. She had never needed anyone in her life as much as she needed her son, and he was so far away. Thousands and thousands of miles. It was like he was on the moon. A lump rose in her throat, and somehow Robbie sensed it. "Are you all right, Mom?"

"Oh sure, you know me. I'm fine. It's a big change and not an easy one, but I'll be okay."

"Jenny's pretty taken with all this." How could he know so much after ten minutes with Jenny on the phone?

"Well, she hasn't looked past all that glitters. Maybe she's not old enough."

"Don't go toe to toe with her on this, and she'll come around. You know what I mean? Give him plenty of rope." Not a particularly Christian remark for a missionary son to make on Christmas Eve, but she didn't care.

"I get it, but it's hard." Sarah wanted to reach through the phone and pull him into the living room. Tears filled her eyes.

"Hang in there, Mom. Everything will be okay. I'm running into Elder Axtell's time slot."

"I love you, Robbie."

"I love you too, Mom. It will all work out. We'll talk on Mother's Day. Tell me the truth in your letters. Quit glossing over stuff. Bye for now." And then, he was gone in an electronic puff of smoke. She sat quietly for a couple of minutes. "Give him plenty of rope." There was no question about what Robbie thought about the return of the prodigal father. Bob might be able to fool Jenny and bend Tom, but Robbie was hers, and she wondered why she didn't feel reassured.

—⁓—

Still thinking about the telephone conversation from the previous day, she rolled off the couch and moved past the Christmas mess over to the oven. Reaching in with a worn hot pad, she jerked the pan toward her and sucked up juice with a turkey baster that looked like an obscenely large eyedropper. She squirted the juice back over the top of the bird and shoved the whole business back into the oven. Would the kids even be hungry when they got home? A blue and white bowl sat on the countertop, and Sarah put a whole cube of real butter in the bottom before she dumped in the steaming boiled potatoes. She shoved in the electric hand mixer and smashed those potatoes with a ferocity they really didn't deserve.

As she sloshed a half a cup of cream into the potatoes, the carport door opened. Tom, stomping the snow off his feet, held the door for Jenny, pink cheeked and smiling, a dusting of snow in her hair. Sarah scrutinized her daughter. How did three hours with her father change sad, petulant little Jenny into this glowing, fresh-faced girl? She could be on the cover of *Seventeen* magazine. What insidious magic was at work here? She was relieved that Jenny wasn't loaded down with gifts. She held a little silver gift sack in her left hand. Pink tissue sprinkled with glitter poked brightly out the top. Sarah abandoned the potatoes to their own devices and followed Jenny into the living room.

"Look, Mom." Jenny carefully pulled out the layers of crushed paper and laid the small plastic cards on the couch. "They're gift cards and IOUs," she explained. An IOU for a shopping trip and lunch with Claire was written on a small personalized note card. Another card was a gift certificate for a pedicure and manicure at a popular spa near the mall.

"Claire said she would go with me if I'll let her know when I make my appointments," Jenny said as she laid the little printed card on the top of the IOU. Sarah rolled her eyes. It must have been painfully apparent to Claire and Bob, as Jenny opened the gifts, that she would never be able to walk into a spa all alone and negotiate the intricacies of becoming beautiful. A third card was for a hair stylist. Tucked in another piece of tissue was a pretty bottle of pink-tinted perfume.

"This is from Dad."

Sarah cringed. She had practiced a calm face and complacent smile in the mirror for a half hour while the kids were gone. She had told her reflection, "That's nice" at least forty-two times until she could say it without growling. Here was the test.

"He said he spent at least two hours at the perfume counter testing different scents, but perfume smells differently on each person, so you never know." Suddenly knowledgeable about perfume, Jenny assumed a different air. She seemed a little older, a bit more removed from Sarah, who had lost any interest in smelling any differently than the cheapest bar of soap.

Sarah kept telling herself, "Rope. Lots and lots of rope," but it was very hard, and she realized she was chewing the inside of her cheek. She relaxed her jaw.

"That's nice," she said, nodding slightly.

She looked over at Tom and asked with her calm smile, "Isn't anyone interested in the condition of the calluses on your feet?"

Jenny raised her eyebrows at her mother's sarcasm. "No, but Tom won the prize."

"And what prize is that?" Sarah asked. She felt as if boulders were being piled on her chest.

"Jazz tickets," Tom responded. "Dad got them from a drug rep, and Claire doesn't like basketball that much." Sarah let that little heresy slide, as she looked at the tickets in Tom's outstretched hand. "They're the bottom section right at mid-court." The price, a hundred dollars each, was clearly printed along with the seat number and the row.

"Sweetheart, a drug rep didn't give these to your dad. He thought of the most wonderful present he could give you, short of a new car, and this is it. I'm guessing that you can take two friends?"

Tom nodded.

"So, you'll drive to Salt Lake in your dad's cute little BMW. You'll have dinner at some trendy restaurant. You'll go to the game. The seats will be perfect. You and your friends will have a wonderful time, and your dad will have the most fun of all. If the Jazz are hot, it sounds like a win all around."

Tom's complete pleasure at the gift turned into a chagrined grimace as though he had suddenly turned into a war profiteer.

"Oh, Tom," now it was Sarah's turn to feel guilty, "it's a wonderful, thoughtful gift from a father who very much wants to have a relationship with you." She could say the right things, but she couldn't suppress the jealously writhing in the pit of her stomach. It would have taken her an entire month's salary to buy these gifts for her children. She felt cheap and overwhelmed.

"Do you think I should take Estee?"

"I think that might be a mistake." Sarah considered for a minute. "You know, if Claire"—and she swallowed hard not to choke on the name—"were going, it would be different, but I think this is more of a guys' night. If you take Estee, you're going to be worrying about her and if she's having a good time. If you take Matt and Jeff, you can kick back and have fun." She should have been pleased to be consulted, but she wasn't. It took every ounce of energy she had not to scream and rip up the tickets. She looked again. "The Jazz vs. the Lakers. It's on a Saturday night. No conflicts. Perfect." She had hoped for a moment that the game would fall on the night of the Valentine's dance, but Bob was too clever for that. He had checked the high school calendar. She thought *Rope* once more and headed back to the kitchen.

The turkey was dry. The potatoes, offended by the previous abuse, had not bothered to stay warm, and the pumpkin pie no longer looked festive. Jenny opened her mouth to say that she couldn't possibly eat another bite after the ham and potatoes and cheesecake she had just consumed at her father's house, but a swift hand slice across the throat from Tom silenced her. By the time they actually sat down to eat the unappetizing little Christmas dinner, a deep gloom had settled over the table. Nothing was the same as last year. Sarah watched Jenny glance around the kitchen as though she were comparing this somber space with the Christmas cheer and the happy banter she had just left. Sarah's arms felt heavy, and she pushed her potatoes around with her fork. The little poinsettia tied with a silver bow in the middle of the table looked sad and tacky. Tom looked a million miles away, probably cheering at the Jazz game.

The doorbell rang. Einstein woofed. Everyone looked up, relieved, as Estee blew in with cheeks red from the cold and a tiny crystal drip at the tip of her nose. She held a wrapped gift in her mittened hand. It wasn't large, and Sarah guessed that it was a CD. Another bit of ribbon peeked out of the top of her coat pocket.

"Oh, you're having dinner," she moaned. Sarah jumped up from the table and pulled a chair over before Estee could make a quick exit.

"Have a piece of pie!" Jenny offered in a very un-Jenny fashion.

"I'm just stuffed. Junk all day," Estee explained, "but pumpkin pie is just like eating vegetables, right? Maybe just a sliver."

Two pieces of pie later, Estee exclaimed over every gift under the tree. She laughed at the new socks and underwear. The new North Valley sweatshirts were pronounced perfect and just the thing. She loved the sweater that Jenny had received from her aunt and uncle, and she examined the small CD player that Tom had really wanted. Suddenly the gifts that seemed cheap and inadequate, compared with the gifts from the house on the Boulevard, were okay again.

"Oh, good," Estee said, giving Tom the present she held in her hand. "This will be perfect." While Tom opened the small package, Estee gave a small gift to Sarah. "It's not new," she apologized with a wince of a smile, "but my mom loved it. She read it at her book club and thought you might like it too." She looked at Sarah for approval, and Sarah remembered that there wasn't a father's paycheck at Estee's house. Estee's skin was so clear, her dark brunette hair was so shiny, and her eyes were so bright that until that very moment, Sarah had never noticed that the cuffs on Estee's jacket were worn and her jeans were never new. She did remember that Tom frequently teased Estee about being a "thrift store whiz."

"What's this?" Estee eyed the small silver gift sack with the glittery tissue sitting on the couch.

"Oh, my dad gave me a bottle of perfume." Jenny pulled the little bottle out of the sack and sprayed the scent on her wrist and held it up for Estee and her mother to smell. The little gift cards stayed unmentioned in the tissue.

Estee turned to Tom. "What did your dad give you?"

"We're going to see the Jazz play the Lakers in a few weeks."

"Cool," Estee responded, more impressed with the perfume.

Tom edged a little closer. "Would you like to stay? We usually have a cutthroat Monopoly game Christmas night."

Clearly pleased with the invitation, Estee hedged for a moment. "I'd like that, but my mom needs me." She was so matter-of-fact that there was no opening for sympathy or even a glimmer of self-pity. "But I'd really like to play another time. We're not die-hard game players at my house."

"Oh," Sarah explained, "we take our game playing very seriously in this family. Bragging rights and all that, but I was thinking Jenny and I might watch *Gone With the Wind*. She's never seen it, and I feel very sure that sooner or later the South is going to win the war. Who knows? Tonight might be the night."

Tom rolled his eyes. "Mom has a great-grandfather who fought for the South."

"Wounded in the hip at Shiloh," Sarah said.

"Maybe I'll go over to Estee's for a little while?" Tom asked.

"Sure, just be home in time to see Scarlet eat that rotten carrot. That's my favorite scene. What a survivor."

Tom went to get his coat, and Sarah put her arm around Estee's shoulders.

"Thanks for the book. I've read the reviews, and it sounds great. I love to relax on the couch with a good book over the holidays. And thanks for coming over. You coming in the door was just like a visit from the Ghost of Christmas Present."

Estee smiled broadly. "Tom says that the Christmas holidays are the only time of the year you don't get up in the morning and make a list."

Sarah laughed. "Well, no point in being compulsive if it doesn't show."

The cold air blew in the front door as Tom and Estee went out to her mother's car. The night was clear but brittle as the temperature dropped.

"Merry Christmas!" Jenny called out, and they could see Estee wave through the front window as she got into the passenger side of the car.

"Pillows and blankets." Sarah shivered. Jenny ran to get her pillow and a soft fleece throw. Sarah turned off all the lights except for the twinkling lights on the Christmas tree. Inserting the tape into the player, she turned as Jenny snuggled onto the couch. Sarah wrapped up in the old flannel quilt. Einstein whined to be included on the couch.

"No way, Einstein." Jenny pointed to the floor beside her feet.

The theme music started. Mother and daughter finished Christmas Day in the dark on the couch, warm and comfortable, as Scarlett and Rhett battled it out one more time.

resistance betrayed

*U*nder arc lights, a cold drizzling rain left the dark parking lot with a wet shine. Piles of dirty snow were melting behind an exit sign. The soles of Sarah's shoes were wet, her socks were getting wetter, and her feet were freezing, but stopping for food after a tournament was a ritual. Gusts of wind whipped around the corner of the strip mall and made standing outside miserable. Her arms, pulled tightly across her chest, held her briefcase against her thin coat. She shook the rain off her hair with a quick toss and watched the last few kids, carrying drinks and sacks, jog toward the bus from Wendy's. She tapped her foot and waved her arm for them to hurry. Rain here meant snow in the canyon, and it would be midnight before she got home. Deciding it was foolish to be standing outside the bus, she climbed up the steps covered in dark rubber matting and stood next to the driver.

Sarah usually didn't do countdowns, but this year wasn't typical. This was the ninth tournament they had attended: Global Issues at Clearview High, the last tournament in January. She ticked off the remaining tournaments on her fingers. Three more in February before Region and then State the first weekend in March. She didn't count today, because today was almost over.

This day had started at five o'clock in the morning when Sarah's alarm clock had jarred her awake. Chan and Ron had been late for the bus. Consequently, the bus was late leaving North Valley. The day had been slow. The cheese and cold cuts in the tabulation room had been nasty. The soft drinks were lukewarm, and the team, as a group, had not done well at all. A handful of students were going home with trophies, but the sweepstakes award was on another bus, and Sarah didn't feel particularly disappointed. She was having a hard time trying to hold all the pieces of her life together. Perhaps it would be easier just to let go. Let everything fly apart. If her feet weren't so cold, maybe she could care, or if she didn't know the ride home would be abysmal. School buses weren't designed for comfort.

She could see Tyler and Brax under the fluorescent lights, sauntering across the parking lot, carrying large paper cups of hot coffee. She hoped it would keep them awake all night. After losing again today, they were surly, trying to pick a fight, hoping to win something, even if it was an argument about keeping the rest of the team waiting. Sarah didn't have enough energy to play. They pushed past her, flaunting their lateness. Tyler flashed an angry stare at her. She looked away as she checked their names off her list. He always managed a well-practiced, smoldering glare, but his look tonight was savage. *What now?* she wondered. *Only six more weeks of that kid.* After Region, he would just be a bad memory, a bump in the road.

She borrowed the microphone from the driver and tapped on it before she began. "Well, this wasn't a great day. We'll do better next time. It's okay to give another school a chance to shine." Nothing she said mattered. Everyone was tired and disappointed. She refused to return ballots to an over-eager sophomore. "The flashlight bothers the bus driver," she explained before settling down to try and relax. The driver ground through the gears as Sarah watched the rain hitting the windshield turn into snow.

The driver swore softly under his breath as the bus slid going up the on-ramp, and from the back of the bus, she heard Tyler tell Mike to take his trophy and shove it. Sighing heavily, she tried to find the energy to reprimand him, but when she turned, Tyler's head was down and he was whispering emphatically to Brax. Oblivious to the insult, Mike was whispering to Melanie, so Sarah turned back to the rhythm of the windshield wipers and watched the headlights of the oncoming traffic.

That afternoon while Sarah had been tucked away in the tabulation room, resolving a judging dispute between two other schools, students were milling around the cafeteria, waiting for the announcement of which teams would advance. Tyler sat down hard on his large Rubbermaid box and rested his hands on his knees, staring down at the floor. Brax was dispatched to stand in the long line of students waiting for slices of cold pepperoni pizza. Tyler tried to convince himself that they had won their second round. He knew they'd won the first and lost the third because they had accosted the judges and badgered them for results, which was clearly against the rules.

He didn't notice the long, loose young man who approached him until the toes of the boy's shoes almost touched his, and Tyler glanced up.

"Dude, how's it going?" the boy asked.

Tyler shrugged his shoulders in annoyance. Mr. Long and Loose and his partner debated for City High and had been winning consistently all year, and Tyler didn't want to hear him gloat.

But the boy wasn't easily deterred. "Dude, what happened to you guys at Gov's Cup last fall?"

Tyler stood up. His height always gave him a little more confidence, and he shook off his anxiety to play the macho adolescent with more assurance than he felt. "Our registration got screwed up. Our coach tried to add us, but the rooms were messed, and we were out."

"You know, we were all looking for you. You were the guys to beat coming out of camp." He nodded slowly, mostly to himself, and went on. "Mr. Kensington was running the policy table. He was watching for your school's registration. You weren't on it. Griffin from East said he saw you in the foyer."

"We were there, but we missed the first two rounds, and the other coaches wouldn't let us add in." Tyler pulled his baseball cap out of his back pocket and tugged it down over his forehead.

"But that's my point, man," the boy continued. "Our coach said no one tried to add you in the second round. What's the story?"

Tyler stared. "I don't know." The frustration that had begun at Gov's Cup last fall had continued through the whole season. It was like no one knew how good he really was, like he hadn't had a fair shot the entire year. Brax had lost his confidence, and despite all the notes Tyler passed to him, he kept dropping arguments. Now at this late date, there was no way to make any kind of a comeback, and Tyler had been floundering and irritated since Christmas, looking for someone to blame.

Mr. Long and Loose's partner was at the postings and yelled for his friend to come. They had advanced. Tyler waited, not wanting to appear too eager, then nonchalantly walked over. He and Brax were out. Wanting desperately to kick at his box, or the table, or the leg of a passing girl, he stood quietly, clenching and unclenching his fists. He had to be cool. Only fools looked desperate. He stood watching Brax in the pizza line until Brax returned his gaze. He shook his head in response to the question on Brax's face. Then he gestured toward kids sitting on the floor by the auditorium doors. Slipping on his leather jacket, he strolled toward the auditorium with a couple of twenty-dollar bills palmed in his hand. A handshake resulted in a quick exchange, and Tyler headed out a rear door and joined a few kids, huddled in the cold, out of sight, smoking dope.

Hours later, in the muffled darkness of the bus, Tyler repeated the conversation to Brax.

"Someone's screwing with us," Brax said.

"She did this to us." Tyler jerked his head toward Sarah, sitting alone a couple of seats behind the diver. "She made sure we didn't win Gov's Cup. That whole routine was bogus. That ugly hag."

"Nah." Brax dismissed him. "That's not her style. She's a total glory hog. She'd never sabotage her own team."

"No one tried to add us in the second round. Why would Kensington lie?"

"To cover his butt. He didn't want his teams to hit us."

"No," Tyler insisted, "you're wrong. It's been her, all year. She's been messing with us all year."

"Are you going to tell your dad?"

"It's too late. What can he do now? Plus, there's no way to pin it down. Kensington doesn't like her, but he'd cover for her."

Tyler silently replayed that day last fall over and over in his head as the bus traveled north through the snowstorm in the darkness. He remembered waiting and waiting in the foyer at St. Mary's, watching the other kids leave, all excited and happy. He remembered wandering around, lost, panicked, and looking for a nonexistent room. The humiliation he had felt all year turned to anger writhing in the pit of his stomach.

He glowered at Sarah, her head leaning against the cold window-pane. She would never have had the guts to treat Sam and Murphy like this. Who did she think she was? Who was she to trash their senior year? Some no-account teacher. Outrage pounded in his head. She'd get hers.

daughter for sale

Sarah didn't like January. She didn't have much use for February either. A blizzard would be better than this. Anything would be better than gray leaden skies. She watched the black branches moving slowly in a chill wind out their small excuse for a window.

"Do we even *have* groundhogs in Utah?"

Meg looked surprised at Sarah's random question. "Who knows? Maybe prairie dogs? Large jack rabbits?" She picked up another batch of uncorrected papers and sighed. "You know, I hate it when I leave all this to the last possible day."

It was a teacher workday, the last day of the trimester. Students were off skiing or sleeping in, and the teachers who were caught up could just roll in, fill in their grading sheets, clean up their classrooms, and vanish out the back doors. Sarah and Meg weren't in that happy group. The debate season was in full swing, and even though they took turns traveling, missing those weekends put them behind.

Their room was quiet as they both flashed though student papers with green pens in hand. Writing a quick comment, Meg said, "You know, I don't think they read anything I write. They just look for the score on the top. This is an exercise in futility."

"Have another piece of licorice." Sarah handed over a box of Red Vines, keeping one for herself. "I don't think setting the thermostat at freezing on work day is really all that economical. Think of the cost of substitutes next week when we're all out with pneumonia." Sarah tucked her coat around her legs and wrapped her scarf around her neck twice. Then she pulled the ends up like a noose and stuck out her tongue.

"Dying from pneumonia doesn't involve hanging. Do you really think they turn down the heat? Maybe it's cold because of the absence of all the little warm bodies." Meg rubbed her hands together, stuck the last bite of a licorice stick in her mouth, and picked up her marker to attack another paper.

Ginger McComber, a tall social sciences teacher, stuck her head in the door. "We're all going to lunch at twelve-thirty. Do you want to come?"

"Where are you going?" Meg asked. "Is it any warmer out in the hall?"

"We're going to Café Grande, and no, it's not any warmer anywhere in this building."

"Do you have your grades entered?" Sarah questioned her jealously.

"I'm close. I might have to come back for a half hour, but maybe not. Well, think about lunch." She nodded when she didn't get a reply. "I think Kathy's going to drive." The door shut behind her.

Meg looked at Sarah carefully. "Do you want to go?"

"I brought a lunch, but you should go. You're further ahead than I am. I'm not going to make the deadline if I take an hour for lunch and gossip. Plus money's a little tight after Christmas." Sarah had twenty dollars in her purse, but it had to last until the next paycheck.

"You know, if you don't go, the gossip could be about you."

"Are you kidding? Other than being a sexual predator, I'm pretty boring."

"Ah, it's that dastardly ex-husband of yours who has everyone talking. Well, him and Claire of the massive chest. It does make for some interesting speculation."

"Oh." Sarah put her head down on the desk. "Say it isn't so."

"Sorry, it is. Maybe you should put your own version out on the street. Every time someone asks me, I do my best."

"What do you say?"

"Well, without going into any of the sordid details that everyone seems to want, I just say the man should be shot at dawn for past offenses."

"You don't."

"I do. I've never been shy about telling the truth." Meg made the statement as though she were announcing an unpleasant weather forecast or the score of a game. "He's been showing up at every single basketball game and almost tripping the players, he's so close to the floor. Of course, it's also very interesting that wherever he stands in the gym, you are as far away from him as you can possibly get. Did you think people wouldn't notice?"

Sarah put her cold hands on her face and pushed her cheeks up until her eyes were small slits. "I really do hate this."

"Of course you do. This is awful. So the question is, do you want to go to lunch?"

"No, I was gone all day Saturday, and I just want to finish and go home." Sarah stared hopelessly at the stack of papers and ungraded quizzes piled before her. "I feel like that woman who had to spin a whole room of straw into gold."

"Gold?"

"You know what I mean."

"No, I don't. I never know what you mean anymore. Is Jenny at home?" Meg asked.

"Jenny is having her calluses sanded off and her toenails painted as we speak. Life in the spa lane."

Meg smiled grimly. "Ex-husband and company are not going away, you know, unless we can plan a clever assassination."

"I've thought of that, but they're not worth the jail time." Sarah smiled.

"Well, we're certainly on arrogant-male overload this year." Meg put her chin on her hand thoughtfully. "You know, we might win Region, but we're going down in flames at State."

Sarah shook her head. "It's just been a horrible year, all around." She stood up abruptly and tossed two sets of quizzes into the wastebasket. "Ten points out of six hundred aren't going to make any difference." She started to whip through a batch of essays, writing scores on the margins without reading a single word. Occasionally, she wrote "good thoughts," or "clear thinking," or "work a little harder on your transitions" as she flipped through the stack.

"I've never seen you do that before."

"That's because I've never done this before. I've been correcting the same stupid mistakes from the first day of school," Sarah said, exasperated. She waved a smudged paper. "This kid writes in stream of unconsciousness. James Joyce has nothing on him."

"Clearly another licorice moment," Meg said as she handed back the Red Vines and checked over her shoulder for witnesses.

Sarah finished correcting in record time and carried the whole mess over to the computer and started to enter scores. "Do we have the attendance printouts?"

"In that large paper explosion on the left side of the desk," Meg responded. "Have you given any thought to teaching English in China? Smaller classes. Interesting landscapes. Black and white bears."

"No, I just want to go home and make something fattening," Sarah muttered.

Meg laughed. "You know, if you stand on your head while you're eating something sinful, it goes right to your chest. I am quite sure that's what Claire's been doing since puberty."

Sarah was entering citizenship grades when laughing and talking in the hall stopped her. She glanced at the clock. *The entire social sciences department must be heading to Café Grande to have my personal problems for lunch*, she thought.

Kathy pulled open the door. "Are you going?"

Sarah shook her head.

"We'll just have to miss you."

Meg waited for the teachers to move on down the hall. "You know, they're all on your side."

Sarah twisted her jaw to the right. "I don't want people to take sides. I just want this all to quietly go away."

"It's not going to go away quietly. Pretty soon you'll probably be the subject of sacrament meeting talks." Meg ducked as a piece of red licorice suddenly became a javelin.

Meg picked Sarah's licorice up off the floor. A tiny piece had been bitten off the end. "Do you ever finish eating anything?"

"What are you talking about? I eat everything."

"No, you don't," Meg said. "You take a tiny bite of a cookie and then you wrap it in a napkin and put in the drawer."

"To finish later. That's not against the law. When did you start paying attention to what I eat?"

"I toss the cookie rocks into the trash every four or five days. You're losing weight. I can see your skull through your skin."

Sarah looked over the top of her half glasses, irritated. "I'm eating, thank you very much. I'm not so good at sleeping, but I do manage to eat."

——~~——

At three fifty-five Sarah finally handed her grades to Gracie in the office. She was not the last, but she had been in the building the longest that day. She was exhausted and her nerves were raw. She hoped Jenny was having a terrible day, but she knew that she probably was having the time of her life. She clomped down the empty halls. Classroom doors were locked. Her echoing footsteps followed her.

"That's nice." Sarah rehearsed to her reflection in the exterior school door as she stepped out into the cold dreary afternoon. She tipped her head to the side and said it again, "That's nice. That's really nice." She spoke to the rearview mirror. "That's nice." The car seat was freezing, and the engine wouldn't turn over. It finally kicked in, but the heater wouldn't start working for another ten minutes. She'd be home by then. Shivering, she drove down Main Street and made a right turn into the gas station on Fourth North. As gas filled her tank and she washed the grit and salt off her windshield, she kept thinking about rope, giving difficult people plenty of rope, watching difficult people hang themselves with rope. She pulled into the carport and saw the tip of Einstein's nose, as the dog watched for her from the front window.

"Hey," Sarah said, sprawling on the couch before she bothered to take off her coat or hang her purse on the closet doorknob. As she patted him on the back and listened to his tail thump on the floor, she couldn't help wondering just how immoral a professional manicure really was. Appalled at the number of women who came to parent-teacher conferences with professionally applied talons painted absurd colors, she wondered how many starving children could be fed with the money those fingernails cost. She shook her head and sat for a moment before getting up to load a few dirty bowls into the dishwasher.

Something was dead in the refrigerator. She wrinkled her nose and gingerly picked past a couple of green peppers to a slimy cucumber. With two fingers, she picked up the edge of the plastic bag, but the troublesome cucumber slid out and rolled against the carrots. Wrapping it in a paper towel, she tossed it into the wastebasket. *Disgusting*, she thought. *I need to stop everything and clean the fridge, but one gross cucumber isn't enough motivation.* A lone, greenish hamburger patty that Sarah couldn't remember also seemed to be contributing to the odd odor, but Sarah slammed the door shut. Jenny had started to clean up the kitchen this morning before she left. That realization cheered Sarah for a moment, and she decided to make chocolate chip cookies.

She was sitting at the counter with a small bowl of raw cookie dough and a spoon when she heard the sound of a car door closing and saw Claire's white Jeep Cherokee pulling out of the driveway. Jenny came in through the back door absolutely shining. Her hair, dyed with blonde and red streaks, was as straight as a stick. Carrying two large shopping bags, *Abercrombie and Fitch* written on one, *J. Crew* on the other, Jenny had to turn sideways to get past the dog wagging his tail happily. *If he sees her hair, he'll go right under the bed*, Sarah thought.

"Rope, rope, rope," she sang softly as she spooned another glob of cookie dough into her mouth.

Jenny dropped the bags on the floor. "You've got to see this stuff, Mom."

"First, the feet!" her mother responded. "Go toes to head."

Jenny laughed. She pulled off her shoes and socks and displayed the light-pink polish and her soft heels now devoid of callus.

"Very nice," Sarah said, smiling.

"My feet have never smelled this good in my life. It took a whole hour, Mom." She paused for emphasis, and then held up her hands. Artificial nails had been applied to the sad little stubs of her fingernails and carefully sanded down to the tips. Jenny's cuticles had been softened and neatly trimmed. For the first time in her life, Jenny's hands looked pretty. Sarah wondered how long it would take Jenny to chew off all that acrylic, and if it was poisonous, whom she could sue.

"Very pretty. But sweetheart, why did you let them do that to your hair?" When she saw the expression on Jenny's face, Sarah wished that she had choked on a chocolate chip, but it was too late.

Jenny's perfectly manicured hand went up to what had been her dark, curly hair, which now had a halo of blonde and red streaks and highlights. The cut framed her face nicely, but the streaks were garish, and Sarah thought she looked cheap.

"Claire and the stylist told me it would be awesome, totally cool." The unfamiliar phrases tripped off her tongue. "I was terrified when the aluminum clumps came off, but they told me it would be fantastic." Her eyes filled with tears.

"Never mind," Sarah waved her hand in front of her face. "The really nice thing about hair is that it has a tendency to grow. If you're not pleased with what you have today, tomorrow will be different. Will it always be that straight?"

"Am I going to look like a freak at school tomorrow?" Jenny wailed.

"No, actually you're going to look like about a fourth of the girls I see every day in Sophomore English, but you're not going to be as unique as you were yesterday." She pushed a strand of hair away from Jenny's forehead. "It's a great cut. Very flattering. Now, show me the rest of your loot." Sarah grimaced. She had let some of the air out of Jenny's balloon, but Jenny shouldn't be impressed with this kind of foolishness. Could a daughter of hers be this superficial?

Jenny started to pull boxes out of one bag, and she proudly showed her mother shirts, blouses, and sweaters that coordinated perfectly with two skirts and a pair of jeans. A denim jacket, a variety of socks, barrettes, pretty silk lingerie, and an impractical pair of fabric ballet flats with embroidery on the toes came out of the second bag.

"My goodness, Claire bought one of everything," Sarah said.

"I think a couple of things were on sale."

"She must really want to make a good impression on you."

Jenny frowned at Sarah like, *Here it comes.* Her eyes clouded over, her smile vanished, and her index finger went right into her mouth, acrylic and all. "She'll never have any kids of her own," she whispered, "and she wants to be my friend. She doesn't want to be my mom, just my friend."

"Why would anyone want the responsibility of parenthood when she can buy friends with her unlimited plastic?" Sarah was being harsh and thought about ropes and the danger of dangling from one of her own, but ugly words seemed to leap out when she opened her mouth. "Do you remember who Claire is?"

"Mom, I've heard this a million times."

"Claire broke up our family. If it weren't for Claire, the five of us would be together, living in that big white house on the Boulevard. Your dad abandoned us when you were a year old because of Claire." Sarah poked her finger under Jenny's chin and lifted her face up so she could look in Jenny's eyes, not at the top of her streaked head. "You want that woman as a friend? Does your love and good opinion come so cheaply?"

Jenny looked over at the pile of adorable clothes on the counter. She slowly gathered up the new clothes that an hour ago had seemed so wonderful. Small dreams of wearing those clothes to school and having people include her started to fade. Without returning the things to their boxes, she pushed them gently into the bags, got down off the bar stool, and walked down the hall to her bedroom, but she turned, before closing her door, and looked hard at her mother.

"Aren't you always the one who says that you can't rewind the tape, that the only path is forward? I didn't do anything wrong. I don't even remember living in Iowa. I don't remember any of it. I only know what you've said."

"And, missy, your point is?"

"Maybe Dad didn't leave us because of Claire. Maybe he left because of you." Jenny shut her door, and Sarah heard the lock click.

She shoved a large spoonful of dough into her mouth and strained it through her teeth, chomping down hard on the chocolate chips. Then she threw the spoon as hard as she could across the room toward the sink. The spoon hit a glass, which exploded, sending shards of glass across the floor. Fuming, she grabbed a pencil out of a drawer, ripped a sheet of paper off a yellow legal pad, and wrote FOR SALE, ONE DAUGH-TER. She pawed through the drawer looking for a half-used roll of scotch tape. She covered the distance to Jenny's bedroom door quickly but didn't stop to listen to the muffled sounds of crying as she taped the sign under a little pink-and-white license plate and a couple of funny pictures that Jenny had stuck there in the fifth grade.

Leaving the rest of the cookie dough uncooked and uncovered, and broken glass all over the floor, Sarah grabbed an old parka and wrapped a thick, wool scarf around her neck as she called to Einstein. The wretched, murky weather was a fitting end to a rotten day. Sarah walked down the block and then turned east. The scarf itched and was too tight around her throat.

—⁕—

The next morning as Sarah hurried down the hall, the sign on Jenny's door was gone. Jenny was waiting for her in the front seat of the car, dressed in one of her new outfits. In spite of the cold, she was wearing the cunning little denim jacket and her hands were tucked under her legs.

hamburgers and basketball

$n$ew snow wasn't falling, but in the darkness the wind whipped through the trees and blew coats and gloves away from bits of exposed skin. Patrons arriving at the basketball game hurried through the heavy doors, stomping their feet and exclaiming against the cold. Sitting in the hallway outside the brightly lit gymnasium, Sarah got a cold blast every time the outer doors opened. She pulled her jacket around her shoulders more tightly. Her fingers were cold, but she couldn't see her breath and assumed death was not imminent. She was doomed, she thought, to a life of frozen ticket taking. Without thinking, she took money, passed over a ticket, and stamped a bear's head onto each person's hand. She wrinkled her nose at the smell of wet wool and bodies in close quarters.

Most nights, if no one was standing in front of the interior double doors, Sarah could see Tom warming up with the varsity team. Unfortunately, tonight was an important game, and people paused, watching in the doorway. Sarah craned her neck around both directions, but she still couldn't see what was happening in the gym.

She could see Mr. Crapo down the long hall, selling tickets. He waved pleasantly to her, and she smiled back. She had wished for the last half hour that she had his spot out of the draft, but when Bob and Claire came down the hall from the south entrance, she was grateful for her uncomfortable post. She didn't think they noticed her, but she saw them, every detail. Claire was in a light-blue down vest with a matching turtleneck, dark, tight-fitting jeans, and high-heeled boots. Sarah put her head down and wound the roll of tickets tightly, but not before she saw Bob guide Claire through the doors with his hand on her slim behind. *She must spend hours at the gym*, Sarah thought. She hoped that those boots would slip on the wet metal steps, and Claire would break her lovely neck. *With no neck*, Sarah thought, *what would hold up that bubble, covered with all that perfectly styled bleached-blonde hair?*

Her nasty interior monologue didn't make her feel better, so she tried to think about Tom and his chances of starting in tonight's game. It didn't work. She couldn't even distract herself with the wonderfulness of Tom. This little town was too small. She knew that every time people noticed the handsome—new to the community, and therefore, a big deal—Dr. and Mrs. Williams, they also turned to look at her. She was the other piece of the very old triangle, and she suffered in comparison. She was sure people looked at her, a faded, tired woman, and didn't blame her ex-husband for trading up. After all, he was a doctor in a small town, a demographic that was notorious for always having the latest model.

The buzzer sounded and the noise of ten boys pounding up and down the court came over the top of the crowd that had stopped moving to watch the beginning moments of the game. She couldn't see anything. She wanted to leave her desk, but people were still coming in. The more people came, the greater the crunch by the door.

The pudgy math teacher, Mr. Thorne, called to her, "Tom started."

So frustrating. Tom was starting, and she couldn't see anything. She stood up behind the kindergarten-size desk, but it did no good. Where did they find these things anyway? She wouldn't be able to see until the half was almost over. The crowd was starting to get noisy. The cheerleaders yelled their rhythmic chants, and Sarah strained to hear the announcer. The crowd roared in unison. Sarah thought she heard him say that Williams had scored three, but she wasn't sure, and no one turned around to tell her. Grousing to herself, she slumped down in her chair for the rest of the first quarter.

She picked at a bag of chips. Subsisting on junk food, cookie dough, and an occasional carrot made her complexion blotchy. Her fingers searched the interior of the bag. She turned it upside down and shook it. Nothing. She frowned. The door opened again, and the new blast of air sent a cold shudder down her spine. She looked into the bag, certain that a couple more chips should be in bottom.

"Did you lose someone?" A deep voice startled her, and she dropped the small sack.

"No, I didn't lose someone," she grumbled, turning around. There inside an industrial-strength coat with a large hood was Clayton McLaughlin. The tip of his nose was red and his eyes were teary from the cold, but he was smiling. How could this man be so perpetually pleasant? Was he impervious to crime and the horror of the human condition? Why didn't his occupation leave him emotionally maimed?

"Shouldn't you be investigating an accident or something instead of opening the door to freeze me?" She thought she should smile, but she was too cross.

"I don't know. You sort of look like an accident to me." Sarah opened her mouth, but he went on. "You've lost weight since last fall," he said, examining her face.

"You've got a lot of nerve," Sarah said.

He picked up the empty bag of chips. "Is this dinner?"

"Well, I left school to go to the JV game, I left the JV game to come and take tickets, and the vending machine doesn't offer a smorgasbord of hot culinary delights. And that is the reality of my life." She didn't need to be reminded that she was starving and that her skull showed beneath her skin.

"Stamp my hand," the sheriff insisted. "I'll be back." He looked at the door as though he had forgotten something, and then he walked back out into the cold.

Sarah could hear the second quarter start, but the knot of spectators at the door hadn't budged, and she wondered why they didn't just go in and sit down. She thought about using her head as a battering ram, getting a running start from the opposite side of the hall, and knocking them all into the gym. She thought about dragging her little desk over behind the knot and standing up on the top, so she could peer over their heads. She thought about loudly demanding her rights as a mother, but instead she withered back down in her chair.

Another late couple came into the hall. She sold them two tickets and thought the temperature must be dropping. *This is getting crazy*, she thought as the door opened again. She turned, glaring, only to see the sheriff. Still smiling broadly, he walked across the hall to a small office and retrieved a gray plastic chair. Opening the side of his large coat, he pulled out a brown paper sack.

"Hamburgers," he said.

"Oh." Sarah smiled because he clearly was intending to share. She didn't care how he had kept them hot. He laughed when she licked her lips and swallowed hard as he handed her a paper-wrapped parcel and a red-striped cardboard container of fries.

"Delicious," she exclaimed as she bit into a greasy French fry. She was a little dubious about the chocolate milk shake until she took a sip. It was wonderful.

"I thought about getting a pizza," he said, "but then I remembered . . ."

She looked up at him and stuck out her bottom lip. He was laughing at her. "I don't think it's very nice of you to remind me of that awful day. It's going to take at least five more years for that to even start being funny."

"Sorry," he mumbled, his mouth full.

"You're forgiven, I guess," she said, putting another French fry in her mouth.

A coach called for a time-out, and the pep band started to play. Sarah put the straw between her lips and drained the rest of the milk shake.

"I think I might live," she said. "It was touch-and-go there for a while."

"So, how's your year?"

"We're not having a very good year," she said, wondering why she chose to confide in this large man sitting beside her. "We're having some trouble in our varsity class."

"What kind of trouble?"

"Spoiled-rotten-kid trouble. It happens. Next year will be better." Sarah shrugged.

"Who are the kids?"

"I really shouldn't say." She added, "I think they're using drugs. That always complicates everything."

"What makes you think that?" Clayton set his drink on the edge of the desk. Sarah told him about her experience being an undercover cop. It had made her aware of the sad, little drug house. She always glanced at it as she drove by. Twice, she confided, she had seen the unnamed boy's blue truck parked in front.

"That's not a good sign."

"It's not a good situation. Kids using drugs always have more trouble with authority. Our relationship's been rocky all year. Drugs are just one piece." She stuck the last French fry into her mouth and looked into the carton with regret. "Can you see the clock?" she asked.

"No, but I think there are about four minutes left in the half. How long do you have to guard the door?"

"Until the half."

"Can I save you a seat?" He smiled and raised his eyebrows. She looked up at his rugged face and remembered Bob's hand on Claire's bottom.

"I need to stay in the lower northeast section. Can you find a spot there?"

"Isn't that a student section?"

Sarah nodded.

"I'll see how brave I'm feeling," he said. Sarah gave him a goofy half smile, and he made his way through the crowd standing near the door.

The girls from the drill team, costumed in glittering bright red spandex, marched off the floor after the half-time show and kept marching until they were out in the hall next to Sarah, where they promptly stopped. She thought they looked like a little group of self-important birds as they twittered to one another.

A petite blonde winked at Sarah and pursed her mouth into a well-practiced little rosebud. "Tom's having a great game. Tell him hi for me." Sarah smiled as the little dancer minced her way down the hall.

She tucked her money box under her arm and walked into the gym. Glancing up and down the rows in the northeast section, she felt a moment's disappointment. No Clayton. *I guess he wasn't feeling very brave,* she told herself, biting her top lip as she motioned to two junior boys to slide over.

She knew Jenny was behind her somewhere up in the second tier of seats. In an amazing moment the night before, Sarah had heard Jenny pick up the phone and call Dorothy for a ride. Not one to dismiss miraculous events, Sarah had said a small prayer of thanks and wondered if this newfound confidence came from streaked hair and mascara. Jenny had discovered makeup and now had the means to mask all her inadequacies. Sarah, looking for her daughter, scanned the hundreds of faces behind her, but the buzzer sounded, and she turned to see which boys were coming onto the court. Tom stayed on the bench.

Too bad, Sarah thought. *He must not have played well the first half.* But at that moment, the senior forward fouled the South Mountain guard. It was too early in the game to be in foul trouble, and Tom went in. Sarah leaned forward, her elbows on her knees. The boys ran down the floor, following the guard dribbling the ball, and there was Bob behind the basket. She couldn't believe it. Leaving Claire up in the bleachers, he was standing with a group of four or five other men too close to the basket. *What's he thinking?*

The gym was newer, the uniform shorts were longer, but the game was the same, and Bob was almost out on the floor with his son, right there, where Bob had been twenty-five years before. She could almost see seventeen-year-old Bob, see his sweaty arrogance as he played to the crowd, see him as he ignored the plays and took impossible shots, and see him grimace theatrically when he bounced off the floor. Somehow he restrained himself from mimicking the action as Tom went up for a shot. She was relieved. It was only when the buzzer sounded for a time-out, and the cheerleaders hurried onto the floor, that she saw him scan the bleachers for Claire's face. She couldn't help herself. She had to watch him. Did anyone notice? He had left Claire too long, but he would need to be there, close to the play, where everyone would see the resemblance and know he was Tom's father, Robbie's father.

The buzzer sounded. Tom threw the ball in and the guard brought it down. As the point guard crossed the mid-court line, Tom broke out to the wing and caught the pass. The bigger, slower defender was giving Tom plenty of room. Ignoring the coach's instructions to shoot only layups, Tom launched a twenty-five-foot jump shot that careened off the rim and was rebounded by the opposing team.

"Come on, Tom, get it inside!" the coach shouted as the teams ran toward the other end of the floor. Tom leapt up to block a shot and sent the defender flying into a couple of cheerleaders sitting under the basket. Tom hit the floor hard as the crowd roared, and the referee's whistle blew. Sure he was going to the foul line for the penalty shot, he looked stunned when the referee indicated a foul and turned the ball over to the other team. The crowd booed. Looking toward the bench, Tom held his arms up in a gesture of disbelief. The coach called time-out.

"Hansen, you're in for Williams. I want you guys to run the offense. Three or four passes, easy shots, no heroics."

"Great play, Tom! Lousy call, ref!" Bob yelled. Sarah rolled her eyes. Her palms felt damp. Tom and his friends on the bench turned toward Bob. The coach looked up from the arrows he was drawing on a small whiteboard and frowned. Bob was oblivious. Sarah put her hand on her forehead. Her eyes darted back and forth between her son and the antics of her ex-husband.

"So dumb," Sarah whispered quietly and shook her head, and then she noticed Tyler Colton, who was casually making his way behind the basketball standard over to the north section of bleachers. A small retinue slouched along in his wake, all very cool guys, two wearing sunglasses, none particularly interested in the game, but each wanting to be where things were happening and kids were congregating.

They worked their way up through the throng of students, past the pep band. Happily ignoring the cheerleaders' frantic attempts to get him to play a song that accompanied their routine, the student band leader seemed more excited about watching the close game than in beating time. Tyler and company circled behind the band, mixing in with the fluid motion of students. Tyler paused on the walkway beneath the top tier of seats and scanned the crowd. Sarah quit watching him and shrugged. Tom was in the game, and her attention was pulled to the play on the floor.

Tyler slowly made his way down the metal seats toward a group of freshman girls. Leaning over the railing, Brax and two other boys remained on the walkway. Jenny was sitting on the periphery of a clutch of freshman girls, who were seemingly arranged by their ability to shriek at the antics of two sophomore boys, or at the ball that skirted the rim of the basket and didn't fall in, or at any scandalous remark made by the three most popular girls, who were sitting right in the center of the group. Jenny desperately wanted to fit in, but just couldn't make herself shriek. Shrieking made no sense to her.

Tyler gently nudged a student over on the bench behind Jenny as Sharon Welling grabbed a ratty looking ski cap off the head of Cody

Jones, revealing messy hat hair. The girls shrieked almost in unison as the hat was stolen, and then shrieked again as Cody climbed over several slender bodies in an attempt to retrieve it, just as Sharon sent the hat sailing over the crowd. Jenny knew that particular hat had an importance beyond its ability to warm the ears of Cody Jones. His signature clothing item was worn continuously, with the exception of Mr. Watt's fourth-hour history class. Jenny witnessed the hat battle at least once a week, because Mr. Watts, completely old fashioned, thought young men should remove their hats in school.

Angry at the loss of the hat that identified him as a snowboarder, even if he was a basketball failure, Cody grabbed Sharon. With the help of his friend, he picked her up and attempted to throw her in the direction his hat had taken. The activity was accompanied by additional shrieking of a significantly higher pitch. The girls sitting closest to Sharon grabbed at her feet to save her from sailing out into the crowd. Jenny reached up her hands too, but she was too far down the row to help. Wistfully watching the mini-drama, she chewed the side of her finger, as the action seemed to push her further away in spite of her new clothes. Pointing and laughing, Dorothy, who was sitting next to her, said, "Sharon's going to have her leg broken if someone doesn't let go." The remark seemed obvious, and Jenny didn't know how to respond, so she was surprised to hear someone speak behind her shoulder.

"Who is that geek anyway?"

"Cody Jones," she answered automatically and then turned around.

"I say we shoot him." Tyler used his index finger to take aim at the obnoxious sophomore.

Jenny laughed. "He's not worth the jail time."

"Justifiable homicide." Tyler smiled down at her.

Why was he talking to her, smiling at her? Jenny looked at the tall, good-looking boy with startling blue eyes, and she immediately became tongue-tied.

Dorothy, eyes widening, looked over and pulled her little shoulder blades back, flaunting her curves, pushed up at an unnatural angle. "We'd all love it if you could get rid of Cody Jones. He's so immature," Dorothy gushed.

Tyler moved away from Dorothy and leaned over Jenny's left shoulder. "Does anyone up here ever watch the game?"

"I do. My brother plays."

"Who's your brother?"

"Tom Williams. He just got back in the game."

"That ref made a bad call. Tom's had a good game. I bet he'll see more playing time on Friday."

Jenny saw him watching the north entrance. He must be looking for other friends, maybe a girlfriend. Those blue eyes. Of course he'd have a girlfriend. As the buzzer rang for a time-out, he stood and turned to climb back up the rows, but before he left, he looked down at Jenny. "Hey, what's your name?"

"Jenny."

"See you later, Jenny." He smiled and blended back into the students making their way down to the vending machines.

Dorothy asked loudly over the noise being piped in for the cheerleaders, "Who was that?"

"I don't know. Some boy."

"You don't know him?" Dorothy said, suspicious, as though Jenny was intentionally withholding information. "Is he a friend of your brother's?"

"I've never talked to him before." Jenny grimaced at a quick memory from the beginning of school, but that was so long ago, and it didn't matter anyway. Dorothy spoke to Jenny three times before North Valley won the game. Sharon winked at her once as the hat saga continued. Jenny managed an odd noise, something between a screech and a groan, when Cody dropped dangerously to the floor below the bleachers to retrieve his precious hat.

Jenny was all smiles when she and Dorothy met Sarah at the end of the game for a ride home, in spite of the fact that her feet were freezing in her new ballet flats.

all the lonely people

O n a cold January morning, Claire had been sitting on a mat, stretching one calf and then the other, waiting for the instructor to arrive, when a woman ensconced in yellow spandex sat down next to her. Without much preamble, the woman asked, "So, how are you getting along with Sarah?" The woman had introduced herself at the previous session, but Claire couldn't remember her name.

"I never see Sarah."

"How can you miss her? She takes tickets at every high school game. I'm sure she sees you." The woman laughed knowingly.

Claire blushed and stammered something stupid. Then she saw two women, standing by the free weights, exchange knowing looks. She left class feeling isolated, homesick, and somehow tawdry. She hadn't been back in weeks, preferring to exercise in the basement with a videotape and hand weights.

Claire woke up every morning wondering how she had ended up here. What had someone said to her? It wasn't the end of the world, but you could see the end from here. Utah felt like a million miles away from Iowa. She'd been so optimistic about making a place for herself. She had found a gym and signed up for a mid-morning aerobics class that certainly would include other women her age. People had seemed friendly initially, but soon Claire realized they were just curious. Questions about the house surprised her until she discovered she and Bob had acquired a landmark. "The Widsoe house on the Boulevard," everyone called it. She'd thought it was just a nice old home with mature trees and a lot of potential. She knew now if she cut down a tree or changed an exterior paint color, it would cause a scandal. But the questions about Bob's children and the pointed asides about his ex-wife made her the most uncomfortable. And everyone knew Sarah. She was an institution at the only high school in town.

Not long after New Year's, a neighbor arrived at her back door on a sunny Saturday afternoon with a basket of fresh cinnamon rolls covered with a checkered cloth and a funny little homemade invitation to an "Enrichment Night" at the local church. The forty-ish woman plopped down at the kitchen table, ignoring the boxes and clutter, and chatted pleasantly.

"Don't let the name put you off," she said, flapping her hand. "It's really just a crafts night. Sometimes we do service projects. It's not a religious meeting," she had insisted. She laughed, telling Claire about a conversation with her husband. "He's so condescending," she confided. When he questioned her about what they would be making, she had told him, friends. "What's more important than that?" she asked Claire, smiling. She rattled on for several more minutes, telling Claire about people in the neighborhood, not needing more than a smile as encouragement.

Coming silently to the dining room door, Bob stood behind the neighbor, shaking his head slightly. Claire's pleasure drained away, and she felt a weary disappointment. "I can't really make any plans until I get out from under this mess. Maybe we could get together some morning next week for coffee—or juice?" she corrected herself quickly.

Noticing Bob, the neighbor hadn't seemed surprised when Claire declined the invitation. "Next week sounds good to me," the neighbor had said, but it had been weeks, and Claire hadn't talked to her again, although the woman waved pleasantly when driving her children to school or lessons.

"You start out painting blocks," Bob had explained seconds after the door had closed, "and the next thing you know, they'll have you teaching Primary."

"Would that be so bad?"

"Babe, you just don't get it." He returned to shelving his books in the study, and Claire picked up the phone, hoping one of her friends in Iowa would be home.

———

Jenny stayed with her father and Claire several times in January when her mother was on an overnight tournament, and after dinner her father would abandon "the girls," as he called them, so that they could watch a movie, or have a facial, or paint their toenails some unnatural color, all things Claire had done with her little sisters. Desperately homesick for her family, she found a natural object for her affectionate nature in the shy girl, but Jenny was reluctant, restrained. Claire was being held at arm's length.

Perhaps it was the furry little puppy that arrived wearing a pink bow Valentine's Day morning, or perhaps it was an isolated young girl and a lonely woman finally connecting, but whatever the reason, Jenny started to find her way after school to the house on the Boulevard.

———

After playing with the energetic little puppy all morning, Claire risked sending a note to Jenny at school.

Remembering the drill from her own high school, Claire called not the main office but the attendance secretary.

"This is Jenny Williams's stepmother. Would it be possible to send a note to her?"

A student answered, "Sure."

Claire sighed. What were the chances a student would tell Sarah she had called? "She's a freshman. I don't know her schedule."

"No problem. I can pull it."

"Could you just say that Claire has a new puppy? And does she have time to stop after school and help decide on a name?"

"What kind of puppy?"

"I think it's a cocker spaniel."

"I'll see that she gets the message. I'll send a runner right now." The student was suddenly businesslike.

Claire had a plate of lemon bars sitting on the kitchen counter when the front doorbell rang at two forty-five. Jenny stood outside the door, glancing over her shoulder at the street. She was chewing on a straggly lock of hair.

I need to help her with the new haircut, Claire thought. *Heaven knows her mother won't.* Brilliant Sarah wasn't smart enough to help her daughter fix her hair.

Claire put her finger to her lips as she opened the door. "Shhhh," she said, "the baby's asleep." Jenny, playing along, tiptoed in. She followed Claire into the warm kitchen and saw a straw basket filled with a pillow and a yellow flannel blanket. A puppy, curled in a little ball, slept soundly.

"Oh," Jenny exclaimed softly. She dropped her backpack on the floor and shook off her jacket. Vital information was shared over cookies and a coke: where the puppy had piddled, what she had chewed, how big was her litter, how she responded to being taken outside in the snow, and most important, was she really old enough to leave her mother? When the little dog didn't wake up and play, their conversation drifted to school, and Jenny described the dramas at lunch. Jenny was merely reporting because she was on the outside looking in, but Claire seriously pondered what Jenny was saying and asked questions about the principal actors, and Jenny supplied the details.

"What time do you need to be home?" Claire finally asked. Was the puppy going to sleep forever?

Jenny looked up at the clock. "I need to practice the piano for an hour before Mom gets home, but she'll be late. They're going crazy trying to get ready for Region."

"Let me show you something fun you can do with your hair," Claire said, nudging Jenny toward the bathroom. Shaking some product from a sleek blue bottle into her palm, she laughed at Jenny's reflection in the mirror. "You look like a drowned rat."

"I don't have much time in the morning, and it's been raining."

"Make time. The difference between looking great and looking blah," Claire tipped her head back and forth, "is about twenty minutes." She massaged the fluid into Jenny's hair and then pulled gently with a large brush and blower, until Jenny's hair curved softly around her face, and the streaks became highlights. "Awesome." Claire stood by the clothes hamper admiring her work. "Don't move; let's put a little color on your cheeks."

An embellished Jenny stood over the basket, looking at the puppy. Her eyelashes were darkened and her chapped mouth was a glossy pink.

"Can you give me a ride home?" she asked.

"Sure. Can you hold the baby on your lap?"

As they were driving up the hill, Claire remembered, "We didn't pick out a name. That was the last thing Bob told me to do before he left this morning."

"You don't want to hurry with a name. It has to be right."

Claire nodded. "That's what I'll tell your dad." She looked down Jenny's street to be sure Sarah's car wasn't in the driveway before she turned the last corner.

Jenny kissed her fingertip and touched the puppy's nose.

"Can I come by tomorrow?" Jenny asked as she got out of the car with a plastic bag containing Claire's extra blow-dryer and a bottle of finishing spray. "I'll be thinking of some names."

———

As the weather got warmer, Claire walked the little dog, Molly, the three blocks to the grassy park around the old granite tabernacle in the center of town and waited for Jenny to walk the two blocks from school. Claire didn't press Jenny for explanations the days she waited and Jenny didn't come. Claire smiled when she saw her and listened and laughed at whatever foolishness Jenny would describe and frowned when Jenny would haltingly describe being left out. When those hurtful stories were shared, Claire would hug Jenny, hold the puppy up to lick Jenny's face, rail against the injustice and shortsightedness of the offender, and describe a similar situation she had survived in high school. In her stories she made sure the villain always got her just desserts, and if Jenny raised her right eyebrow skeptically, Claire would laugh, "Well, that's what should have happened."

Sitting on a small wrought-iron bench, as the puppy gamboled about, Claire would watch small groups of girls, twos or threes, meandering down Main Street. They would gawk in the store windows or stop at the Bluebird for jellybeans or a couple of chocolates delivered in a pale-blue sack. Claire wished Jenny would bring a friend to meet the little puppy, but Jenny always hurried along alone, her face paying careful attention to the cracks in the sidewalk. One blustery March day, Claire, the wind whipping her hair around her face, was surprised to look up and see Jenny arriving in a truck driven by a good-looking young man with blond hair and startling blue eyes.

you can't say you can't play

Several weeks after the mock trial season began, Tom was driving his dilapidated truck up the Boulevard and giving some serious thought to the defendant, DeVon Kelmar, who claimed that post-traumatic stress disorder was the reason he had gunned down Cory Jackson. Tom frowned. It was going to be tough to prove, particularly within the strict time limits. He was trying to envision the scene in the parking lot after a high school basketball game where the murder occurred.

He wasn't sure why he had started driving home up the Boulevard. Fourth North was more direct, but the Boulevard was a pretty road. Trees lined the street, and older, more graceful homes stood elegantly on wide lawns. A pale-green suggestion of leaves covered the lofty trees whose branches almost touched as they reached across the road.

Tom never stopped. His dad was at work, and he had no interest in a friendship with Claire. Nothing a dope like Claire had to say could interest him. But he was surprised to see a blue truck parked in the driveway of his father's home, so he pulled over. He sat in his truck, looking at the house, and wondered what Tyler Colton could be doing there.

Tyler was trouble, trouble Tom was going to have to deal with soon. Matt Swaim had told him on Monday that Tyler was paying attention to Jenny. Tom had blown Matt off, but when he had looked at his friend's face, Tom knew something was up.

"What are you talking about? Tyler Colton and Jenny? That doesn't add up," Tom had protested as they drove to soccer practice.

"Hey, it doesn't make any sense to me either," Matt agreed, "but no kidding, I saw him walking with her down by Howell's classroom. I asked my little sister about it. She said they were going out."

Tom guffawed. "They're not going out. My mom would kill Tyler first and then lock Jenny in the basement. It just wouldn't happen. Besides, who's less Tyler's type than Jenny? You saw that girl he had at the Christmas dance. Scary." That remark ended the conversation because Jenny was an innocent, painfully shy girl. Neither Tom nor Matt had any use for Tyler Colton, and they were glad to talk about anything else, but the seed had been planted, and when Tom saw the blue truck, he was puzzled. Several minutes passed before it occurred to him that Jenny might be inside the house also. She was always home when he arrived after school.

Tom didn't relish confrontation. When Robbie would plow head-first into trouble, Tom trailed two steps behind. His role had been wing-man, and he wished Robbie were here now and not a continent away. But Tom was the best brother Jenny had at this particular moment, and he slowly opened the truck door and stepped down onto the strip of grass. He wasn't sure how this would play out, and he thought quickly about the murder in the mock trial case and wondered with a grim smile if Tyler carried a knife or a gun.

Tom was big, broad, and muscular, but his real strength was the grin that played on his face and his easygoing manner. He decided, as he rang the doorbell, that he would get rid of Tyler somehow, and then he would reason with Jenny. He'd appeal to her intelligence, and he wished, as he waited by the door, that Estee were around to tell Jenny the truth about Tyler Colton.

Tom rolled his eyes as the doorbell played "Take Me Out to the Ball Game" and Claire bounced into the entry. Astounded to see Tom, she recovered quickly and invited him in to the kitchen.

"We're making cookies," she chirped. "Come on back." The kitchen was in the rear of the house, and a large-paned window looked out over a brick patio and enclosed yard. Tyler was sitting at the oak table in front of the window. His long legs were stretched out across the floor. A tall class of milk, half empty, stood on the table beside his hand, and a cookie was sticking out the corner of his mouth. Seeing Tom, he sat up abruptly and swallowed hard. Jenny's back was turned to both of them, Tom in the doorway and Tyler at the table, and she was reaching for a spatula in the drawer. Immediately struck by the ease with which Jenny knew her way around this kitchen and Tyler's relaxed stance, Tom knew this little tableau had been played out here before.

"Look who's here," Claire sang in a nervous soprano to the occupants of the kitchen, including the sparkling dishes and red enameled pots and pans. "Tom must have smelled the cookies from the street." So pleased to have Tom stop by unannounced and uninvited, her smile enveloped her entire face. She moved quickly to the large sub-zero refrigerator to get him a glass of milk. Seeing Jenny's face blanch, she exclaimed, "Jenny, what's wrong, honey?"

Jenny was caught, not red-handed doing something wrong, but caught in a situation, pleasurable and unexpected for a girl who had few friends and no illusions about ever being popular. Her eyes widened and she dropped the spatula on the floor. Claire, beaming in her crisp blue shirt, turned with the jug of milk in her hand and tipped her head at Tom as though he were her favorite high school beau.

"I need to take Jenny home." He grinned at Tyler and nodded his head slightly. Tyler glowered up at him. No one was eating cookies. No one was engaging in the easy flirtatious banter that Claire had been modeling for Jenny. Claire's forehead wrinkled, and she slowly turned back to the refrigerator and set the milk on the shelf next to the lettuce crisper. She gave Tom a quizzical look and stooped to pick up the spatula Jenny had dropped.

"Oh, come on, Tom. Just one cookie?"

Did she think one cookie passing into his mouth would ease all the tension in her perfectly decorated kitchen? Tom knew her Martha Stewart after-school moment was being spoiled, but he just shrugged. She smiled at him and bounced her shoulders up and down in a practiced manner. *Give it up*, he thought. *You're not a cheerleader, and you're not cute.*

Tom didn't have time for Claire, her chocolate chip cookies, or her red enameled pots and pans. He gazed intently at his sister, and then he turned and locked eyes with Tyler before he spoke. "I'll take Jenny home. I'm sure you've got things you need to be doing."

"Oh, Tom," Claire wheedled, "sit down. No one needs to leave yet."

He ignored her.

The boys stared at each other. No way Tom was going to blink first. He waited, gauging Tyler's reaction. He'd never seen Tyler back down, but he usually had his little gang in tow, and this afternoon he was alone. Tyler slowly finished eating his cookie before he stood up languidly from the table.

"Yup," he said as though it had not been minutes since Tom had spoken, "I've got places to go and people to see." He turned to Jenny. "Call me tonight if you get a minute."

"Don't hold your breath," Tom said gruffly. Jenny didn't say a word. Her eyes were open wide and her hand, holding the oven mitt, trembled.

"Later," Tyler said with a contemptuous smirk. He sauntered through the dining room, but the front door slammed behind him, and the three people standing silently in the kitchen heard the sound of his tires squealing as he accelerated down the street.

Jenny's bottom lip quivered. "He'll never come back," she whispered at Tom. "It's over."

Tom didn't understand. In Jenny's head the small beginnings of social status and inclusion had vanished out the door with Tyler. Tears filled her eyes as she looked at her brother, the student body officer and athlete, who couldn't possibly understand what he had just done.

"Let's go home, Jenny." Tom said quietly, seeing that his sister was on the verge of a meltdown.

Claire looked between the brother and sister and shook her head. "Someone needs to explain what's going on here."

Tom sighed heavily. "Jenny and I need to leave." Large tears were starting to roll down Jenny's cheeks. He nodded at his little sister, and she tried to collect her belongings, but the tears were falling more rapidly, and she looked stupidly around the room. Tom picked up her backpack and located her jacket where it had fallen behind a chair. He put his hand on her shoulder and guided her down the hall, but the storm broke before he could get her out the front door, and they both sat on the bottom step of the stairway. He could smell the new wallpaper and felt the crush of expensive carpeting under his feet. They didn't belong here. He put his arm around her, and she buried her face in her jacket and sobbed, her heart broken into a million irretrievable parts.

"Jenny, none of this makes any sense," he whispered. He wasn't sure where to go with this and wished again Estee were here to explain.

"He doesn't go for girls like you. You know what I mean. Nice girls won't go out with him." He was repeating the conversation with Matt, but Jenny wasn't having it. She just cried harder. He tried a new tactic. "Jenny, he and his friends are all stoners. You don't want to be there when they're getting high. That's not what you're about." She looked up at him with black streaks of mascara running down her cheeks, and she clearly didn't believe a word he was saying.

"Geez, Jenny, look at how he's behaved to Mom. Meg and Mom can't stand him. He's ripped their team in half. Mom would have a fit if she knew what was going on here."

"But look at all the things Mom told us about Dad," Jenny cried into her jacket, "and they weren't true. Dad's great, and Claire's not a monster. Mom could be just as wrong about Tyler." The sobs continued, and Tom wondered how he was ever going to get her home and cleaned up before his mother arrived.

"Look, Jenny," he whispered insistently, "nothing Dad says or does now can change the fact that he left us, three little kids, and Mom. He left us, Jenny, with no money. That's pretty rough, and Claire played a big part in all that. I mean, that's just the bottom line."

"Are you going to tell Mom?" Jenny jerked out her question between sobs.

"No way. If you haven't noticed, Mom is just about at the end of her rope. She doesn't need any of this." He chose his words carefully, looking over his shoulder toward the kitchen. "And what's all this buddy-buddy stuff with Claire? What are you thinking? You need to treat her with respect when you have to be over here, but . . ."

"You're wrong about Claire," Jenny protested, as the heaving sobs became more sporadic. "She's nice. It isn't always push, push, push. Being with her is fun. It's fun to go shopping. Do you know what it's like to go shopping with Mom? There are two rules: cheap and ugly. That's it. If it's not on the sixty-percent-off sale rack, forget it."

"Jenny," Tom whispered again, "have you ever stopped to think what would have happened to us if Mom had left us the way Dad did? What if she had gotten tired of three little kids and decided to do something she wanted? What if she had just walked away and gone to Europe? We'd have grown up in foster care." He grabbed Jenny's possessions. He had a break in the storm, and he wanted to make a run for it.

No one in the house had heard Bob come in because the house was old, and the garage wasn't attached. He walked in the back door and through the dining room. He saw Claire eavesdropping and chewing the edge of a dish towel, tears running down her face, and he saw Hansel and Gretel sitting on the bottom stair, lost in the woods. He shook his head before he walked over quietly to Claire and pushed her toward the kitchen. Then he strode into the living room.

"Who died?" he asked quietly. "I mean besides John Lennon and Kennedy."

Tom gave him a wry smile. "No one died, and we're on our way home." Tom stood with all the dignity his seventeen years could muster and said, "Jenny, wait for me in the truck, would you please?"

"Well, I would like to talk to both of you, if you don't mind." Bob was quietly emphatic, but Tom didn't budge.

"Jenny, the truck." He nodded toward the door. She gathered her things quickly and scooted past him.

"Hold on. Tom, who's the parent here?"

Tom didn't respond because he felt like the role of father had been dumped on him, and he didn't particularly like the additional weight. Finally he said, "Look, I'll be straight. Jenny's been seeing this guy, Tyler, here, at your house." There was almost a drum roll and a scene of the crime placard. He didn't accuse his father of being an accessory, but he wanted to. "The guy's a complete jerk and not someone Jenny should ever be around."

"I've met this kid a few times, and I don't think he's a bad sort."

"Look, Mom's had this kid in debate for three years, and he's always causing trouble."

"So this is about your mom?"

"No, this is about Jenny."

"How about if we trust Jenny to make some of her own decisions? She seems to like this kid."

"I mean it, Dad. This stops now, today." Tom was dying to say, "Or I'll tell Mom," but he knew that would be a mistake. "You've got to trust me on this one. I know this kid. Really, he's not okay." He had pulled out all the stops. He didn't know how to be any more emphatic, but he could see his dad was getting his back up. The more he said, the less his father would be inclined to go along with him. He turned and went out the door and walked across the lawn to his truck. Jenny was waiting on the front seat.

"Please start," he said under his breath as he put the key in the ignition. He couldn't imagine anything worse that having to get out and push the truck to get it going with his father watching out the front room window.

The engine turned over, and Tom sighed in relief. He put the truck in first gear and slowly pulled away from the curb. There was no screeching of tires. Tom knew how much tires cost.

—∿∿—

That night, not expecting any help from his father or Claire, Tom brought in heavy reinforcements. He took the handset downstairs after he got home and called Estee. Listening to Jenny practicing the piano in the background, he took half an hour to tell Estee about the disaster that afternoon, how worried he was about Jenny, how much he hated Tyler Colton, how ballistic his mother would be if she knew, and how clueless his father was. Estee signed on to help, and after dinner, Tom and Estee took Jenny out to get a milk shake and gave her the full-court press. Tom was encouraged. He couldn't conceive of anyone not being persuaded by Estee, and he smiled and squeezed her hand as he dropped Estee off at her house.

"This is all going to be okay," he told Jenny. "You'll meet someone else, and this will all just be a dumb thing you did when you were a freshman." Jenny tried to smile. She really did want to please Tom, but she knew what he said wasn't true. Tom felt like the problem was resolved. Jenny was on board. Tyler was history.

But Tyler wasn't on board, and he was only history for a week. How could Tom know that Jenny had been keeping track of time in relation to the blow-up? Three days since the blow-up. Five days. Seven days since she had seen Tyler. She was training herself not to look for his blue truck. She was careful to avoid the halls by his classes.

On the ninth day, post blow-up, after fourth hour, she found a note wedged in the crack in her locker door.

I need to talk to you. I'll meet you at the corner by the Tabernacle after school.

—∿∿—

Jenny didn't have a best friend she could ask for advice. She thought of finding Estee, but she didn't want to hear what Estee would say. She was afraid that Tyler might be unpleasant and accuse her of being a wimp. She was a wimp. After school she followed the crush of students to the front entrance and down the main steps to the area where four large yellow school buses transported the totally uncool kids who didn't have friends with cars.

She started to stand in line, but her feet just seemed to change direction on their own, and she found herself walking to the tabernacle grounds. Tyler drove up moments later and held open the door. He had a handful of daisies on the empty passenger seat, but the broad smile on his face lacked warmth, and she wondered if she should get into the truck with him.

arresting developments

Sarah fingered the business card in her hand, flipping it over ner-vously as she waited for someone to answer the phone. After huffing over her shoulder to Meg that it was a good thing she wasn't being held hostage in a bank robbery, a secretary finally answered, "Sheriff's office."

"Hi, this is Sarah Williams. Could I talk to the sheriff for just two seconds?" She stood flipping the business card until she heard Clayton's voice. "Hi," she said. "I wondered if you had a couple of min-utes to answer some questions for me about our mock trial case. It's a murder, which is a lot of fun, but I have a couple of questions about fingerprinting and the trajectory of bullets—you know, stuff like that. A policeman is one of our characters, and they always end up being the secondary defendant." She slowed momentarily for a breath, and Clayton laughed.

"I'm in the middle of a meeting right now."

"Oh, I am so sorry."

"Don't be. When are you through with school?"

"Around four," Sarah answered, embarrassed at having interrupted him.

"Can you stop by my office on your way home?"

"Or I could just talk to you on the phone."

"No, I'd like to look at your materials."

"Well, I'll see you at four then." Sarah hung up the phone and turned back toward Meg. "He wants to see my materials." She raised her eyebrows and laughed wickedly.

"I'll bet he does. It's only taken you six months to figure that out." Meg moved the apple sitting on top of the mock trial booklet and flipped through the pages until she found the witness statements. Taking a healthy bite, she chewed for a moment, and Sarah wondered if she was going to be questioned about the sheriff or the case.

Meg swallowed. "Have you cast this little drama yet?"

"No, but I'm close. I've got the issues laid out." Sarah changed the direction of the lunchtime conversation. "Do you know what my hair stylist said to me Saturday?"

Meg raised her eyebrows.

"She asked me if I ever wore any makeup."

"Really?" Meg said, not knowing where this was going but wondering if the final destination might be Clayton's office at four o'clock.

"Yes. I told her I did, but not when I was going somewhere to put my head in a sink." Sarah grimaced. "But her implication was clear. She was hinting, rather broadly, that I would be improved by a little paint. What do you think?"

"You know what they say about old barns?"

"No, I don't know what they say about old barns."

"Well, even old barns look better with a fresh coat of paint." Meg sucked in her cheeks to keep from laughing.

"So now I'm an old barn?"

"No, I would say that you're an almost-middle-aged barn, and I think you should gain ten or fifteen pounds." Meg was having fun with her analogy. "However, all things considered," she started, as Sarah pulled a little mirror out of the lost-and-found box and examined her face, "I think your materials are in pretty good shape."

Sarah picked up the mock trial booklet and flapped it in Meg's direction.

—⁓—

At five minutes past four, Sarah arrived at the sheriff's office. The door into the interior office was open, and before Sarah could give her name to the secretary, Clayton walked out and extended his hand.

"So, tell me about this really fun murder. None of the murders we investigate could be classified as fun. I don't even have a file for fun murders." He led her into his office, closed the door firmly, and gestured toward a chair that faced his desk. The head of a stuffed deer with large brown marble eyes looked down at her. Another animal head—she thought it was some sort of mountain sheep—glared blankly down from the north wall. She stared at both of them for a moment.

"What did they do?" She pointed at the mounted heads. "Rob a fish and game office? I think stuffing a defendant might constitute cruel and unusual punishment."

"Well, I guess you could characterize them as recreational murders." He laughed and Sarah found herself smiling and apologizing for characterizing a murder as fun.

"But it's a great case. The kids love a good murder." Sarah stopped and laughed again. "Good murder. I'm sorry; my mind set is just different from yours."

"Is this the case?" Clayton reached for the small blue booklet that Sarah had placed on the large desk, cluttered with folders, an empty soda can, and two well-used blue volumes.

"It really is interesting, particularly for high school students. They're written to appeal to kids. One boy's been harassing the other. He almost ran down the perpetrator in the parking lot after a ball game. He threatens him in class and bullies him in the halls. Finally, the boy who's being harassed brings a gun to school to defend himself, supposedly because the bully always carries a knife." Sarah stopped to catch her breath.

Clayton looked up from perusing the booklet and nodded for her to continue. "Kendall thinks that the bully is going to knife him, and so he shoots him with a handgun. Kendall's defense is that he's suffering from post-traumatic stress syndrome and was acting in self-defense. Unfortunately for Kendall, the bully wasn't carrying a knife, and the prosecution has a good case for premeditation."

"So it's not clear cut."

"Oh, the cases are never clear cut. On first reading it always seems like the cases are slanted to one side, but they never are."

Clayton left the booklet open to the policeman's affidavit and leaned back in his chair. "You've gone over this pretty carefully. What can I do to help?"

The booklet was underlined in several colors, notes were scribbled in the margins, and several questions were jotted on the top of the page. She wiggled uncomfortably. Did he think she had cooked up a reason to see him? She took a few deep breaths to calm down and keep from making a mad dash out the door. Pulling the yellow legal pad out of her bag, she flipped over to the list titled, "Questions for Sheriff." The title was underlined, and the questions were neatly numbered.

"The first is about the bullet exit and entry positions in the body. It's really going to be a problem that this kid shot the gun three times. We're wondering if the position of the victim's arm is defensive. Could one bullet cause two injuries? The second is how easily a semi-automatic weapon fires repeatedly. No one in the class has any experience with guns, thank heaven. Then any technical questions that the officer would be expected to know makes the character seem more credible and, consequently, gets us more points."

Clayton nodded at her again and turned to the officer's statement. He discussed the behavior of the police officer, and Sarah took notes on a clean page. When he got to the medical examiner's report and diagram, he paused, analyzing the sketch of the body. Looking up, he caught her, pencil in hand, studiously watching him, and he laughed. She frowned, not understanding the joke. Mock trial was serious business, and she had been thinking about this case for the last two weeks.

"I'm sorry, Sarah," he said giving her name a pleasant lilt. "You don't strike me as person who would get into all this true crime stuff, to say nothing of the gore and mayhem."

Sarah had started to relax. "Oh, I'm not, but I'm all about winning. Plus, this really is a wonderful educational tool. Kids have to write, and speak, and think on their feet. They've all either experienced or witnessed bullying at school, so the issues are real. It's really a good thing." She paused. "It's good for me too. It stretches my mind a little. The cases are different each year, and of course, it's a different bunch of kids. It's not like teaching *To Kill a Mockingbird* year after year after year. I love that book and save it for February and March, the dead months, but it's still the same old thing."

Gradually their conversation turned from business to chitchat. Sarah found herself talking freely, something she rarely did with anyone except Meg. She thought what she was saying was interesting to Clayton. She didn't realize that anything she said would be interesting to him, because he was interested in her, watching the animation in her face, the tilt of her head, the motion of her hands. She rested a finger on her bottom lip, as Clayton said that his son's progress in school was a worry. It was apparent to them both that he needed to turn off the video games and pick up a book, but the boy didn't enjoy reading, and Clayton didn't like to nag.

"Oh, don't think that you can be a friend to kids this age. They need a parent, someone to create boundaries. It really is scary. A fif-teen-year-old is making decisions that a thirty-year-old is going to have to live with."

Clayton nodded. "Home was always downtime for me. Not any-more. Now coming to the office is a relief, and this isn't a low-stress occupation. Some days are quiet, but others can be intense."

"Do you have any help with the nuts and the bolts at home?"

"Actually, I do. My daughter comes over twice a week. She cleans a little and does the laundry, and that helps." Clayton admitted. "The kids have really held together pretty well." He paused. "I saw a thera-pist, a grief counselor, for a couple of months after my wife died, and he pretty much said that the kids will do as well as I do."

"What a luxury," Sarah said, "to be able to grieve for a spouse and not just dislike him intensely."

He leaned forward over the desk and studied her carefully. She was suddenly conscious of a small orange juice stain on the front of her sweater and wondered how much her hair had expanded during the course of the day.

"Jenny's the one I worry about," she said.

"Jonathan says she a nice girl."

"Right now she's so confused by her father moving back to town that she doesn't know which way is up. Her stepmother's filled her head with makeup and clothes and turned Jenny into a wannabe cheerleader type."

"And that's bad?"

"It's awful. She's losing any sense of self and trying to be something she's not. What am I going to do with a really smart girl who suddenly wants to be a piece of fluff?" Sarah pressed her fingers to the sides of her head and sighed. It suddenly occurred to her that she might have put her foot in her mouth. "Are you a fan of cheerleaders?" She remem-bered somewhere in the back of her brain that he had two older daugh-ters, and she wondered if she needed to cook up a quick apology.

He smiled. "Would you like a donut?"

Now it was her turn to laugh. She turned her head sideways, fluttered her eyelashes, and patted her chest lightly. "Oh, be still my heart."

He smiled, unsure of the joke. He reached up to the top of his filing cabinet and lifted down a box of Krispy Kreme donuts. It had been several long hours since the apple and half a tuna fish sandwich she had eaten for lunch.

"You know, I never met a donut I didn't like." Sarah appreciatively picked out a donut covered with chocolate frosting. She chewed thoughtfully and sighed. "Do you always have a stash?"

"No, the secretary had to go to the post office." He casually explained that refreshments were not something he usually offered visitors, particularly if they were wearing handcuffs. Sarah laughed and popped the last bite into her mouth and started to put her legal pad back into her bag. She was tempted to take another donut, this time one with caramel icing, but restrained herself. Clayton watched her preparing to make her getaway.

"Can I keep this for a couple of days, maybe over the weekend? I have some ideas, but I'd like to think about it for a while." Clayton closed the cover of the booklet and walked from behind his desk.

"That would be great." Sarah smiled to indicate just how great it would be.

Without any warning, he put his large warm hands under both of her arms and lifted her up, with very little effort, onto a couple of thick volumes sitting on the top of his desk. She was almost at eye-level with Clayton, but felt precariously positioned and at a significant physical disadvantage, and there was no graceful way to extricate herself.

"So that was your plan," she laughed nervously. "You got me here under false pretenses to ply me with donuts and have your way with me." Her eyebrows were raised and her tone was an odd mix of indignation and flirting. Clayton's face was uncomfortably close. She thought for a minute that he was going to kiss her, and in the next instant, she thought that it had been too many years since anyone had kissed her, and she was woefully out of practice, but who was this guy to put the moves on her uninvited? Bombarded with conflicting emotions, her palms started to sweat. But he didn't kiss her; he put his head back and laughed loudly, and Sarah took a quick nervous look toward the outer office.

"No, I'm not going to have my way with you." His look was so warm and his voice was so gentle that Sarah felt disappointed. "I'm lonely, Sarah Williams, and I would very much like to be your friend. I would like to have someone to go to the movies with, or talk to when my kids are driving me crazy, or sit with at games, or eat a pizza with, or whatever. You know, friend stuff." He lifted her chin up softly with his finger so he could look in her eyes, and Sarah thought, *Here it comes.* But a kiss was not in the offing. Instead he continued, "What do you think? Is a friendship with me anywhere in your future?"

She knew the best answer was a simple yes, but she was suddenly frightened. Her heart started to pound, and her cheeks felt flushed. Maybe he thought he was asking her to take a very small risk, but it wasn't small to her. It was enormous, and she hedged.

"My life is going to be nuts until the trials are over. They're on the weekends in Salt Lake usually. I work with attorney-witness teams every night." Her voice trailed off, as she saw the embarrassment in his face. "We finish on May 1, Law Day, you know. Can I call you then?" She was giving herself a little time and him a little hope. "Is that okay with you?"

He didn't speak for a couple of moments, and then he said, "Sure." But it didn't sound like sure, and Sarah wished she could backpedal, but she really was crazy busy during mock trial season. He just stood there for a moment, and finally Sarah gave him a funny sort of half smile and said, "If you're going to keep me up here, you should probably have me stuffed too." She looked down at the distance to the floor. A slight smile returned to his face, and he lifted her gently down. Suddenly, leaving just seemed like the entirely wrong thing to do. What she really wanted was to bury her face in his chest. She wanted to hide from obnoxious students and their parents, and her ex-husband and his pretty wife, and Jenny's insurmountable shyness, and the scarcity of money, and all the other slings and arrows that always seemed to come her way.

But she didn't. She squared her thin shoulders, slung the straps of her bag over her left arm, and extended her right hand. "Thank you so much," she said, "for the donut and the help and everything. I really will call you, May 1."

He nodded at her and smiled. "Would you like me to send you my ideas in a memo? Maybe a fax?"

She dropped her chin and studied her shoes. "Yes, it is true. I am a very dumb, smart person, a lethal combination." She shook her head. "I'm just on overload and not thinking clearly. I really do need your help."

"I'll meet you. Next week. Thursday night, neutral location, seven-thirty. How about the Bluebird? We'll probably have the place to ourselves."

She turned to leave when he caught her arm and kissed her on the cheek.

"For luck," he said. "Your cheek's warm."

"Luck? Kissing non-relatives is not something I typically do. I don't count being accosted by a very strange geometry teacher in the faculty lounge on my thirty-fifth birthday. I mean, who would count that? He was a bow-tie type with lots of hair . . ." She pointed to her nostrils and her ears. "The really scary part is he thought he was doing me a favor, like maybe I needed to be serviced." She shuddered, her hands fluttering, before she headed out the door and left the sheriff leaning against his desk, laughing.

interceptions

$\mathcal{A}$lmost April. Sarah rolled her shoulders and extended her arms. She scanned the classroom of young faces reading and she smiled. She had survived. It had been close, but she made it. Tyler and Brax would soon be long gone. Only two months left in the school year. She always saved *Romeo and Juliet* for the spring. It was perfect for sophomores. They were just as crazy and hormone-driven as Romeo and his friends. That was the point she was trying to make second hour on a beautiful, warm day.

"So, let's forget, for just a minute, that Romeo is a character Shakespeare created four hundred years ago. Is he real? Do any of his behaviors ring true?" She deftly acknowledged the hands that habitually went up with a quick smile and called instead on students whose hands were lying comfortably in their laps. "Jorge, then Micah, then Andy. We'll go in that order, and then we'll open this up to anyone." She repeated the question. "Do any of his behaviors seem real to you? Have you ever behaved like Romeo? Have you ever seen any of your friends behave like Romeo? Jorge, what do you think?"

The boy near the back of the room paused for a minute and then pushed his dark hair away from his forehead. "Well, you always want to have your friends around."

"Okay, boys seem to travel in groups, maybe packs? What about girls? Do they travel in groups? Did Juliet?"

Amy, a girl with a pretty face coated with a thick layer of makeup, raised her hand and started to speak before being called on. "Juliet might have been with friends at the party." Sarah gestured for the girl to continue. "But I don't think they let girls go out in public like the boys did. After she and Romeo got serious, she doesn't seem to have anyone her own age to talk to. Just the nurse."

"Does Romeo confide in his friends about how serious he is about Juliet? What do you think, Micah?"

Micah sat up a little straighter in his desk. "No, his friends would think he was crazy. He was just in love with that other chick on the way to crash the party."

"Good point." Sarah tried to look impressed even though she had listened to this same discussion dozens of times. "What's driving this relationship? In a couple of days, these kids are going to be married. Do things happen this quickly? What do you think, Andy?"

Andy was not the best choice for that particular question because he had been involved in several quick relationships and had been shaving every morning since Halloween. Boys in the back of the room snickered.

Andy huffed as though the question were a no-brainer. "Sure things can be that quick, but people don't get married. That's dumb."

"Okay," Sarah picked up the ball, "you're saying that Romeo is totally motivated by his raging hormones. Did you know that the average adolescent male has a sexual fantasy every thirty seconds? How much of your own behavior is driven by the need to impress or attract the opposite gender?"

Andy shrugged.

A hand waving in the second row caught Sarah's attention. Sarah nodded and Lizette, a redheaded girl, started to speak. "But he died! He thought Juliet was dead, and he killed himself. That's not about hormones; that's about true love."

"Okay, Lizette and Andy are coming at this question from two different perspectives. Romeo is about your same age. What fits? What doesn't?" Sarah was getting ready to make the assignment when another hand shot up on the right side of the room.

"Mrs. Williams, it's only been seventeen seconds, not thirty!"

Sarah started to laugh. Clearly it was a mistake to encourage the class clown, but she couldn't help it. Her laughter was the signal to the class that it was okay for them to laugh too. Tears spilled out of her eyes, and she sat down on the riser to catch her breath.

"Oh, Jeremy, we don't want any details," she said.

With an intermittent giggle, she told the class they had fifteen minutes to create a concept web for their papers and turn them in to her. "Okay, pencils need to be moving." She pushed the class to begin and not just pack up their belongings and stare immobilized at the clock.

Two girls in the middle of the room wrote furiously. Using a bright pink marker with sprinkles of glitter on the shaft, one girl carefully covered her notepad with her web. The paper underneath was written in highly stylized printing. Small pink hearts dotted every *i*. The girl looked around the room carefully for her teacher. Discovery would mean instant and painful death. She pulled the top sheet down near the tip of her pink pen.

She tucked the note inside the sophomore literature survey and passed it across the aisle to her friend. She raised her eyebrows up and down significantly. Meghan took the hint and cracked the book open to the page with the slight edge of paper and pink ink showing. She read the note quickly and nodded across the aisle.

Sarah noticed the exchange from her vantage point at the back of the room. She should chastise the girls—neither was a particularly good student—but she vacillated when she saw two minutes left on the clock.

"Put your webs on the front desk," she called out over the sudden noise of students stuffing backpacks and bags. "I'll hand them back tomorrow before we head to the writing lab."

She walked down between the desks, leaned over Meghan, and whispered in her ear. "Let's see what's more interesting than your assignment." Meghan fluttered, trying to make her book evaporate, but nothing worked. The grim expression on Sarah's face was not to be denied. She handed her book over to Sarah, who deftly pulled the note out of the second act of *Romeo and Juliet*. Without reading the note, she folded it in half and stuck it in her pocket. The bell rang and Sarah pointed to the door.

"Tomorrow, no note writing. Do I make myself clear?"

Meghan nodded, her eyes wide and unblinking. She was having a near death experience; she knew the minute Mrs. Williams read that note, her life on the planet would end.

Meghan grabbed her friend's arm, as they hurried out to the hall, and whispered loudly, "I'm not coming to class tomorrow. No way. I'll get any deadly disease they want to give me. I'll break any bone. I'll throw myself in front of the bus, but I'm not coming to class tomorrow."

Her friend gulped painfully, knowing she was the author. "I'm not coming either." They were quiet until they got to the stairs. When danger was no longer imminent, they continued the conversation begun with the note. How could Jenny Williams have a senior boyfriend when they were both struggling to find sophomore dates to the April Fools' dance? Jenny wasn't even old enough to go. What a joke. They were way cooler than Jenny.

Sarah forgot about the note until the bell rang for lunch, and she felt in her pocket for any loose change that might add up to a cookie. Her forgotten lunch sat on the kitchen table at home. Instead of two quarters and a dime, she pulled out the note, read it quickly, and dropped it in Meg's lap as though a snake had bitten her hand.

"What's this?"

"Read it."

> *I can't believe she's laughing. She's Jenny's mother? At least she has a sense of humor. Jenny is the most boring person in the history of the world. Absolutely no personality.*
>
> *Jenny told Dorothy she is going out with a senior, but no one believes her. What a loser. I mean why would a senior want to go out with her? What would they talk about? Math facts?*

Sarah pursed her lips and rocked back and forth, toe to heel, getting angrier by the moment at the girls who had written such a cruel note about her daughter in her own class.

"Do you think there's anything to this?" Meg set the note down on the desk.

"Which?" Sarah said. "That there's a whisper campaign about Jenny being a loser, or that she has a loser boyfriend? When would she see someone? She never gets calls at night." Sarah tried to put the puzzle together, but she didn't have any pieces. The cardboard puzzle box was empty.

"Well, one thing is for sure," Meg offered. "He's probably just as shy as she is. I don't think you have much to worry about. She's probably worried sick about asking you if she can go to the senior prom with him, whoever he is."

Sarah bit her lip and shook her head. "I don't like sneaking around."

"Oh come on. Do you give her any other choices? Look at how you're responding. Jenny didn't meet you yesterday. She's probably been seeing him at lunch or after school. Maybe he's on the math team."

"Brax Martin is the only senior boy on the math team. The other senior is a girl, Karen Ogden." A cold tingle ran up Sarah's back. "Brax Martin, the world's worst boyfriend."

"Sarah, you've got to give Jenny more credit than that."

angst and anger

*S*it down right there, missy."

Jenny slumped down on the couch and dropped the cumbersome pink-striped canvas bag on the floor.

"It's four thirty. Where have you been since school's been out? How did you get home?"

Jenny's deep blush didn't help her cause a bit, and Sarah had immediate visions of Jenny, embraced in the front seat of a car by some nondescript male body. Sarah's lips made a pale thin line across her face.

"I've been at Claire's playing with the puppy." Jenny's tone challenged her mother. "She brought me home."

The Claire buttons were always close to the surface, and Sarah didn't feel any relief; she just added disloyalty to her truckload of issues.

"So, I guess we're just skipping the piano?"

"Sometimes I practice at Dad's house."

I bet you do, Sarah thought, *but practice what? Being a ditz.* Sarah put one hand on her left hip and said sharply, "Jenny, I'm just going to put my cards on the table. I picked up a note between two airheads in my second hour that said you have a boyfriend who's a senior. Is that true?"

It was a straight shot, yes or no. No equivocating. Jenny chipped at the polish on her fake fingernails instead of looking at Sarah.

"You do have a boyfriend, don't you?" Sarah looked at her watch and ran her fingers through her hair. "I've missed half of Tom's soccer game waiting for you. Can we please talk about this? I don't mind a boyfriend, but I think a senior is really too old."

Jenny sat silently on the couch, her brow furrowed. She was in the midst of some interior dialogue that didn't include Sarah. She reached down to pick up her bag.

"Oh, no you don't. No slinking off into your bedroom. No way. We're talking about this right now. Who is this mystery person?"

Realizing there was no way to detonate a nuclear bomb in small increments, Jenny looked up at her mother and said "Tyler Colton" in such a miniscule voice that Sarah thought for a moment that she had misunderstood.

Cheeks flushed, Sarah smiled. "Right." She knew this adolescent trick. Tell your parents something a thousand times worse than the truth, and then the truth feels like a relief. She wasn't falling for that old ploy. Then she looked at the panic on Jenny's face. Suddenly, Sarah's mouth felt parched. She couldn't swallow. How could she have believed that Tyler would go down without some miserable last hurrah? Some last body blow. Using her daughter to wring every last drop of blood out of her heart.

She shoved a stack of old newspapers and a couple of books off a chair and sat down hard and stared at Jenny. Her immediate inclination was to scream and shake Jenny until the braces popped off her teeth, but she didn't do anything. Panicked, she looked at her daughter, teetering on the brink of a dangerous precipice, and wondered how she was going to save her from falling.

"Okay." Sarah sighed heavily twice and extended her hands as though she were proving she wasn't hiding a weapon. "I'm going to tell you some things, and I want you to listen very carefully to me until I finish, and then we'll talk about anything that you want."

Jenny turned her head away.

"Tyler is not a good person. He's angry and spoiled and blames other people when things don't go his way. I'm pretty sure he's using drugs. He expected to be ranked nationally this year, and he's done badly, and he needs someone to blame, so he's blamed Meg and me."

"He blames you," Jenny shot back. "You've screwed him over all year."

Sarah cringed at the ugly slang. "Jenny, that is just not true."

"You could have added him in at Gov's Cup, and you didn't. Some guy from City High told him. You've helped Eric all year, but you've ignored the policy kids."

"Okay, so Tyler has a million reasons to hate me. What better way to get even than to mess with my girl."

Sarah realized she was in deep water, and she had started out badly. Tyler had been prepping Jenny. He had known this was coming, but Sarah was caught, blindsided. She scooted her chair closer to Jenny and whispered guardedly as though she was confiding a secret.

"Tyler isn't interested in you romantically. He's using you to punish me because he's had a bad year. That's all this is. You're being used."

"Maybe." Jenny looked up at the ceiling, her eyes filling with tears. "Maybe that's why he noticed me at first, but now he likes me, just me. It doesn't have anything to do with you. You always think everything's about you, but it's not."

"That's not fair."

"It's the truth. We all get to be perfect, so you can be the brave little single mom who raised great kids all by herself. We have to go to every single church everything, and then you come home and snipe at half the people in the ward. We have to get straight A's. We have to be smarter and better than everyone, and maybe Tom and Robbie could pull it off and make you look good, but I can't, and I don't want to." Jenny clenched her hands and glared at her mother, but hot tears betrayed her defiance and gummed up her mascara.

"Jenny, I just want you to be who you are, not some cheap imitation of a stereotype." Sarah looked at her daughter as though she hadn't seen her for months. Jenny's pretty hair was highlighted with blonde and red streaks. Her skirt was too short, her makeup was thick, and glitter sparkled across her cheekbones. Sarah shook her head. "Look at you. You don't have any idea who you are."

"I know who I was—a geek with no friends." Jenny spoke slowly. "I was invisible. Yeah, Mom, just like that article said. Do you know how awful it is to dread lunch every day, because there's no place to go? You just have to wander around. It's like announcing to everyone that you're nothing."

"Oh, Jenny, this isn't the way. Who are all your friends now? I haven't heard the phone ringing off the wall," Sarah said, desperation creeping into her voice.

"People notice me. People say hello. When I sit down with Dorothy's crowd at lunch, they don't all get up and leave. That's a major change in my life, and you haven't even noticed because I'm invisible here too. No, that's not right." Jenny shook her head. "I'm not always invisible. Sometimes you notice me because I'm a disappointment."

"Sweetheart," Sarah dropped her shoulders and tried to swallow her fear, "you are not a disappointment. I don't like the direction you've been going lately, but I want you to be happy. Tyler isn't going to make you happy. Tyler's trouble. Let me tell you what Kristen said he did to a girl in middle school."

"Kristen hates Tyler. You hate Tyler. You say he's just trying to get even, but he wouldn't want to if you hadn't been so horrible to him. You always have all these people that you hate. You don't like the bishop. You hate Dad. You always talk about him like he's some sort of monster, but he's not. He's great. He loves me. I don't have to get straight A's for him, or be a student body officer, or play the piano perfectly. He loves me just the way I am, and Claire does too."

"Oh, your dad loves you, and I don't?" Had her real daughter wandered away when she wasn't looking? Didn't Jenny understand that sacrifice meant love? "Did he love you when you had chicken pox or when you broke your arm? Did he love you enough to sell tickets at a million games to pay for the orthodontist, so kids would stop calling you Dracula?"

"Give it up, Mom. I've heard it all before, and I'm not buying any of it. You pushed Dad away. You tried to control him just like you try to control all of us." Jenny marshaled her courage for a final blast. "You should have controlled yourself."

"What do you mean?" Sarah felt as if she had been clobbered flat on her back in the ring with the ref making the final count.

"Everyone's been talking about it all year."

"Oh really, and what has everyone been saying?" Sarah bit off each word.

"That people saw you with Jason Wolcott last summer."

Contempt is an ugly thing to see in a daughter's face. Einstein whined and pushed at Sarah's hand with his nose. She shoved the dog away. "I suppose Tyler told you that too, and you, of course, believe the much-maligned, put-upon Tyler."

"I heard it from other kids. Tom has too."

"And because Tyler has spread that little bit of filth around for the entire year, that makes it true?"

Jenny shrugged her shoulders and looked away from her mother.

"Jenny, Jason's gay."

Jenny's eyes widened and her jaw dropped.

"Did you think I didn't know about Tyler's little smear campaign?" Sarah's voice rose. "The principal called me in months ago. Parents have been calling. I could lose my job. My professional reputation has been wrecked. But I always assumed that people who knew me and loved me would never believe it. How stupid was I?"

"Dad said it wasn't true," Jenny admitted softly.

"Some character witness."

"Why didn't you say anything? Why did you let Tom and me be humiliated all year and not do anything?"

"It's Jason's secret to tell. Not mine. Jason's my friend. He's Robbie's friend." Sarah rubbed her forehead. "Plus, he wasn't involved in any of this."

"Neither was I. But Jason's privacy is more important to you than we are?" Jenny's voice grew louder and she breathed rapidly. "I can't stand you. You're selfish and stingy, and you're cheap. You don't care how I feel or look. You are the worst mother anybody could ever have." She grabbed her bag and inadvertently bashed Einstein in the head as she ran down the hall and slammed her door.

Sarah followed her, the heels of her shoes clicking sharply against the floor. She rapped on the door and tried the handle. It was locked. "Jenny, what you think about me doesn't matter. I am not going to let you ruin your life. You're never to see that kid again. Period, the end. I am dead serious about this. I'll send you off to Aunt Katherine if I have to."

The only response from inside the room was complete silence. Standing, waiting outside the door for several minutes for the second round, Sarah's shoulders drooped. She had no energy. Moving slowly down the hall, certain that she was hemorrhaging quarts of blood from the battering she had just received, Sarah sagged into the chair. She dropped her hands over the armrests and leaned her head back.

Her mind started doing instant replays of Jenny's face making ugly accusations. She tried to slow the tape and look for bits of truth. Did she use her children as some sort of moral currency? Had Jenny really interpreted Sarah's anxiety as disappointment? The tape spun round and round in her head like a VCR stuck on fast-forward. Did Jenny mean the things she said? Sarah wanted to run outside screaming. She wanted, she wanted . . .

Unable to hold still, she tried to grasp the arms of the chair, but her hands, contorted and chalky white, twitched at her sides like spastic claws. *I'm hyperventilating again*, she thought. Remembering Meg's face, she tried to breathe in and out slowly. She looked at the clock on the piano. Four breaths every thirty seconds. Soon her hands tingled. She shook them until the color returned.

Einstein whined deep in his throat.

"Be quiet."

She didn't realize how long she had been sitting until she heard the truck pull in. Tom bounded through the kitchen door smelling like sweat and newly cut grass. Dirt streaked down the side of his wide grin and his knees were covered with grass stains. He glanced down at his cleats full of dirt clods. "Sorry, Mom." Then he grinned. "We beat South Mountain, and I put my application in to run for student body president. My hat is in the ring." Tired but excited, he unstrapped his shin guards and peeled down his muddy socks.

When he finally noticed his mother looking a little pasty, Tom kicked his cleats under the kitchen table.

"So what's up?" Tom sighed and stared up at the ceiling, as if a moment's happiness in this family was too much to ask.

Sarah lifted her head off the back of the chair and turned stiffly as though dozens of pins were poking her neck. "I don't know where to start. Did you know about Jenny and Tyler?"

Tom nodded slowly.

"Have you heard the garbage about me and Jason Wolcott?"

Tom nodded again. "Mom, I could be way off base, but I've always thought that Jason was gay, so I sort of didn't think that anyone would believe it." He shrugged. "I guess I could have said something, but I don't think it's very cool to out your friends."

"Did Jenny ask you about it?"

"I told her it was crap and to forget it."

"Meg thinks it originated with Tyler." Sarah choked on his name.

"That wouldn't surprise me. They were the first ones who bugged me about it." He breathed deeply. "Mom, I thought I had put a stop to this thing with Tyler and Jenny. She promised me she was through with him. He's just using her. She's not his type. At least, she didn't used to be. Mom, I'm sick of Jenny. She's so screwed up."

"Where is all this coming from?"

"Claire."

He's been worried about this for some time, Sarah thought.

Tom went on. "She and Dad just don't get it. Claire thinks having a boyfriend will make Jenny popular and solve all her problems. Plus, Tyler has them snowed. He's such a creep."

"So what do I do now?"

"I don't know. I guess you could lock her up or let her do whatever she wants, but one thing is for certain, she won't listen to reason. I've tried that."

two runaways

*b*ob shifted the paper gown slightly and listened to the old woman's heartbeat. The scent of Mrs. Steiner's perfume and hair spray filled the small exam room, and Bob thought about installing a gas mask next to the blood pressure cuff. For the life of him, he didn't understand why these women thought a doctor's appointment was a date to the prom.

"Okay, take a deep breath for me." The woman inhaled. A knock on the door interrupted him. He had been an hour behind all morning, and his stomach growled. His prom date smiled.

Carol, a medical assistant with straight hair and freckles, stuck her head into the room. "Dr. Williams, your daughter's in the waiting room." Carol acted imperious, as though she had just announced the arrival of the queen or perhaps an exotic endangered species needing specialized treatment.

"Jenny?" She was the only daughter he had, but the visit was so extraordinary that he had to double-check his facts. It was on the tip of his tongue to ask what she was doing here on a Wednesday morning, but not wanting to provide grist for the office gossip mill, he said, as though endless numbers of daughters arrived daily, "Have her wait in my office, would you please?"

Carol nodded and closed the door.

Bob jotted a quick note in the chart. "Mrs. Steiner, I'm going to change your medication." He spoke loudly, enunciating each word. "I think we can alleviate the swelling in your feet with a different diuretic."

She smiled complacently as he scribbled a few lines on a prescription pad.

He spoke brusquely to the nurse standing in the hall. "Mrs. Steiner needs her protime checked and schedule her back in a couple of months."

He felt like his office was crowded with large female birds, constantly moving, constantly chirping. It made him nervous. Stopping by the mirror in the hall, he adjusted his red tie, unbuttoned his lab coat, and smoothed his hair. The twittering stopped. Glancing at the front office, he saw the receptionist, the nurse, the medical assistant, and Mrs. Steiner—all watching him. He hitched up his pants and strode into his office.

His little girl was sitting in his green leather chair. She swiveled back and forth slowly, looking out the west windows. Her eyes were swollen, and she sniffed three times before she turned toward him. He sat in the chair usually occupied by patients, and scrutinized Jenny as if to say, "Well?"

"Dad." She flopped a bit as though in the battle precipitating this visit, she had lost three fourths of her vertebrate. She sniffed again without saying anything. Ten years earlier he would have demanded impatiently, "Get to the point. I have a clinic full of sick people." But Bob walked carefully with these adolescent children he was courting.

"Dad," Jenny started again, "I want to come and live with you and Claire."

He leaned back and dropped his hands over the armrests on the chair. Staring at her a couple of long moments, he finally said, "I would love to have you come and live with us." He didn't say, "But what will your mother say, or do, or think," but it hung in the air between them. Jenny started in with the quick inhales Bob knew preceded a large wail that would be heard by the entire office.

"Jenny, let me cancel my patients after lunch, and let's get out of here." The plan allayed the tearful onslaught, and Bob picked up the phone and spoke to his receptionist.

"Barbara, would you move my afternoon patients into next week?" He didn't wait to hear her protest. "Let's go," he said with a smile. He touched Jenny's left shoulder to direct her toward the stairway. "Did you walk all the way over here from the high school?"

Jenny nodded.

"You just took off?"

Jenny nodded again.

"Shall we go get a hamburger?" He finally got a response.

"But I don't want to go in anywhere."

"Fair enough," he said as he opened the passenger door of his car.

She had just settled down into the soft leather car seat when Bob leaned over the gearshift and put his arm around her.

"Jenny, I don't know what's going on, but it's going to be okay. If you need to stay with us for a while, that's fine. Believe it or not, none of this is going to jolt the earth out of its orbit."

Then the argument with Sarah came out in bursts and spurts and a smattering of tears. Fishing a tissue from his pocket, he mopped Jenny's eyes and nose. "Aunt Katherine. That's grim," he said as he drove through the take-out lane. Sarah's aunt in Boise had a husband with Alzheimer's. That condo would be in permanent lockdown. "Well, that's not an option. Why don't you just come and stay with us until school's out?"

"Will you talk to Mom?"

"I think I might be sick that day."

Jenny laughed. "Are you afraid of Mom too?"

Bob pulled away from the drive-in window with his hamburger balanced on his left knee and a French fry sticking out of the corner of his mouth. "Was Davy Crockett afraid of wrestling a grizzly bear? He was if he was smart. I'll call your mom tonight." *Long distance,* he thought. "Do you want to go by and get some of your stuff while nobody's home?"

Jenny nodded. Five minutes later they pulled into the carport at Sarah's house.

Holding the kitchen door open for her father, Jenny asked, "Aren't you going to come in?"

"Sure," he responded, but he felt intrusive, as though he were a burglar casing the joint. Jenny ran down the hall, and Bob looked around. This was the first time he had been inside the home where his children had grown up. He recognized some of the beat-up furniture and Sarah's haphazard housekeeping style: cereal boxes on the counter, open kitchen cupboards, shoes scattered by the door, a complete lack of organization. But the house was filled with more than just clutter; it was filled with the stuff of his children's lives—their papers, pictures, piano books, and appointment cards. A couple of trophies stood on the mantel and an MVP brass grizzly held down a collection of newspaper clippings. He picked up a framed picture of the three kids on the front stoop of their duplex in Iowa. Touching their faces with his finger, he walked over and looked at snapshots taped to the fridge. Robbie in his missionary suit grinned amidst a group of Venezuelans outside a cinder block church. He read Sarah's lists and notes to herself.

Startled when Jenny called to him, he walked down the hall but paused at Sarah's bedroom door. A dress and a black slip hung over a chair. The bed was unmade, and the sheets and pillows were rumpled. Her scent enveloped him, pulling him back fifteen years into Sarah's bed and Sarah's life. In danger of being inundated with nostalgia, he asked Jenny if she was ready, just as she dragged an old Barbie doll duffle bag into the hall and caught him standing in her mother's bedroom doorway.

She watched him silently before she asked, "Dad, why did you leave us?"

He shoved his hand into his pocket and played with his car keys. Chaos and contention, he had told himself multiple times, but he couldn't say that either.

"It was a million little things that seemed important at the time, but not so important now."

"That's not really an answer, Dad."

"I know. I was buying a little time." He grabbed the duffle bag and followed Jenny out of the house.

———

He turned to Jenny as he pulled into his garage. He had blown this same conversation with Robbie years before. He wasn't going to make the same mistake now.

"It was my fault the marriage broke up, Jenny."

She didn't say anything, nor did she make a move to get out of the car.

"When I got to Switzerland, I was pretty sure I had made a mistake. Several mistakes, actually. One thing's sure, I really missed you. I wrote to your mother, but she never answered any of my letters. I guess she'd finally had enough. I had a friend of mine go by the house to see if you guys were okay, but you had moved." He wasn't sure how much more she wanted to hear, so he paused.

"Uncle Carter came and got us," Jenny added.

"So I understand." He jingled the key in the ignition. "Jenny, it was a mistake to start a relationship with Claire before I resolved things with your mom. I don't want you to think that was okay. It wasn't. Claire came over after Christmas, and I was lonely, and one thing led to another. Don't misunderstand," he corrected himself. "I really love Claire. We're very happy, and to tell you the truth, I thought your mother would have remarried by now."

"No way. She hates men." Jenny thought for a minute before she confided, "Mom's very prickly."

"Well, that's probably my fault too, but that's a waste." He decided to go out on a limb. "There were years when I was absolutely crazy about your mom. She was funny, and pretty, and smart, but some people just aren't a good fit in a marriage." He interlaced his fingers and then stuck his index finger up. "Fidn't dit." Jenny laughed and dismissed thirteen years of father bashing in seconds.

When Bob heard Jenny upstairs opening drawers and getting settled in her new room, he called Sarah at school. At least he tried to call Sarah but was informed by a tart voice that teachers were never interrupted by personal calls when they were in class. Leaving his phone number, he felt relieved.

"I tried to call your mom, but I got a professional interceptor." He leaned against the doorjamb and watched Jenny organizing her few possessions.

"Gracie." Jenny guessed and made an *X* with her fingers to ward off evil. "Knows all, and tells more than she knows."

Bob laughed, not knowing that Jenny was quoting Sarah's tight circle of friends. For a moment Jenny's sun went behind a cloud, and he was puzzled. She sat down on the edge of her bed and looked through the starched white curtains as though she could see directly into her mother's classroom. "Mom's friends are going to be bummed about all this. I mean really bummed."

"Well, that's her problem, isn't it? I'm sure she'll have an explanation. I kidnapped you, or I bribed you, or I had you hypnotized." He tried to make her laugh again, but she cupped her chin in her hand and talked to the little blue flowers on the wallpaper.

"It's going to be my problem if I have any of them next year, or the year after that, or the year after that. I mean, Dad, they really stick together. I'm in there before and after school and hear what they say." Jenny stopped abruptly, and her father finished her sentence.

"But you won't be doing that anymore, and you're afraid they'll be talking about you? You've stepped outside the circle forever?" Jenny looked up at him. "You know, kiddo, we can take you home, and no one will be the wiser."

Jenny shook her head. They both heard the puppy yipping in the kitchen.

"Claire's home." Bob smiled. "We better go and face the music. One more starving mouth to feed."

Following her father through the living room, Jenny closed the lid over the keyboard on the baby grand piano, and Bob turned and saw her doing a small celebratory dance step.

—◇◇◇—

After dinner Bob stepped into the living room, supposedly out of earshot, with a telephone in his hand. Jenny and Claire stood in the dining room like a couple of guilty conspirators, listening to his one-sided conversation with Sarah.

"Well," he said speaking into the receiver, "we really haven't thought this through carefully. There's no plan here. She showed up at my office this morning pretty upset." He paused, waiting for Sarah to make some explanation, and when she didn't, he continued with the small speech he had been rehearsing.

"I thought that maybe she could stay with us for a little while, maybe until school's out. You know, just a little downtime. Maybe after school's out, we could all sit down with a counselor or a therapist or someone and figure out where to go from here." Again he paused and waited, but Sarah didn't say anything.

Bob continued, "So is there anything that I should know? Any appointments, drug allergies, school stuff that you want to pass along?" He waited and then said quietly, "Come on, Sarah, say something. This isn't easy for anyone."

He listened for several minutes and the expression on his face darkened. He had forgotten what a shrew she could be. "You're right,

I really don't want to hear what you think of me. This is about Jenny." Why had he thought she would be reasonable? "Okay, I'll ask her." He put his hand over the mouthpiece.

"Jenny, do you want to stay on the mock trial team, or do you want your mom to put in an alternate?"

Jenny looked around the door and shook her head.

Now, he didn't know what to say. In spite of the ugly bit of tongue-lashing he'd just received, if he had a minute alone with Jenny, he would have told her she was making a mistake. His lips pulled away from his teeth, and he lied into the receiver, "I think she feels like she's not contributing to the team. Maybe someone else would be a stronger witness?" He knew he sounded like a total dope.

"Listen," he hurried to fill the gap, "I'm totally on board with homework and the whole piano thing. I'll make sure she practices," but he was talking to a dead line. Sarah had hung up.

bluebird encounter

Sarah stirred a teaspoon of honey into the steaming peppermint tea and wrapped her hands around the warm mug. A piece of lemon meringue pie sat on a small blue and white plate with *Bluebird Cafe* written in script on the rim. She caught her melancholy reflection in the mirror above the dark wainscoting.

She sighed. "I guess I don't understand how we're going to explain the trajectory of that bullet to the judge and make it convincing."

Sitting across the small table, Clayton pulled a pen out of his pocket. "I saw this done in court once. Use a pencil to make the flight of the bullet plausible. Have a kid assume the position of the victim. It will work. Try it." He handed her the pen and held his arm in the position outlined in the booklet open on the table. She aimed the pen past his arm and poked him in the chest.

"That will do," he said. "I don't need to be impaled." He took the pen but continued to hold her hand. He stroked her fingers gently.

Sarah tried to smile. "Seriously though, bullying is such a problem. Everything in this case could be real." She pulled her hand away.

"Have your kids been bullied?"

"Ha!" Sarah exclaimed. "You don't know Robbie. You remember that great Clint Eastwood line, 'Make my day?' That would have been Robbie's response to a bully. Sort of like a starter's pistol. Tom was always right there in Rob's shadow. Not a problem."

"What about Jenny?"

"Jenny?" She blinked back tears and pressed several crust crumbs under the edge of her fork. She listened to the echo in the old building as a busboy called to a waitress. The high ceilings and a pink marble soda fountain along one wall dated back to the 1890s. Bar stools with swivel seats, covered in green leather, were bolted to the floor. The large mirror, behind the nozzles and the flavor bottles and the rows of glassware, reflected the display case across the aisle, filled with dozens of different kinds of chocolates. Three tables away, an old woman, having the dinner special, was the only other customer.

"You know," Sarah murmured, "my grandparents used to bring us here for Mother's Day when I was a little kid. If I behaved perfectly, on the way out my grandfather would hold me up and let me choose any chocolate that I wanted. They're still making the exact same candy. Maybe it's the very same stuff. Petrified."

He watched her intently. "I was afraid you weren't going to come tonight."

"I wasn't sure I was going to come either." She touched a bit of meringue to the tip of her tongue and let it melt. Holding the fork up to her face, she studied him between the tines. He was nice looking but not handsome. His nose had been broken, probably more than once, he had a noticeable scar on the right side of his cheek, and his hair was mostly gray, but he looked like a man who had stood at the bow and weathered his share of storms and not broken. He was solid, not skittish, but what was she? She wasn't sure.

"What's wrong?" His rough hand reached across the table and covered hers.

"Jenny ran away," she glanced over at the old woman and swallowed hard, "to her father. She's dating an absolute walking disease. He's so horrible that my skin just crawls at the thought of him with Jenny. I've got trials next week and I can't focus. I need to do well, because we lost Region, but I can't seem to think about anything except Jenny."

"I'm so sorry. Have you tried to talk to her?"

"What's there to say? 'Oops, I made a mistake. Tyler's a great guy'?" She shook her head. "Nothing's changed. Tom's furious with her. Her dad and his brain-dead wife are encouraging her. I don't know what to do." She broke off a piece of piecrust with her free hand, contemplated it for a moment, and then dropped it on her plate.

He reached over and tucked a curl behind her ear. "You'll figure it out."

"You know," she spoke slowly, "you've got to love life's little ironies. Jenny was a surprise, and Bob was furious. He was humiliated for nine months. He didn't want another baby. Two little boys were somehow manageable, but three kids were an army. Plus, there was no way he was ever going to leave academics, and there was absolutely no way that he was ever going to practice in his hometown. Now he's done this big mid-life flip-flop. He can't get enough of Jenny. He buys her whatever she wants and tells her whatever she wants to hear."

Clayton listened intently, occasionally making small sympathetic noises.

"He wasn't even there for the delivery. She was two weeks early. He told me he was working, but he didn't answer his pager. He wasn't in the hospital." She plucked at the paper place mat.

She couldn't believe she was telling him this. She'd never admitted to anyone that Jenny was a mistake, part of the 3 percent failure rate for oral contraceptives. She remembered Bob storming around the duplex, ranting that he wasn't going to be one of those Mormons in white shirts and baggy polyester pants, driving a rusted-out station wagon stuffed with car seats.

"She was such a beautiful baby, but he never bonded with her. She was colicky and cried for six months straight. That whole time is just a blur, an exhausted blur. I was up all night with her, and when she slept during the day, I had two crazy little boys to herd around. When I finally came up out of that fog, my marriage was over. So this feeling, like I'm bleeding to death, isn't new."

"There you were with three little children."

"I can't explain how frightened I was. I didn't know what to do. When he finally left, I came home and tried to make things work. It hasn't been perfect, but it's been sort of okay. Now, he's stolen Jenny, and he's throwing her to the wolves, some sort of weird sacrifice to his fatherhood, and I don't understand, because he never wanted her in the first place. I was the one who really loved her, and now she hates me." She pushed her temples with her fingertips.

"She doesn't hate you. He might be more protective than you think. Fathers have long memories about adolescent males."

"Well, he's not being very protective right now. He's shoving her at Tyler. By the time he makes all his mistakes, her life will be ruined."

"Maybe not. Kids make mistakes, and if we're lucky, they learn from them. My daughter broke our hearts, but I think she's going to turn out okay."

"What did she do?"

"Nothing in high school. She wasn't popular, but she had a few girlfriends, went to a few dances. She seemed pretty happy. College was a different story. She hooked up with a football player from Detroit. He was a thug. There's no other way to describe him. He was booked a dozen times as a kid. Did some time in a reformatory. Then he got recruited and came out here to play. A new start. With my daughter." He whistled softly through his teeth. "We talked to her nonstop, but she didn't hear anything we had to say."

"What finally happened?"

"My wife got sick. It was a wake-up call for Becky."

"Where is she now?"

"She's married to a nice young man and lives here in town. She has a baby girl, nine months old."

Sarah gasped, "You're a grandfather?"

He chuckled. "Guilty as charged." He looked at her seriously. "Sarah, trouble comes in waves. When everything seems completely hopeless, something will change. That's one of the great lessons in the Book of Mormon."

She looked at him out of the corner of her eye. *Here comes the lecture. The easy moral conclusion. The tidy ending.*

"You have to be patient. 'And it came to pass' is mentioned one hundred and seventy-four times in the Book of Mormon. Nowhere does it say 'it came to stay.'"

She scrutinized his face, cut a piece of pie with her fork, and put it into her mouth. "Well, my problems don't seem to be going anywhere. I feel like that witch in *The Wizard of Oz* that had a house land on her. *Splat.*" She slapped her hand on the table. The old woman quit cutting her meatloaf and stared at them.

"Tyler would have been enough for one year, but then Bob moved here, and then Tyler targeted Jenny. And then this really nasty rumor has been circulating about me that just added fuel to the mess."

He held up his palms. "I know. I've heard it."

"You're kidding!"

"Come on, Sarah, it's a very small town."

"It's not true."

"Of course it's not true. Let me tell you what's true. You're pretty. You're single. You're funny. I've been entertained with Mrs. Williams stories at dinner all year, so you're high profile at the high school. I'd be willing to bet plenty of boys have their first crushes on you."

"I don't flirt with students. I think it's disgusting."

"You don't have to flirt. Their hormones will do all the work. They've been sitting in class, bored, entertaining themselves with fantasies about you for months, so it isn't much of a stretch for them to think that someone's fantasy was fulfilled."

Sarah rolled her eyes.

Clayton reached over with his fork and stole a piece of her pie. "Even grandfathers have fantasies."

Her cheeks felt hot. *I'm blushing*, she thought. She looked down at the mock trial booklet. She didn't know this man. She didn't have any history with him. Why was she confiding intimate details of her life to this guy? She glanced at him out of the corner of her eye. He was watching her. She inadvertently shook her head and frowned.

"This isn't a little problem," she said. "If I'm formally accused, I'll be suspended, even if I'm innocent. I could lose my job and end up teaching in some horrible little podunk town. Plus the poor kid whose name was linked to me is doing a semester abroad. His mother heard all this and wrote to him, telling him to come home and repent. She thinks I'm a predator and the reason he didn't go on a mission. I mean, it just goes on and on." She took a sip of tea, but it was cold.

"So, what are you going to do tomorrow?"

He's acting like a grandfather, or maybe just an alpha male giving me directions. Mildly irritated, she arched her back and tipped her head to the side. "Tomorrow? I'll implement your ideas. Rehearse with the attorneys, and maybe I'll see if Meg or Bill Cottle will intervene with Jenny. Jenny loves Bill. Maybe she'll listen to him." She didn't know if Bill could work some of his magic on Jenny, but it felt good to be making a plan.

He stood and swung his jacket over his shoulder by his thumb. "Things will work out. I think your behavior is absolutely perfect in the face of so much trouble. How about if I buy you a chocolate?"

"How about if I buy you one?"

"Do I need to ease up on the throttle?" An anxious look passed quickly across his face.

"I didn't know there was a throttle."

———∽∾∾———

He offered her a bite of his peanut cluster, and she broke off a small piece of her dark chocolate mint and stuck it in his mouth. He took her arm and tucked it under his. When he opened the exterior door outside the vestibule, a brisk April wind, blowing through the parking lot, caught them off guard. Sarah's sweater blew open and she shivered. He wrapped his jacket around her and, without asking, he kissed her. Her foot bumped against a small concrete planter filled with daffodils, the city's latest beautification project. Her arms were crunched against his chest.

"I can't have a romance," she protested, feeling her wrist for a sprain. "I'm up to my armpits in alligators. My life is falling apart."

"Relax, Sarah. I want to try this one more time. I'm not the geometry teacher."

She started to smile, but he drew her arms up to his shoulders and pulled her tightly against his chest. He kissed her gently. He tasted like chocolate and peanuts and smelled like musky aftershave. Standing next to him she was sheltered from the wind and she felt warm. His kisses became more insistent. She felt curiously observant as though watching from afar. The wind whipped her hair, and she heard the beep-beep of an automatic car lock. They had an audience. Sarah ducked behind his shoulder. Two women in waitress uniforms were trying not to stare as they hurried under the streetlights in the other direction.

"Oh great, the brazen hussy is now kissing the sheriff, a grandfather, in a public parking lot." She arranged her face into a frown.

"No one will ever blame you. There's something about a man in uniform." He glanced down at his striped shirt. "Okay, so that doesn't work. How about authority figures?"

After a pause, he carefully began, "Sarah, I don't want to add any more complications to your life. I want to help."

"You know, I'm pretty used to driving my own boat. I'm not sure if that's your MO." She hurried to finish her thought. "The kissing is very nice, you're very nice, but I'm really very independent. I don't think I'm a couples sort of a person." She ran her tongue around the inside of her lips tasting the chocolate.

"Don't decide anything right now. Let's go slow. Try it out. See how it feels."

She didn't like all these imperative sentences. "I'm not a used car that you can take for a test drive around the block." Her hand went automatically to her hip.

He laughed. She stepped back and bumped into the planter, and he was kissing her again.

She knew what he wanted, and it wasn't a bi-weekly kissing assignation in the parking lot behind the Bluebird. The backseat in his SUV or a stadium blanket in the canyon wasn't going to be his destination either. He wanted her with a ring on her finger. No trial runs. Two middle-aged adults dragging their mismatched baggage into the bridal suite.

How did people merge totally different lives? Children? She thought of Jenny sharing a house with two non-brothers. She would die a thousand deaths. How could you give up your home? Whose toaster won out? Her appliances were hashed, but they were old friends. How could she give up her garden and fruit trees that were really starting to produce? How did people just start sharing bathrooms, and money, and keys to the car with middle-aged strangers? A grandfather, for heaven's sake.

What if he snored? He probably did. Snoring was the bane of her married middle-aged friends. She had heard, with a degree of relief, of white-noise machines, of sleep apnea, of nights on the couch. She only remembered Bob snoring once. He had been coming off an exhausting long weekend on call. He had been flat on his back at two o'clock in the morning, and she couldn't believe the horrible cacophony coming out of his mouth. She had listened for a few minutes and then pounced on him. Upset, startled out of a deep sleep, he had chased her across the bed, only to be belted with a pillow. Tommy's stuffed giraffe, revealed in the glow of the Winnie-the-Pooh nightlight, became a sword in Sarah's hand. He trapped her against the headboard. His hand held her arms captive. Breathing hard, he had whispered silly threats about being awakened. She had giggled, and the giraffe had slipped through her fingers. Now he played those games with someone else. All those memories, stagnating in her brain, were clogging up her life.

Opening her eyes, she looked over Clayton's shoulder at the stars. She felt his warm breath on her neck. Leaning into him, she wondered, what were his memories? Who was this man? She didn't know him. He was lean and strong and used to capturing the bad guys. He had a badge in his back pocket. Almost involuntarily, she nestled against his chest.

A couple of boys in a battered Chevrolet sped down the alley. One rolled down his window and yelled in their direction, "Get a room!"

"Tell me they weren't my students," Sarah groaned pulling away. She rustled in her purse for her car keys.

"I'm sorry, Sarah. I got a little carried away."

She raised one eyebrow.

He had felt her responsiveness. A pleased little-boy smile covered his face.

"Right," she said. "I guess it's springtime even for grandfathers."

He reached for her, but she held him at arm's length.

"Do you think you might have a hero complex?" she said. "I'm sure it's an occupational hazard. You know, rescuing people from wrecked cars, burning building, bears in the mountains. Please don't feel like you need to rescue me."

"Sarah, listen to me. I liked you the minute I walked into your classroom at Back to School Night, before there were alligators any-where in the vicinity. Don't close the door on this without giving us a chance."

"May 1," she called, running in the direction of her car. Her sweater flapped in a gust of wind, and her hair, out of control, swirled around her head. As she stuck her key in the car door, she realized that for the last fifteen minutes, she had forgotten about Jenny.

first time father failure

*b*ob stood by the window and listened. He heard a siren in the distance, maybe heading toward the canyon. He turned and paced over to another window, moving the lace curtains aside. In the darkness, he saw the trees in the front yard, a few red tulips in a flower bed, and twinkling lights on the bluff across the valley. He glanced down at his watch and tapped nervously on the face as though he could jostle time. One-thirty. He pushed his fingers through his thick hair. He'd grab that kid by the neck and shake him until his teeth rattled. He walked over and picked up a magazine from the carefully arranged stack on the coffee table, but he dropped the magazine as he heard the sound of a car coming up the boulevard.

As a car door slammed, he flipped on the porch lights. He was ready. "Where in Sam Hill have you been with my daughter?" sat coiled in his mouth, but the truck squealed out of the driveway as Jenny came in the door alone.

"Hey, Dad. You didn't need to wait up for me." Her pupils were dilated.

"I didn't wait up—until twelve-thirty. For the last hour I've been planning your funeral. That is, after I headed up a search and rescue team for several days." Jenny turned away from him and burped, but he smelled the beer and noticed the buttons on her shirt were out of sync. A couple of dry leaves were tangled in her hair. His heart sank.

"Jenny, Jenny, what have you been doing?"

"Just hanging out," she mumbled incoherently.

Too many years moonlighting in an ER had taught Bob that there was no point in talking to anyone who was chemical. *Tomorrow*, he thought. But what would he say to her?

Relieved she was home, he nodded toward the stairs. "Head up to bed, young lady. You've got church in the morning." He couldn't believe what he was saying. Words imprinted in the back of his brain fell out of his mouth. He was quoting his own father, who had used religion as a punishment and church as a place to feel guilty.

Jenny, already starting up the stairs, looked at him quizzically. "Church? With you and Claire?"

"With your mom."

"Right."

He stood outside her bedroom door and listened to her vomit over and over again in the perfectly decorated Laura Ashley bathroom. Finally he heard dry heaves and thought about going in to help her, but his feet felt permanently attached to the soft blue carpet. *She needs to be miserable*, he thought.

Around two a.m. he heard her crawl into bed, and he moved down the hall. Claire rolled over and looked up at him with sleepy eyes.

"Is she okay?"

"She's been puking up her socks, but I'll think she'll live."

"Poor little bug. I'll go give her some Tylenol." Claire made a move to get out of bed.

"Not a chance. I want this to be a headache she won't forget." He paused. "Sometime tonight, she put her shirt on in the dark." He felt sick just letting the words come out of his mouth.

Claire giggled. "That's what high school is all about, drinking beer and making out in the backseat. Why are you being such a hard guy? I bet you tossed back your fair share."

"No, I didn't. I was the token athlete on the seminary council." He spoke as though that single fact guaranteed the moral high ground for life. He had such a rigid idea of what was right and wrong for his little girl, and whatever had gone on tonight was horribly wrong. He remembered Tom's face and heard his warning. Tom knew this guy was trouble. He had been too quick to be the understanding parent, the lenient parent. What would Tom think if he knew about all this? What would Robbie say? Why did this happen on his watch? He groaned thinking of the mess he was in.

He set his head gingerly on his pillow. "Such a small town. This will be all over by Monday morning. Jenny's reputation is shot. Sarah's going to kill me." *And rightly so*, he thought.

"Everyone needs to take a deep breath and relax. Jenny hasn't done anything wrong. She's finally acting like a normal teenager."

"No, you don't understand. She's crossed a line. Good Mormon kids don't drink beer. No one's going to wink at this. She's out of the paddock and into the woods."

Claire whispered in his ear as she tugged him gently toward her. "Nix on the beer, but I bet you had your fair share of fun."

"With Queen Sarah? You've got to be kidding. Sarah allowed only small incremental advances spread over years leading up to the big wedding night finale. Actually, I think Sarah was more of a prime minister than a queen."

"So if Sarah was the prime minister, what does that make me?"

"You, my dear, are a hussy," Bob said. Claire giggled and left the light on.

———

Bob opened one eye carefully the next morning and glared at the phone, but it wasn't making noise. Claire had her head sandwiched in a pillow, a clear sign he'd been snoring. He could see just the tip of her nose. Light was coming in the window, and it wasn't early morning light. The whining started again, and he rolled over and looked down at the puppy standing near a wet spot. He elbowed Claire.

"Your dog just peed on the carpet."

Claire went from out cold to bolt upright in five seconds flat. "Oh, poor thing. She'll feel so guilty."

Bob took another look, this time with both eyes, at the little dog that had stopped whining and started to wag her tail at the sound of Claire's voice. He looked at the clock and felt the sinking feeling in his stomach that had started last night. He rolled over and pulled Claire's pillow over his head. He should have stayed in Iowa. He groaned as he heard Jenny bumping around in her bedroom and listened to her vomit halfheartedly a couple of times. "You can't puke up guilt," he wanted to tell her. He pondered the approach he should take. He could shave and put on a shirt and do the whole father-child interview thing.

How many times had he been hauled into his father's study? Maybe he should just go in now and get it over with? Just be straight? Just be informal and scruffy and then make waffles or scrambled eggs? His stomach growled.

He tapped a couple of times on her door and then walked in. Her face was pale gray-green and her knees were pulled up under the checkered yellow quilt.

"We need to talk."

"Dad, I really don't feel so good. Could we do this later?"

"No, we're going to do this now. There's a reason you feel awful, kiddo. What went on last night was no good." He started to say that he was terribly disappointed in her, but he stopped. "Listen, Jenny," as though her eyes weren't riveted to his face, "I've worked in ERs enough to know that too much alcohol combined with anything is a disaster. It's just trouble. So what happened last night?"

"I don't feel comfortable talking about this with you." Jenny started to pull her quilt over her head and slip to that faraway Jenny interior space.

He was sitting on the side of her bed, but he felt like they were at opposite ends of a long hallway, and she couldn't hear him. "That's too bad, because we're going to talk." He paused for a minute and rested his hand on her knee. "So you had a few beers? Was that it? Any pot?" He tugged the quilt off her face.

"I don't know how to smoke. I didn't want to look stupid."

"Were you up the canyon? How many kids?"

"I don't know, maybe thirty, maybe less."

"You know by eight o'clock on Monday morning, this will be all over school. Tom's going to hear about this even if your mother doesn't." Jenny's face tightened as she flopped back onto her pillow and closed her eyes.

"Brothers," she groaned.

"Do you know how this feels to me?" he asked. "This feels like you came to live with me and let everything go. You don't practice the piano. I don't see you studying much. Your first weekend here, you were drinking and making out with a boy that Tom and your mother think is a jerk. Somehow this is all going to end up being my fault. I can feel that train coming down the track." He rubbed the bristle on his face and frowned at her. "Well, you are about to discover where the bear sleeps. Was Tyler drinking and smoking pot?"

Jenny didn't answer. She opened one eye and tried to glare at him.

"He drove down the canyon with you in the car?"

She didn't answer. No defense.

"This Tyler kid is bad news. He's too old for you. He used lousy judgment, and he broke the law. Underage drinking is against the law; that's all there is to it. Driving drunk is inexcusable. I hope we're not going to add statutory rape to the list, because, Jenny, I will go after him. We're through with this kid as of right now."

"Is that what Claire thinks too?"

"Claire's your friend. I'm your father." His tone dismissed Claire's opinions as though she were an errant child. "Jenny, I don't want you to look back on the day you came to live with us as a terrible turning point in your life. You'll end up hating me too. I couldn't stand that." He waited for a hug or some assurance that she could never hate him, but it didn't come. He sighed heavily.

"Drinking and carousing are not what you should be doing." He thought the conversation was over, and he stood up, starting to think about scrambling eggs, when he heard her whisper.

"I was funny last night, Dad. I made people laugh. Those kids liked me."

Helplessness engulfed him. He reached down and pulled Jenny tightly against his chest as though he could protect her.

family trials

$g$rateful the April rain wasn't some freaky March blizzard, Sarah maneuvered the district van up the parking ramp and into the evening. The eight students, fledgling attorneys and witnesses in the back of the van, were laughing, jostling one another, and searching through backpacks looking for their money. Before anyone could relate horror stories they had heard from friends who worked at any particular fast food restaurant, Sarah decided on a McDonald's near the 33rd South on-ramp. She was sure that the fat content in the hamburgers would be through the roof, and multiple rats had drowned in the hot French fry oil, but hopefully, none of her students would die a sad and lingering death tonight.

The darkening clouds and the light spattering of rain on the plate-glass windows at McDonald's created no sense of urgency in the students. In the midst of hamburgers and grease-stained papers, drink cups, and wadded napkins, they had started to relive the trial with their own comic interpretations.

Walter Nichols ribbed Tom about his cross-examination. The team from the opposing school had thrown them a curve: the bully/victim and the perpetrator/victim were both girls, an unexpected gender switch.

Tom, the most experienced attorney for the prosecution, had moved carefully. He had established that handguns are only used to shoot people. The defendant left home with a gun in her pocket for one purpose: to shoot Cory Jackson. The witness demurred. The gun was only for her protection. Tom questioned her quickly. Did anyone else pose a threat? His voice was so calm and non-confrontational that the witness's attorney didn't make any objections, didn't interrupt the flow of Tom's questions.

"You didn't see a knife in Cory's hand, did you?"

"I thought I did," she protested.

"But we know from the police report that Cory wasn't carrying a weapon, don't we?" Tom spoke quietly.

"Yes," the girl responded.

"So, you couldn't have seen a knife, could you?"

The girl had to give him the answer he wanted.

"You pulled the gun out of your pocket, didn't you?"

"Yes."

"You fired the gun at Cory Jackson, didn't you?"

"Yes."

"You murdered an unarmed person, didn't you?"

"Yes" had come automatically, and then the girl started to sputter and try to inject another answer, but Tom was quick. "No further questions, your honor." The witness was dismissed. Bingo!

———————

Sarah and Tom had rehearsed the questions the night before until Tom stopped abruptly. She expected him to say, "Enough practicing already," but he had looked hard at her and said, "You know, Mom, if I owned a handgun, I'd kill Tyler Colton." He wasn't shouting or angry. He spoke in the same steady, calm voice he rehearsed. This frightened Sarah more than if he had thrown her favorite philodendron across the room.

It had not been an easy week. Monday morning, five minutes into first hour, 95 percent of the student body was whispering about a raucous party up the canyon Saturday night. Rumors of drugs and alcohol and girls dancing around the campfire partially dressed were on everyone's lips. Sarah didn't pay much attention. Wild parties in the canyon were a rite of spring. Several students in sophomore English couldn't look her in the eye, but she was so consumed with her own heartache and anger that nothing registered until Tom interrupted her class second hour with a cold expression on his face and motioned her out into the hall.

"Jenny was at that party," he said, staring down at the linoleum floor. "She was wasted." He didn't want her to hear it from some student enjoying the shock value, he explained, but he looked at her as though he expected her to intervene, do something—dismiss school, call out the National Guard, jail Jenny—to correct this hideous mistake. He didn't mention that Thursday would be a close primary election for student body president and that a four-year leadership scholarship hung in the balance. Jenny obviously hadn't given any thought to that. Layers and layers of trouble. Sarah leaned back against a locker and grabbed the handles to keep from sliding onto the floor. Now sickening rumors about Jenny would be added to the tawdry lies about Sarah. What chance did Tom have? What chance did their family have?

"I told him about Tyler," Tom continued in a cold voice, "and he didn't even listen. He's so full of himself. He makes me want to puke." It took her a second to realize he was talking about his father. She reached for Tom and put her arms around him.

"Go back to class," she whispered over the lump in her throat. She couldn't cry, or scream Jenny's name, or tear out her hair, or even comfort her son. She had to behave as if nothing was wrong. She had to go back into that room with thirty-five sophomores who had been whispering about her daughter. They would be scrutinizing her face for any hairline cracks, any little slips. "Does she know?" they would ask each other. A family's calamity made such exciting fodder for lunchroom gossip. It had been a horrible week.

———w———

The pretty blonde defendant on the stand had confessed. Tom turned back to the attorney table and gave his team a silent thumbs up. The attorney for the witness tried to repair the damage on redirect, but Tom had nailed it. *Yes!* Sarah wrote empathically across her legal pad.

Estee, thrilled to be included as the bailiff, came back from the judges' chambers fifteen minutes after the last speech. She had a toothy smile on her face and winked at Sarah.

Darling Estee. She had come into the debate room Friday after school with a dark storm cloud hovering over her head. She gestured impatiently for several students to leave before she closed the door. Startled, Sarah dropped her papers and Meg stopped sorting debate certificates.

"I don't know what to do," Estee began.

"What's happened?" Meg put her arm around Estee's shoulder.

"Is Tom okay?" Sarah's only expectations were trouble. Fate has singled out her family, and bad news waited on every corner.

"Tom's fine." And then she stammered, "But no, he's not fine at all."

"Is he hurt?" Sarah wanted to shake her.

"No." She paused. "Yes." She started to cry.

"Sit down. Take a deep breath." Meg gently pushed Estee over to a desk. "It's okay," Meg mouthed at Sarah.

Estee tried to explain between sporadic gulping sobs. "Jenny came up to Tom after fourth hour. She told him how great it was that he had made it to finals."

"It was a miracle," Sarah mumbled. "Given everything that's happened this year, it's a miracle."

"She offered to help with his campaign. She wasn't asking to be a big deal, or be in the skit or anything. I know she wasn't. She wanted to make posters or help paint Tom's outdoor display, anything."

Estee stopped talking and looked from Sarah to Meg to see if they understood the enormity of what she was saying.

Meg asked, "What did Tom say? Is he going to let her help?"

"He didn't say anything. He just looked at her with so much hate. Finally when she quit talking, he turned his back on her and walked away."

"What did Jenny do?" Meg said.

"She called out to him, and so did I, but he kept walking. Then Jenny ran in the girl's restroom and cried, and I went with her and cried too. I don't know what to do. Jenny's heart is broken, but I think Tom's heart is broken too." Estee put her head down on the desk and sobbed.

"There's nothing you can do," Meg said. "They'll have to figure out how to forgive each other, and it might not happen quickly." Meg sat down next to Estee and hugged her. "None of this is your fault. You shouldn't feel so bad." She patted Estee on the back but looked up at Sarah.

"This," Sarah whispered, "is why I didn't want Bob to come back."

Bill Cottle picked that moment to tiptoe into the back of the room and wipe imaginary tears off his cheeks. "What's happening?"

he mouthed at Sarah. She just shrugged at him, and he backed out the door, but the minute Estee left, back he came.

"I saw that puddle moving down the hall. I guess that makes it a wave?" No one laughed and he tried again. "I couldn't decide who was the sympathy sobber and who was the real thing. Has Jenny had a change of heart?"

Meg shook her head. Suddenly exhausted, Sarah couldn't make her mouth work. She couldn't expel enough air to be heard. She felt like this weight was squashing all her life force out onto the floor.

"It was a very sad scene," Bill said. "Two little girls, coming out of the restroom, crying their eyes out." He looked from Meg to Sarah. "It looks like two middle-aged girls are going to be doing the same thing. I think I'll leave."

―――∽∾∽―――

Sitting in a booth at McDonald's, Sarah tried to push the stop button in the back of her brain to put yesterday on pause. She rolled a small French fry around on her tongue. When North Valley had won, decorum had flown right out the window. The fledgling attorneys became high school students and acted like a three-point shot had just won a tied game with a rival team.

Now, Estee laughed as Walt mimicked the courtroom drama. He batted his eyes at the small audience and said, "I'll confess to anything if you'll take me to the prom." Everyone laughed, and Kristen threw a French fry at him, which he caught in his mouth, chewed quickly, and swallowed in a large gulp.

"Can you believe the gender switch? Unbelievable." Emily Glass was appalled. "Girls can be nasty, but they're never as overt as that witness statement. Whatever they gained in surprise, they lost in credibility."

The postmortem went back and forth. Sarah knew if she didn't get them in the van soon, they would replay the entire three hours. She stood up and made a show of looking at her wristwatch.

"Let's head out," she announced. There was a slow move to collect belongings and unfinished drinks.

Waiting in the van, Sarah fantasized briefly about a seamless life with a tall man with graying hair and a badge in his pocket, but those possibilities felt hopeless, her future shrouded in a deepening fog. Those moments with Clayton in the parking lot seemed long ago and strangely irrelevant. She revved the engine to let the stragglers know that she meant business.

Kristen slipped into the passenger seat to keep Sarah company, and they were the only occupants of the van who noticed when the April rain came down harder, and in spite of the rhythmic motion of the windshield wipers, it was getting more difficult for Sarah to see the lines on the road as they finally drove out of the canyon and past small farming communities. Relieved to be out of the heavy rainfall in the mountains, Sarah wanted to deposit the students at school and go home.

Only a few highways accessed North Valley. Another road circled up through the small town past the college campus and wound its way up near a golf course nestled in the foothills. Not a route to be taken on a stormy night, the highway passed a dam and followed a river flowing wildly with spring runoff. Steep shafts of granite, interspersed with slopes covered with dense pine, rose steeply on each side of the river. Periodically, a gravel road would break away into a side canyon. The forest was home for wild creatures but an unfriendly environment for adolescents who frequently used the road as a deadly racecourse, or sought its darkness to cover behaviors best hidden.

where's jenny?

*t*oo tired to sleep, Sarah wandered around the kitchen, talking to the dog and idly loading a few dishes in the dishwasher. The rain rattled on the roof, and she listened for Tom to return from taking members of the mock trial team home. Estee had been in that group, and when Tom didn't come back by twelve o'clock, Sarah nodded knowingly to her reflection in the hall mirror and remembered her own behavior when she was seventeen. Determined not to plague herself with memories that would keep her awake, she went to bed with a book she had been reading, one page per night, for two months. It didn't work. She knew he was standing there. Irritated, she glanced up at the ghost, a composite of the boyfriend, young husband, new father, and despised nemesis standing near her bed.

"You can't be here tonight," she snarled. "You stole Jenny, and then you threw her away. You dumped her in front of a semi. Wasn't trashing my life enough?" She turned the pillow over and tried to concentrate, but his face kept getting in the way. She shoved him aside, but he just kept returning.

She picked up her book, but when she tried to focus on the print, all she could see was that persistent ghost. All that love, the tenderness of his touch, and the promises: all lies. Even when she had been so young, she had intuitively known something was wrong. *You could divide people into two groups,* she thought, *givers and takers, and Bob was a world-class taker.* He was going to love her forever? He had cast her off, without a thought, like old clothes, like yesterday's news. Now he had taken Jenny, and he didn't care about her either. She was just a novelty, valued for a season but easily discarded. Hot tears rolled down her face. The ache in the center of her being felt like a black hole, sucking away her life. Sarah sobbed, choking sobs that no one heard, sobs that continued until she was exhausted. She fell asleep in the light of the bedside lamp.

In the middle of the night, the ringing of the telephone awakened her. Thinking immediately that something might have happened to Robbie, she startled awake and grabbed for the phone.

"Sarah," Bob's voice started, "I'm sure it's nothing, but could you check and see if Jenny's there? Is she in her bed?"

Sarah, horrified, didn't say a word. She took three steps across the hall to Jenny's empty room. All her maternal instincts were on high alert when she picked up the receiver. "Isn't Jenny with you? Don't you know where she is?" The digital alarm clock read 3:32. Frightened by the hour and the message, her knees felt watery, and she couldn't collect herself enough to ask coherent questions.

"I don't mean to frighten you. I'm sure it's just a flat tire, or some car thing. There's bound to be a reasonable explanation," Bob floundered. When he had woken up at one a.m., he was immediately uneasy, and around two a.m. he had let go, his imagination racing. Claire was standing at his elbow, and when he shook his head at her, her eyes became round and frightened.

Sarah grasped for information. "She's not here. She's not there. Where is she? When did you see her last?"

"She left here about nine o'clock to get pizza with some friends. They probably went to someone's house to watch a video."

"Friends? What friends? Jenny doesn't have get-a-pizza-and-watch-movies friends," Sarah said.

"She didn't actually say. She just said that she was going to hang out with some girls."

"Who? What are their names?"

"Well, that's what I mean. She didn't actually say. If she had, I'd be calling them and not you. I thought maybe she wanted to help Tom with his posters and decided to stay for the night." He paused. "Or something."

"Jenny's hasn't spoken to me since she ran away. Why would she come here?"

Words were sticking in Bob's mouth. "We had a disagreement," he admitted. "I told her she couldn't go out with that Colton kid anymore. I thought if she was mad about that, she might have gone home."

"You're afraid she's with Tyler."

"It's crossed my mind."

A strange noise erupted out of the pit of Sarah's interior, a primordial groan of maternal anguish. Startled, Bob held the phone away from his ear. He uttered feeble protests trying to convince Sarah not to overreact, but he found he wasn't speaking to a person, just a quiet handset. Sarah had dropped the phone and was frantically pawing through her purse.

Tom, partially aroused by the phone ringing, heard the pattering of his mother's feet on the floor above him. Glancing at his own clock, he wondered what on earth she was doing. He grabbed an old terry-cloth bathrobe and ran up the stairs, two at a time, into the kitchen. Every light was on, and his mother had dumped the contents of her purse out on the kitchen table.

"Mom, what's wrong?"

She didn't answer him. She was searching through the appointment cards, wrinkled receipts, coupons for a free loaf of bread, and other various scraps of paper accumulated in the bottom of her bag. Finally seeing the business card, she grabbed it. She held up the little card in front of Tom's face and shook it hysterically, as she stepped quickly to the phone.

"Jenny's lost." She punched the keys and took several deep breaths as she waited for Clayton to answer.

"Sheriff McLaughlin."

"Oh, Clayton," she blurted, "I think Tyler Colton's taken Jenny."

"Okay, Sarah. I need you to give me exact information. Why do you think she's with him?"

"She's not here. She's not at her dad's. It's the middle of the night." It seemed obvious to Sarah. Tyler had lured her away.

"Who saw Jenny last?"

"Claire."

"What was Jenny wearing?"

"I don't know."

"What kind of car does the boy drive?"

"He drives a new blue truck."

"Can you describe Tyler?"

How could she describe Tyler Colton? He was a bad kid. He was spoiled and rich, condescending and crude, and he used drugs. In all her years of teaching she had only had two students that she thought were really bad people, scary revengeful people, and Tyler was one. Her little girl was somewhere at the mercy of that horrible boy? Her hand holding the receiver shook.

"He's blond, a senior."

"I think I'll come over, and we can sort all this out. In the meantime, let me get her information out to anyone who's patrolling. What does Jenny look like?"

Sarah shook her head stupidly. "She's about five-six. She used to have dark curly hair, and she's only fourteen years old." Sarah started to sob.

"I'm on my way. We'll find her."

She handed the phone to Tom, who placed it carefully in the cradle. Sarah's intuition was receiving crazy signals. She was sure Tyler had plied Jenny with drugs and alcohol. Sickening images of her little girl exploded in her mind. She started to gag and grabbed a dirty dish towel.

Sitting on a kitchen chair, her head in her hands, Sarah rehashed the previous months and did the "if only's," trying to recreate junctures where Jenny could have made different choices, where Sarah could have made different choices. What if Tom had asked Jenny to spend the weekend designing posters? What if she had gone to Bob's house and begged Jenny to come home? What if she had asked Jenny to forgive her? When the clock on the stove read four o'clock, Sarah thought, *What if Jenny's hurt? What if she's dead?*

The thought clutched at the pit of her stomach. She grasped her hair on both sides of her head and pulled back and forth. Tom sat hunched on the couch, watching her. She wanted to cry, but her eyes were dry. She lifted a glass out of the cupboard to get a drink but left it sitting on the counter. Finally, she unlocked the kitchen door and slipped across the damp grass until she was standing in the middle of her garden.

She pushed her toes into the earth matted down by the winter's snow and rain. She held her arms straight out from her body and looked up at the sky, still dark.

"What did Jenny ever do to You? What did she ever do to anyone? Couldn't You aim Tyler at someone a little more deserving?" She waited for an answer, not very patiently. She hated to be a scold, but she didn't have time for the long-suffering routine. "She's only fourteen. All she needed was a couple of friends, not the world's worst boyfriend." In her head she watched Jenny, an isolated little calf wandering along behind a herd that clearly wasn't paying attention. Here came the wolf ready to rip her throat out, and none of those stupid cows knew. They didn't even care. "Please, please, please let Jenny be okay. I'll do better. I'll be a better mom to Jenny. I'll love the rotten kids at school, I promise I will, if You'll just let Jenny be okay."

—∿∿—

Tom heard the knock on the door. He let Clayton in.

"Where's your mom?

Tom gestured to the window over the kitchen sink. "She's out in her garden talking to God. She's lost it. This has been coming all year." They both looked out the window at Sarah, standing in the dirt in worn, threadbare pajamas, speaking at the dark, cloudy sky. Tom held on to both sides of the sink, full of dirty dishes, and put his head down on the cold porcelain.

"It's cold out there," Clayton said, zipping his jacket.

"Well, she doesn't feel it," Tom mumbled into the dirty dishes.

Moving quickly, Clayton grabbed the old flannel quilt off the couch. In about three steps he was out the kitchen door and walking deliberately toward Sarah, as though she were a wild animal he didn't want to startle. In one deft motion he picked her up, wrapped the quilt around her and held her close to his chest. He carried her over to a white plastic lawn chair and sat with her on his lap. Pushing her wet hair back from her face with his hand, his lips softly touched her forehead. She started to cry. He shushed her as though she were a small child.

"I'm so frightened. I don't know where she is."

Clayton exhaled. "A highway patrolman found Jenny."

"Is she okay?"

He held onto Sarah tightly. "No. She's not. She's been life flighted to St. Vincent's in Atherton."

little girl lost

Clayton reached across Sarah and pulled a device from the glove compartment. The wires trailed over her lap as he rolled the window down and slapped the magnetized light on the top of the car. Moments later the siren was wailing and the light was flashing. The windshield wipers moved back and forth rhythmically. He stepped on the accelerator, and the car sped past the few cars on the wet road in the gray morning light.

He patted Sarah's leg as he reached for the radio to call dispatch.

"Marilyn, this is Sheriff McLaughlin. Contact Dr. Bob Williams and tell him his daughter is at St. Vincent's, and he probably needs to head over there quickly, if he doesn't already know. Thanks."

Looking over his shoulder at Tom, he said, "It wouldn't surprise me if someone in the ER called your dad before they flew her over. Maybe he'll meet us there."

Tom had retreated into the corner of the backseat and didn't answer. His baseball cap was pulled down low, concealing his eyes.

"How much longer?" Sarah asked.

"Ten minutes."

"Did they tell you anything else? A head injury—was that all they said?"

"I'm not holding anything back, Sarah. They flew her over because the helicopter was right there on the tarmac, and St. Vincent's has a neurosurgeon. That's all I know."

He flipped off the siren when he was within a few blocks of the hospital. Making a right turn, he rolled into the parking space designated for emergency vehicles.

"Let's go," Clayton said, but Sarah was already out the car door and headed for the glaring lights of the emergency entrance. She ran to the desk and accosted the clerk making computer entries.

"Jenny Williams? Where is she?"

The clerk glanced at her disheveled hair and gave Sarah a blank look before making a few clicks with his mouse.

Clayton, standing behind her, said, "She just came in on that helicopter. A fourteen-year-old with a head injury."

"Right." The clerk looked at the screen. "Are you the mom?"

Sarah nodded.

"The neurosurgeon saw her when she came in."

"Can we go to her?

The clerk looked over Sarah's head to Clayton. "You the dad?"

Clayton shook his head.

"Well, they're planning on taking her right up to the OR. I have a few things that I need you to sign." He pushed a form in Sarah's direction. "Do you have your insurance card with you?"

Sarah leaned forward over the counter until she was inches from the clerk's face. "I want to see my daughter. I want to talk to the neurosurgeon. Right now." Her hands were shaking, and she gripped the edges of the Formica counter top. She was breathing quickly, almost panting.

The automatic door opened with a whoosh, and Bob ran into the reception area. He stopped, ashen-faced. Tucking his wrinkled flannel shirt into his pants, he took two deep breaths.

He's putting on his doctor face. She could almost see him counting to ten. *I want to kill him*, she thought.

Bob hurried to the desk. "Where is she? Where's Jenny?"

"The clerk said they took her right up to the OR," Sarah said. "She had a CT scan at North Valley. That's all that we know."

"That CT scan's why they shipped her." Quickly, he looked around the waiting area, avoiding Sarah's eyes, and then stepped to the counter. "I'm Dr. Williams. Which OR suite are they using?"

The young man nodded. "Number two." Bob turned toward the elevators.

"Dad, can I go with you?"

Bob shook his head. He reached over and squeezed Tom's shoulder. "Let me find out what's going on. I'll be right back. There's a waiting room over there." He gestured with his hand. "Wait for me."

As though they had anywhere else to go. Sarah watched him hurry toward the elevators. She wanted to follow him to see Jenny, to know how badly she was hurt, but Clayton grabbed her arm and ushered her across the hall. He draped his corduroy jacket around her shoulders and pushed her gently onto the couch. She sputtered, "I'm not a shock victim," but he put up his hand to silence her.

"Yes, you are. Can I get you anything? A drink? A sandwich? Stay with your mom, Tom. I need to make a couple of calls." He walked away.

"Women and children into the life boats while the manly men go off to do their manly men stuff, and no one will talk to me about my little girl. No one will let me see my little girl." She made a motion to stand, and Tom stopped her.

"Mom, no one is going to let us see Jenny right now. It's too late. We should have seen Jenny yesterday, last week, before this all happened. I should have gone over to Dad's house and brought her home."

"But we didn't, did we?" Her fingers tightened on the armrest on the side of the couch.

They sat huddled together. Tom studied his palms, and Sarah watched the second hand on the clock go round and round and round. Bob had been gone an hour.

The sky was growing light. Sarah cracked the window open a couple of inches and wondered where the birds were she could hear chirping. People were talking in the reception area. The shift must be changing. A custodian was vacuuming the mauve carpet near the door. Clayton came in carrying donuts and hot chocolate. Tom took a Styrofoam cup and set it on the napkin on the end table. Sarah held up her hands in refusal.

"If I eat that, I'll puke."

"We've already done that, haven't we?" He smiled kindly at her. It occurred to her that their only inside joke involved vomit. Pulling a chair over, he faced Sarah and Tom. "Well, this is what I've found out. Someone made an anonymous call from a public phone at that 7-Eleven on Sycamore. He said Jenny was seriously hurt and that she was at the Bird Hollow picnic area up the canyon. Clark Liddell, he's a highway patrol officer, found her. He couldn't revive her at the scene. He called for an ambulance. He reported a lot of blood, but he's young and a little blood goes a long way. It was raining pretty hard by the time he got there and the temperature was dropping. He didn't see anything or anyone. Detectives will go up this morning. They might already be there, but this rain is going to obliterate any tire tracks." He didn't tell them that Jenny's pants had been jerked down around her knees, probably causing her to lose her balance and fall against the granite outcropping. Her wrist looked broken, and she had a black eye and facial contusions that probably occurred previous to the fall. He wasn't going to mention that either.

"Up the canyon?" Tom asked.

"It would have taken us days to find her if we hadn't received that call. Do you think she might have been with other kids besides Tyler? A group?"

Sarah bit her lip and shook her head.

"I'd be willing to bet it was just Tyler Colton." Tom's voice was so quiet, so cold.

Clayton bent over and put both of his hands on Tom's shoulders. "Then who called? We aren't going to know anything for sure until Jenny can talk to us, or until this mystery caller comes forward. I don't want you to go off and do something stupid that will cause your mother more grief."

Sarah clenched her fists. "He'll have to stand in line to murder Tyler Colton. If anything happens to Jenny, I'll strangle him with my bare hands." Then she paused, realizing that something had already happened to Jenny, and they were sitting here waiting to hear how terrible that something was. Clayton rested his hand on her shoulder. The gentle weight was comforting, but he couldn't protect her. He couldn't erase a head injury. He couldn't make the second hand on that clock move any faster.

He reached over and held Sarah's hand. "A forensic nurse will come this afternoon when Jenny's out of the OR to collect physical evidence. It's routine in a situation like this."

"What will they do?" Tom asked. Her face blanched, Sarah sat tight-lipped, not speaking.

"They'll want the clothes she was wearing. They'll take photographs. They'll be looking for DNA. Anything under her fingernails, in her mouth. They'll do a rape kit."

Sarah whispered so quietly that Clayton had to lean forward to hear her. "But she won't know, will she?"

Clayton nodded. "I don't think so. I imagine that the detective will be paying Tyler Colton a visit this morning to see where he was last night. They'll probably be talking to Claire and your husband later today."

Sarah leaned her head against the back of the couch, opening her eyes periodically to look at the clock. Eight-thirty, nine o'clock, quarter to ten.

Bob finally appeared at the waiting room door. Exhausted, his shoulders sagged and every line on his face was etched more deeply. "She's out of surgery."

"Where have you been for so long?" Sarah demanded. "Is she going to be okay?"

He shrugged. "I wanted to see the films post-op. We won't know anything until the swelling goes down. Her skull's fractured. She had a big hematoma on the right side of her brain, which was causing the brain to shift. They evacuated that. Stopped the bleeding. They'll try and use medications to control the swelling. That's the immediate risk, the swelling."

"Explain," Sarah said.

"When the brain swells, there's no place for expansion to go. It forces the brain down into the brain stem. That's fatal. If Jenny had been up the canyon a couple more hours, she would have died—up there alone in the rain. I can't stand this." His hands trembled, and he sat down heavily in a chair. Dark circles hung under his eyes.

"Whoever made that call saved her," Tom said quietly.

"What call?" Bob asked.

"Someone called," Clayton said. "Someone told us where she was and that she was hurt."

"Hey. More information." Sarah tapped insistently on Bob's knee. "What if they can't stop the swelling?"

"They could lift a section of her skull, but I don't think that's going to happen. Don't borrow trouble."

A short, balding man, Bishop Richards, came through the door. "Sarah, how's Jenny?"

She looked up at him, and suddenly, for no reason that made any sense to her, she started to cry. All the terror of the last few hours welled up inside her and came out in wrenching sobs. So what if Bob and Clayton saw a pudgy man who probably voted a straight Republican ticket; she saw the bishop.

Ingrained since childhood in the back of her head, the arrival of the bishop was just like the cavalry coming over the top of the hill to save the settlers who were down to their last bullet or morsel of food. He was hope. His coming would set her little Mormon congregation in motion. She didn't know what would happen to Jenny, but she did know that starting in a couple of days, women would bring a kind word, and a hug, and dinner, for weeks if she needed it. The scout troop would arrive on a Saturday morning to spring-clean her yard. Her dirty laundry would vanish and reappear cleaned, pressed, and folded. But most important, this man would stay by her side as long as she needed him.

He sat down on the couch, nodded at Tom, and held Sarah in his arms. She couldn't talk. Her chest heaved with noisy sobs, and no one else spoke until Bob whispered behind his hand to Tom. "Who is this guy?"

"Bishop Richards."

"Is he tight with your mom?"

"No, she doesn't like him."

"If I live to be a million, I will never understand your mother." Bob watched the bishop, who, with small hushing noises and little clichéd phrases, calmed Sarah.

"Doesn't church start in fifteen minutes?" she asked, because the bishop wasn't wearing a suit. He looked more like he was ready for a ward work project in a faded cotton shirt and baggy jeans, but he just waved a hand to dismiss her question.

"Dave Jones can handle it. This is where I need to be." He listened patiently to Sarah's halting description of the previous night. He bowed his head thoughtfully for a moment before he said, "Well, we need to have the ward fast and pray for Jenny. I'll call Dave in a minute. He can announce it at sacrament meeting. Has Jenny had a blessing?"

Sarah shook her head.

"Tom and I will need to do that first thing when she's out of recovery. Is there anyone we need to call?"

"Oh, my brother, Carter. How could I have forgotten him?" She started to cry again.

"With all you've been through last night, I'd be surprised if you can remember your name. Don't beat yourself up. We'll have Tom call him."

Clayton chose this minute to leave. He touched Sarah's shoulder and told her that he would call her later. Bob stood up and shook his left leg, standing on it gingerly as though he wasn't sure it would support his weight.

"I'm going to check on Jenny," he grumbled.

The bishop sat between Tom and Sarah and held their hands. "We need to remember that God has a plan for Jenny, and we need to be strong enough to understand that His will is what's important, not ours. Sarah, I know you're strong, maybe not today or tomorrow, but you will be. You'll survive this, and whatever happens, we know, absolutely, that Jenny will be loved and cared for. Everything is going to be okay in God's time." He bent his head and started to pray fervently.

A young nurse waited patiently by the door. Hearing the prayer, she automatically folded her arms across her chest and bowed her head. After the final amen, she spoke softly, "Jenny's out of recovery. She's been moved up to Two South. Dr. Williams wanted me to tell you."

The ride up the elevator was a blur. The bishop gripped her elbow and guided her down the corridor and past a nurse's station into a secondary hallway. Everything beige melded together, the walls, the chairs, equipment, but bland colors didn't calm the feeling of panic surging in her head.

The rooms in the surgical ICU were small and clustered around the nurses' station. Four of the beds were occupied by patients, no longer people, victims covered in faded pastel sheets. Jenny was unrecognizable. Most of her hair had been shaved away. The top of her head was loosely bandaged in white gauze, tinged with pink where blood had oozed through. Her features were small protrusions on a face twice its normal size. Her eyes were narrow slits. Purple bruising on the left side of her face made Sarah shudder. A plastic tube secured with white surgical tape filled Jenny's mouth and forced air into her lungs as a machine next to her bed hissed and moved its mechanical diaphragm. Lines and wires connected Jenny to bags of fluid and electronic monitoring devices, and above her bed six multi-colored blips made their way across a monitor.

Sarah moaned.

A young man in a white lab coat looked up from the chart he was discussing quietly with Bob. "You're Jenny's mom?"

She nodded. She didn't have the energy to open her mouth, certainly not enough energy to speak.

"We're not really going to know the extent of Jenny's injuries until the swelling goes down. I want you to keep something in mind the next few days. If this had happened to my mother, it would have killed her. If you had this serious an injury, you wouldn't recover completely, but Jenny's very young. She's still capable of producing new neurological pathways. Her strength and her age are a huge advantage." His eyes flicked toward Bob. "This is not the time to give up hope. I know she looks terrible right now, but she took quite a beating, and the surgery was pretty traumatic. Try not to be influenced by how she looks."

He left the chart in Bob's hands and went on to the next room.

Tom and Sarah clung to each other. *My baby,* Sarah kept thinking. *She's going to die. What did I think was so important?* She wanted to hug Jenny, pull her up off the bed and hold her in her arms. She wanted to tear out all the wires and tubes and take her home, but instead she clutched Tom's arm more tightly. Her eyes moved back and forth between Jenny and the monitor. Bob stood on the opposite side of the bed, watching them, watching Jenny. "I'm going to call Claire." He coughed roughly into his hand.

"I can't handle having Claire here right now, Dad," Tom said. He shook his head slightly, looking down at the linoleum. Bob shrugged. He covered his mouth with his palm.

"It's our turn now, Tom," said the bishop. "We won't be anointing her head, and that's okay. Let's wash our hands, and instead of putting our hands on her head, we'll touch her gently on the shoulders. I think God and Jenny will understand, don't you?" He smiled and went over to the sink.

The bishop moved deftly over to Jenny's bed. "Okay, Tom, I want you to muster all the faith you have and all the love you feel for your sister."

Tom mumbled in a thick voice, "She needed me and I turned my back on her."

The bishop looked down at the swollen, distorted face, and the smile left his lips. "We all failed Jenny. I failed. Her Mia Maid teacher failed her, the girls in her class. Your mom, your dad. We all failed Jenny. We were slow to love and quick to judge. But I think God's going to give us a second chance. We'll sort out all of those feelings, but not now, Tom. Right now I want you to focus on Jenny getting well. Are you with me?"

Tom looked in the bishop's eyes. The creases across Tom's forehead eased, and he gave a quick nod and softly put his hands on Jenny's shoulder. Bob sidled toward the door. He jammed his hands into the pockets of his jeans.

"All right, let's begin. Sister Jennifer Sarah Williams, by the power I hold . . ." And he blessed her. He blessed her that if it was God's will, she would heal and be well and strong. Her mind would be quick. He reminded her of her family and how much they all loved her and needed her. As he spoke, Sarah thought about her little Jenny and resolved for the hundredth time that day to fix what was broken between them, if she only had time.

She felt the tension in her forearms start to relax. Maybe Jenny would be okay, but as she peeked out her left eye at the figure on the bed, she had to fight down a wave of anguish and hopelessness that threatened to knock her down. After amen had been pronounced, everyone traded weepy hugs, and Sarah glanced over to see Meg standing in the door with a large chocolate cake in her hand.

"Clayton called me. I didn't know what else to do." Looking at Jenny out of the corner of her eye, she said, "You know, besides going out on the porch and screaming."

The bishop included Meg in his effusive smile. "You were inspired. This is just what we need. Tom, ask the nurses for some napkins."

How does he do it, Sarah thought. *How does he keep us all moving forward?* She felt like a dead weight being hauled over icy slopes up Mount Everest. *He keeps finding little jobs to keep Tom busy.* Her inclination was to curl up in the fetal position under Jenny's bed and cry until sleep-induced amnesia freed her.

"Food and rest." The bishop nodded significantly. "For the next two weeks it's going to be very important for everyone to get plenty of sleep and remember to eat regularly. Let's start with that cake."

Sarah took a large glob of chocolate frosting on her finger and stuck it in her mouth. It tasted like paste. Everyone started to whisper. Meg asked the nurse questions about the monitor. The bishop grasped Tom's arm and said, "Tom, in a couple of days, I want you to spend some time thinking about what we can all do to help Jenny. You're closer to her than anyone. I want you to be the point man on this."

Meg apologized to the nurse for having a cake in the ICU. The middle-aged woman, previously all-business as she checked an IV line, grinned at Meg. "Families heal," she said.

Bob stood at the door, his shoulder leaning against the doorjamb. He stared stupidly at the group, blinking, not talking. He refused a piece of cake. Sarah was the only one who noticed him leave.

election speech

*W*hat am I doing here? This is so worthless. The lighting was directed at the stage, right in his eyes. Tom couldn't see the faces in the auditorium, but he knew they were there watching him, whispering about him, about his family, about his sister lying in a hospital bed looking like a monster. Someone had ironed his shirt, and a red carnation with a gold ribbon was pinned onto his chest. That morning he had pulled on a pair of khaki pants from the pile on the basement floor and given them a shake, checking for spiders. He knew he looked rumpled, but no one would notice his pants, not when they could gossip about his family. He rubbed his hand across the perspiration on his forehead and looked at Lucy Bennett at the podium. She must have said something funny. Everyone was laughing, everyone but him. He was up next, the last speaker.

Nothing like a scandal to heighten everyone's senses. Everyone knew about it. A girl had been lying in the hospital for six days, maybe dying. Maybe she'd never wake up. She'd been left for dead up the canyon. Who left her there? What had they been doing? How did she hit that granite rock so hard that her head nearly exploded? How scintillating. What a buzz Monday morning. He felt nauseated.

Bill Cottle, his mom's friend, had organized his campaign, breaking all school rules, but who cared. "I've seen a million of these, kid. I know what sells. Don't give it a thought. We've got it covered." And

Bill did. He pulled together a handful of Tom's friends and put on a campaign. Estee and Matt hung his posters. Uncle Carter built his display on the school lawn. But Tom had written his own speech. It was there folded in half, in his pocket. He wiped his sweaty palms on his knees.

He should be grateful. He was here—pretty much in one piece. His mother had implored him with her eyes in Jenny's hospital room. "You can't quit your life, Tom. That won't help Jenny. She'll probably be fine by the time school starts next fall. This is a very bad patch, but you've got to keep going." So he did, but this morning, he had driven to the hospital instead of going to school. He didn't know why. Maybe to see Jenny, maybe to get his mom's blessing, he didn't know, but he had arrived just in time to hear his parents carving each other up.

Claire wasn't there. She'd been a fixture in the small alcove outside Jenny's room since Sunday, sitting in the same chair in the corner, quietly wringing her hands. She sat there with her fussy hair and her fussy face, like an elaborate dessert no one wanted to eat, guilt all over her face, untouched knitting in her lap. But this morning, no Claire. Something was up. His parents didn't see him as he paused by the door. They were locked onto each other.

His dad, sitting next to his mom, was holding both of her hands tightly like he was afraid she was going to run away or, worse, hit him. He was telling her that Jenny might not be the same. A personality shift, he said, maybe subtle, maybe dramatic. The longer it took her to wake up, the worse it was likely to be. His dad was frightened. Tom could see it in his face. His dad had told him the night before that Jenny's brain scan looked like a stroke victim.

"And what if Jenny doesn't wake up?" his mother had asked.

"Don't go there," his dad had said, irritated. "She'll wake up. Quit borrowing trouble."

"But what if she doesn't wake up?" His mother pushed to the edge of the worst possible scenario.

"It's no life," he had said. All the crazy stories you hear about people waking up in ten or twenty years. They're one in a million, but they get a lot of press, so people think they're the norm. A persistent vegetative state is no good, existing in an institution, curled up in the fetal position, and alive with tubes. "There are worse things than dying," he kept insisting.

His mother had given him a withering look. It was as though she had been in slow motion for the last five days. It was like she was taking her time, sharpening her knife before she sliced into his dad.

"So Jenny's life might not be the same?" she questioned. "What life? When did Jenny ever have much of a life? The little dignity she had was trashed when you came back. You did this to Jenny. If you had stayed in Iowa, none of this would ever have happened. Fathers are supposed to protect their daughters, but you fed her to the wolves. Being a parent isn't the party you thought, is it? Why don't you slink back to Iowa?" she had finished, and his father had looked like she had nicked his carotid and all the blood had drained right out of his face. His hands trembled slightly when he looked up toward the door, but Tom had left. He ran down the back stairs and out to his truck in the parking lot.

He had driven back to North Valley, missing his first two classes. He stopped to get a couple of donuts and a pint of milk at a drive-in. He could handle the milk, but when he tried to eat the donuts, he started to retch. He opened his car door and threw up on the pavement. Finally making his way to the school auditorium, he stuck his head under the faucet in a dressing room and then stood patiently as Estee helped him into a white shirt and pinned the corsage on his shoulder.

"You can do this, Tom." She smiled up at him. "Everything's going to be okay." But, of course, nothing was okay. Nothing would ever be okay.

———◆———

"I hope you'll vote for me." Lucy was hitting her time limit. "But if Tom wins," and she turned to give him her thousand watt smile, "I want you to know that he'll have my support. One hundred percent." Applause exploded in the auditorium, and Lucy's supporters started to chant, "Lu—see, Lu—see."

Tom paused for a minute. His knees didn't seem connected to the rest of his body. He pulled the folded paper out of his pocket and smoothed it on his leg. He rolled his eyes back and looked up at the curtain, knowing if he started to cry that would be all anyone ever remembered about this assembly. The boy sitting next to him gave him a nudge, and Tom hauled himself over to the podium.

"I've never really been into history," he started. History? No laughs there. What had he been thinking? He plowed ahead.

"When Mr. Cottle started to drag us through the Civil War last December, I was totally not interested." A few courtesy laughs. He thought he could hear Estee. "But then my mom told me that I had a great-great-grandfather who was wounded in the Battle at Shiloh and left for dead on the battlefield. He was only seventeen. He'd never left home before, but when they mustered a regiment in Selma, Alabama, he went with them. The men in his regiment were all guys he had grown up with. Their captain was his cousin's stepfather. That would be like all of us walking out the front door and climbing onto trucks to go and fight a war together. I can see us electing Coach Thornton as our captain"—he got some laughs here; Mr. Thornton was a large grizzly-bear sort of man, who coached the basketball team—"and if it was like the Civil War, we would all be together. Until some of us were killed.

"There was a famous regiment from Maine that held the Union flank at Gettysburg the second day by fixing their bayonets and charging when they were out of ammunition. The third day at Gettysburg, this same regiment was given a rest assignment at the center of the Union Line. Picket's charge came right at them. At the end of the third day of fighting, of the eight hundred members of that regiment from the same town in Maine, only a hundred men survived.

"Brothers, friends, men who had grown up together would march, fight, and watch each other die. There were no dog tags. At night soldiers would go back to the battlefield to find their friends before the corpses were unrecognizable. Can you imagine searching a field in the dark with a lantern, trying to remember where your brother or your best friend had fallen? That would be pretty tough.

"There are lessons to be learned from struggle and the value of friends during difficult times. We aren't going to march into an artillery barrage with General Pickett, but we'll all have battles of our own that threaten to destroy us. Most of the time we just march along together, but when our friends get into battle, there's no safety in watching from the sidelines. We can't look at the struggle and say, 'I'm glad that's not me.' No, we have to help.

"We have to take our lantern and go out onto the battlefield and look for our friends, secure in the knowledge that if the situation were reversed, if we were lost or hurt, they would come and find us." He paused for a moment to swallow the large lump that had been building in his throat.

"My great-great-grandfather's friends came and found him. He had a terrible leg wound and limped badly for the rest of his life, but he lived.

"Saturday night," he said—and the rustling in the auditorium hushed—"someone made a phone call that saved my sister's life, probably someone right here in the auditorium. She was left for dead, and you saved her. I don't know who you are, maybe I never will, but I want to thank you for Jenny's life."

He straightened up and pulled away from the microphone. The audience didn't erupt with enthusiasm and no one chanted his name, but slowly students began to stand and clap politely until the entire audience was on their feet, and Mr. Schuback stood up to dismiss them to fourth hour. Tom knew he'd lost, and he didn't care.

—◊◊◊—

The nurse brought a lunch tray into Sarah. "Mrs. Coleman is down having a procedure. I thought you might like her lunch."

Sarah smiled. Everyone was trying to fatten her up. Standing at Jenny's bedside, she dabbed a Q-tip covered with Vaseline under the feeding tube threading into Jenny's left nostril and rubbing against her cheek. She glanced up at the sound of a knock on the doorjamb. Terry Schuback was waiting there, not speaking, with a small white envelope in his hand.

"I just wanted to bring you this," he said, averting his eyes from Jenny's limp form. "We're all praying for you, Sarah." He handed her the envelope and then slipped away as quietly as he had come.

She tossed the Q-tip into the wastebasket and flipped open the seal on the envelope. She pulled out the card with a North Valley crest in the corner. "Congratulations, Mom, it's a president."

Sitting down on the chair, she started to cry.

pick up your handcart and go

*S*hafts of sunshine breaking through the rain clouds came in the west windows, warming the room, and Sarah, listening to the rhythmic whir and hiss from the respirator, fell asleep. She jerked awake. Bob was touching her shoulder lightly, a serious expression on his face.

"Go home, Sarah. You're exhausted. I've got the afternoon off. I'm going to sit here and hold down the fort." Bob held a couple of thick medical journals next to his chest like a shield.

"I can't leave her."

"Sure you can. She's going to be okay. Go celebrate with Tom. Whatever. I won't leave this room. I guess you've been sleeping on that chair?" He nodded skeptically at the hospital issue recliner in the corner. "I can do that too."

She looked dubious.

"Really," he said. "Sleep in your own bed. Come back in the morning."

Her eyes narrowed. "How do I know you won't unplug her while I'm gone?"

Suddenly flushed with anger, he took two steps in her direction, grabbed her wrist, and yanked her out of a chair. "Stop it, Sarah, stop it. You've cut me out and pushed me aside for the last time. I'm sick of it. I love Jenny too."

Her heart was racing. She was so close to him she had to tip her head back to look into his face and sneer. "What do you know about love? How much did you love her when she was a baby and you were out with Claire every chance you could get?"

He gasped, as though she had slapped him. "You need to learn the words to a new song. That one's worn out. The perfect mother. The evil father. Some creep hated you enough to do this to Jenny. How does that fit your martyr status?"

She wished she could spit at him, but she had never learned how. She needed to be taller, bigger. She wanted to slap him, but he wrenched her wrist hard until it was touching his chest. She yelped. He was hurting her. She could smell the starch in his shirt and got a whiff of his cologne. She winced as his fingers squeezed her more tightly, and he whispered, "Do you know how many times I've closed my eyes and seen your face telling me that my kids, my own kids, would grow up hating me?"

"You deserved it."

"What about you? It wouldn't have killed you to answer my letters. I was the one who wanted counseling. You wouldn't even meet me halfway. You wouldn't even try. You just wanted to twist the knife. And when I came back, you and your sick old witch of a mother hid the kids from me. What a fool I was, standing there with a puppy and a sack of presents."

Her eyes widened. "What letters?"

He dropped her hand and stared. "The letters I wrote from Switzerland."

"I never got any letters."

He groaned and sat down awkwardly on the chair next to Jenny's bed and buried his face in the white cotton blanket.

Anguish welled up in her, a wail or a sob, and her mouth opened, but nothing came out. She felt like her stomach had dropped seven stories, leaving her body behind. She gazed at the back of his head for what seemed like an eternity. Finally, she touched his shoulder with the tips of her fingers.

"Go home, Sarah," he mumbled into the blanket. "Nothing will happen to Jenny while I'm here."

She stared at the monitor for a minute before she picked up her purse and sweatshirt and headed out the door.

Then she stopped, leaning against a gurney in the hall until the walls stopped moving. He had written to her? Multiple times? He had come back to her after he got home? How had she missed this? Hiding the kids? How had she not known? Why hadn't she tried? She couldn't get her head around what he had said. Clearly he was telling the truth. But she had been so sure. How could she have been so wrong? She imagined her mother sneaking letters out of the mailbox. Her brain felt like it was choking.

—⁓—

She closed the kitchen door with her foot. Slowly, she walked from room to room in the dense quiet, picking up her children's belongings and setting them down again, looking but not seeing. She was so tired. She lay down on the edge of Jenny's bed and fingered the old stuffed monkey Jenny loved. She didn't need to hear Jenny play the piano or be a witness in mock trial. It would be enough to have Jenny home. Jenny could hang out in Sarah's classroom after school and laugh at Bill and feel safe with Meg. Sarah wouldn't push her away. It would be enough. She pushed her nose into the rough fur and tried to close her eyes. Sleep wouldn't come.

She paced down the hall and kicked off her shoes by her bedroom door. Her bed was made and a pile of laundry was folded neatly on the bedspread. She heard Einstein lumbering up the stairs. The last few days, he had been hanging out in the basement with Tom, sleeping under the bottom bunk. He wagged his tail and pushed under Sarah's hand with his nose.

"I love you too, old friend." She hugged the dog. A note from Tom was sitting on the kitchen table.

Mom, I called the hospital, but you weren't there??? Sister Wartle wants you to call her if you don't want her to bring dinner at five-thirty. Maybe I'll bring Estee over.

He had underlined *don't* three times. She wondered where he was. Celebrating? She glanced at the clock on the stove. One-thirty on Friday afternoon. He was at school. Was school still happening? She wasn't there. She'd forgotten her life, her responsibilities for six days. Who was taking her classes? Who had written lesson plans for the sub? Meg and Bill, she was sure. The freshman mock trial team should have played on Wednesday. Did they win? Bob had written to her and wanted to try a reconciliation, twelve years ago. Her mind wouldn't engage.

The sun's rays were coming through the windows. The rain, drizzling or coming down in torrents for the last week, had finally stopped. Einstein barked twice at the kitchen door. Slowly, she followed him out to the carport. Her digging fork and her gardening shoes waited for her in the corner by the bag of fertilizer and an odd assortment of terracotta pots. Sitting on the bottom step, she smacked both shoes on the concrete, checking for anything creepy, before she put them on. With the digging fork over her shoulder, she wandered through the damp grass toward her garden. Most of the blossoms had fallen off the apple trees, creating smudges of pink and white in the grass. New leaves were so small they didn't show much yet, but each tree had a shading of that wonderful chartreuse color of early spring.

Everything was blurred; she felt as though she were standing in the middle of a Monet painting. She dropped her digging fork, stretched her arms out, and started turning in circles until she was twirling. When she was a little girl, her mother had sewn a wonderful skirt specifically for twirling. She would twirl and twirl and twirl, with her skirt lifting around her, until she fell onto the couch. Now the fruit trees, and the garden, the back of her house, and neighbor's fence went round and round. Too dizzy to stand, Sarah fell down and lay still with the grass poking her face.

She rolled over to pick up a dirt clod, sniffed it, and crumbled it between her fingers. She closed her eyes and turned her face up toward the sun pushing back the clouds after so many dark days. She felt its warmth on her face and the promise that spring really had arrived.

Standing up, she waited for the yard to quit spinning. She squared her shoulders and shoved the digging fork into the packed earth. She put all her weight on the rim before the fork went down into the dirt. As she turned the fork load over, a fat pink earthworm wiggled back to safety. She worked without any set pattern, turning over the earth, pulling out straggly, dead tomato plants, thinking about what she would plant. She worked hard until perspiration trickled under her arms and her back ached, then she lay down in the damp grass next to the pile of weeds and dead plants and watched the gray clouds moving slowly in the jet stream.

Her mother, dead for five years, buried and safe from the horror of what she had done. Her mom had spent her whole life being afraid in a world full of secrets. Had she been alone all these years because of her mother? But what if Bob had been a serial adulterer? What if it had happened over and over again? But what if they had sorted it out and been happy? What would Jenny be like? Ideas flitted into her head, ricocheted around her brain, and vanished. She couldn't grasp a thought and wrestle with it until she understood.

What had he written in those letters? What had her mother done with them? He had tried. It didn't absolve him, but he had tried. He had tried and she hadn't. If she had called him, when he was reaching for her, would Jenny be lying in that hospital bed? Her whole body ached for Jenny. She shook her head.

"What now?" she whispered up to the sky. It was so still. She could barely hear a neighbor backing out of his driveway. A pair of robins was poking around a flower bed looking for building materials.

She sat straight up, her hand shielding her eyes. "What do You mean, pick up my handcart and go? Go where?" Sticking a single blade of grass in her mouth, she tried to think. She looked up at the sky again.

"I don't think there's any point in being so cryptic. You know, no one understands Isaiah."

She lay back down in the grass and looked up at the clouds. Then she rolled over onto her stomach to watch the birds hoping around the garden, poking at bits of dead grass. She pushed a couple of twigs toward them. "Think of me as Home Depot," she murmured.

Suddenly, she saw herself sitting out in the middle of nowhere in Wyoming, completely alone. A trail cut through dry sagebrush stretched all the way to the horizon. Her handcart was bogged down in deep wagon ruts. Tears tracked through the dirt on her cheeks. Everyone had gone on without her. How long had she been sitting there, in the dust and the stifling heat, cradling a dead marriage in her arms?

"I need to pick up my handcart and go," she said. "You're right. You're always right, but why did You wait so long to tell me?"

The robins hopped over to the garden, looking for the worm in the newly turned earth.

"Why did I wait so long to ask?" She bit down on her knuckle to keep from crying.

—⁂—

A gray-haired woman put a breakfast tray on a cart while an ICU nurse pushed past with a tray full of medications. Dodging the early morning bustle, Sarah, her hair still wet from the shower, paused at the door. Bob was sitting close to the side of Jenny's bed, holding her limp hand, slowly kissing each finger.

He looked up at her with red-rimmed eyes before he spoke in a gruff voice. "Sarah, she just squeezed my hand."

"She's going to get better?"

"Maybe."

The room was quiet except for the soft electronic whir of the monitors.

"Where's the respirator?" she asked. The tube in Jenny's mouth was gone.

"They started weaning her from the ventilator yesterday afternoon, but she wasn't quite ready. They let her rest overnight and tried again early this morning. She did better, so they pulled the tube. She's been breathing on her own since then."

"What do you mean she wasn't ready?" She tried to keep the panic out of her voice.

"The sedation didn't wear off as quickly as they'd thought, and they didn't want to extubate her at night."

"Why didn't you call me?" She tugged on her fingers with her right hand.

"Because I was afraid you would act just like this if we didn't get her off the ventilator. I can't handle anything more. I'm worn out—just plain worn out."

She nodded her head and stood at the end of the hospital bed, rubbing Jenny's foot for several minutes before she moved the blanket out of the recliner and sat down. Bob wouldn't look at her. A pink ball of Claire's yarn rolled across the floor. A sack of stale donuts sat on the windowsill. Sarah reached in and broke a piece off and chewed thoughtfully for a moment.

"I don't love you anymore," she said.

"I can probably live with that."

"You don't understand."

He put one palm up in protest. "That's okay. Please don't explain." He tucked Jenny's hand under the covers and turned toward Sarah. "I thought about us most of the night. I even thought about going back to Iowa, but I'm not going to leave. When Jenny's well, I'd like us all to get some sort of help, some sort of counseling, and try to work through all this anger and bad feelings. I don't know if there are any decent answers, but I think Jenny's seriously introverted, and this is going to make all of that worse. A brain injury exacerbates any personality traits a person already has. I can't have Jenny vanish."

He paused, waiting for a tirade that didn't come. Scrutinizing Sarah's face, he said tentatively, "Maybe we could have a goal of being on a better footing when Robbie comes home."

Home, she thought. *I'm home. You're not home. Robbie's coming home to me.* She thought of the disaster last Christmas had been. She opened her mouth but closed it tightly before a mean retort could flit across her tongue. She looked down at the pink sunburn on her arms and imagined picking up the crossbar of her handcart and pulling as hard as she could.

She sighed. "I'll want Jenny with me this summer."

"Jenny could be in a rehab facility for months."

"Let me finish. For whatever's left of the summer, I want Jenny with me, but in the fall, when school starts, maybe she should live with you." She fought with herself to get the words out. "And Claire. Jenny needs you. She always has." And Sarah started to cry, not a torrent, more of a trickle. "I'd want her on the weekends to go to church with Tom and me." She sat down on the chair and wiped her nose along the sleeve of her T-shirt. "I'm so sorry we've screwed things up so badly for our kids."

He stared out the window, his back toward Sarah until he turned, dumbfounded. He squinted as though he couldn't see her clearly, and then he put his hands on her shoulders and squeezed gently.

"You'd let me have Jenny?"

She gave him a barely perceivable nod.

"We can't go back and undo anything, Sarah. We can only go forward."

"Pick up our handcarts and go," she said.

He gave her a wry smile. "Whatever works."

admissions and confessions

*L*ocker doors slammed behind him, as Brax went from an excited walk to a trot up the stairs and down the math hall. His red hair was rumpled, a letter waved in his hand, and a manila envelope was tucked under his other arm. He didn't smile until he turned into Mrs. Beale's room and saw her correcting tests.

"I'm in at Michigan." A huge smile split across his face. "I was wait-listed and didn't think that I could go anyway, but I got in, and I think I can swing it." He tossed the letter on her desk. "I'm so glad I took the SATs again," he continued in a rush. "I think bumping up my score probably made all the difference, plus the math team taking second at the five-state regional. That probably really helped. I can't believe I got in there. Nobody gets in there. I mean, kids like me don't get in. I can't believe this."

He bounced back and forth across the front of the room, slapping the tops of desks joyfully, until he ran out of breath and sat down in a front-row seat.

Mrs. Beale smiled at Brax, one of her diamonds in the rough. "Well, this is a happy, happy day, and of course, you deserve this. You're on your way." Thinking of hours she had spent after school tutoring him, she chuckled softly. "Have you communicated with the financial aid office?"

"That's the first thing I did. When I got the letter, I mean. I called them. They didn't have my mom's financial stuff, but the lady was nice and tried to ballpark things for me. I can apply for a couple of scholarships and a grant that will cover tuition, but it wouldn't be near enough. Not for living and books and everything." His smile faded. "I was up at Tyler's to show him the letter. I thought maybe he had gotten in somewhere too, and his dad talked to me."

Mrs. Beale placed her pencil carefully on the letter and studied an uncorrected test on her desk, as the crease between her eyebrows deepened.

"He said how grateful he was that I've been such a good friend to Tyler all these years. He said he tries to help one deserving kid each year, and he wrote me a check. Not for the whole thing, but what the grant and scholarships probably won't cover. He even added enough money for me to come home at Christmas and see my mom." He tugged at his bottom lip nervously.

He doesn't want to know, she thought.

Brax hurried on. "He added five hundred dollars a semester for books. He just sat at his desk and wrote me this check for a truckload of money." He shook his head in disbelief.

Mrs. Beale put her elbows up on her desk and rested her chin on her hands. She studied him for several moments without speaking. Then she tapped her cheek with her delicate fingertip.

"Brax," she said as though she were about to explain a difficult algebraic equation, "you saved Jenny's life, didn't you?"

The color left his face. His shoulders sank, and the jubilant expression on his face ebbed away. He opened his mouth several times, but nothing came out. Finally, scrutinizing her face carefully, he said, "How did you know?"

"You just told me." She spoke with adult calm. "It is very important that you act quickly, now, to save yourself."

"I don't get it," he whispered.

"A moral compromise of this enormity will eventually crush you. Mr. Colton is using your dreams to tie you to his son's disaster. You've got to break free."

He turned away from her and looked past the bright red geraniums through the windows as though watching his dreams vanish like a kite when the string snaps.

"Jenny Williams almost died," Mrs. Beale said.

He shook his head, and then he put his face in his hands.

"Were you there?"

"Not when it happened." He didn't speak for several minutes. "I was up the canyon with some guys. Tyler and Jenny came up later. They didn't stay where we were. They kinda walked further up to another campsite, and we took off."

"What prompted you to call the police?"

"He left her there in the rain. He knew she was hurt, really hurt. He came by my house to warn me off. He wanted me to say he'd been with me. He took off in a hurry, and I walked over to the 7-Eleven and called. That's pretty much it."

"Did the police question you?"

He nodded, picking at the dirt under his thumbnail. "I covered for him. I told the cops he was with me."

Mrs. Beale leaned forward and patted his hand.

He looked up at her, tears filling his eyes. "You know what the crazy thing is? He didn't even know Jenny. He didn't even like her. He was using her to tick off her mom, to get even." He coughed twice, rubbing his eyes with the back of his hand.

"You've got to tell the truth. Jenny deserves the truth."

Brax wiped his face on his sleeve. "I know all that. But you don't know how much I need this," and he ran his finger over the letterhead from the University of Michigan. "My mom's worked two rotten jobs forever. Who knows where my dad is. My little sisters are up for grabs. I've got to give my mom something to hold on to. Give my sisters a reason to hold up their heads. It isn't just about me."

"There are other ways, Brax," she insisted.

"Not for me. I'm on my own."

"You and I are both very clever. Surely we can come up with something," she promised. "But now, we're going to the hospital. We're going to see Jenny and tell her parents the truth."

He shook his head. "I don't think I can do that."

"Yes, you can. I'll be with you every step of the way."

———*∞*———

Several gurneys, a crash cart, and a couple of wheelchairs crowded the nurses' station. Mrs. Beale clutched Brax's arm tightly. Noise and confusion followed the nurses as they whisked into patients' rooms with medications or gloved themselves quickly to change a dressing or assist doctors. Mrs. Beale stopped a tall woman holding a clipboard.

"We're looking for Jenny Williams's room. Can she have visitors?"

"Sure, but she won't know you're here," a nurse explained quietly.

"We would like to see her parents, at least. If that is possible." Mrs. Beale nodded at the bouquet of daisies Brax was carrying awkwardly. The nurse pointed toward the west end of the ward and continued making notations on the clipboard.

Sarah flipped a light blanket over her daughter when they appeared at the door. A handsome man, absorbed in the information on a chart, glanced up. Mrs. Beale assumed he must be Jenny's father. A blonde woman stood up, fluttered her hands, and then sat down again without saying anything.

A familiar person squeezed past them and set a white sack from Big Blue Take-out on the windowsill. He turned to stare at the unlikely pair. "Mrs. Beale?" he asked. "I'm Clayton McLaughlin."

She looked at him for a clue as to whom he could be. "Are you an old student?"

"I'm Becky McLaughlin's dad."

"Of course, I should have remembered." She smiled, but Mrs. Beale didn't understand his presence at the bedside until Clayton, as though he sensed trouble, stepped next to Sarah.

Sarah pointed a slender finger at Brax. "Why is he here?"

Mrs. Beale waited a moment, wanting to give Brax the chance to explain, but he couldn't take his eyes away from Jenny's discolored face, her shaved head covered in white bandages, and the purple slits that were her eyes.

"Is all this from hitting the rock?" Brax asked in a low tone of voice.

"Someone slapped her around pretty good before that," Bob answered angrily. "Most of the swelling is from the surgery." He looked hard at Brax. "What do you know about this?"

Mrs. Beale cleared her throat quickly. "Brax is the boy who made the phone call." She held on to his arm protectively. Bob's face colored, and Sarah stared through Brax's red hair and acne as though she could shove her way into his mind.

"You know who did this to my daughter?" Sarah asked sharply.

Brax breathed in and out several times. He avoided Sarah's eyes and stared at Jenny. "Tyler," he said.

Clayton pulled Sarah to his chest quickly, whispered into her hair, and released her. He grabbed a couple of sandwiches out of the sack and headed out the door, gesturing for Brax to follow him. Bob moved to go with them, but Clayton held up his hand.

"Let me talk to him alone."

Mrs. Beale arranged the daisies in a vase on the dresser. "I believe there are some things you should know. In coming here today, Brax is refusing not an insignificant amount of money, money that would have enabled him to attend a very prestigious university this fall. More importantly, I think Brax thought of Jenny as his friend, probably all year."

"Well, it all fits, doesn't it?" Sarah asked.

Feeling the weight of too many years, Mrs. Beale said, "Yes, dear, I'm afraid it does.

A thick silence filled the room. The air, warm and heavy with the odors of disinfectants and sickness, smothered Sarah. Opening the window, she pushed her face against the screen and felt the roughness on her nose. She smelled lilacs in bloom somewhere close on the grounds. She turned away from the window and looked from Jenny to Mrs. Beale. "There are some pieces I don't understand," she said. "The detective told us Brax gave Tyler an alibi. Why is he changing his story now?"

"Brax mentored Jenny all year on the math team. They were friends. This abuse," and Mrs. Beale gestured toward the bed, "ended that friendship. Brax has two little sisters of his own, not much younger than Jenny. He's quite protective of them."

Agitated as though the room was shrinking, Sarah looked down, half expecting to see ants crawling up her forearms. She shook her hands. "Can you excuse me for a minute? I need to call Tom and remind him . . ." Mumbling the rest of her sentence, she was out the door. She questioned the nurse at the desk. "Did you see where Clayton and that red-headed kid went?"

"They were headed toward that atrium by the elevators."

"Thanks." Sarah jogged down the hall. Her heart beat rapidly, and she had to stop to catch her breath by a large rubber tree. Clayton and Brax were sitting in two upholstered mauve chairs. Late afternoon light from a large bank of windows filtered through the leaves of artificial trees. Brax was talking, gesturing with his free hand. He had a sandwich halfway to his mouth when he saw her. He held it midair for a moment; then he took a large bite and swallowed almost without chewing.

Clayton followed Brax's eyes and saw her. He patted the chair next to his, gesturing for her to come over.

She crossed the room quickly, her nostrils flared, and started to speak before she reached the chair. "Did the Coltons try to bribe you? Did Tyler's dad know about Jenny?"

Brax slouched in his chair. "Tyler said his dad didn't know. I don't know if he guessed. Mr. Colton cut me a check for a lot of money, but I don't know if it was a bribe, or if he was sticking it to Tyler."

"You're not making sense," Sarah said.

"They don't get along. All year Mr. Colton's been on Tyler's case. He's worked hard all his life to be able to send Tyler to one of the best schools in the country, so Tyler should do what he has to and get in. But Tyler didn't get in anywhere except here and the U. He didn't even get wait-listed. His last rejection came the night Jenny got hurt. His dad was ballistic. Maybe he was rubbing it in that I got in and Tyler didn't."

"So you all headed up the canyon?" Clayton asked.

Brax nodded.

Glaring at him, Sarah said, "You were there?"

"Not when it happened." He turned away from Sarah and looked down at a family through the window as they wheeled a child with a bandaged leg toward the parking lot. Redbud trees were blooming on both sides of the sidewalk. A little girl was helping a stuffed Elmo jump over the cracks in the concrete.

Sarah turned to Clayton. "If Brax covered for Tyler, how did they have enough probable cause to get samples of Tyler's DNA to match against what was under Jenny's fingernails?"

"Claire told them Jenny was going with Tyler that night."

Sarah gasped. "She knew?"

"That's what she told the detective. She encouraged Jenny to go."

She tightened her grip on the arm of the chair. "Does Bob know that?"

Clayton looked at her curiously. "I don't know what Bob knows. The detective questioned them separately. I hope she's smart enough to tell him the truth before this all comes out."

Sarah leaned back into the chair. Behaving like some stupid adolescent, Claire had encouraged Jenny to ignore both of her parents. *No wonder she's not talking to anyone. She's waiting for us to jump down her throat.* Sarah ran her fingers through her hair and sat up straight.

"Brax," she said, "you saw more than you're telling us. Who were you with?"

"Brian Schiffman and David Conger, but they were both so drunk, they don't remember anything."

"You weren't drinking?" Clayton asked.

"I was the driver."

"So you remember?"

He nodded. "Tyler didn't want to stay with us. He and Jenny walked further up to another campsite. I went up to tell them we were leaving, and I could hear them arguing."

"Jenny, arguing with Tyler?" Sarah asked.

"Yeah, it was mostly Tyler."

"Why were they arguing?"

"I don't know. He was wired. He gets real aggressive when he's using meth." Brax studied his palms, avoiding Sarah's eyes. "He's been doing more the last few months. It's really messed him up."

"Did you see him hit her?" Clayton asked.

"No, but I've seen him knock her around before."

A cry escaped from Sarah as though she were the one being struck. Clayton reached over and held her arm.

Brax winced. "Tyler's not an a bad guy unless he's using meth."

Clayton looked at him intently. "What happened?"

Brax stared past Clayton's shoulder. "When I walked up to tell them we were leaving, I heard her crying. He was yelling at her. I should have made her leave." He rested his head in his hands. "Maybe he was pressuring her. He probably smacked her hard a few times, and she tripped and hit her head on the rock."

Angry and confused, Sarah squeezed her eyes shut. Jenny in the light of a campfire, frightened, crying? Why didn't she leave? Sarah clenched her jaw. Adrenaline pounded through her and tied her stomach in a knot.

"Why? Why would Tyler hit Jenny?" she said out loud.

Disgusted, Brax raised his head and stared at her. "Because he couldn't hit you. He hates you."

Clayton frowned. His eyebrows became a straight line across his forehead.

Brax kept talking. "We tried to tell you what we wanted to do the first day of school, but you laughed at us. You wouldn't help. You could have talked the school board into letting us go to an out-of-state tournament. But you wouldn't even try. Then a kid from City High told us what you did at Gov's Cup. You planned that whole thing." He shook his head. "And no one ever found out who dumped the honey in our files, did they?" He sneered. "Tyler thinks it was you."

She tried to keep her voice calm. "The board would never have allowed it."

"If we had won any of those tournaments, it would've looked great on an application. It might have made the difference for Tyler."

Sarah closed her eyes.

Brax saw Mrs. Beale coming down the corridor. He pointed his finger at Sarah. "If it weren't for you, Tyler wouldn't have given Jenny a second thought." Wadding up the paper wrapper, he fired it into a trash can as he rose to join Mrs. Beale, who waved her hand pleasantly in their direction before she stepped into the elevator.

Sarah pushed her fist against her mouth. As she watched, a fat bumblebee bumped angrily into the plate glass windows over and over again. *How did it get all the way up here?* It would never escape. In a few days, she thought, the tiny corpse would be caught between the windowsill and the glass, and a custodian would vacuum it up.

Clayton took a last bite of his sandwich and folded the paper over and over, creasing it carefully each time with his thumbnail until it was a small square that he tucked into his shirt pocket. "Was there any truth to what he said?"

Sarah looked over at him. "About me?"

Clayton nodded, looking out the window into the fading afternoon light.

"It's more complicated than that," she said, "but I'm not proud of what I did."

"I see this every day, Sarah. People who feed antagonism can wreck a life beyond repair, and it's usually their own."

He seemed so careworn and discouraged, but she couldn't explain what she had done. It wouldn't go away. Her daughter was lying on a hospital bed in a coma. She could rationalize and say the price was unfair, outrageously high. If she had known the end at the beginning, she would have done things so differently. The resistance fighter had been captured. Standing on the scaffolding, a noose inches from her face, suddenly the hangman had shoved Sarah out of the way and grabbed Jenny instead, tightened the noose around Jenny's slender throat, and then sprang the trap door. Sarah was forced to watch as Jenny paid the price for what Sarah had done.

bedside revelations

Sarah cracked open the window half an inch, and a cool, almost-summer breeze wafted into the room.

"Can you feel that?" she asked over her shoulder to Tom.

She looked out at the first evening stars. A soft florescent light over Jenny's bed cast the room in shadows. A half dozen helium balloons bobbed eerily in the corner. Jenny's eyelids fluttered. She had been opening her eyes for the past week, but today she had looked at Sarah—and smiled.

"Soon," Sarah said to Tom. "She's coming around. The doctor said the swelling is resolving. I was reading to her this morning and when I quit, she squeezed my hand." Sarah tapped the lotion bottle into her palm. Massaging Jenny's foot, she asked, "What's the talk at school?"

"Kids want to know if you're coming back before the end of the year. Mr. Cottle has been threatening your sophomore classes. If they torture any more subs, he'll have them drawn and quartered. No one knew what he meant, until he told them to watch the last scene in Braveheart."

Bob walked in the door and dropped the stack of charts he had been carrying on the floor. He slumped down in the recliner and loosened his tie. Rubbing the dark stubble on his chin, he glanced down at his wristwatch. "Any changes?"

"She's in and out, but more out than in."

"I'm starving. Maybe I'll bring something back up here. Walk down to the cafeteria with me, Tom?" Bob asked.

Tom stood up. "Can I bring you anything, Mom?"

She shook her head. She rubbed more lotion into Jenny's calf after they left. "Jenny," she sang, "come out, come out wherever you are. I need to talk to you, because this is too weird, weird, weird. Your father's always materializing, unannounced," she hummed to Jenny. "I can't get used to it."

"What's weird and who's materializing?" Clayton, wearing a wrinkled olive-green uniform, was leaning against the door watching her.

"Well, that would have to be you. You know, serial murderers dress up in police uniforms to dupe their victims. Do you have any ID?"

He laughed. "I came straight from work. Does the uniform put you off?"

"No, when I like someone, I'm not easily put off." She busied herself with the lotion bottle. "So what brings you here? There's a smashed-up biker with about a million tattoos in the next room. He might need arresting. I could introduce you."

"You're not going to make this easy, are you?"

"I don't know what this is." She turned toward him slowly, her hand on her hip. "I'm sure it was difficult for you to hear what Brax said." She covered her abdomen with her hands. "But I felt it right here, a sucker punch to the stomach. Brax Martin was everyone's golden child that day, but I don't think of him as much of a character reference."

"I couldn't believe you'd do something like that, Sarah."

"Well, the bottom line is you don't really know me." She reached over and held Jenny's hand. "You have no idea how much I wish I could undo that stupidity, but I can't. I stand here and look at Jenny and beat myself up all day." She ran her fingers through her hair until the curls lifted like a strange horizontal halo. "So if you're here to do the whole disapproving thing, do it somewhere else."

"I want to understand, Sarah."

"It's taken you a week to figure that out?"

"I can forgive anything, if you'll just explain."

Stepping away from Jenny's bed, she stood up straighter. Her arms gripped the railing on the bed. "Forgive me? I don't need you to forgive me. I'm the one who has to live with my ten zillion mistakes, not you."

"I'm not saying this right."

"It doesn't matter. Not hearing from you for a week said it all." An overwhelming sadness weighed her down, and she sat heavily in a chair. "Just because I was born with a 'kick-me' sign attached to my back doesn't mean I haven't learned to dodge feet." Sarah took off her reading glasses and chewed on the earpiece.

"How's Jenny?" he asked.

"She squeezes my hand to answer questions, and when she opens her eyes, she recognizes things. Now, if she'll just stand up and recite the Gettysburg Address, it will be another perfect day."

He gave her a disapproving look. She watched without moving, waiting for him to leave, but he sat down in a chair near the foot of the bed.

"Why do you think I'm here?" he asked.

She shrugged.

"Okay, I was upset by what that Martin kid said. I've had a hard time understanding the connection between Jenny and Colton since you first told me about it, but suddenly it made sense."

She bristled and pulled the earpiece out of her mouth. "Well, some of the pieces fit, but what he said doesn't begin to describe last year."

He grabbed the back of the chair and set it next to Sarah. "A couple of months ago, I watched a backhoe operator dig up a pasture looking for the remains of a sixteen-year-old girl who had been butchered by a man who raped her. I knew who it was, but we just couldn't nail him." He raised his eyebrows. "Who has a hunting knife that clean? He thought he'd gotten away with it, the smug. . ." His voice trailed off. "It all started out as one of those phone calls in the middle of the night. 'Kristy's never come home, and I don't know where she is. Can you help?' "

Sarah leaned over and put her hand on his shoulder.

"I understand why you would feel powerless and driven to do things out . . ." He stumbled around looking for words that wouldn't offend her. "I'm telling you this because I thought of a hundred dirty tricks to let that guy know that I knew, that I was watching him: letting the air out his tire and coming by to help him fix it, standing behind him in line at the grocery store, pulling him over for no reason, but I couldn't do anything to jeopardize the case or scare him into taking off. I hate that guy. I hate what he did. You don't know how terrible it is to ring a doorbell in the middle of the night and see desperation on a parent's face, and in a small town, it's usually someone you know."

The bell rang on the IV monitor, and Sarah pushed the call button for the nurse. Smoothing the blanket under Jenny's hand, she said, "Did you know that girl's family?"

"I went through school with her dad."

"But you didn't do anything."

"No, but I wanted to." He lifted Sarah's chin with his finger. "Sarah, men and women are so different. Women view men pretty realistically, but men think the women they love are perfect. Imperfections can be something of a shock. I needed time to think it through."

She turned her head away. Pinching her bottom lip between her thumb and forefinger, she studied him. He had dirt in the cuffs of his pants, and his shirt was dusty.

"Where have you been?"

"You haven't been reading the paper?"

"No."

"I'll tell you about it later. Is Bob around?" he said.

"He's scavenging for food."

"Tyler was booked last night and arraigned this morning."

"They kept him in jail overnight?"

"Yes, his parents were livid. They handcuffed him at home and took him away in the middle of dinner. No dessert."

Bob and Tom walked back into the room. "Does anyone care if I eat? I'm starving." Bob shoved his plastic fork into the stew, nodding at Clayton as though giving him permission to speak.

"Well, as I was telling Sarah, Colton was arraigned this morning. His father's attorneys had him out in about ten minutes."

"No surprise there," Sarah muttered.

"He's denying everything," Clayton said.

Sarah pursed her lips. "That kid will never see the inside of a prison. If it looks like things aren't going their way, Tyler will vanish. I bet there are contingency plans under way as we speak. *Whish!*" Annoyed, her hand zoomed across the front of her chest. "He'll spend the rest of his life in Budapest, hiding."

"So how is this going to play out?" Bob raised his eyebrows. Clayton put his arm on Sarah's shoulder, but she leaned away.

"If the evidence looks conclusive," Clayton said, "the Coltons will probably take some sort of a deal. If it goes to trial, the jury will decide."

"They'll never risk prison. He'll vanish." Sarah bit the side of her thumb and looked over at Jenny.

"You really think he's a flight risk?" Clayton asked.

"Do chickens have lips?"

Tom straightened his long legs and got up off the floor. Picking up his backpack, he asked Clayton, "Did they ever find those three guys?"

"Late this afternoon."

"Are they okay?"

"Hungry, tired, and embarrassed, but okay. Thirty-five people and two airplanes looked for them for three days. These East coast kids who've hiked the Appalachian Trail think they can handle the Rockies with a bottle of water and sturdy shoes."

"Didn't they have a terrain map?" Tom asked.

Clayton shook his head. "They thought they could follow the river out. They're lucky they didn't drown. It's been a long three days and I still have a report to write." But he didn't leave.

Tom kissed Jenny on the cheek and waved good-bye to Sarah.

Bob picked up Jenny's chart and examined the labs drawn that afternoon. "We're going to see some improvement soon. I really think we will." He smiled at Jenny and walked around to the side of her bed. "Tomorrow, pumpkin, I want you to open your eyes and say something." He picked up her hand and bit her little finger gently, but she didn't respond. "Can I walk you out to your car?" he asked Clayton.

"I need to talk to Sarah for a minute."

"Oh," Bob said and lingered as he positioned his charts carefully in his brief case. Taking a last look around the room, his brow furrowed, he said good night and left.

Sarah opened the top of the Tupperware container and reached in for a last, slightly stale, rice crispy treat. Offering half to Clayton, she said, "You've had a rough few days. I guess I did some conclusion jumping."

"It's okay. Walk with me out to the elevator?"

The atrium was dark. The only light was coming from the bank of elevators on the east wall. Pausing in the shadows under the windows, he reached for her, but she took a step away and looked out the atrium windows at the night sky. Rubbing the end of her nose, she said, "I thought you were a specialized Sarah rescuer. I didn't know you rescued people wholesale."

"Sooner or later, we all need a little rescuing."

"You know, I missed you. It hurt that I wasn't worth a fifteen-second phone call." She put her hands up defensively. "I've been picturing you with a woman at work who doesn't have a mean temper. It's not okay for me to be feeling those things, not right now. I don't have any emotional energy for romantic entanglements. I need to be focused on Jenny."

"So now I'm an entanglement, not a friend?" He shoved his hands into his pockets.

"Oh come on, we both know a line had been crossed. I was starting to fantasize about not sitting alone at basketball games. It was nice to have someone to talk to about Jenny besides the great Doctor Poohbah." For the last few weeks, she had indulged herself in the little illusions born of hope. Life with two incomes. Nearly new cars. Never selling another ticket again in her life. Maybe travel to some places she had only imagined. Coming home each day to a person who loved her. *Good grief,* she thought, *I'm going to cry. A little dignity, please.* She bit down hard on her bottom lip. Could he see her face in the shadows?

"I'm so sorry, Sarah. I didn't mean to hurt you; that wasn't what I was thinking about."

"Spoken like a male member of the species."

Exasperated, he shook his hands on both sides of his head.

"It's okay," she said. "It wasn't much of a hurt, more like a skinned knee. I'll survive. I always do." How many times in her life had she said that? She was breathing and both of her feet functioned to propel her forward, but was that surviving?

They stood uncomfortably for several minutes until he whispered, "I've got to go home."

Sarah nodded, looking out the window. "You don't think Mrs. Colton will sneak in here and try to smother Jenny with a pillow?"

"No, I don't think she'd risk it."

"I guess they don't let professional manicurists visit their clients in prison. But, no kidding, should we have a guard outside Jenny's door? To be safe?"

"Promise me you'll quit watching *Law and Order.* The Coltons aren't going to dig this pit any deeper. They'll use the courts. This will go on for years."

She sighed and looked up at him.

"I have Saturday off," he suggested tentatively.

"You must have a million things to do. Plant your garden. Play golf. Stuff animals with antlers. Oh, that would be uncomfortable. I'm glad I didn't end up on your wall." She straightened up. "Hey, thanks for coming by with all the info about the super creep."

Three steps toward the elevator, he turned around and caught her wiping tears off her cheek with the back of her hand. "You were starting to trust me, and I blew it, but this is a mistake. Letting go of this is a mistake." He pointed his finger at her. "Think about that." And he stepped into the elevator.

Think about it yourself, she thought.

———∿∿∿———

When Sarah came back into the room, the only light the nurse had left on was the dimmed light above the bed.

"Jenny," she whispered, "I always manage to screw things up so badly."

Jenny's eyelids blinked twice and she opened her eyes.

Sarah picked up Jenny's hand. "Can you understand what I'm saying?"

Jenny squeezed her hand lightly.

"Can I do anything for you?"

Jenny spoke so breathlessly that Sarah had to lean forward to hear her. "Water."

She hurried to find the water pitcher. Lifting the back of Jenny's neck very gently, she put an ice chip between her lips. Sarah laid her head back against the pillows. "I don't want you to choke."

Jenny tried to speak, let out a breath of air, and closed her eyes for a moment, before trying again. "What happened?" she whispered.

"You were hurt, cupcake." A nickname Sarah hadn't used since Jenny was a little girl. "You're in the hospital and you're going to be fine, but you've been unconscious. Your head was hurt and you have a broken wrist, but you're getting better."

"Tom?"

"Tom just left. He's been here every day. He loves you so much. He's so sorry he was mad at you. He won his election. The mission president let us call and talk to Robbie. We've all been here waiting and watching. Your dad comes twice a day. We're actually speaking to each other without yelling. It's a miracle, and it's all because we love you so much."

Jenny smiled slightly and closed her eyes.

She tucked Jenny's good hand under the sheet and whispered, "I'll be here all night if you need me."

clayton at the hospital

Sarah wiped carefully around the edge of Jenny's bandages and sang little snatches of songs. She gossiped about teachers at school and told her all the family stories she knew about departed relatives. She tried to keep up a steady flow of talk, pleasant human noise that Jenny might hear. She couldn't bring herself to leave the room. Jenny might wake up again.

When Sarah had wrung every bit of news out of her own head, she picked up a worn copy of *Rebecca*. Pulling the bookmark out, she began reading the conversation between Max De Winter and Mrs. Van Hopper. "He's going to marry Rebecca," she confided to Jenny, "and he doesn't need any help from Mrs. Van Hopper. Thank you very much." Sarah added a smug aside. "I think the author named her Van Hopper because she's such an ugly old toad."

Mrs. Van Hopper had just told the girl that she didn't think she had it in her to be Mrs. De Winter, when Claire cautiously peeked in the door.

She offered Sarah a brown paper sack and said in a rehearsed rush, "I stopped by your house to pick up a few things for you. There's a call room down on the first floor with a shower. The nurse said no one uses it after nine o'clock and that you'd be welcome."

Sarah examined Claire's face. *She's trying to help,* Sarah thought, *but she's afraid of me. What did I ever do to her?* The morning had been happy, but now she felt cross.

Claire moved over to the bed. "Has she said anything else?" Claire smelled fresh, some nice perfume that Sarah had noticed last week. Her clothes were clean and looked new, and she had somehow found time to paint her toenails a light shade of peach.

"She asks the same questions. Why is she here? Where's Tom? Can she have a drink? Simple sentences. Can you stay for a while?" Sarah asked, suddenly aware that whiffs of a funky smell were coming from under her own arms.

Claire held up a bag of yarn and knitting needles, "All day."

"Good grief, I thought knitting and malingering away the afternoon playing bridge had gone the way of the dinosaurs."

Claire's face collapsed. "I don't play bridge."

"I'm sorry. That wasn't very nice," Sarah said. She took the sack and headed for the door. "Thanks." She stopped and turned on the ball of her foot. "What are you making?"

"Scarves. Make sure you lock the call room door. There are lots of stories about people being surprised." Claire rolled her eyes.

Sarah smiled. "We don't need any more gossip, do we?"

—◆◆◆—

Sarah ambled down the hall, which, over the last few weeks, had become as familiar as her own street. She scarcely noticed the patients in the rooms she passed. Thinking about how good a shower would feel and opening the sack to make a quick inventory, she nearly ran into Clayton coming the other direction. He was carrying a sack too and looked like he was moments out of the shower. His gray hair was damp, and he smelled like shampoo and aftershave. She was fairly sure the crisp plaid shirt he was wearing was new.

Sarah nodded at the sack he was carrying, "If that has soap and a change of underwear in it, I am going to know that I have been totally offensive to everyone."

Clayton looked her up and down and laughed.

"Well, that's what's in here." Sarah held up her own sack. She smiled at him and continued a couple of steps down the hall, then she turned. "Say, why are you here at ten o'clock in the morning on your day off?"

The smile left his face. He regarded her seriously. "Because I love you," he said. "And God knows you need to be loved."

A telephone rang in the nurses' station, the ward clerk hurried by with some lab reports, and the chaplain drifted past with his hands behind his back, but Clayton didn't move. He stood firmly in the middle of the hall, looking at her, waiting.

Sarah's eyes flicked back and forth twice. She licked her lips nervously, pointed at her chest, and then gestured with her index fingers down the hall. "Shower."

"Sarah, don't run away from me."

"Is that sort of 'stop or I'll shoot'?"

"Yes, that's exactly what it is."

"I'm prickly, not a very lovable sort of a person," Sarah said, pulling at a scraggly lock of hair.

"I know, but you could be." His face was deadly serious.

She looked over at 12C because the stroke victim in that room had pushed the mute button on her TV remote.

Clayton took advantage of the distraction to grab Sarah's arm and pull her into a small family lounge. He shut the door with his foot and drew her down to sit next to him on the couch. He kissed her lightly on the mouth.

"I'm disgusting," she said.

"I know."

"I mean," she said indignantly, "I haven't had a shower in three days."

"I know exactly what you mean, and I don't care." And he kissed her like he hadn't had lunch in a week.

Sarah finally pushed him away to catch her breath.

He held her face between his hands. "Sarah, neither of us should spend the rest of our lives being alone. It's just too hard to face all of this by yourself. I don't want to be an entanglement. I want to be a partner, and you need me. I never thought I'd ever feel this way about anyone again, but I do. I love you. That's all there is to it."

She didn't answer him. She kicked off her shoes and pulled away, sitting on the arm of the couch with her knees tucked up close to her chest. "What about being AWOL for a week? That didn't feel *I love you* to me."

"I was wrong. I should have talked to you. I think I was giving myself a test. Can I live without Sarah? I can, but I don't want to."

Sarah tipped her head to the side and examined his face closely.

"Clayton, my dad had a favorite saying: 'People change, but not much.' I'm not going to become a calm, easy-to-live-with sort of person."

"I don't want you to change."

She loosened her grip on her knees. "Do you want me to tell you what I did yesterday at three o'clock?"

"Okay, I'm game."

"Tom stayed with Jenny, and I took my engagement ring to a jeweler and sold the diamond. I'm going to buy a new sofa, and a coffee table, and maybe a couple of chairs. I want to have things be bright and cheerful when Jenny comes home."

"That's okay with me."

She started again. "My point is, that ring's been in my drawer for years. I don't seem to be able to move quickly on these relationship things."

"I can be patient."

"That wasn't a patient kiss. That kiss was a rush sort of a kiss."

"Do you want the truth?" He pulled on one of her loose curls.

"Truth is good, yes."

"Sarah, I don't want to date. What I really want is to be married. I want a home with you and your kids and my kids, and your big yellow dog. I don't remember his name."

"Einstein." She tapped her chin with her index finger. She laughed nervously. "Shower," she said looking toward the door.

"Will you come back to me?"

"Did you bring food?"

"Apple fritters." He picked up the white sack and shook it at her.

"Then I'll be back." She had her hand on the doorknob, when she turned suddenly. Putting her arms around his neck, she pressed her face into his chest and felt his arms encircle her. She stood, not wanting anything more than this physical closeness. She'd survived—she always did—but maybe she deserved a little more than that. Maybe she deserved a little happiness.

teacher checkout

Sarah walked in the back classroom door.

"I'm over here," Meg sang, waving her hand over the stacks of AP American Government texts piled high on the mauve carpeting. Using a book stack as a writing surface, she was filling out a triplicate form requesting replacement texts. "How could anyone lose a book this large? It makes no sense."

Leaning over the desk, Sarah picked the teacher check-out form with her name written across the top. She recognized Gracie's handwriting. "Why is she writing in fluorescent orange?"

"All your check-out signatures have to be in that color of ink."

"So much for trust."

"I think they've had problems. Who wants to find thirteen different people this afternoon? Forgery becomes an excellent option."

Sarah stood in the center of the room. The posters, stacks of books, unclaimed trophies, discarded papers, stains on the rug, it was all the same. Nothing had changed. She had stood in this spot a year ago. Maybe this last year had been a merry-go-round of bad dreams. Had time stopped while she went on a nightmarish journey? Everything was familiar, but not immediate, as though she were standing in front of a house she had lived in twenty years before.

"It seems like I've been gone for years."

"Well, at least weeks. I've really missed you." Meg smiled.

"Thanks for covering for me. I don't know what I would have done, if I'd had to zoom back and forth arranging things for a sub."

"It was easy. I just pulled out your black poetry folder and there were outlines, handouts, and tests. After the little beasts had two subs for lunch, Terry Schuback came in for three days. They were thrilled to have Mrs. Miller back."

"Terry subbed for me?" Sarah sat down hard on the riser.

"He owes you. Of course, now everyone is saying they knew Tyler Colton was evil all along."

Sarah looked down the list of things she had to accomplish on the check-out list and sighed. "What a terrible year."

"Next year has to be a major improvement. Five kids from the sophomore class are going to debate camp." Meg came around the stack of books and sat on a student desk. "Look, Sarah, I'm sorry I wasn't more understanding about everything that happened last fall. Maybe it wouldn't have been so hard if I'd been more supportive. You know, with you all the way."

"No, Meg, you were true north. I was the one who was off base. I spent so much energy being angry. What a waste."

The back door opened and Bill Cottle leaped into the room wearing horrible Bermuda shorts and a Smashing Pumpkins T-shirt. "You're back."

"I have to check out."

"How's Jenny?"

"Well, she was moved over to a rehab facility on Monday. She can walk a little, use the potty, and eat pudding. She remembers more every day. She remembers going up the canyon with Tyler, and she remembers seeing Brax, but that's it. A part of me doesn't want her to remember anything else. She gets confused so easily. I can't imagine her on a witness stand. Huge on sympathy, lousy on credibility."

"But," Bill tilted his head to one side, "she validates that Martin kid's story. Everyone knows Tyler was lying when he denied being with her that night."

Meg held up her finger doing her Perry Mason impersonation. "Were you lying then, or are you lying now?"

Sarah tried to smile. "Every day there are a few less cobwebs. It's slow, but she's improving. When I read out loud to her, she understands the plot for a few minutes."

"You read aloud?" Meg asked. "That's so nice."

"That's what she asks for every morning when I get there. She sees the book on the nightstand and wants me to read. We haven't done that since she was a little girl."

"You're friends again?" Bill asked.

Sarah's eyes teared, and she brushed the back of her hand across her face.

"Well, there's nothing like a head injury to help you remember that your mother is your mother," Bill said, patting her on the shoulder. "You're going to be okay."

"How long will she be in rehab?" Meg asked.

"I'm not sure. Probably until the end of July, depending on how she does. Then she'll come home. When school starts, she's going to live with Bob."

"No!" gasped Bill. He held up his wrist and tapped on his watch. "Count down to Armageddon. You're going to let Jenny live with them after all they've done?"

"Jenny needs him. She's just got this large hole where her dad should have been all these years. If she can do a partial schedule, Claire can drive her back and forth. It seems to fit, for next year at least."

"What about her hair?" Bill flashed his fingers in and out.

"Well, her head's shaved right now, but we talked about that, last night in fact."

Two patients in plaid bathrobes were finishing a board game as several others on a couch in the corner watched television. The doors to the patio were open, letting in a warm summer breeze. Sarah stood to the side, watching, as Bob squatted in front of Jenny's wheelchair. He usually came straight from work in a starched shirt and tie, but today he had on a golf shirt and jeans. He must have taken the afternoon off. Both his hands on her knees, he asked Jenny what she had eaten for lunch. What had she done in physical therapy? How much time had she spent out of her wheelchair? Her brown eyes, so large in her gaunt face, focused on him. Her facial bruising had healed, the swelling almost gone, but her thin smile was so melancholy. The attendant interrupted him.

"I need to get Jenny ready for bed."

"Give me another minute." He reached down into a sack by his foot. "I brought you a present." He helped Jenny tear off the wrapping. A small leather book rested in blue tissue on her lap. "It's a journal. I want you to write in it each day. Keep track of your progress. In a few months you'll be able to look back and see how much you've improved." He leaned forward and gave her a hug. "Promise me you'll write in it?"

Jenny nodded and kissed her dad on the cheek.

Efficient and pleasant, the attendant wheeled Jenny down the hall.

"I'll be there in a minute," Sarah called. Jenny waved over her shoulder with her good hand.

Bob stood up and one of his knees popped. His eyes followed Jenny being wheeled away. "If I let myself, I can get so angry that I want to find that kid and tear him apart. Shooting him would be too easy." He clenched his fist and his biceps moved under his short-sleeved shirt.

"He's an easy kid to hate. Believe me, I know. I hated him all year."

"Sarah, I'm sorry I threw that at you. You know, about that jerk hurting Jenny because of you."

"It's okay. You're not the only one who said that to me. I absolutely indulged my hatred for Tyler Colton. Sort of like I did with you."

"That bad?"

"Worse." She looked down at the floor. His shoes were always polished. Didn't he ever step in the mud? Or get scuffed? How could anyone be so immaculate?

"I never felt that way about you," he said.

She rolled her eyes. "Congratulations."

Sarah analyzed the leaves on a potted ficus tree. When she turned, Bob was watching her intently. His eyes were so brown and deep she wanted to reach up and touch his cheek. Instead, she said, "There are some things we need to talk about. I mean the whole hair thing."

"Her hair's only a half an inch long."

"You know what I mean. The hair and the makeup. The extreme clothes. That's not who Jenny is. Can Claire sign on with all that?"

"Believe it or not, Claire and I have already had this conversation."

"And homework. She's so bright, it's a shame for her not to do well in school." Then the realization that Jenny might not be a math whiz hit her again. Several times a day flashes of this new reality pounded at her. She looked at him, her own fear reflected in his eyes, and she started to cry. He held her as she trembled. "Is she going to be all right?"

"I don't know. I hope she will be, but I don't know for sure."

They held on to each other tightly until Sarah's quiet sobs subsided into several large gulps. Then he whispered into her hair, "Oh, little Sarah, this isn't what we had planned, is it? But we did make great kids together."

Her heart was racing, but she pulled away from him, her fingers wiping under her eyes, mopping up a few errant tears.

Handing her a tissue from his pocket, he said, "You know, when I was a little kid, I always wanted to be a big deal in the Church, maybe a bishop or a stake president. I used to turn over an empty garbage can in the garage for a podium, and I've give extremely profound sermons to the rakes, and the snow blower, and my dog Ralphie."

She sniffed and tried to laugh.

"Didn't I ever tell you that?" She shook her head. "I probably did. You just weren't listening."

"Are you kidding?" she asked. "I hung on every word. I was mesmerized, just like Jenny is now."

"Mesmerized?" he asked.

"Totally." She managed a laugh.

"Sarah, I want my family back." He held her forearms with his hands.

"You want us in your camp, even me."

He looked at her curiously.

"Your camp. You know, on your team. You'd be the quarterback, the paterfamilias, but I don't think that's going to happen. The best we can do now is sell hot dogs and programs. We're not the main event. We blew that. I can't see us doing happy family Sunday dinners with dogs and grandchildren and all that. It's not in the cards."

"It could happen. If we wanted it badly enough."

The pied piper had nothing on this guy. His handsome face, those soft brown eyes pleading with her. All that wonderful chemistry, it was still there, but it wasn't enough, not anymore.

"I have an agenda of my own," she said softly.

"That sheriff's too old for you."

"He's only four years older than you are." She poked him on the shoulder.

"Really?"

"Look in a mirror. We've gotten older."

"You mean I'm not twenty-three anymore?" He gave her a crooked smile.

She smiled at him. "No, you're not. Neither am I."

"Listen, Sarah," he said, tugging on her little finger, "you can't expect Claire to do things your way. She's not like you. She won't insist on piano practicing. She doesn't proofread papers. She's not aggressive or demanding."

"So what is she?"

"What's Claire? She's quick to smile."

—*w*—

"That's it?" Bill sputtered. "Quick to smile? A three-word character analysis? He dumped you for quick to smile?"

"Maybe that says everything."

Meg interjected, "Maybe that's what Jenny will need for the next little while. Who knows?"

"So what's the story on this elderly sheriff?" Bill looked at her over the top of his glasses. "Does this mean you're withdrawing your application to be a member of my harem?"

"He loves me."

"And you're eating." Meg smiled.

"Oh no." Sarah stretched out her hands in protest. "Now you're going to tell me that there's some sort of symbiotic relationship between kissing and eating?"

"Kissing?" Bill straightened his long neck, turning it side to side as though he were a flamingo in khaki shorts. "Did someone mention kissing?"

"No," Sarah said coyly. "Someone said happy. Brief, sporadic bursts of happiness. That's the best anyone can hope for."

The back door opened, and Kristen and Rachael Beck came in carrying large red books covered with embossed gold letters.

"Mrs. Williams, will you sign my yearbook? We looked all over for you yesterday."

Sarah sat cross-legged on the floor. She glanced through the pictures and the notes written by friends, until she came to the debate page. On a warm fall afternoon, their picture had been taken on a jungle gym at a nearby grade school. Harry and Mike were hanging upside down from their knees. Eric was smiling shyly, towering above the other students. Kristen, Rachael, and Chan sat stacked up behind one another on a small slide. Other faces poked out at odd angles, laughing, being obnoxious for the student photographer. Tyler and Brax, baseball caps pulled low over their foreheads, stood in the back. At the right, Sarah had her arm draped over Meg's shoulders, clowning for the camera. Meg was laughing. They did look joined at the hip. She wondered if she could get a large glossy print from the yearbook staff to put on the back wall. Maybe they could eliminate Tyler with an airbrush or, at least, paint bars over his face.

She took the pen from Kristen's outstretched hand and wrote carefully on the top of the page.

"We don't see things as they are, we see them as we are." Anais Nin

She signed her name, closed the book, and handed it back. "Kristen, thanks."

"For what?"

"For everything. For trying so hard. For watching my back."

Kristen stepped closer and gave Sarah a hug. "Mrs. Williams, you're the best." Kristen stopped by the door as they were leaving. "What about you and Josh McLaughlin's dad?" She raised her eyebrows, and both girls giggled as the door closed behind them.

Sarah looked over at Meg and Bill. Bill was rubbing the top of Meg's head in a circular motion, looking into her auburn hair as though he were peering into a crystal ball. Meg was trying hard to keep a straight face.

He looked up at Sarah with his eyes half closed. "I see a cake in your future. A large cake with white concrete frosting. Small pink flowers cover the cake, also made of concrete. A man with a badge is damaging the cake with a knife, because *he's old.*" Bill paused waiting for Sarah to finish the joke.

"But he's not dead," Sarah said, laughing. "I get it."

"Finally," Meg said, sighing.

About the Author

Annette Haws was raised in a small college town in northern Utah. She graduated from Utah State University with a degree in English Education. She has done graduate work at the University of Iowa and the University of Utah. A schoolteacher for many years, Annette has set aside denim jumpers and sturdy shoes to pursue her interest in writing fiction. Currently residing in Holladay, Utah, Annette and her husband are the parents of four above-average children and have one spectacular little grandson.

If your book group plans to read *Waiting for the Light to Change*, Ms. Haws would be delighted to phone in and join your gathering via speaker phone. She can be contacted at Annette_Haws@yahoo.com. Discussion questions for *Waiting for the Light to Change* are also available on her website at www.annettehaws.com.